ONE OF TWO

46. ASCENDING

S. R. CRONIN

This book is a work of fiction and, with the exception of news
items, public figures, and cultural information, the events,
characters, and institutions in it are imaginary. No individual
character, organization, or group of people included as part of the
fictional narrative is intended to represent any real person or
group.

Table of Contents

The Third Law of Thermodynamics
It Doesn't Get That Cold, Even in Antarctica.

Defying Entropy

More Information

A Dedication to My Mom and More

I know my mother expected me to do great things. Negotiating a lasting peace would have been fine, or solving world hunger. She was a woman with big ideas, filled with fierce objections to the injustices of life. Early on, she saw that fire burning inside me, too.

Yet, she didn't get a fighter. She got a daughter with a fascination for science and a smoldering need to tell the stories inside her head. I know it's not what she expected, but I also know her fire glows in the tales I tell.

I dedicate this book to her, with my thanks for the many ways she encouraged that flame. It has turned out to be the part of me I like the most, and it is my favorite thing about my main character Lola, too.

This book is also meant to celebrate the people who struggle everyday to nurture and care for someone. It isn't easy to keep another safe, yet the very act of looking after another person raises us higher.

No wonder most of us love the idea of a guardian angel. At one time, we were raised by flawed angels, people who struggled to develop their own wings while they helped us grow ours.

Previously in the World of
46. Ascending

A lot has happened since Lola Zeitman became a telepath in 2009, but most of it doesn't matter as you read this book. However, if you're curious, here is a timeline and summary of the other books in this collection.

2009	2010	2011	2012	2013
One of One: Lola becomes a telepath				
	Shape of Secrets: Zane improves his shape-shifting			
	Twists of Time: Alex revives his time-warping skills			
			Layers of Light: Teddie trains for out-of-body experiences	
			Flickers of Fortune: Ariel's prescience makes a difference	
				One of Two: Lola leads a fight for a better world

One of One

Lola, a Texas geophysicist in her late forties, takes a new job with a Nigerian oil company and draws the attention of a young telepath needing assistance in rescuing her captive sister. This woman ends up helping Lola develop her own psychic powers as they both become part of a worldwide organization of telepaths called x^0. Lola also gets training from Maurice, an elderly friend in her hometown who made a similar transition a decade earlier.

Shape of Secrets

Zane's first job out of college is with an unethical pharmaceutical company. A few months after discovering his employer's transgressions, he becomes involved with a murder in the South Pacific. Attempts to prove a friend's innocence force him to use his secret shape-shifting skills in ways he never imagined. An online group of philosophers known as y^1 offers him a new direction in life, while his romance with a fire-dancing islander shows signs of becoming long-lasting.

Twists of Time

High school physics teacher Alex used to slow down time on a basketball court. He has to relearn and refine the skill when a growing white nationalist movement at his school threatens his teaching and his outspoken daughter. Xuha, a new student, becomes Alex's tennis protégé and star pupil, and draws the ire of this hateful crowd. Fortunately, Xuha has secrets of his own, and one of them is the way he can slow down time too.

Layers of Light

Sixteen-year-old Teddie becomes an exchange student in India, encountering a frightening world in which young girls are bought and sold. As this crime touches her friends, Teddie learns she has a special ability for locating others. An ancient group of mind travelers known as c^3 offers to train her to save her friends. In the end, Vanida, a young traveler from Bangkok, and Yuden, the grandmotherly head of c^3, join Teddie in a daring rescue.

Flickers of Fortune

Clairvoyant Ariel is annoyed by her visions of the future; then she takes her first job with an investment company in Dublin and encounters two groups of seers. The first, known as d^4, has learned to make huge profits from their abilities. The second, lead by the prophet Cillian and his shape-shifting friend Nell, is obsessed with preventing a dark future for humanity. Both groups do their best to win Ariel's allegiance.

And ...

There is more information about the 46. Ascending collection at the end of this book. Also, the last pages have a list of characters, where it is easy to find while you read.

Who has what superpower?

South of Forty Degrees

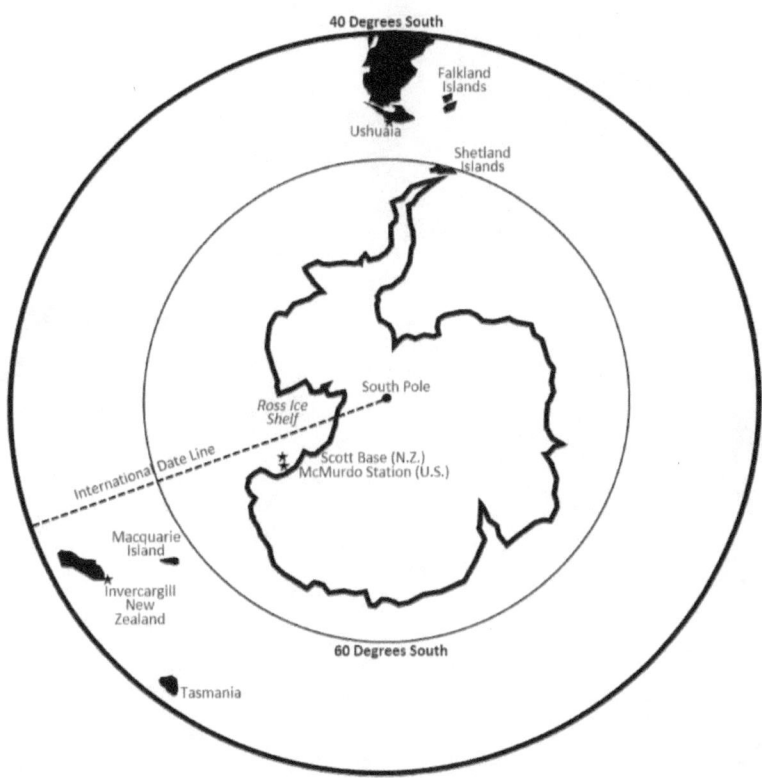

The Zeroth Law of Thermodynamics

You Must
Play the Game.

1. Not Today

Lola Zeitman had her first telepathic experience in 1986. It lasted about three seconds and she ignored it.

The next morning, at nine months pregnant, she made a presentation to the president of her company. It involved everything she'd done so far as a newly hired geophysicist and it went well, if she ignored the smarmy jokes the executives made about her advanced state of pregnancy. She did so, because people were always telling her she had to learn to get along. She just wished she felt better about it.

She failed to follow that advice when she joined her co-workers for a celebration later in the break room. A geologist made a pathetic joke involving the deaths of black children. She objected to the joke while holding her hands protectively over her own belly. It was a meek a protest, too meek, yet everyone was embarrassed by her violation of social norms.

Disgusted, Lola gathered up her things to leave. She didn't intend to speak to anyone, but she ran into Mary in the hall. Mary was a draftsman who had the dual distinction of being the only professional woman in the office with a child and the division's lone black employee. She took one look at the irritation on Lola's face and shook her head.

"They say you have play the game," she said.

"Not today I don't." Lola gave her swollen abdomen a pat. "I've got a doctor's note saying I can get out of here."

Mary laughed. "You know they call it the Zeroth Law of Thermodynamics, right? You trying to defy the laws of nature?"

"I'm thinking about it." Lola gave Mary a wave as she waddled towards the exit.

The next day she gave birth to her first child. As she held her newborn she wondered if she'd really heard her baby's thoughts two nights ago. Then he began to fuss and for the next twenty three years she was too busy to think about telepathy.

2. First Fuzzy Wall

In 2009, thanks to repeated interactions with a Nigerian woman who was determined to contact her telepathically, Lola's natural abilities grew until she became a full-fledged psychic. She was lucky an organization of telepaths known as x^0 discovered her. Old family friend Maurice turned out to be a telepath, and the elderly man took her under his wing and trained her well.

Over the next few of months Lola accomplished things she'd never dreamed she could do. In December of 2009 she and the Nigerian woman worked together to rescue her younger sister from an abusive husband and his terrorist plans. Christmas Eve of 2009, Lola was safe in Nigeria and ready to come home.

"You'll be in Houston in time for a nice holiday meal with your family," she was told.

As she walked through airport security, the overload of input felt like a bright light shining straight into her eyes. She wasn't sure if she could handle this new gift. Then, for the first time, she figured out how to put up a fuzzy mental wall to muffle the unwanted input.

There you go. That's the way. You'll figure this out. One of the telepaths got the message through to her.

You're right. I will.

Over the next three years, she did. That's when this story starts.

The First Law of Thermodynamics

You Can't Win.
The Best You Can Do
Is Break Even.

November 2012

3. The Interview

How could this lady possibly be a telepath?

Violeta watched the nervous American woman squirm in her seat as she prepared to be interviewed on live television for the first time. She straightened her necklace and patted down her unruly, coppery-brown hair. Yet, there was no doubt about it. In spite of her nervousness, the woman sought the minds of others as she waited, hoping to find helpful information.

Well, this does answer one of life's burning questions.

Violeta had finally found someone outside the grasp of Reel News with well-developed psychic gifts. Under other circumstances, she'd approach the woman and try to make a new friend. However, that was out of the question.

The woman had reason to be nervous. No matter how well-spoken she was, Violeta knew the interview would be awful for her. Violeta produced this news program, and she'd prepared questions to ensure it would be. For some bizarre reason, her bosses wanted to make this woman look like a fool.

Violeta was puzzled by why a giant conglomerate like Reel News wanted to swat at a fly, but she'd stopped trying to follow the palace intrigue at this company long ago. Perhaps she asked too few questions of her employers, but it kept life simpler.

As far as the lady went, the good news was Violeta's boss Gabriel and several other network telepaths in the studio today hadn't noticed what the woman could do. Yet. Violeta knew she'd have sensed their surprise if they had.

The woman's own wall of protection was inadequate, but the monads, as they called themselves, weren't expecting a clairvoyant interviewee. Until the show started, they would pay no attention to her. Once the interview came on the air, they might listen in and pick up on the woman's skills.

Violeta knew how paranoid the upper management of Reel News was about other telepaths. They were always sharing rumors and checking leads, and never tired of discussing how far they'd be willing to go if such others were ever found. What would they do if they discovered a lone adept right in their own office? Violeta guessed they'd pounce on her like cats on a grasshopper.

There seemed no way this woman deserved those consequences after the awful interview she was about to have. She looked so harmless.

Violeta sighed as she accepted the inevitable. She took down the well crafted wall she held in place around her own mind and extended it outward to include the nervous lady as well.

I wish I hadn't agreed to this.

Lola squirmed in the studio chair, waiting for the interview to start. A few months ago, a popular magazine published an article of hers and it received more attention than she expected. When a news outlet in New York invited her to appear on this broadcast, she was so honored, she didn't hesitate.

Her tongue-in-check essay about achieving world peace by encouraging people to get to know each other was based on her decades of working with different cultures in the oil business. Lola was baffled when people attacked her premise and proclaimed such naïve ideas made the world more dangerous, not less so.

The invitation for this appearance was presented as a chance to explain her side. Yet now that she was about to go on the air, every instinct told her this was a huge mistake.

She looked into the dimly lit area off stage and saw the well-dressed Latina with long black hair who'd greeted her as the producer of this show. In spite of an otherwise strong, almost regal, body, the woman walked with a cane. A small amount of underlying pain was evident in her eyes and the rest of her mind was a gauzy grey. Odd.

Lola's misgivings were so strong she considered walking off stage, feigning illness. Then the words "on in five" blared, the stage lights grew brighter, and the chirpy host she met a few minutes ago walked to his seat. The next thing Lola knew, he was saying, "Meet today's guest, Lola Zeitman, a quiet geophysicist from Houston who stirred people up with her little article called 'Face Painting for World Peace.'"

As he said the words, Lola finally picked up a clear thought. This interview had no other purpose than to make her look like a fool.

Telepathy isn't as useful as you'd think.

******

Violeta felt Lola's puzzled probe and worked to remain hidden until she heard the five-second warning. Then the woman's attention turned to the host as he made his way to the stage. Violeta relaxed and put her own focus back on the other ways she had to be so careful.

She was careful to speak English, of course, and careful to keep her injured body safe in the bustle of so many busy people. She was careful to keep up the walls holding back the emotions of millions of strangers, lest they overwhelm her in ways the familiar people of Argentina did not.

She kept her innermost thoughts away from her boss Gabriel because although he knew she was telepathic, he wished to believe she had only enough ability to be a useful spy for him, and not enough to ever be a threat. She hid her talents entirely from the other thirty-four mind readers who called Gabriel their leader. They lived in cities all over the world, running the largest subsidiaries of the news conglomerate, but they often visited New York and were always curious about her. She worked to keep Gabriel's secret, appearing to be his loyal assistant while adhering to a barely spoken understanding the two of them reached years ago.

As the interview went on, Violeta pushed the strong wall around her own mind out to encircle Lola too. Several of the monads were watching the show now in their offices. Violeta let the power of her wall increase by absorbing their strength.

She knew more than most about how to use the power of others. Twenty years of judo training had taught her far more than holds and kicks and the painful injury that ended her judo career a decade ago hadn't diminished the mental skills the martial art had given her. Through the long 20 minutes of the show, her wall held firm, and the strength of her protection grew.

******

"It wasn't that bad," Alex said, giving Lola a hug.

Her husband had been in the audience, and his large, sandy-haired form was a welcome sight backstage as soon as the show was over. Lola tried not to read her husband's mind, but she couldn't avoid sensing his irritation at how the host had treated her.

"Not that bad? He said I was the kind of person who hurt America, by giving people the childish idea others around the world were like us. He asked me what it felt like to be providing aid to our enemies!"

"He did. He was ridiculous and I'm furious for you." Alex saw her faint smile. "Oh hell, Lola. No sense lying to a telepath. The guy was an asshole and we both know it. If I wasn't an old hippie pacifist, I'd rearrange his face for you."

Her smile widened. "Please don't."

"Look, you did as well as you could." She was comforted to feel he meant it.

Then, probably because she was using her gift, she felt the faintest probe into her mind. She'd been trained to think of it as a knock on the door. This knock was barely discernable, but she knew there was another telepath nearby.

Come in.

She used the imagery of opening a door. Instead of the other making themselves known, as expected, the door in her mind was pulled open wider. Who was making such a rude entrance? She saw an image of an empty prairie stretching to the horizon with hundreds of tumbleweeds blowing by as a jackrabbit took off into the distance. How odd. She slammed the door closed against the dust and wind.

"Talking to someone else?" Alex looked at her with obvious discomfort.

"Sorry. There's more creepiness to this place than I realized. Can we get out of here?"

"No objection from me."

******

Violeta watched Gabriel come backstage as the segment finished. Her wall held firm as Lola went offstage to meet her husband. An assistant asked Violeta about the upcoming piece on France recognizing the new Syrian rebel coalition, and Violeta stopped to recall the name of the group's leader. In that instant of distraction, Gabriel noticed Lola.

Violeta felt him seek out Lola's mind, prompted by an idle desire to enjoy the woman's humiliation. Before Violeta could get her wall back in place, she felt Lola's invitation to him to enter. She watched while a surprised Gabriel recognized another telepath and jumped in fear.

Seeing the vain and sometimes contemptuous Gabriel scamper like a rabbit made Violeta smile for a second, but the humor didn't last. She knew Gabriel understood what he'd found. Soon the monads of Reel News would realize they weren't alone. Then they'd find Lola, because no one could hide from the Entelechy. If Lola had a teacher, they'd find her teacher, too.

Violeta had failed, for a split second, the same way she'd failed in that match in Córdoba years ago. She glanced at the cane in her hand, still needed to make walking easier when she was on her feet for too long. She should know better than anyone how much could be lost in an instant.

Worse, they'd wonder why they'd remained unaware of Lola's talents while she was sitting in their own studio. Their questions could lead them to look places they'd never looked before. If that happened, no wall of Violeta's could stand up to their combined direct scrutiny.

All of these arrogant men would know Gabriel's secret: his assistant worked as a psychic spy on his behalf. Gabriel could wonder if she was less dutiful than he liked to think. Reel News might figure out she wasn't the supporter of their agenda they'd supposed, given she'd chosen to protect Lola.

No one was going to like any of this new information.

******

Lola and Alex planned to go out for a fancy dinner after the show but Alex could tell his wife was in no mood to be around crowds. He cancelled the reservation as they left the studio. They walked back to the hotel, surprised by the mild November day in New York.

A little exercise worked its soothing magic, relaxing them as they strolled along holding hands. Lola told Alex of her mental encounter after the interview. Alex had learned of Lola's telepathy three years ago, but still had trouble understanding how experiences in his wife's head could be so real to her. Tonight he was a little annoyed she was more spooked by some door experience in her mind than she was angry at the obnoxious TV personality who had treated her like an enemy spy.

"The incidents are related. I know they are," she said. "The energy in the studio was weird. Everything was muffled, like there was some mental soundproofing in the building. I've never come across anything like it."

"The philosophy of Reel News can be, kind of, I don't know, fear-mongering," he said. "I mean they do push a viewpoint that everyone is out to get America."

"Only on their more extreme shows. As far as I knew, they didn't push that message on their mainstream programming, or I wouldn't have agreed to this in the first place. But I felt all that muffling for a reason."

Alex considered. "Do you think this intruder knew you were a telepath before they, uh, entered your head?"

"No. I keep up shielding as a habit, and they were at least as surprised as I was."

"Maybe it's a telepath who thought they were the only one in the world?" They approached the doorman at the front of their hotel.

"Good evening, ma'am. Good evening, sir." He opened the door for them. They paused their conversation as they entered.

"Well, this telepath knows about me now and I don't think they were happy about the discovery," Lola said as they reached the elevator. "Maybe we should fly home tonight?"

"You don't even want to order room service?"

"Physical proximity plays a role in telepathy, especially between strangers. I'm afraid this person will come looking for me and I'm pretty sure I don't want to be found."

He followed her logic. "So you want to vacate this perfectly wonderful room and take a red-eye flight back to Texas?"

She nodded, and he wrapped an arm around her shoulder.

"Okay, let's get packed. I don't want any creepy telepaths finding you either."

4. The Edge of the Earth

The last flight of the night to Houston was sold out, so they ended up at an airport hotel with a 6 a.m. flight. Lola didn't expect to sleep, but she tried to lie still so Alex could get some rest. Every time she dozed off, she woke up more exhausted.

Then she started checking her gear, making sure she had the food and water she needed. Did she need first aid? Of course she did. There could be no doctors where she was going.

Why was she headed somewhere so remote? She must be running from the evil telepath. No, she'd planned this trip long ago. She wanted to walk to the edge of the Earth, following the coastline south. She ought to get a map and a Spanish dictionary. People spoke Spanish where she was going.

She looked down and saw her feet covered in mud. Maybe she was so tired because her shoes were so heavy. How had she gotten out into this marsh? She'd been walking for weeks. Or months. Perhaps the Earth had no edge?

Then there it was. After a rocky scramble up over boulders, she could see waves crashing underneath her, a hundred feet below. She was on a windy cliff, watching ocean swells coming from two directions as they exploded in a giant spray of noise and foam. It was the Atlantic and Pacific colliding at the tip of South America, and it was incredibly beautiful. She started to cry because she knew this was where she needed to be.

"Lola, it's okay." Alex was sitting up in bed next to her. "You did everything you could today. Don't be upset."

She looked up at Alex, confused. What was he doing here? Rather, what was she doing here? The dream faded.

He wiped a tear from her check. "Tough day."

"It's not why I'm crying."

"Why then?"

"I have to go to Tierra del Fuego."

"You mean in South America? What on Earth for?"

Lola sat up and looked out of the small hotel room window at the moonless sky. She pulled the worn bedspread closer around her and shivered.

"That's the problem. I have to go, and I have no idea why."

******

After his encounter with Lola, Gabriel went back to his office without saying a word to anyone. Violeta took a cautious mental peek and discovered he was alone, considering with whom to share his discovery and when.

Smart man. Violeta knew the other thirty-four monads expected any newfound telepath to be like them: smart, successful, and attractive. Male. Healthy. They believed they found each other because they were brothers of the soul, gifted in ways other humans were not. Telepathy was part of the package.

Gabriel, of course, had his own views, because Gabriel knew about Violeta. He accepted inferior beings could develop a milder version of his ability. Violeta was the only example so far, but he saw no reason to think she was unique. Gabriel thought he was open-minded, believing such others could make worthy assistants once found.

News of an American woman in her early fifties who was well trained in the clairvoyant arts would upset the monads' world. If Gabriel wasn't careful, the ensuing turmoil could oust him as manager of this group of cagey alpha dogs.

Violeta picked up two encouraging facts. First, Gabriel was considering keeping quiet about Lola, at least for now. Second, the idea of Violeta somehow shielding this woman from his notice hadn't even occurred to him. At least not yet.

She needed to avoid Gabriel for a while. She had a good chunk of vacation time to use. She'd saved it, hoping one of her relationships with men would mature into a romance warranting a vacation together, but both potential boyfriends had dallied out the door before things got serious enough to plan a trip.

That made this an excellent time to go home. It was spring there, and she could enjoy her mother's cooking and check in on her brothers and their families. She texted Gabriel that she had to go back to Argentina to deal with sudden family matters. He wouldn't object.

Maybe she'd go see the penguin colonies at the tip of Tierra del Fuego. In spite of her injury, she could still manage to make her way up those rocks to a vantage point. The sight of waves from the world's two biggest oceans crashing together, colliding in a giant spray of noise and foam, never failed to fill her with wonder with its dreamlike power and beauty.

******

Family and friends had followed along as Lola wrote her article, and those closest to her were quick to offer their support once she got home. Her sister called first.

"You've got to understand, they brought you on their show to make a point. That network is owned by folks who make guns and by people who do mercenary things for the army, too."

"You mean companies suppling contractors to the military?"

"Yeah. Them. I've heard that's where the real money is. Waging war for profit. These people can't afford grassroots peace movements, so they trot someone like you out once in a while and make them look ridiculous." After other friends made similar comments, Lola wished she had been more cautious about the invitation.

Teddie, Lola's seventeen-year-old daughter, was the only one of her three children still living at home. More grown woman than child, Teddie often seemed wiser than those who were older.

"I know you feel like you let down some cause, but it's not true," she said. "The only people who watch that stupid show wouldn't like you no matter what you said, and you probably wouldn't like them either."

"I like to think the world isn't that black and white."

"I *know* you do, mom. That was the point of your article, and why they have no use for you. They sell fear and hate. I don't know why everyone pretends they're a legitimate news outlet when they've got such a clear agenda."

"Hmmm. It wasn't all that clear to me until a few days ago."

Only one group of her friends ignored the situation. The telepathic organization x^0 had found and trained Lola three years earlier and they had a clear policy of tolerating all views. Lola's octogenarian friend and mentor Maurice was far more conservative than she was, and Lola was sure he watched Reel News. He liked the network, but not all of the network. Maurice was too good a telepath to want to encourage more fear and hate in the world.

He contacted Lola by phone the day after she got back to Houston. He didn't want to talk about politics; he had other concerns.

"Something happened that spooked you," he said, not bothering with pleasantries. "I can feel it all the way out here in West Texas."

Lola wasn't surprised. Close telepathic friends kept a light finger on each other's emotional pulse, by mutual consent, and often began verbal conversations with no introduction.

"You're right. Before I send up an alarm, I need to ask you an odd question. Is there another secret group out there like x^0?"

Maurice laughed.

"What? One secret organization of telepaths isn't enough for you? No, Lola. I've never heard of another group. If there was one, I suspect we'd merge with them, to be honest. You know how telepaths tend to get along."

"What if there was one not inclined to be friendly?"

Lola knew she had Maurice's full attention now.

"I don't think that's possible. The ability to sense the feelings of others breeds empathy. By the time a full-fledged telepath develops, he or she is always a highly compassionate person."

Lola pushed back.

"What if their telepathy developed differently? I don't know. Maybe the world made them think they deserved special treatment. What if each of them was just a hostile person?"

"Then we'd really need to get the rest of x^0 involved. If you think you've found an evil telepath, they need to hear about it."

"I know, but evil is too strong a word. Selfish, maybe. I sensed a presence that wasn't friendly. But here's the thing. He, I think it was a he, was just as surprised by me. We both jumped."

"So we need to find out more. Lola? Let's do that *before* you offer the mystery man an olive branch, okay?"

Lola understood. She wouldn't try to make a new friend until the rest of x^0 was consulted.

******

Ushuaia felt like a village to Violeta after New York, even though her hometown had grown into a tourist destination of sixty-thousand. Her three nieces and little nephew smothered her in hugs as she arrived at her mother's door. Violeta was single at forty-one, and knew her family had decided it was unlikely she'd be a mother. So her two brothers and their wives made an extra effort to give Aunt Violeta a place of honor with their own children when she visited. Her brain switched over to her native tongue as she greeted her mom, two brothers and both sisters-in-law.

The most predictable thing about each visit was how the old house never changed. To her mother, it was a shrine to her dead husband, a police officer killed in the line of duty almost a dozen years ago. The man had been a hero to many, and the source of Violeta's own passion for martial arts. It always pleased Violeta to see her old room. Its soft lavender walls and white bedspread covered in lilacs waited for her with open arms, giving warm continuity to a life holding more twists than Violeta would have liked. She took a few moments to relish the familiarity.

She was unpacking when her youngest brother walked into her room and broke the spell.

"Your company has developed a liking for our area."

"You mean Gabriel's BNA news subsidary? They've owned a station here for years now."

"No, I mean the U.S. company that bought Gabriel out after you started to work for him. Reel News?"

"Yeah, that's them. Gabriel and I work for Reel News, although in Argentina BNA acts like an independent, nationally owned company. What would Reel News want in Ushuaia? Most of their viewers don't even like people unless they speak English."

Her brother shrugged.

"They're building a giant complex out on the edge of town. Offices, apartments, who knows what? Word is that they want something extremely remote for a second corporate headquarters."

"Well, we are remote," her other brother laughed as he walked into her room. "We can use all the foreign money here we can get. I hope they build more."

Violeta disagreed. She'd heard nothing about this project back in New York and she was fairly high up in the organization. Her resentment was about more than office politics, though. This town, this place at the end of the world, it was her refuge. It was her place to run away from them. They had no business picking it as a place to run to themselves.

$$******$$

Lola's other mentor and instructor was a Nigerian super-telepath named Olumiji. She knew the call from him was coming.

She was listening to a news report about how the latest Israeli attacks on Gaza resulted in airstrikes from both sides. It seemed like it never ended. She considered how x^0 estimated one percent of people had an innate ability to receive thoughts and feelings from others, although only one in ten recognized it. These seven-million or so often used their gift to excel in sales, politics, and even negotiating peace treaties. Why weren't any of them negotiating in the Middle East now? Maybe they were.

Lola also knew less than a hundred people in x^0 could communicate complex ideas mentally, and she was one of this small group. She'd met or encountered most of the other advanced telepaths, and she knew the dozen or so who informally ran x^0. None was a closer friend, or more instrumental in running the organization, than Olumiji.

So, Lola knew the call was coming, and she anticipated his first question.

"Should we worry about this telepath trying to harm you?"

"No. Not yet." She used words because a voice conversation was more efficient, but her feelings went as well.

"Take your time and tell me everything. This is important."

"I know so little." She told him her story.

"Perhaps this entity is part of a group like ours," he said. "Did you get any sense of that, and if so, how large?"

"I thought that could be the case, but I got no information about any others."

"Okay. Did you sense a desire to be destructive?"

"No, not really. I mostly got surprise and fear, but the whole studio sort of, I don't know, reeked of a destructive purpose."

"You are talking about the corporate headquarters of Reel News, aren't you, Lola?" It was impossible for her to ignore the tone of amusement that came with the question.

"Apparently the network has more of an agenda than I realized," she conceded. "I haven't paid much attention to them, honestly. But yes, the place felt dedicated to a goal they don't consider malicious. It's an agenda they believe in. This telepath felt tied into that purpose. I can't say how."

"I see. Well, you knew more than you thought." Lola felt her mentor and friend's appreciation, and his pride at how much her abilities had grown. The she felt his request and responded before he could speak.

"Don't worry about putting me in danger. Of course I'll help any way I can. What is it you want me to do?"

"We'd like to find a way to bring your mental intruder out where more of us can examine him. He has to have been intrigued by you, and we think he'll try to learn more. We want to pick the time and place. How would you like to make a fool of yourself on the air again?"

She had to laugh. "I was hoping I could contribute with more dignity, but I'll do what's needed."

5. Perpetual Motion

Gabriel spent days deciding when and how to mention his mental encounter with the woman pacifist to Warren Moore, the head of Reel News. He knew stalling meant taking a chance. He and his fellow monads seldom admitted to prying into each other's minds, but they all did it now and then, and they all knew it. The longer he kept his silence with Warren, the more he risked another monad discovering his secret.

He ran his hands through his thick head of jet black hair. Gifted with a tall muscular stature and rich bronze skin, Gabriel knew he was the picture of an Argentinian heartthrob, even though he'd stopped listening to the thoughts of teenaged girls as he walked past them. Well, he'd mostly stopped listening to them.

He forced his mind to the problem at hand. Each one of the other thirty-four monads was eager to take over Gabriel's job. Each sought ways to lower Warren's opinion of him. No sense in handing them an opportunity. He could use some advice.

If there was any monad Gabriel could call his friend, it was Rafael from the Philippines. The man was the odd one out; shorter, older, and frankly less attractive than the rest. However, in spite of his receding hairline and pudginess, he had a quiet dignity. He was smart, and multi-lingual, which was an advantage with this bunch. His fluency in Spanish had started the bond between him and Gabriel. They'd joked about being named for angels, and their friendship had been cemented with laughter at the absurdity.

Rafael was also in New York when the woman pacifist was interviewed. A few nights after the program, the two men shared dinner at a favorite restaurant. Rafael mentioned he'd sensed

Gabriel's concern over the last few days. After downing the last gulp of his beer, Gabriel decided to risk confiding in Rafael.

"I don't think any of us is naïve enough to think there aren't more telepaths out there with some variation of our talents," Rafael said. "Obviously we'll stumble on some sooner or later. This woman is simply one of them."

"But she's nothing like us. She's a flaky, middle-aged peacenik."

"Exactly. So how much danger can she pose? She's a nobody." He cut into a cheese enchilada oozing grease. Gabriel looked away in distaste.

"You do have a point, Rafael. It takes money to make our talent useful. We owe our influence to Warren."

"That's right. This woman, what does she have? Read minds, don't read minds. Does it matter for a housewife from Houston?"

"I don't think she's a housewife, but that's not what concerns me. Our encounter was only a few seconds, but I could tell her abilities were well practiced."

Rafael looked surprised. "You think this woman has received some sort of training?"

"Yes. I'm pretty sure she has."

"Oh." Rafael took a sip of his beer before he spoke. "Then, of course, someone has trained her. That someone has you rightfully worried."

"Some *ones*," Gabriel corrected him. "I got the impression there was a group of telepaths who had her back."

"A group? And we've never heard of these people before?"

"I sensed this group goes to great pains to remain hidden."

Rafael's expression was changing. As he finished his beer he turned to Gabriel with worry in his eyes.

"Think about it. If they are hiding from us, they must be up to no good. Why else hide? You need to talk to Warren now."

******

"You do want me to act like an idiot," Lola said.

It was Sunday evening and her good cheer was starting to fade as the reality of the charade sunk in.

"No one wants you to go that far," Maurice said. "Just get on another show and appear indignant, like you can't let this thing drop. If you make enough noise, you'll draw out whoever found you. He's probably looking for you anyway. Then the rest of us will figure out who the hell he is."

"You don't have to go off the deep end," Olumiji added. "Just get his attention. We'll do the rest."

******

Warren Moore hadn't gotten to where he was by trusting any man, and as a matter of principle he trusted women even less. However, he knew he had to rely on others. One couldn't remake society without help.

In the dozen years since he'd taken the reins from his father and turned his family's modest broadcasting company into an international news conglomerate, he'd taken surprising strides towards improving the world. His first stroke of genius was recognizing he needed lots of money to expand. What did he have to sell? Public opinion. So he found people with lots of money, who stood to gain from influencing what people thought.

Other news outlets were squeamish about not reporting everything they knew. Warren Moore was happy to run a news enterprise reporting only the part of the news serving the weapons manufacturers and military consultants that were his investors.

His next stroke of genius was recognizing his company had to be watched, believed and liked. That was journalism. So he searched the world over for other small broadcasting companies experiencing unexpectedly high growth in popularity. He hoped to model his techniques after them.

He found Gabriel and his company BNA in, of all places, Argentina. Warren wasn't fond of Latin America. He didn't know Spanish and never intended to learn it. However, Gabriel and his staff were English-speaking and surprisingly cosmopolitan. They appeared flattered by Warren's curiosity and opened their offices to let him observe.

Warren was baffled. The network didn't seem to be doing anything unusual. They didn't take polls or engage social media in any new way or use outside experts any more capable than Warren's own. Gabriel just seemed to know what people wanted to hear. If he guessed wrong, he figured it out almost instantly. Over and over, his programming was right on the mark. His interviewers asked the perfect questions. His ads had appeal.

"What the hell is going on here?" Warren finally asked the inexplicably successful Gabriel. "You read minds or something?"

The question was met by a long silence.

Then, Warren did the most courageous and brilliant thing he'd ever done in his life. He listened to Gabriel's answer. By the time Gabriel was done talking, Warren believed in psychic abilities and he had a plan.

Gabriel could find others like himself, if they existed. Warren would finance trips to major cities around the world to meet journalists. The field of communication must attract psychics. Most wouldn't have the good fortune to own the company, like Gabriel, but Warren could seek out unusually successful men in journalism and find out what each could do.

Warren could then buy their companies and put the telepaths in charge. Gabriel would train the mind readers, and Warren would turn his simple company into a worldwide conglomerate of unusually popular news outlets. The only caveat was the news had to remain slanted to serve the needs of those paying the fiddler.

That last item turned out to be his final piece of good fortune. Guess what people wanted to hear from the news?

They liked hearing things that scared them. All over the world, in all types of cultures, people would tune in to stories that left them frightened. Or angry. The emotions that fueled the hostilities that made the money for his investors were *exactly* the emotions people wanted from a newscast. How lucky was that? But wait, it got even better.

The stories that caused the emotions that fueled the hostilities that made the money were also the same stories of which there were no shortage, at least for a network willing to continually report the part of the news that suited their agenda. Hell, just today Hamas had launched several hundred rockets, with some hitting Tel Aviv. What more could he want?

Best of all, the more Reel News covered the pieces of the story that riled up the people, the more people got riled up and created more material. It was like a perpetual motion machine. It was like making energy from nothing. It worked so well that it defied physics and logic and it had made Warren Moore rich beyond all reason.

He was practically running the world, even if much of the world didn't realize it because everybody was too busy trying to put out all the flames Warren had fanned.

Warren was feeling pretty damn proud of himself when Gabriel, his original weapon on this road to success, strode into his office to tell him there was problem. It appeared someone else had formed a group of powerful telepaths as well. Gabriel guessed they wanted to rule the world too.

Damn. Just when everything was going so well.

******

Violeta enjoyed the simple comforts of being at her mother's house, as her struggle to keep information out or in melted into a more diffuse sense of loving and being loved. She could see how someone could be a telepath in this situation and hardly know or care.

She'd never spoken of her gift to anyone in her family. As a child she hadn't known it was unusual. As a young teenager, it was an asset on a judo mat, and she'd been afraid it would disqualify her from competition. Never mind that her long hours of practice, and focused mind were more responsible for her wins. To this day, none of her family knew.

No one at all had known until the horrible year her father died. In the sad months after, she lost her decade-long battle to keep her body in the lightweight class, and had to fight larger women. One of them pushed her off the mat forever.

Then a man who interviewed her offered her a better job than she deserved at his television company. He said it was because he knew what she could do. Violeta thought he referred to her budding talents as a reporter, but once she looked closer at his remark, she saw he'd picked up on what she could *really* do, because he could do it too. She took the job and did her best to please this amazing new boss.

She had romantic hopes at first. He was good-looking and they shared a special bond. Sure, she worked for him, but she wasn't the first girl in the world to find her boss attractive.

Then she learned how telepathy could hurt. It wasn't long before she felt the way her injured, less-than-perfect body, repulsed him. She sensed how women fighters weren't his type for girlfriends. She felt him dismiss her telepathic abilities as trivial compared to his own, even though it seemed to her they were on par. Soon she felt how he dismissed her journalistic skills as well. Violeta finally got it. He wanted her for a subordinate, and nothing more.

A younger Violeta would have fought for his attention and admiration, but the grown woman was cagier. She was well paid. Was it worth leaving this easy job so soon? Being underestimated had advantages.

The romance angle withered. She watched his affairs with a string of seemingly perfect women, and noticed how he was too infatuated with himself to care about them. It seemed to Violeta most of the women were much the same.

Her plan was to stay a couple of years, build her resume and move on. It was a good one. Then Reel News bought them, and he offered her a position in New York as his full-time representative at the corporation's headquarters. On paper, she'd be a producer in her own right as she coordinated efforts between the parent company and its Argentinian subsidiary. In reality, her task was to use her unique talents to gather useful information for Gabriel.

Her English had always been good, better than his, really, and by then she and Gabriel had reached an understanding about her telepathy. He understood her talents were small, and she could be trusted because he would know immediately if she couldn't be. She understood her abilities were actually greater than his and she could keep him from knowing anything she didn't want him to know. They were both content with the arrangement.

Once she moved to New York, Violeta was happy to be away from him and to have a glamorous adventure in another country. In fact, she was so thankful for the opportunity that she didn't give much thought to what a U.S. communications conglomerate wanted with a clairvoyant Argentinian manager. Instead, she watched as Gabriel and his new boss traveled the world, bringing back more companies, each with a telepathic and telegenic new executive.

Gabriel's duties shifted to coordinating this group, which Warren dubbed "the monads." Violeta's focus turned to dampening her own talents as the number of telepaths at Reel News kept increasing.

Sitting in her mother's kitchen, it was clear to her she should have been more concerned about what Reel News was trying to do. Warren Moore was likable enough in a rich I-don't-have-time-for-you kind of way. But he used a strong hand in guiding how his reporters and subsidiaries handled the news. They didn't just report it; they shaped and filtered it for a purpose. Because he had a hand in so many different countries now, there wasn't so much an obvious political slant as there was an emotional bent to his message. If Violeta had to put it in a few words, it would be this. *Be afraid. Be very afraid.*

Why would anyone want that?

For that matter, why would anyone want to build a second headquarters in a place as out-of-the-way as Ushuaia? Most of the world couldn't even pronounce the beautiful name "ew SWAY uh." Sitting mere kilometers from the tip of South America, there probably wasn't a more remote city in the world.

That's it. Reel News is coming to Tierra del Fuego because it's the most difficult to reach populated place on any continent.

That made her shiver. A few dozen telepaths, possible control of the world's news, and a bunker sheltered from most of humanity. This couldn't be good.

6. Less Chaos

Lola was surprised by how easy it was to get an interview with a local NPR station. On the Tuesday before Thanksgiving she called Olumiji to let him know.

"They'll interview me next week. Will this get the attention you need?"

"Easily. And it sure beats having this unknown get your address and park outside your house to get a read on you."

"True. Anything special I should do during the interview?"

Olumiji laughed. "Yes, and it's the last piece of advice I'd normally give. Focus on your fear. Really let it overtake you."

"Seriously?"

"We want this person to learn as little about you as possible. Stay distracted. If you start to calm down, move on to being mad."

"Angry at Reel News? Or just general pissiness?"

"I'd try for the first. When your mind drifts to x^0, and it will, because it's so hard *not* to think about a topic, try to diminish what we are. Think of a single person, maybe Maurice. Elderly, well meaning, not threatening."

It was Lola's turn to laugh. "I wouldn't tangle with Maurice."

"Neither would I, but we'd like them to see you, and us, as harmless. Once you work your way through fear, anger, and helplessness, move on to general pissiness at your own discretion."

Lola could feel her friend's wink in her mind, and she sent one back.

"I got this."

"Good. Because while you're busy overreacting, I'll have the best team of telepaths possible trying to figure out who the hell this person is."

******

Violeta spent much of the next day fretting about Warren Moore's secret building project in Ushuaia. Why keep something like that hidden? As far as she knew, Gabriel knew nothing about it, and Warren seemed to include Gabriel in on everything. The lack of openness on this project was frightening.

Maybe it was time to leave Reel News. She had enough experience now to get a decent job some place else. She could live here with her mom while she job-hunted. Her mom would love it, and there was no safer place in the world to be.

No wait. Her mom's house would be within miles of the Reel News complex. In fact, her family and everyone she loved would be at the epicenter of whatever Warren Moore was planning. This could be the worst possible place in the world to be.

Could she get her family to move? She was sure they wouldn't consider it based on the sketchy information she had now. She could stay here and try to protect them, but from what? The fact was, she could learn more about what Warren was planning if she was back in New York.

The judoka inside of her began to wake up. Violeta Delgado hadn't fought for anything in the eleven years since she was carried off a mat, afraid she might never walk again. She'd moved cautiously since, working to stay unnoticed and unhurt.

Open your eyes. You have people to protect.

"I wish you could stay longer," her mom said that night, when Violeta told her she was heading back to New York. Violeta took both of her mother's hands and wrapped her own around them like a blanket.

"So do I, mom. But I can't take that chance."

Her mother gave her an odd look, but said no more.

✱✱✱✱✱✱

When Lola got home from work Tuesday night, Alex and Teddie were in a heated conversation. She thought of all the possibly reasons why and none of them were good. Then she stopped to listen.

"It's not funny, dad. It's seriously depressing."

"You don't have to look at it that way."

"Of course I do. You spend a whole week deriving these complicated, awful equations and right before a holiday you tell a bunch of vulnerable teenagers you've proved the universe sucks."

Alex was a teacher at Teddie's high school, but this was the first time he'd had her in class. They'd both tried to avoid the situation, but he taught the school's only advanced physics course, which Teddie had been determined to take.

"What are you studying?" Lola asked.

"Thermodynamics." Alex whispered it.

"Mom. Did you know that when it comes to chaos, it is always increasing and you can't do a thing about it?"

"You're talking about the silverware drawer? Or entropy? Either way, I know the problem."

"Stop it, mom. I'm talking about how the universe is getting worse every second, and dad thinks it's funny. He told us thermodynamics proves you can't win. At best you break even. Then he laughed."

Lola gave Alex a look.

"The law says disorder stays the same or increases, not that things *get worse*. I was just trying to say it in a way teenagers would listen to me."

"But don't you care about the fate of the universe?"

"Honestly, no," Alex said.

"Chaos doesn't have to grow around you," Lola added. "You can create order and beauty. These laws are on a grand scale; they don't dictate your personal life. Okay?"

"I suppose."

With that, the tiny place in the universe known as the Zeitman's living room returned to a state of less chaos.

Lola's oldest child Zane arrived Wednesday to celebrate Thanksgiving. Teddie was happy to have her big brother around, and Lola wished middle child Ariel could be there, too. But their twenty-four-year-old daughter had accepted a job in Dublin a year ago, and she was knee-deep in her own problems. The next day, as Lola prepared the family feast, she sensed her daughter's apprehension.

Before dinner, they dialed Ariel for a video chat. Teddie and Ariel knew about their mother's telepathic capabilities, so it didn't surprise Lola both girls usually kept their mental guard up around her. As the family talked, however, Lola was pleased Ariel wasn't trying to conceal her concerns.

"Things have gotten shaky over here," she said. "Some of my clients are involved in some serious shit. I'm trying to do the right thing, but I'll be in danger in a few days."

Lola felt Ariel's permission to enter her mind and learn more, so she let the others visit while she did. Her daughter needed information about a man in Iceland who posed a threat to her.

"I wish I knew someone in Iceland, but I don't." Lola interrupted the conversation. "I'll find out if my friends do. Please be careful, dear. I'll try to find someone who can help you. Let's talk in a few days."

"Thanks. I love you all." Ariel signed off.

As they waved and laughed and said their goodbyes, Lola was already coming to terms with what she'd learned about her daughter and was reaching out to her network for help.

Lola didn't have much more information when she called Ariel back early Sunday morning, but she promised her daughter she'd keep trying and would maintain her own loose mental surveillance over the next few days.

"Definitely. Do anything you can to help me, please."

"I will," her mom promised. "You won't sense my presence, but you can count on me to be there."

After she got off the phone she shared her frustrations with her husband.

"Not a lot of well-developed telepaths in Iceland. I have one lead so far, but what are we going to do about it?"

Alex looked puzzled. "I thought your group x^0 would send a team racing over to Reykjavik, no questions asked."

Lola shook her head. "Maybe under normal circumstances but right now they're all in a tizzy about this telepath I found."

"How serious is the trouble Ariel has gotten herself into?"

"It's hard to tell. She let me know—how can I say this—she seems to have an ability to sense what will happen. She's had it from birth and kept it from everyone, but yesterday I could see how she does it. It's caused the trouble she's in. One of her clients has the ability too and he uses it to beat the stock market."

To Lola's amusement Alex walked right by the issue of precognition.

"Do you mean to tell me my daughter could use prescience to invest in stocks? That's brilliant. She could get rich! Think she could help us with occasional investment advice?"

"Alex, she could be in a lot of trouble. Worse yet, she's afraid this man may try to kill her to ensure she doesn't put a stop to what he's doing."

Lola watched as various emotions played out across her husband's face. It was easy enough for him to accept Ariel had an unusual ability. His family was full of people with odd gifts. Ariel was the only one who had appeared to be normal, except for him. But this future thing made sense. It even explained a lot of Ariel's past behavior.

"Her clairvoyance is a lot like my telepathy. She doesn't know everything she wants to know, and she can't make it tell her what she needs it to. But she knows she is in danger."

Lola felt Alex switch into dad mode.

"Then I'll go to Iceland. I'll find this telepath you've heard about and I'll bring her to Ariel. What are dads for?"

"I think you're supposed to be my protection detail while I go do this *other* thing tomorrow. You know, the interview to bait the evil telepath. Besides, I'm not sure anyone should run off to Iceland. People in her company are trying to help her, and Zane's friend Toby…"

Lola hardly got Zane's name out of her mouth before she and Alex both knew who needed to go to Iceland.

"Do you think he'll have to take incompletes in his classes?" Lola asked. "I hope not. I hate to ask this of him now. He's supposed to leave for the airport today to go back to school."

"Zane can handle his studies. He's the right person for the job. He can find your telepath, and give Ariel a hand, and he can do it better than anybody, because he can look like anyone he needs to while he does it."

Lola had to agree. Zane had spent years developing extraordinary control over tiny muscles most humans remained unaware of, and as a result he could alter his body shape and facial features.

"First I need to tell him his mother reads minds," she said.

"Yes," Alex agreed. "That conversation is way overdue."

Zane shared his father's outward calm, and, in spite of his need to pack, he listened to his mother's detailed explanation of her past few years. He seemed almost amused when his mother finally got to her confession of her abilities.

"I was afraid it would freak you kids out; I thought you might not want to be close to me," she said.

"Mom, we always thought you read minds when we were little. So, turns out you didn't start until I was in my twenties. I can accept that." He was more disturbed by his mom's upcoming attempt to bait a potentially unfriendly telepath.

"It's under control," she assured him. "I've got this part to play tomorrow, and then it's out of my hands. But that's why I need your help."

She described Ariel's situation and was surprised again.

"Mom, I already know about that. I've been relaying messages between her and my friend Toby, and I promised Ariel I wouldn't tell you guys how she's a natural-born fortune-teller."

He looked thoughtful.

"Do you think we need, like, family therapy or something to get all this who-can-do-what stuff out into the open?"

Lola couldn't help laughing. "You have a point. When you get back from Iceland we need to talk about Teddie."

"Her too? Sheesh, mom, what did you do? Take some kind of weird vitamins when you were pregnant?"

"How come I'm getting blamed?"

"Because dad seems to be the only normal one in the family."

"He acts like he is, but I'm not so sure."

"Family therapy it is, then. No question. Maybe over Christmas."

As Alex predicted, Zane cancelled his flight back to campus, made arrangements to miss school, and booked a flight for Reykjavik the next day to meet with Lola's lead, an elderly telepathic woman in the Icelandic countryside.

Lola gave Zane all the contact information she had with a skeptical shake of the head.

"It's okay, mom. I got this. Go be a superhero. Be glad you got kids that can do the same."

Lola got ready for bed that night, trying to calm her nerves as she went through the routine of laying out her clothes for the morning. Maybe the soothing color of her favorite purple dress would help get her through the stressful day.

She reached for the jewelry box that held her best earrings, and the little porcelain angel sitting next to it caught her eye. It was one of the few relics from her childhood, a tiny figurine of a young girl in a sparkly purple dress with beautiful white swan wings and a gold halo above her head. It said "Tuesday's Child Full of Grace."

Lola guessed it represented the guardian angel of those lucky to be born on a Tuesday based on some obscure nursery rhyme. She picked the little figure up and studied it. Part of one of the wings had broken off, but the other still had the swirly white feathers she'd loved as a child.

She crawled into bed, expecting hours of tossing and turning, but the next thing she knew the alarm was waking her up with its song.

November 2012

7. Quarantine

The second interview went well. The host of the show was sympathetic and a little amused by Lola's animosity about her first interview. Lola tried to be as nervous and angry as she could be and kept the internal turmoil up until she left the studio.

No one expected the mystery telepath to cause her harm, but Alex came with her anyway and insisted they stop for ice cream on the way home. She'd almost calmed down when they pulled into their driveway and she saw a woman from a courier service ringing their doorbell.

The envelope had to be signed for by Lola Zeitman. Lola felt her hand shake as she scribbled her signature on the touch screen. She tore it open and read:

Hi Lola. I hope this arrives soon after you get home. You handled the interview well. We located the telepath and are sifting through what we learned. We've already gathered enough information to know we're dealing with a large and powerful group. Because of this, we must quarantine you immediately.

Olumiji wants you to know we've got an impenetrable wall of white noise surrounding you. Yes, we can do that. The good news is you can relax and think about anything you want.

The bad news is you won't be able to communicate with anyone until we lift the wall. We know this is bad timing because your son Zane left for Iceland this morning and you want to know how things are going for him. Rest assured we'll do our best to provide support as he makes contact with the telepath there.

We also know your daughter's situation is urgent. We know how hard it will be not to reach out to her. However, contact from you could endanger your children, as well as the rest of us.

Please don't use conventional communication to ask me or anyone else for details. x^0 will also quarantine anyone you contact.

This will take a while to fix. We'll be in touch once we can.

Lola stared at the note, signed, "With love and affection, Maurice."

Her first reaction was disbelief.

Never in her life had she needed her powers more than now. She'd promised Ariel she'd be there for her. Her own daughter, far away and in danger, had for the first time in her life asked her mother for help. Ariel would think her mother was listening, standing by in case of emergency, ready to alert police or send others rushing to the rescue.

Lola would not be there, and she couldn't even let Ariel know she wasn't there.

Lola felt sick to her stomach. She started to cry. She knew the quick tears were the aftermath of frothing up her emotions during the interview, but in seconds she was furious. The one time in her life this damn telepathy would have been useful, she was banned from using it. Anger was followed by a cold, hard fear for her daughter, then followed by a horrible sense of loneliness and the unfairness of it all. The tears had worked into gasping sobs as Alex came back outside.

"Is everyone okay?"

Lola glared at him. "*Everyone* is fine. Maurice sent me this note to tell me I've been kicked out of x^0 for now. They've put some kind of psychic wall around me. I can't help Ariel. I can't keep tabs on Zane. I can't do anything and my kids have never needed me more."

"Why would they do that to you? You did everything they asked."

"They think I'm a liability. They found out there's another group out there, and can't afford for me to draw these people to them, or even to my own family, until they know more."

"Oh. It does kind of make sense then. You don't want us dangled as bait." At Lola's look he softened his tone. "Look, I know you want to be there for Ariel, but Zane is capable, and

Maurice knows your situation. He'll monitor her just like you would. She's going to have the help she needs."

Lola realized Alex was right about Maurice. She could trust her friend. Before she had time to raise other objections, Alex took her by the hand and pulled her inside while he looked for a subject change. Lola loved to travel.

"Hey, we haven't talked about a vacation in a long time. How about this summer we go somewhere interesting?"

He watched Lola consider letting go of her worry. "I dreamt about Tierra del Fuego again last night. This time you and I were going to sail there. We could go somewhere and learn to sail."

"I don't think sailing is such a good idea. But, hey …. we could look into a trip to Argentina. Could we afford it? See Buenos Aries. Visit vineyards. You look at rocks in Patagonia. We learn to tango."

"We could end up at Tierra del Fuego!" The water in her eyes was being replaced with fire, and Alex knew there was no undoing what he'd started.

"Exactly. You've got some spare time now that you aren't mind-chatting with your friends, so instead of worrying, why not plan a dream vacation for us?"

She looked so happy. Alex tried to think of something positive about a twelve-hour flight, but all he could come up with was where they'd be going was extremely remote. Surely no place on Earth was safer from a gaggle of evil telepaths than the tip of South America?

******

Warren had assumed his innate intelligence and considerable wealth would be enough to keep three dozen men beholden to him, in spite of the fact they could all do something he could not.

Now that he was in a room with all of them for the first time, he reconsidered the wisdom of that assumption. They were communicating with each other, there was no doubt. Even he could tell from the nuances of expressions and gestures that silent exchanges were taking place.

Gabriel told him telepathy communicated feelings and the recipient supplied words in his own head based on the emotions transmitted. This made it a vague tool, useful for some kinds of things, like naturally spanning language barriers.

Warren guessed these men were sharing their feelings, and judging by the way the men kept glancing at him, those emotions had to do with him. Well, enough of this.

"Ahem," he said, taking the mic. "I took the extraordinary step of bringing you all together tonight because we face an unprecedented challenge. I know many of you traveled far and several of you are listening to my words through a translation program. Thank you for being part of this momentous first meeting of our entire Entelechy. I hope to make this an annual event."

He paused. The men looked at him with expressionless faces. He wished he could read a crowd half as well as any of them.

"Our company is becoming the main source of news for the citizens of Earth." He tried to interject a warm smile and failed. "That success is due to your thirty-five media outlets." This got a nod or two of appreciation.

"You men were catapulted into leadership roles because you possess a rare talent. Some of you knew it before Gabriel came along, others were less sure. Gabriel has helped each of you develop your abilities well beyond what they were when we found you. I understand he's done a fine job with this."

Murmurs of agreement followed.

"My job is to help you become adept businessmen, a skill that is just as necessary. Many of you lack experience in management or finances, but we're fixing that. With the resources I offer, your success is guaranteed."

There. Let's get the part about my usefulness out on the table. He noticed several polite nods. He'd have liked to see a little more energy in them, but he'd take what he could get.

"I was told there must be more adepts like you out there who are untrained and confused about what they can do. We'll continue to seek them out, but you men will always be more powerful." He paused to make sure he had their attention.

"I've been thinking a lot about that over the past few days. What if we were to face opposition from a group like our own? I think that could cause a problem. Maybe some of you think no such thing could exist without our knowing about it."

He waited. The faces in front of him waited without expression. Damn, why wasn't this telepathy shit something he could be taught, or catch like a virus, or buy from one of these guys like an organ?

"The other day, we had a woman in our studio. Gabriel determined she was a well trained telepath, on par with many of you. No, I didn't think females could control their emotions well enough to be good at this either." He let the chuckles finish before he went on. "She doesn't scare me. She can go home and have all the silent conversations she wants with her cats."

More laughter.

"What bothers me is Gabriel is certain she has a teacher. We think he is an old man who is part of some larger group. They could be some cluster of aging pacifists. What sounds more harmless than that, right? Yet, even old men can influence others, and pacifists are dangerous. Do you know why?"

This time Warren only paused for a second, because he had every intention of answering his own question.

"These particular fools would convince the world to forsake or limit the production and sale of arms. In the name of peace, they would give up the ability to defend themselves. Do you have any idea of the horrors that would be inflicted on the human race if good men like us gave up our ability to protect ourselves and those we love? Ban the bomb? Recall automatic weapons? Sign treaties? Forsake information-gathering in the name of privacy or for humanitarian considerations? Please. This is a dangerous world. We think this woman is affiliated with dangerous people.

"So, we're looking into her. She did an interview on the radio yesterday, and several of you worked with Gabriel to learn more about her. You said she appeared harmless, and I believed you."

To Warren's satisfaction he saw a few surprised faces in the audience.

"But you were wrong. Gentlemen, she tricked you. How do *I* know? Because while your telepathic abilities were being toyed with, I went at this the old-fashioned way. I hired a private detective in Houston, where Lola lives."

Now there was a bit of restlessness in the room as various men shuffled in their seats.

"That's right, her name is Lola. When I showed this woman's picture to my PI, he knew her! Turns out four years ago, my guy Harold was hired to find some dirt on Lola's family. Guess what?"

Warren paused to enjoy the attention he was being given.

"Four years ago, Lola walked up to Harold in a parking lot and started rattling off things to him about his personal life and his private indiscretions. That's right. Even Harold recognized she'd read his mind and done a real good job of it, too. Scared the heebee jeebees out of him, and when he asked her how she knew this stuff she started to brag. She told him she was a telepath with a whole lot of telepath friends, and if he knew what was good for him he'd go back to his client and say he'd found nothing. Harold was smart enough to do just that. He doesn't want anything to do with her even now, but he kept his file on the family. I bought those files from him yesterday.

"Lola is our entry point into this dangerous organization. We have to find them—all of them—and we need to use every tool available to us. No less than the safety of our world depends on it."

Even Warren could sense the surprise in the room and the increase in respect he was being afforded. He didn't try to hide his self-satisfied smile. It would have been pointless, the telepaths all felt it anyway.

******

Violeta stayed in the background, finding ways to assist Gabriel as he prepared for Warren's first meeting of the Entelechy. She was glad she'd made it back from Ushuaia for this, in part because she could tell he didn't want her around for the meeting. She made motions to leave each time he dismissed her, then thought of one more helpful thing to do. Finally, as the others arrived, Gabriel became too distracted to continue ushering her out the door. She'd counted on that.

She remained busy enough to justify her presence, keeping up the soft white noise she always held when several of the monads were around. They all ignored her. As Warren began to speak, all eyes and minds turned toward him.

Violeta studied the man. He was physically impressive, tall and well built for his age, with thick white hair. His personality took over a room, keeping everyone else on edge with his questions and demands. She sensed how he loved being in charge and thought he was good at it. He worked to keep a firm hand on the till of society, and believed society was the better for it.

However, he also radiated fear. Not nervousness, but a deep dread of any society in which men like him weren't in complete control. He loved the present order of things, which made sense, because the present order of things was quite good for him.

He feared power or influence in the hands of anyone he deemed as "other." These others included females not captivated by his charms or who lacked charms by his definition. At one time it had also included males of other ethnic groups, but Warren had seen the necessity of overcoming his own racism in forming the Entelechy. Now, inclusivity of the strongest males of other ethnic groups was a means to an end for him.

What was that end? It had to do with Warren being an honorable man. He felt loyalty to those who'd given him his power, and he intended to do right by them. He and his Entelechy would nurture the concerns that prompted the wars that required the weapons being built by the stockholders who'd allowed him to grow his company. Violeta listened to part of Warren's short speech, planning to leave before Gabriel noticed how long she'd stayed. She'd picked up her purse and coat when Warren's words turned to how powerful and dangerous the woman Lola was.

"Lola is our entry point into this threatening organization. We must find all of them. We must understand what they do, and we must neutralize them. The safety of our world depends on it."

Good Lord. They were going to go after this poor woman *again*?

The sport of judo has a history of honor, and of protecting the weak. Decades ago, young Violeta bought into that philosophy, and, deep within, she still embraced it. As she listened to Warren speak, she knew what she had to do. She added Lola, and Lola's own, to the circle of people she was sworn to protect.

So be it. Warren had his ethics, and ample weapons. He was a worthy opponent. She bowed softly in his direction. Let the match begin.

8. An Awkward Question

It hurt Maurice to think of his friend and protégé Lola without her powers at a time when she needed them so much. He wished he'd been able to offer more information or even more comfort to her in the short note he'd been asked to write, but Olumiji insisted he be terse and vague.

The one thing he could do for her now was watch her kids like the proverbial hawk. Others were busy this morning looking into emergency resources available in Iceland, and awaiting Maurice's word to send help if needed. However, because Maurice was the telepath closest to the Zeitman family, he was the most qualified to monitor Ariel and Zane's emotional states.

Thanks to time differences, his day of being a hawk started at 1 a.m. He made a good strong cup of hot cocoa and prepared to spend the wee hours of the morning doing what he needed to do.

An hour later, a wave of embarrassment jolted him awake. Not his own, but someone else's. He felt Zane's awkwardness as he leaned against the glass door of a grocery store freezer, listening to an elderly woman yell in a strange language. Oh good. Zane had made it across the Atlantic. This tiny emotional woman had to be the Icelandic telepath.

Maurice put out feelers for Lola's daughter and felt the young woman had a plan of her own. So far, her plan was on track. Very well. Instructions were to let Ariel proceed unhindered unless she made it clear she needed help.

Maurice rubbed his eyes. Looked like he wasn't quite as good at staying awake as he'd been back in his seventies. Time for a second cup of cocoa, maybe with a little instant coffee mixed in.

As the day wore on, Maurice went for three walks and splashed his face with ice water every fifteen minutes as both youngsters proceeded with their plans. Finally, Maurice felt a pang of frustration from Ariel as she was forced to change tactics. He felt her mind race with possibilities. He wished he could get more details, but he was pretty sure planes, boats, and wetsuits were involved. Wetsuits? Yes, definitely wetsuits. As Maurice splashed his face with ice water one more time, he was positive the young lady needed to get her hands on some high quality cold water apparel.

Maurice sought out his counterpart in Oslo for help.

"Somebody has to know someone in Reykjavik who owns a sporting goods store," he pleaded. "Learn more about what's happening at this office. Who else is there? We don't need the police to barge in. We need to help her carry out her own plan."

✻✻✻✻✻✻

From the beginning, Gabriel helped Warren ferret out data on competitors and news sources. It gave the conglomerate an edge. It wasn't much of a leap to get information on enemies of Reel News. On occasion, he gave Warren information to be used as leverage for coercing others, personally as well as professionally.

Because he'd helped Warren vet the other monads, he knew the group was remarkably homogeneous. No one had fervent political or religious feelings; Warren regarded both as a flaw. Every member believed the strong were entitled to enjoy their lives, without wasting time or money on causes.

Every one was endowed in multiple arenas. None were sadistic or psychotic, attributes which would have deemed them unworthy. Passion to do evil, or even passion to do anything, was considered a weakness during the screening process. Two potential members had been disqualified merely because of the intensity of their emotions.

One man who barely made the cut sat across the dinner table from Gabriel tonight. Fifty-year-old, balding Rafael was no great physical specimen, but he'd been included because of his exceptional telepathic powers, his intelligence and his inner strength. He also wrote poetry and had amazing soulful eyes, but that was window dressing.

Gabriel would have pegged him as the monad least likely to cause trouble, and yet, it felt like Rafael was about to do just that. Gabriel's attention wandered over the dark wood booths and red leather seats giving this steak house the feel of a rich man's den. He noticed the care with which Rafael was choosing his words.

"I know you're beholden to Warren, and I'm talking to you as his second, as well as my friend. He has an agenda and it's not one he told us about when we formed our business alliance. Last night when he spoke, it was obvious the idea of peace bores him."

Gabriel understood. "He was unusually frank with us because these new telepaths have gotten under his skin. If you must know, Warren sees his politics as protecting what's good in this world. He thinks he's a cautious realist, not a warmonger."

"Really? It seemed to me he wants to play with toy soldiers."

"Maybe he does. So what's it to you?"

"There isn't a man in the Entelechy who minds if Warren controls world news. But using that power to keep the world in conflict could cause a rift between him and the monads."

"Why? Do *you* have moral objections to his beliefs?"

A small smile formed on Rafael's lips. He understood the chess game that had begun.

"Not particularly. I'm not fond of killing, of course. No sane man is. But I fear Warren's zeal for stirring up wars will hit close to home, eventually. Even monads have family." He paused. "And friends and lovers. When you fear for the safety of those you care for, moral objections follow. Warren would be well served to find different investors and leave his old allegiances behind."

"I understand your concern, but he doesn't want to do that. So is our ultimate loyalty to Warren or to the Entelechy he formed?"

The waiter arrived with two steaks. Rafael looked at his hungrily, but Gabriel turned up his nose at the smell. Why could no one in New York equal the tender aged beef of his homeland?

As the waiter moved off, Rafael answered.

"I'm not trying to make trouble; I'm trying to avoid it. I don't know how a conflict between Warren and the Entelechy ends but we're both powerful and could do considerable damage to each other."

"I think we hold the better cards," Gabriel said. "Warren is hard to read, but I suspect he thinks we have the advantage, too. I catch a whiff of concern under his take-charge words."

"Then perhaps you could encourage Warren to be less involved with how we convey the news? The subsidiaries all want less direction. He has more pressing business matters to attend to."

"I can try," Gabriel said. "But I doubt he'll back off from doing what he loves. He doesn't want to own a news conglomerate; he wants to shape what happens. From his point of view, why shouldn't he?" Rafael was too engrossed in garnishing his baked potato to answer. "I know you mean well. Look, I don't get to steer the ship much, but I promise I'll try to head it toward more peaceful waters. Okay?"

The older man nodded with his mouth full. He was, from all appearances, totally engrossed in enjoying his steak. The conversation was over.

******

Lola had settled onto the couch with her laptop hoping for some distractions when the call came. Maybe it was Zane, contacting her from Iceland? She was disappointed when she heard an unfamiliar female voice with a faint Spanish accent.

"You're who?"

Out came a story of working for Reel News, and how media magnate Warren Moore had formed an improbable league of telepaths, and now it was an awful mess and going to get worse.

Lola knew she was on her own, isolated from x^0. Any effort to help this woman was too risky. "I feel bad for you; Violet was it? I do. I just can't be of much help right now."

The woman laughed. "You're confused. I don't want *your* help."

"Oh." Lola wasn't sure what to say.

"The name is Vee oh lay tah. With an ay tah on the end. We met in the studio two weeks ago. *You* are in danger. I'm offering you my protection, but only if you wish it. Yes or no?"

Well, this was awkward.

"Yes. I suppose."

Violeta explained she'd made the call intending to form a working mental connection but had encountered the psychic wall of fuzz surrounding Lola and guessed its purpose.

"Do you know when your people will take down the wall?"

Lola had no idea, but she hesitated. If Violeta's offer of help was a ruse, "never" was the best answer.

"I think there's a good chance they never will." She realized the barricade around her brain kept her from knowing if Violeta was telling the truth, but it also kept Violeta from detecting her lie. The deception worked.

"You're probably right. It would be the safest path for your teachers. You don't need telepathy for me to look out for you. Be patient, I'll find other ways to stay in touch."

As she hung up, Lola wondered if her lie had been the truth. Could her mental gift be gone forever?

She woke in the middle of the night, nauseous and afraid. She was sure Zane and Ariel's experiences were getting through to her on some low frequency, emergency mom channel. It didn't matter though. She couldn't help them.

In the morning, she called in sick. After Alex and Teddie left for school, she put on a pot of coffee and considered her next move with Violeta. Her instincts said to trust this woman, but she lacked her usual supporting information. She had to know more.

Okay. x^0 had taken away her telepathic abilities, but the internet still worked. Lola searched Warren Moore and the rest of his explosively popular conglomerate. Probably should have done that sooner.

Reel News was publicly held, so a wealth of information was available. About a decade ago, Warren Moore had gone on an unprecedented buying binge, acquiring a foothold in thirty-two countries over a few years. His new subsidiaries rose in popularity and become a major news source, in every single case.

Lola found the "in every single case" part odd. Had Warren Moore become a telepath ten years ago? It would explain a lot.

She found videos of interviews done over the years. Being a telepath didn't fit. He had enough manners to not be rude, but his awareness of the feelings of others was minimal. He wasn't the mind she'd encountered.

She looked at the subsidiaries. Most of their chiefs were from nations across the globe. Argentina, Australia, Austria, Belgium, Brazil, Canada, Egypt, France, Germany. It looked like an inventory of the thirty richest countries on Earth. Well, not counting China and Russia, but she assumed there were barriers to owning subsidiaries there.

She examined the thumbnail photos. My goodness. When had she seen such a collection of attractive men?

When she got to the top of the list her gaze settled on Gabriel Varela, head of the Argentinian company BNA. Lola could feel the tiny hairs on her arm stand up. It was him. She knew it. Her mind sought him and encountered the fuzzy wall around her. Right. She couldn't find him, but then again, he couldn't find her. For the first time, the wall felt comforting.

She clicked on his photo, and was taken to a page giving information about BNA and its talented personnel. There she was. Violeta Delgado was chief liaison between BNA and its parent company. She was the woman who'd greeted Lola at the New York studio, and produced the disastrous interview.

Her long dark hair framed a finely chiseled bronze face. She was attractive, in a fierce way. Lola hadn't found the woman to be friendly, although she'd been difficult to gauge. In spite of her fashionable business attire, and the cane she leaned on, Lola got the feeling there was a warrior deep inside.

Now that she had a last name, her fingers flew. She didn't expect much of an internet footprint, but she was wrong. Violeta Delgado had once been a rising star in Argentina's robust women's judo program. Articles noted she'd fought well throughout her twenties before an injury ended her career. A fluff interview for the 2000 Olympics claimed twenty-nine-year-old Violeta was the darling of Tierra del Fuego.

Tierra del Fuego? *Really*?

She flipped back to the BNA page. Violeta began working for Gabriel in 2001. The timing fit. She'd been a close assistant since. He must trust her, and she him.

Why the bizarre phone call offering Lola protection?

******

Olumiji had never seen x^0 in crisis mode like this. There was a team working to keep Lola isolated. Another was protecting the team trying to figure out who these men at Reel News were. He had a side group tending to Lola's children while another worked to keep those children off of everyone's radar screen.

All this fuzzy wall nonsense took so many people. Olumiji preferred a world where telepaths got along.

******

Wednesday night Lola did everything she could to calm down. A bubble bath with wine. Yoga with soft spa music. A half-pint of ice cream. It combined to create a weird inner peace. She was headed out the door in the morning when her phone played Zane's ring tone. She couldn't answer it fast enough.

"Mom. Everything's okay."

"They let you call me?"

"You're my mom. I call you. There's no 'let.' I'm at the airport in Reykjavik about to board. Ariel's fine."

"How do you know she's fine?" She heard her son's sigh.

"Because the asshole who tried to kill her is in a coma. Look, I'm glad I came; I had a lovely time. I met your friend in Iceland. Ariel and I got to go skydiving together and go for a boat ride."

"You had time to do tourist things? Isn't it a little cold in Iceland for skydiving?"

"Yeah, it's a bad idea this time of year. Listen, we'll fill you in on the *whole* story later, but stop worrying. Ariel says she sees the holidays as being a little shaky. We'll be there. I'll call you once I'm back at school. Bye."

Lola looked at her phone and shook her head. She had so many more questions. Yet it was enough to know Ariel and Zane were safe. She tucked her phone into her purse, and resolved to do everything she could to have a normal day.

December 2012

9. Never Here

Olumiji was glad Lola's children were out of danger. Not only was it great news, but it also freed up more of his best telepaths to look into the Entelechy. For now, x^0 had the advantage. They'd learned Warren's telepaths were also his top employees, making them easy to find. Olumiji wanted to learn all he could before this balance of power changed.

He took on the task of probing into Warren Moore. The head of Reel News presented challenges. Warren was a person with no telepathic skills who knew he was surrounded by telepaths, so Warren worked at being hard to read. He didn't think about anything for long. When he wasn't engaged in work-related tasks, he occupied his mind with sports and entertainment. When he wanted to be safe, he played with words games and puzzles, sandwiching bits of analysis in-between a lot of gibberish. It was clever, and it spoke of the deep distrust Warren felt towards others. It also seemed like an exhausting way to live.

Distrust appeared to permeate Warren's organization, too. As Olumiji spent time in the man's head, he learned more about these monads. They made frequent furtive darts into Warren's mind, hoping to find information to gain them an advantage over their brothers. Each feared being detected by another while snooping; none stayed long enough to understand Warren's deeper motivations.

For the past few days, the swooping monads hadn't sensed Olumiji's presence. They didn't expect him and didn't probe deep enough to find him. After two days, Olumiji thought he'd spent more time examining Warren than his own telepaths had, and he knew something those closest to him did not.

Warren had a secret, a secret so big he couldn't afford to think about it. Olumiji struggled to fathom the self discipline such a feat would take. The secret was wrapped up in Warren's fear of his own men, and his dread they would someday decide they didn't need him. His distrust of those not like him fueled what he'd done, or was doing, or was going to do. No matter how deeply Olumiji burrowed into Warren's brain, he couldn't get more information. Warren had trained himself to pick up a Sudoku puzzle anytime his mind wandered in that direction.

Right now, Warren was reviewing the days headlines and Olumiji felt the man's pleasure as he read of the strife in the world. Olumiji shuddered. Until now, he'd believed there was no such thing as an enemy. People made bad decisions, and they had different tastes and beliefs. There were misunderstandings but honesty, forgiveness and tolerance cured all. However, Warren was an anomaly. He was as devoted to perpetuating conflict as Olumiji was committed to peaceful co-existence. Getting along with him was impossible by definition. Olumiji faced the uncomfortable fact that he could have an enemy after all.

Warren moved on to reading a report he'd bought from a private investigator in Houston. Odd. Olumiji felt Warren's curiosity. This investigator had looked into Lola's family a few years ago and amassed pages of details. One page discussed a family friend named Maurice. Warren was happy. This Maurice sounded like the elderly family friend Warren's people claimed had trained Lola. Warren picked up the phone to get someone to look into Maurice immediately.

Damn. These guys are close to finding x^0. So much for having an advantage.

Olumiji wondered how Warren and this private eye had found each other. Warren was thinking about the same thing. No, he was laughing about it. Laughing about how lucky he was Lola Zeitman had marched up to this detective years ago and told him she could read minds and was part of a big scary organization of telepaths.

Lola did what? To be fair, it didn't sound like her. Yet the private eye had told him this story. *Lola, what were you thinking?*

Olumiji put his head in his hands. It looked like Lola needed to come out of quarantine. Now that Warren knew of Maurice, there was no point wasting the energy to isolate her. Also, Olumiji needed to get some answers.

******

When Lola woke up early on Saturday, the wall was gone. She could feel the blurry questions in her husband's head as he puzzled over something in his dream. Upstairs, Teddie was in a deep sleep. Further away she felt son Zane gulp the last of his coffee, while even further away, Ariel stood under the cold, bright blue of the midday sun. They were all well.

Lola settled into the cozy feel of her own mind, all of her own mind, and enjoyed being whole. Then, it occurred to her to wonder what had happened.

******

Maurice got out of bed to make his second trip to the bathroom. He was as healthy an eighty-eight-year-old as he could have hoped, but even then the nightly bathroom trips came with the territory. As he swung a foot onto the floor, he felt it. For the first time since his wife died a decade ago, the voices in his head were silent and the parade of emotions had stopped. He was alone.

Maurice fought down the wave of fear accompanying the realization. He'd obviously been found by the others and was now a risk to x^0. These Entelechy people must have broken through the wall around Lola, which was horrible. He hoped she was okay.

A second wave of fear came with the idea that evil strangers were trying to force their way into his head. In his years of being a telepath, he'd never encountered an entrance by force. What was his best move now? He could add a wall of his own. He could use distractions. Maybe watch TV or look at his bank statement. All good ideas. But first, he should go the bathroom.

******

Judo had taught Violeta battle skills. Feint. Wait. Surprise. Yield. Pivot. Roll. Attack.

Could these combat techniques be used psychically? To look out for others, she needed to know more about what Warren intended, and she had to find out without arousing suspicion. Who were the most dangerous monads? Were there any potential allies? Who knew what was planned for the business complex in her hometown? Those techniques could help her get answers.

Violeta knew how to practice and she began adapting old skills to new problems. She sought out the secrets of the old woman in the apartment next door. Feint. Wait. Surprise. She tried her techniques with the doorman. Yield. Pivot. How about the family running the little bakery across the street? Of course. Roll. Attack.

By Sunday night she felt ready to take on Warren. Violeta knew he had a younger wife who was often gone and a hoard of servants, but tonight a lone employee brought him his standard Sunday night cold supper to eat while he worked. Most of his household took Sunday off.

Violeta paused. This intrusion seemed ruder with someone she knew. *This is a battle. Press on.*

She felt how Warren liked working. He liked it a lot. He knew his wife was out having fun with people who'd bore him, at loud flashy places he didn't enjoy. Having a pretty young wife was expected, but he didn't want her around most of the time. He preferred his work.

Incredible. This man is not particularly fond of his wife, but loves his work so much that he spends time thinking about how much he loves it.

Violeta burrowed in further and got the impression there weren't many things Warren let himself ponder for long, because he lived in fear of his own monads being in his head. Of course he did. One safe topic he could always allow his mind to linger on was how important his job was. He did nothing less than protect the human race.

Really?

Warren understood the sad truth. Men were prone to laziness at best and violence at worst, and had to be prodded into productivity. Their aggression needed direction. Guilt and fear were crude tools, but without them civilization would fall. Humans would revert to barbaric chaos without organized religion, strict formal education, and the need for conventional full-time employment. The traditional family had to be preserved, and roles well defined. An occasional war was necessary to maintain order, boost economies, and encourage self-sacrifice.

Violeta was fascinated by this alien perspective. She was hoping Warren's thoughts might move on to Lola, or to the tip of South America, but Warren felt he'd done enough thinking for one night. He picked up a book of crossword puzzles to quiet his mind before he returned to the safety of accounting and numbers.

She left, doing her best to visualize picking up all the crumbs as she went, so no snooping monad would detect her visit.

I was never here. Never.

She didn't know if the words or images would work, but in her experience with the mind, such techniques were surprisingly effective.

******

Olumiji acted fast as all efforts to shield Lola were redirected towards Maurice. Both parties were strong enough to handle the abrupt shift and wise enough to understand its necessity.

The x^0 leadership agreed Lola's indiscretion concerning a secret society was uncalled-for, however it happened. The full truth was needed, even though no one was sure what the consequences ought to be. x^0 was not a group prone to punishment. Members who transgressed always had justification, regret for problems caused, and a desire to make things right. Everyone who knew Lola expected this to be the case. The problem was her carelessness had put the group in more danger than anyone could have foreseen. Did that make her more liable?

Olumiji gave her the rest of the weekend to get back on her feet, sending only the faintest whisper on Saturday morning about a need to talk. She would receive a video call Sunday night.

******

Lola sensed the cold in Olumiji's whisper. She let it be and kept busy. Teddie wanted to go Christmas shopping, and there was a tree to put up and holiday lights needed on the front porch.

Twice on Sunday she sensed a stranger seeking her out. It felt like Gabriel, the one who'd found her before. Both times, she made her own best wall, and both times he got bored and left.

She also felt the faint touches of others in x^0, some checking to see if she was okay, others seeking information about something she'd done. What had she done? Wanting no trouble, she brushed each one away. Sunday afternoon she explained her predicament to Alex and he invited Teddie to go see a movie with him.

Lola felt nervous when Olumiji contacted her from his Monday morning in Japan. A Japanese woman Lola had only heard of, and an older man from India she'd met once, were with him. He told her how Warren Moore was certain x^0 existed, thanks to the surprising story told by a private detective in Houston.

Lola's eyes widened as she listened.

"Yes. I did try to scare that man away. He was investigating Zane. I don't remember my words, but I was desperate to protect my child. I figured he would decide I was a kind of nuts and had gotten info on him some other way. I mean, who thinks somebody will believe you when you say something so outrageous?"

All three telepaths knew Lola felt awful, and Olumiji knew she was about to feel worse.

"Lola, the PI had a full report on you from 2009. He has a reputation for taking cases with dubious ethics. It's our bad luck Warren picked him or we wouldn't be having this conversation."

Yet we are. Lola felt it from the other two telepaths.

"Was there anything particularly worrisome in his report?" she asked. She knew the answer before she heard it.

"There is lot about Maurice. You were meeting him often then. Harold was hoping you were having an affair or, better yet, prostituting yourself, but even he had to conclude it seemed more like Maurice was teaching you something."

"Shit. They found Maurice."

Lola realized her wall was gone so x^0 could redirect power to protect her friend in West Texas.

"This is horrible. What can I do?"

"Nothing." They all three said it and knew it was the worst answer they could give her.

"We believe they consider you a trainee, and will focus their efforts on Maurice. Let us focus on him too," the man from India said.

The Japanese woman spoke. "You are a wolf, Lola. Independent, passionate, and powerful in your defense of your cubs. We can't ask you to be otherwise, but your human brain needs to temper your actions. For now, stay busy with small tasks. The less you do, the less concerned we have to be about you."

She didn't speak unkindly, but there was no warmth.

"Of course." Lola accepted banishment to the sidelines as her punishment.

After they hung up, she stared at her screen for a while. She was angry with herself for the harm she'd caused, but she was angry with x^0 as well. That last bit had been pretty condescending. These people were all about empathy; how about a little appreciation for everything she was going through?

As she tried to calm down, the word "one" kept drifting through her head. It was how the members of x^0 referred to the group, sort of an inside geeky joke. Any number raised to the power of zero equals one, and the group held the oneness of all humans to be a sacred concept.

You're not treating me like I'm part of this One. I don't have to stay in your organization, you know. You're not the only path to the top of the mountain.

She was pretty sure that last part was a Buddhist saying, and if it wasn't, it should have been.

✱✱✱✱✱✱

Gabriel contacted Warren late Sunday night to tell him the teacher Maurice had been found. Warren was delighted, until he learned the teacher, too, was surrounded by a wall of impermeable energy.

"This group is stronger than I feared."

"Maybe not," Gabriel said. "The wall around the woman has weakened. It means they've had to move resources to protect the elder."

"Well then, get more info from her."

"It's still strong," Gabriel said "and we're not sure she has much else to offer. We're encouraged they can only do so much at once."

"Yes, that is good news. You do fine work, Gabriel. I don't mean to imply otherwise. I just think you're hindered by the careful way we're going at this. How much more effective would you be if you had the old man sitting in a chair in front of you?"

There was a second of silence. Warren supposed Gabriel was reading his mind.

"I don't think kidnapping anyone is a good idea."

"Bullshit. It doesn't have to be *kidnapping*. I can find ways to finesse this. We need information. Would having this Maurice in a room with you help you get it?"

"Of course it would. A lot."

"I thought so," Warren said. "Then this nonsense has gone on long enough. I'm sending a car to your place tomorrow morning at six. You'll fly on my jet to San Antonio. Most of the Entelechy is still here in New York, so take two of your best monads with you. When you land, another driver will take you to Maurice. There will be some muscle with him; they are totally at your disposal. This shouldn't be hard. He's an old man. I want to know *everything* about this organization. Do what you need to do."

Warren hung up before Gabriel could object.

10. The Good News

When the alarm went off Monday morning, the first thing Violeta did was go back to Warren. He was wide awake, proud of the few hours of sleep he required compared to others.

He sipped hot tea as he waited for news. Warren drank tea? He did. Coffee was hard on his stomach. What was he anxious about? Today, it was the kidnapping of Lola's teacher Maurice.

What? Violeta threw the covers back and lunged for her phone. Forget subterfuge. She had to call Lola now. She was searching for the scrap of paper with Lola's number when she was surprised to feel the woman's presence in her head.

✶✶✶✶✶✶

The encounter with three leaders of x^0 left Lola uneasy. Concern for Maurice, guilt over the trouble she'd caused, and irritation with x^0 were all causes, but there was something else. Lola knew what is was when she woke up at five in the morning.

The phone call from Violeta. She hadn't mentioned it to x^0. In her defense, they hardly let her speak and there were graver matters to be discussed. Nonetheless, the last thing she needed was to cause more trouble by withholding information.

She reached for her phone to call Olumiji. Then she looked over at her sleeping husband, snoring softly. His alarm would go off soon. She should move to the kitchen and let him rest.

As she fumbled for the light switch in the hall, she decided she could check on this Violeta woman first. Now that the wall was gone, a stealth peek into the lady's head would give her a feel for whether this offer was benign, or not. Surely it would be better to know before she contacted Olumiji.

Lola was concentrating on Violeta's face when she was surprised to feel the woman's presence.

******

Violeta was taken aback by Lola's mental powers. What a strong presence this woman had. Well, she practiced her arts every day, so of course she'd be adept with them.

Violeta calmed her mind and worked to be open to the other woman. Lola was considering how her group had freed her. Why? Never mind. Violeta needed to get a message across, and using telepathy would be more secure than by phone. Were her own skills up to it?

******

Lola felt the woman's distress, then realized Violeta was trying to reach her with a message. She was clumsy at it, letting other feelings interfere as she struggled to convey with clarity. Well, this woman had spent years trying to be difficult to read. Of course she'd have trouble transmitting information.

Why was she contacting her like this before dawn? Never mind. Violeta was agitated and doing her best to express the idea of a teacher and to convey danger.

Teacher? Teacher. They thought of Maurice as her teacher.

Danger. Lola focused and saw images of cars and people headed to Maurice's house. They were going to take him somewhere. Warren had had enough of this mumbo jumbo. He wanted Maurice interrogated now. Lola could have sworn that both her breath and her heartbeat stopped.

******

Gabriel decided to bring the monad Ezra from Tel Aviv because he'd once been in an interrogation unit in the army. For the second man, he considered several before picking Chidi, the Nigerian. Chidi's mental abilities were immense, and even when Chidi smiled he looked scary to most people. Gabriel was betting few things would terrify an old man from Texas more than being at the mercy of an angry Nigerian.

Unfortunately, once the three boarded Warren's jet, it became apparent this particular Nigerian objected to the mission.

"I'm an educated gentleman, and was raised to respect the elderly. I do not to try to force information out of old men."

"You don't have to do anything but stand there and look pissed," Gabriel said. "We'll do the rest."

Ezra was chuckling. "Don't worry. I used to be so good at this, and no one knew why, not even me. I just got ideas about what was the truth. After a while, they let me run with what they called 'my instincts.' Once I started picking at secrets I had no way of knowing, the captive would break like glass." He gave Chidi a friendly punch on the arm. "No violence needed."

Gabriel hated to derail this good cheer, but he reminded Ezra about the psychic wall surrounding the old man. "Your point is good, though. We need him to believe he has no hope. We'll have to find other ways to do it."

"I don't understand why we can't ignore these people. They seem simpleminded and harmless, with no ambition other than to stay hidden," Chidi said. "In my country, we have enough trouble. We don't go looking for more."

"Warren calls the shots." Ezra shrugged. "He wants us to be the only organization of telepaths in the world. I say we thank him and eliminate the competition."

******

Lola shook Alex awake, gripping him harder than she intended. He jerked his arm away from her as he rubbed his eyes.

"I can't get Maurice on the phone, and I've got to warn him. I need a second opinion quick. Do I call 911 in his hometown? Before you answer you need to know this involves telepathy and x^0 frowns on indiscrete behavior like getting the police involved. Or do I contact x^0? Before you answer you need to know they've already told me I've been benched for past indiscrete behavior, and if I do contact them I might not even be allowed to help Maurice."

He opened his mouth to talk but never got out a sound.

"Alex, it's only seven hours, six if we drive fast. I think we should get in the car and go."

"Slow down. Whatever the problem is, six hours is too long for us to be help. Let's not go off the deep end, okay?"

"Alex, we're got to do something!"

Alex typically woke up fast. Under these circumstances, he was coming to quicker than usual.

"Don't you know anyone in your hometown you can call? Send someone over to check on Maurice. Make up any story, but get them over there. They can have him call you, and then you can warn him."

"You're right. That makes more sense."

She took a breath and started looking for phone numbers. After a few tries, she found her junior high English teacher who she'd talked with a few times over the years.

She kept the pleasantries short by explaining she'd gotten a partial text from an elderly friend in town. He wasn't answering her calls, and she needed to know if he was okay but hated to embarrass him by involving police or an ambulance. The woman, who'd always been a kind soul, agreed to drive by his house on the way to work and call Lola back.

As the family met in the kitchen, Teddie asked the inevitable questions based on what she'd overheard.

"Is Uncle Maurice is hurt?"

"He's not." Her father gave her an overview as he cleared a space at the end of the cluttered counter and started to make a sandwich for his lunch. The family was lucky Teddie had done so well accepting the oddities of her mother's gift. It helped that she'd been coming to terms with unusual talents of her own.

"He's probably sound asleep, and this is a lot of commotion for nothing," her father added.

Lola felt her former English teacher's fear as the phone rang. She answered it expecting the worst.

"I don't think he has a medical problem, dear," the woman said. "But his front door is open, his house has been ransacked, and he's not here. I do think I should call the police."

"Yes, of course, please do," Lola said, giving Alex a desperate now-what look.

"The police will find him," he said as she ended the call.

"How? I know who's responsible for taking him and they haven't a clue."

"You want to drive there and find him, don't you, mom?" Teddie said in her calmest voice. She'd found a spot at the other end of the counter and was pouring milk into a cereal bowl.

"It's a bad idea. It would take you hours to get there, and then you wouldn't have the faintest idea of where to look."

She set the milk down, and both her parents saw tears forming in her eyes.

"Uncle Maurice would probably be dead by the time you found him. Wouldn't he?"

Lola and Alex both realized where this discussion was going.

"Isn't it amazingly lucky for Uncle Maurice that there *is* somebody who can find him, and can do it fast and well? That this somebody spent months in India training to be really good at doing exactly this kind of thing? And that person loves Uncle Maurice and maybe even owes him her friends' lives because he took really big risks for her?"

"Honey, you told us both you never wanted to have another out-of-body experience again," her father said.

"Given everything you went through over there, we don't blame you," her mother added.

"I'm pretty sure I've also said some things about not letting people I care about die." She shoved her cereal bowl away. "I can do this. Uncle Maurice won't know I've found him, but I'll get a good look at where he is, then you can find a way to get him help."

She looked at both of her parents as they looked back at her.

"There isn't a better plan and you know it."

******

Maurice woke up in the trunk of a car. He'd always been a positive sort of guy, so he made himself focus on what was good about the situation. Well, it was a large trunk. It was probably a luxury car. Could have been worse. And, he was the only person in it. Plenty of space and no unpleasant dead bodies lying next to him. He'd seen this sort of thing in movies, and no dead bodies was always good.

His hands were bound loosely behind his back, but he could wiggle his legs around for comfort and there was no duct tape over his mouth, so breathing was easier. Better yet, it felt like he'd been drugged, presumably in his sleep. The lingering effects were effusing him with such a nice sense of serenity.

On the down side, the wall that x^0 was holding around him was as impermeable as ever. And he was in the trunk of a car. That was definitely a minus. He drifted back to sleep.

******

Teddie walked into the living room and closed the blinds. She gave her parents an annoyed look when they followed her.

"Shouldn't we be here with you, in case you need help or something?" her mother asked.

"No, you should not. I need to go into a trance and that won't happen with my parents sitting here watching me. All I need is quiet, low light, and solitude. Dad should go on to school. You go do something else, anything else and I'll come find you when I have information about Uncle Maurice. Remember, this isn't instantaneous. It takes a while."

Once the parents were gone, Teddie got comfortable on the couch and let her mind wander. She found the memory of the Bhutanese man who'd trained her.

"Ask people if an apple will always fall to the earth once it breaks free from the tree and one hundred normal adults will tell you it will," he'd said. "But a child will say, 'Maybe not, because it could float into the hand of a magic genie.' A mystic will tell you he could levitate the apple if he wanted to. A physicist will instruct you on stronger and weaker gravitational fields and then move on to warped space, and, if you're still listening, may begin to discuss probability functions. They're all scratching at the same truth, that the universe is more complicated than our day-to-day experiences lead us to believe."

Teddie remembered the scene. It was the day after her first successful out-of-body experience, and he was beseeching her to unlearn many of her most basic assumptions.

She focused hard on remembering the feelings of that night. She wasn't tied to her physical body. She was an entity of mist, or, more correctly, of energy, but she liked the word mist. Never mind the words. She could float, she could fly, she could command her body of light to find those she knew.

"Let's go to Maurice," she said. She gave the sleeping body of solid Teddie a glance as she floated though the sliding glass doors and began to move westward, about ten feet off the ground, passing through the occasional tree branch or electrical wire like it wasn't there. As her confidence grew, she picked up speed.

******

The next time Maurice woke up, he was duct taped to a chair. He was thirsty, and his muscles ached, and of course he needed a bathroom. Three well built men were standing in front of him, staring at him.

The slightest and youngest of the three looked faintly Arab.

"Sleeping beauty wakes up," he said. "She can have such an easy morning if she chooses."

The menace in his voice was clear, almost practiced.

They've brought in a professional interrogator?

"What a shame your group shrouds your mind and protects you," the tall, good-looking Latino added. "Now you'll have to tell us everything by talking. Such a cumbersome process, but we'll make it work."

Maurice turned his gaze to the third man, a muscular African, a little older than the others.

"That's Chidi, my friend from Nigeria," the Latino said. "He's backing us up. Trust me, you don't want him to be the one to question you."

"Nigeria?" Maurice's face lit up. "I've friends from there. What part? Are you Ibo?"

"I am." Chidi could not conceal his joy at having his tribe recognized. "But I live in Lagos. I work in broadcasting."

"I recognized the Ibo name. I mostly know engineers over there and geologists in the oil business. I spent time in Lagos."

"You survived the traffic." Chidi laughed.

The Latino and Arab exchanged looks. This wasn't going according to plan.

******

Teddie was relieved to find Maurice unharmed, even though his hands were taped to the back of his chair. Three men were talking to him. Maurice and the black man were laughing, which was a good sign. The other two men looked less happy.

One of the many frustrations of travel in the abode of light was the lack of sound. She could pay attention to expressions and gestures, but the actual conversation remained out of reach. Best to start exploring for other clues.

Two more guys were in the hallway. They had guns and were nowhere near as friendly looking. Teddie guessed Maurice was using his natural good cheer to stay safe, but she also guessed it would only work for so long.

She headed outside to get some idea of where she was. She needed to figure out what town this was, then what part of town she was in, and then remember how the building looked. Keep it simple. Where was she?

Teddie wasn't fond of heights, but she nudged her body higher. This was a big city. How big was Midland? Not this big. There had to be some defining feature. Okay, that was a river. Didn't they all have rivers?

Wait. She knew that building over there. It was the freakin' Alamo. Teddie was sure there was only one of those, and she knew exactly where it was.

December 2012

11. Tea

Violeta's anger grew as Monday morning wore on. She'd never considered Reel News a humanitarian organization, but she was abhorred Warren would hurt a helpless man. The problem was she still didn't know the first thing about the news complex in her hometown. The more reasons she found to cut her ties with Reel News, the more important it was to stay and learn more.

She went for a walk at lunch. The crowded streets of Manhattan were a better place to use her telepathy to check in with Lola and check on Warren.

Lola. Violeta focused on the connection the previous contact had forged. The woman was so full of information and so nonchalant about conveying it with her mind. Through her years as a judoka, Violeta had spoken little and listened much. The monads, too, were silent observers, while x^0 had evolved a more expressive style of mental communication. It would take some getting used to.

Violeta peeked in on Lola and found her driving her daughter to school. Both were going in hours late. Because? Because Lola had believed Violeta's warning and done something. Done what? The woman wasn't thinking about that. She was thinking about how much she loved her daughter and how proud she was of her.

Well, wasn't that sweet. Why wasn't the woman thinking about Maurice?

Frustrated, Violeta moved on to Warren. She sensed no monad nearby, so she entered and found Warren more frustrated than she was. Police had been called to the building in San Antonio where the three monads and two guns for hire were holding Maurice. Gabriel had sensed the police seconds before they came through the door, with time enough to pull the old man out of restraints.

Warren's mind was full of appreciation for Gabriel's quick thinking. But how could police possibly have been alerted by an anonymous call? Who would know Maurice was being held there against his will? Warren could think of no way.

The police had been dubious about Gabriel's assurances the men were having a sensitive business discussion, with guards hired to protect their privacy. They took a hard look at Maurice and put him in a separate squad car, while bringing the others in for questioning. Now, a team of his lawyers was working to get the monads released. Worst of all, he still needed to question Maurice. Warren swore there would be no mysterious rescue next time.

******

Once Maurice was in the police car, the seriousness of the situation hit him. Going home was a bad idea. He could visit his son in Seattle or the one in Upstate New York who'd been trying to get him to move there for years. Right now, though, he didn't want to be with anyone likely to try to take charge of his life. He wanted to stay in Texas, and be with people who understood him.

He began the phone call with, "Lola, I've got a favor to ask." He wasn't surprised when she insisted he stay at her house, but he was surprised when she seemed to know more about his problems than he did.

"I'll explain it when you get here," she promised.

"How will I get there? It's not like these guys were nice enough to bring along my wallet. And I'd like to go home first and get some stuff."

"That's what I figured. The cops will get you to the airport in San Antonio and through security. There's a ticket waiting for you. Take the puddle jumper out to Pecos County. You'll have a police escort waiting to take you to your house."

"Goodness no. The police don't have time for that."

"They do. Your home was broken into and ransacked."

"What?"

"I know. It's one of the biggest crimes in your hometown in a decade. They'll wait while you look things over and pack up belongings, then they'll get you back on a plane to Houston. I'll meet the plane."

"Lola, you're sure?"

If he had his damn abilities right now, he wouldn't have to ask. He'd know. Then he realized he knew anyway.

"Thanks. I'll see you late tonight."

******

Warren scheduled a last meeting of the Entelechy on Monday night, before many of them headed home. As he prepared his address, he wished he could hide the failure to obtain information from Maurice, but Gabriel, Ezra, and Chidi were still being held in San Antonio. No doubt, many of the men knew the full story.

Why hadn't he found men with some other superpower to help him build his empire? Guys who could fly faster than a speeding bullet would have been cool. They probably wouldn't have been as useful, but they'd be easier to deal with.

He gave himself a mental slap and reached for a word search puzzle. He worked on finding words having to do with travel and kept circling groups of letters until his mind was clear.

Then, he focused on the situation. He now knew how dangerous this other group was. They'd located three monads they'd never met and pinpointed their exact address when even the men hadn't known it. That defied the rules of telepathy, at least as they were explained to Warren. This new need for fear would be the perfect introduction to his speech.

He stood up at his desk and practiced tonight's closing remarks in his best thunderous voice.

"Once you arrive home, I want every one of you to become a hunter. Everyday, everywhere you go, look for their telltale signs and bring me back at least one of them. That's right. Bring me one evil telepath, and more is better. I know you can, because if they can find you, you can find them, too."

Warren sat down satisfied. He was certain the speech would be well received.

******

Lola could see the pain in her friend's eyes and knew the hardships of the day had taken their toll on him. He took the cup of herbal tea she gave him as he settled in the guestroom for the night, but he stopped her as she turned to go.

"Lola. I'll sleep better if I know what's going on."

She understood, so she gave him the short version of the facts about the woman who'd contacted her twice now to help her and how the second time had been an alert about Maurice's situation.

"I'm incredibly lucky."

"In more ways than one. I was frantic to find you when my daughter reminded me this was something she's quite good at."

"Teddie?" Lola saw more pain in Maurice's eyes. "She told me if she never had another out-of-body experience in her life it would be too soon. Oh no. She didn't. She shouldn't have."

Teddie had been waiting out in the hall, wondering how much of the story her mother was going to tell. She had the unsuspecting Maurice engulfed in a hug before he knew what hit him.

"And let those horrible men do awful things to you? I don't think so."

"Actually the Nigerian was rather nice. I think the others were just doing a job."

"Whatever. No way I don't go find you, Uncle Maurice. There were exceptions to my declaration."

He laughed. "Well then, I'm doubly lucky I made the list. Thank you Teddie."

Maurice snuggled under the covers to fall into an exhausted sleep, appreciating the day ending far better than it began

******

Warren hated being asked about things he couldn't think about. He tried to keep his feelings vague as he answered the construction manager in charge of the new complex being built in Tierra del Fuego.

"Yes, the primarily purpose is to keep intruders out. State of the art security system, as obvious as possible. I want my people to feel safe there from nuclear war, zombie apocalypse, and viral Armageddon. You get the idea."

"That was in the original design, sir, although we've added a few things I'm sure you'll like. The area I need more guidance in is the one you left rather grey. To what extent do you need to keep people in?"

I need that area to stay grey, you idiot. Warren recited a couple of nursery rhymes in his head before answering.

"That's a contingency concept, on the off chance, uh, unexpected circumstances arise. Just being prepared. You keep that function concealed and don't give me details. Give me a manual or something I can access in an emergency."

"You want a manual?"

"Better yet," Warren said. "Why don't you do this part on your own initiative? You know, in case I have needs down the road I don't anticipate. Don't skimp, but bury the costs and don't mention it to me again."

"Sure, boss. Whatever you say."

The man hadn't risen into management without being able to read a situation. He was being told to build an impenetrable fortress that could secretly double as a prison, and to pretend the second function was his own idea.

******

Maurice woke up to the sound of Lola singing. Or humming. No, more kind of a...

He sat up in bed. There was no sound, just the feeling of his friend a few dozen feet away, letting a song run through her head as she loaded the dishwasher. She'd gotten off of the phone with a young man who'd lived with the Zeitmans for a few months and he was arriving Friday to spend his Christmas break there. She was happy.

Maurice was happy too. It was nice to be a telepath again.

He stepped out of bed, and felt the tug of a request for contact. Olumiji? No. All the leaders of x^0. Lola felt it too. They were being summoned. Lola deflected the request. *Give him a few minutes to wake up.*

"Got coffee and tea out here when you're ready," Lola called from the kitchen. She was no longer singing in her head.

Ten minutes later, Maurice and Lola sat side by side on the couch in front of Lola's laptop. There were a dozen of x^0's leaders on this call, at ten different locations. The audio was slow and the video was spotty, but this group could augment the technology.

Several telepaths had become aware of Maurice's plight over the last several hours. Concern had led them to discover Violeta, to learn of Lola's contacts with her, and to become aware of Teddie's rescue mission. They had a few questions.

The woman from Japan took the lead. Lola answered as though she was on the witness stand. No, she hadn't willfully withheld information about the employee of Reel News helping her. The story about the private investigator had distracted her the last time they talked. Yes, she considered contacting x^0 when the Argentinian woman alerted her to Maurice's plight but concern for her friend prompted her to turn first to those who could do something faster. She had every intention of checking in with x^0 this morning once Maurice woke up.

Lola was defensive. Olumiji stayed silent. The woman leading the conversation *had* called her a wolf last time they talked. Maybe it wasn't meant as an insult, but she was realizing she and Maurice belonged to the less regulated part of this organization. Parts of x^0 seemed to prefer more of a bureaucracy.

"You're right," a man with a heavy Australian accent responded to her thoughts. "There's plenty of us who do what we do and wouldn't have it any other way. The rest of x^0 tolerates us. There are also plenty of telepaths you don't know who are more committed to community. They'd never act as you did without the advice and consent of their mates."

He laughed when Lola winced.

"No one is asking you to be like them," he said. "But you've drug a right old mess into x^0 too, now, you know."

Lola started to respond but the Japanese woman cut her off.

"Yes, we all know you're sorry. Don't need to hear it again. Many of us didn't even *know* about the organization c^3 until now."

She seemed upset Lola had known about it and she hadn't. The older man from India spoke up.

"We understand why you'd turn to your daughter's skills first and how your friendship would prompt you to provide Maurice with a night's sleep before reaching out to us. It's not how I'd behave, but x^0 doesn't require its members to act alike."

"I wouldn't have lasted long in it, if it had," Maurice said, opening his mouth for the first time. All eyes turned toward him. "Look, I appreciate the sympathy I'm feeling, but there's no need for this to be an inquisition. Lola did her best to help me. We know you can't keep protecting us; we've got to find another solution."

"There is only one," the Japanese woman said.

"True," the Aussie agreed.

Lola was feeling around, trying to find this obvious solution, when an older woman with a heavy British accent spoke up.

"Indeed. We're going to invite them for tea."

The Aussie laughed. "Or a pint if they prefer, Lillian. Listen, you two. You've brought these sharts into our group. We can't crawl under the couch and hide forever, and this nonsense of kidnapping our olds and sending nippers off flying through the air on rescue missions has got to stop."

"We'll tell them everything they wish to know about us," the man from India said. "We'll seek out common ground. Perhaps some of them will join us and we can work together on projects."

"So go on about your day." The British woman was smiling as she talked. "We understand how this happened, and there's no need to hide anything, from us or them."

Neither Maurice or Lola responded.

"If it turns out we've opened the tiger's cage, we're confident we can handle the tiger," the man from India added.

Lola understood she was forgiven, and she and Maurice were being dismissed. It was a relief, and she projected a courteous smile as she logged off. These were smart people. Surely they understood what they were doing.

But what if there was a whole cage full of tigers? Could an army of wolves, bats, kangaroos and bumble bees survive if they went up against a team of skilled predators?

It was hard to imagine.

12. New Friends

The monad Rafael was glad to be home in Manila, comfortable in his role as a late-blooming business star in the community. He took his instructions from Warren seriously, as befitted a man who owed another much of his success.

So at lunch time, he went for a walk. Instead of keeping his mind closed, shutting out the suffering around him in his usual fashion, he went so far as to seek information. Everyone buzzed it back at him, and he blinked his eyes as though blinds had been opened to admit a bright sun.

He felt a couple of low-level telepaths in the crowd. Both were unaware of their talents so Rafael disregarded them and looked further. Nothing, nothing, then there she was. A woman barely twenty-years old sitting on a park bench looked up from the book she was reading.

He felt her *hello*. When he failed to respond, she spoke aloud.

"I'm the telepath you're seeking. Would you like to get lunch?"

Rafael was sure lunch wasn't what Warren had in mind. Then again, she was a pretty girl and he did need to eat.

"Sure."

He'd find a way to put a better spin on this when he mentioned it to Warren.

******

Warren waited four long days for the report on the search of Maurice's home. His men examined every email on Maurice's computer, every scrap of paper in his drawers, and every message on his phone. From this they compiled a list of suspicious contacts called "potential psychics."

Warren scanned the names. No special ability was needed to notice the surprising amount of time this retired geologist spent communicating with people from Africa, India, and East Asia. At the top of the list was a man named Olumiji who'd spoken with Maurice every week for years. Who was this Olumiji?

To Warren's surprise, the contacts weren't even the real gold mine. The computer yielded a secret website visited by Maurice almost daily. Warren chuckled. Who'd have thought a group of telepaths would maintain a website?

Access required two massive passwords, and Warren's team supposed Maurice did what most older people did. He wrote his passwords down. It was to his credit the two were kept in separate places, but eventually the right combination was found and a pleased IT expert showed Warren how to log into the website of a group called x^0.

"Real nut case stuff," he confided. "You're gonna get a kick out of this nonsense."

"I'm sure I will." Warren squinted at the screen and said no more until the man took the hint and closed the door behind him.

I've got you people right where I want you.

Warren skimmed the content for anything useful, making notes as he went. Yes, this was good. That was filler. That was garbage. Wait, this gave an idea of the size of the organization. Good Lord, there were hundreds of these people! Could they all read minds?

The phone rang, annoying him with its interruption. Then he guessed who was at the other end of the line. *I hate goddamned telepaths.* He picked up the phone.

"You're correct. My name is Olumiji and we're quite capable of changing a password before you use it. But we didn't. I trust you're enjoying our website?"

The deep voice resonated with the melody of Africa.

"I'm finding it interesting, thank you."

"Wonderful. My group and I have decided it's a waste of valuable time for us to play hide and seek with each other, simply because we have different philosophies. Needlessly dangerous as well, don't you think?"

"It hasn't been dangerous for me."

There was silence.

"What is it you want from me?" Warren asked.

"We'd like to meet you. Have you over for tea, so to speak. See if there are areas in which we can work together while we eliminate our mutual fear of the unknown by learning to understand each other."

"No thank you."

There was more silence.

"You don't even want to meet us?" The man sounded genuinely baffled.

"Not really," Warren said. "We're not looking for new friends. My telepaths have work to do, and I don't have time for play dates."

His eyes flicked to the screen. He'd been logged out.

Don't underestimate their technological capabilities.

"Correct. You'd be well advised not to underestimate any of our capabilities."

Warren winced.

"But suit yourself. Perhaps the monads who choose to tell you about their encounters with us over the next few days will suggest you reconsider."

"Encounters? How do you know about the monads?"

Warren got no answer. The line went dead, then the screen went dead, and then the lights went off.

"Cheap trick." For once he hoped every telepath out there could hear him.

******

"You'd be well advised to not underestimate any of our capabilities," Olumiji said to Warren in the most menacing voice he could manage without feeling utterly ludicrous. "But suit yourself. Perhaps the monads who choose to tell you about their encounters with us over the next few days will suggest you reconsider."

The line went dead, the screen went dead, and, just for good measure, the lights went off. The first two were easy enough to manage, and the latter was courtesy of a helpful x^0 member who worked at Con Edison.

It was a cheap trick, and Olumiji knew it, but this guy was starting to really piss him off.

******

Lola sent a mental request to Violeta for a conversation. The two of them had established the connection so essential to telepaths, so it was the obvious thing to do. But Violeta didn't respond. Lola tried again. Still no answer. The third time she attached a feeling of urgency. Once she got no response back, again, she reconsidered. The woman was new to this kind of friendship. Perhaps she was expecting too much.

A day later, Lola got a call from a blocked number.

"You understood my warning. You saved your friend." They were statements, not questions, and the speaker was happy.

"Yes, Violeta. I can't thank you enough."

"Your acting on my information was all the thanks I needed. I'm happy you have your capabilities back. I'm trying to learn what Warren is planning, but so far I have nothing."

Lola took a breath. Either she trusted this would-be protector or not. More information would help. Lola peered directly into Violeta's mind in a way she wouldn't with others. It felt invasive, like staring directly into a stranger's eyes. What she saw was that Violeta had little training in dealing with others. Direct contact confused her. Lola confused her.

Most of Violeta's day-to-day efforts involved keeping others out of her head, but with Lola she didn't bother. It was easy to see the basic honesty swimming below the surface. Lola felt the chronic pain caused by the old judo injury. She saw a woman who often distracted herself with superficial pursuits to deal with hurts of all types. She saw a woman who would go out of her way to avoid hurting another.

Lola made her decision. "Let me tell you what I know." She described her group, with its thousands of members and its amorphous leadership. She explained how x^0 decided hiding from Warren's telepaths was a waste of time. Finding a way to co-exist was the only answer.

She was surprised to hear the sound of Violeta's laughter.

"I said something funny?"

"You did. There is nothing Warren hates more than those bumper stickers saying co-exist. He rants to everyone about them. If you used that word in your invitation, I'm sure he declined."

"I don't know what words Olumiji used, but you're right. Warren said he didn't have time for us."

"He believes there's room for only one group like his, because he thinks of winners and losers. Tell me, does he have any idea how large x^0 is? It seems you can squash him like a bug."

"That's not true. We're not as powerful as our numbers make us sound." Lola started to explain what she knew about the various stages and levels of telepathy.

"Seventy-million people have this skill? No way."

"Most of them are empaths, people who barely pick up feelings. Only about seven-million even realize they are doing it."

"So how many telepaths do you think there are?"

Violeta whispered the question. Lola could tell it scared her.

"We've been studying this a long time, and we think one-in-a-thousand self-aware empaths develops telepathic skills. So about seven-thousand."

"Even that's incredible."

"Not really. Telepathy is a gradational thing. Most only get vague information. Maybe one-in-a-hundred can do what we do."

Violeta was doing the math. One-in-a-hundred was seventy.

"How many of them are in your organization?" she asked.

"Ninety or so, but only about three dozen are as adept as us. It's not like we give tests. The boundary is fuzzy. How many are in yours?"

"There are exactly thirty-five monads," Violeta said.

"Doesn't leave a lot of room for a third group, does it?"

"Those numbers can't be right. Do the math."

Lola was a little annoyed and ran through her calculations again. She found no mistakes. "I don't see the problem."

"Really? Are all three dozen of yours women?"

"Oh no. Telepathy is distributed amongst all demographic groups."

"That's what I'd guess. My group is all men, except for me. Are *you* willing to accept three-quarters of the world's best telepaths are male? I'm not."

Lola laughed. It looked like the two women had found common ground.

"Me neither. Okay, maybe some third Amazon group is yet to be discovered, but I think it's more likely there are a few dozen adepts yet to be found. No surprise, the bulk of them are females, perhaps uneducated and isolated from the outside world."

"We need to find them and fix this," Violeta said.

"I agree. Until then, looks like it's just your group and mine."

Lola could feel Violeta's grin as she said, "So, if one of our groups is going to run the world, I prefer your people."

It was Lola's turn to laugh. "That's good to know, but we don't want to run the world."

"Well, Warren does, and if you don't, he will."

Yes, that is exactly the problem.

"I want to quit my job." Violeta had moved on. "But I won't, yet, because I can help you where I am."

"That's a dangerous game."

"One I'm used to. If I learn something helpful, I'll let you know. If you must tell me something, ask me to call, like you did."

I'm not used to waiting days for a response. It slipped out.

"I'll call when it is safe. Not before."

Sorry.

No problem. "I'm sure Warren intends to eliminate x^0 because he'll never feel safe as long as you exist. If I can learn more about how, I'll be in touch."

"Eliminate us? He'd actually kill hundreds of people?"

"I don't think so. He's not a mass murderer, but I'm sure he'd kill to defend what he believes in. Is it the same thing?"

Lola didn't answer, but she spent much of the day considering the question.

✱✱✱✱✱

The monad Cenk was glad to be home, surrounded by the familiar sounds and smells of Istanbul. He always had second thoughts about his alliance with the untrustworthy American, and every day he considered walking away from the wealth it brought him. Then each time, he looked at his wife and saw the hope in her eyes. Hope he would keep the job, hope the expensive medicines would keep working, hope their son would live another month, another year.

In truth, it was a home filled with sorrow, and Cenk left it each day to find solace in the growing broadcasting company he ran at Warren's behest. The business was interesting, and the people who worked for him were fine. What troubled Cenk was Warren's continual push to cover the troublemakers and to present the news in ways to make others angry.

Warren called it good journalism, but Cenk thought it was more like stirring the coals of a fire. As if there wasn't enough fire already in his part of the world. Who wanted more trouble?

His thoughts were interrupted by a man he thought was an accountant standing in his doorway. Why had his secretary let this man pass?

"Your secretary wasn't at his desk," the man explained. "I was hoping I might have lunch with you today."

Impertinent.

"I realize that and I apologize. But I have information about Warren and his behavior."

Cenk looked at the accountant, puzzled, and noticed he was holding a flat cardboard box.

"I brought a tuna and egg pide. Your favorite. We could eat it here."

Cenk took a whiff. Well, anyone who claimed to understand Warren Moore was worth a few minutes. Besides, he had to have lunch somewhere.

******

Teddie got home from Darjeeling six months ago, and she was still recovering. One of her roommates had fled school to avoid being sold by a greedy uncle, while her fellow exchange student Michelle was kidnapped by an angry crime lord and sold to a brothel. Teddie was proud of how she'd helped rescue both friends, but out-of-body experiences brought back the worst of those memories. It was why she didn't travel in her energy body.

She'd made a friend during this experience, one whom she'd never met in the physical world. Vanida was raised to perform in the sex shows popular in Bangkok. An avid reader and clever multi-lingual survivor, Vanida had kept her dignity and love of life in a world that usually robbed young women of both. She was a traveler like Teddie. The two of them had met on this other plane, and worked together to rescue Michelle.

Vanida now had a job in Bangkok with the research arm of the organization of travelers known as c^3. She checked in with Teddie often to see how Michelle was doing. She didn't understand why Teddie had stopped traveling, so she listened with interest to Teddie's tale of helping to rescue family friend Maurice.

"Didn't it feel good to be flying again?" she asked the American friend she called Teda. "Light and free and moving as fast as you choose?"

"Yes," Teddie admitted. "It did."

"So maybe you're ready to meet me somewhere? We can turn cartwheels on the beaches in Tahiti? Watch the sun rise as we fly over the Pacific? Come on, Teda, you can have fun with this gift."

Teddie shook her head. "Maybe someday I'll be ready to fly for fun, too, but right now I travel only in emergencies."

"Well, I do wish you few emergencies. Look, should I be worried about you with this crazy group of kidnappers?"

"I hope not. My mom says it'll all be solved soon."

"If you need a helpful traveler, you know I'm only a phone call away."

"Thanks, but I don't think this will turn into a big enough deal for that."

As Teddie hung up the phone, she felt the cold fingers of a superstition buried deep in the human unconscious. Don't tempt fate. Don't ever tempt fate.

Damn. I probably shouldn't have said that.

13. Normal Enough

Lola's informal foster child, Xuha, was arriving today to spend his Christmas break with them. She'd already decided tomorrow she'd fill him in on everything he didn't know, including Teddie's out of body travel and Maurice's telepathy. He was going to be at the Zeitman house for weeks, and it was hard to predict how the situation with Reel News would evolve. He had a right to know what was happening and how everyone fit in.

Lola recalled how the young man had surprised them with his fighting abilities during his senior year. He was on the small side, but his incredible quickness allowed him to hold his own against multiple larger bullies and he'd shown the same adroitness defending Teddie from an attacker. He was a useful ally; involving him in their current situation made sense for many reasons.

"I need to ask you both something," she said to Teddie and Maurice once she got home from work. She explained the need to give Xuha information. "I'd like to give you each the chance to talk to him yourself if you'd rather."

They both gave the same answer.

"No, you go right ahead."

When Xuha drove up an hour later, dinner was nearly ready. His second family, as he called them, engulfed him in hugs.

******

"Why haven't you answered my emails?"

Violeta heard the frustration in her mother's voice, and felt bad. The cozy world of Ushuaia seemed so removed from her troubles in New York and she didn't know how to explain her situation to her mother. It had been easier not to try.

She let her brain move into the well worn pathways of her native tongue, seeking an answer to soothe. A truth, even a partial one, was best.

"I've been thinking about quitting my job and I wanted to decide before we talked. I'm sorry it's taken so long."

"Are they putting too much pressure on you? Is your boss mistreating you? Oh, cara, are you homesick for Argentina?"

Violeta laughed. "All of them, but I've decided not to quit, at least not now. So no, I won't be home for Christmas. Yes, I'll miss you horribly."

Violeta sensed her mother expected as much and was trying to decide whether to share a piece of news or not.

"Is everyone okay there?"

"Yes. Your brothers, their families, we're all fine."

The silence grew longer. "What's worrying you, mom?"

"You always can tell when I'm upset, can't you? Ever since you were a little girl."

"What's upsetting you, Mom?"

Her mother's sigh could be heard in New York. "It's your boss."

"*My* boss?"

"Yes, and this compound he's building."

"It's ugly? He's not paying his bills? What's the problem?"

Violeta kept her voice nonchalant, but her instincts were moving toward red alert.

"He has people there working 'round the clock now. His construction managers are all outsiders, of course, but the workers, many of them are local, and they talk."

"Some people like attention. What are they saying?"

"That it's a fortress. Or a prison. I've heard rumors of both. Don't get me wrong. Everyone understands a U.S. company is going to have a security system. But who has their windows made from unbreakable bullet proof glass? Who puts in escape tunnels? Who wants security checkpoints along the perimeter and elevated platforms with assault weapons mounted to turn full circles."

"That does sound extreme. Are they making this up?"

"These are people I trust, Violeta." Her mother's voice went from defensive to secretive. "They're not broadcasting these things in bars, trying to get free drinks. They'd get fired. They're sharing their concerns with the local police. I hear about it at work."

Violeta's mom Alma had worked as a police dispatcher since her husband was killed. Most thought the job had been offered to the widow as a form a charity, but over the last decade Alma had proved herself to be an asset to the force.

"Okay. I believe you. Honestly, I'm not much of a fan of Reel News these days. Um, I guess you should know I'm *not* quitting because I'm trying to get information for people who have concerns about Warren Moore. How about I see if I can learn anything for you while I'm at it?"

"I was hoping you would. The chief of police was impressed when I told him your New York news company was the same as these people. I know he'll be happy for anything you can find out."

My worst fears about this building project could be true. What in heaven's name does Warren want with such a place?

******

A small group of high-powered telepaths had made the decision to dispatch thirty-five x^0 members to contact Warren's monads. As other members of x^0 learned of the decision, they all understood why it had been made, but they didn't all think it was a good idea. Disagreement was probably inevitable. They were, after all, discussing the survival of their organization.

Those who opposed it coalesced behind a single idea. *We're the larger and more evolved group. We shouldn't stoop to playing their games. We should ignore them.*

As was the custom with a controversial decision, the leaders of x^0 sought out more opinions. While they did so, selected members continued to contact the monads as they'd been asked. Some met with minor success, others with hostility, but each encounter added information about the threat they faced and forced their enemy to learn more about them as well.

******

The grey of winter had settled into Toronto, and the monad Dave admitted he wouldn't have minded another week in New York. The climate wasn't better, but somehow the lights did a better job of fighting off the gloom.

But Warren Moore had said go home and find evil telepaths, so here he was at the Toronto Zoo late on a Friday afternoon, shivering as he walked through the ten-acre Tundra Trek, featuring polar bear habitat. He was thinking he should have explored the Gorilla Rainforest instead when a young boy who couldn't have been more than ten walked up to him.

"We are *not* evil," the child said.

Dave blinked hard, thinking he must be mistaken.

"That's right." The boy answered the thoughts in Dave's head. "It *is* unusual for a child my age to have this kind of ability. They let me do this to make a point to you. We are children and old people and pregnant women and men that could be your brothers. You don't need to fight us. You need to get to know us. Yes, it was hard to find you out here. Any sensible man would have walked around the rainforest exhibit."

Dave started to probe into the boy's mind, and he felt a sharp, defensive wall rise up to stop him. He sought out its source and sensed the woman on the other side of the bushes before he saw her. She stepped out in plain view. Good lord, she had to be at least eight months pregnant.

"Come here, Dave. Now." The child ran toward her.

"His name is Dave, too," she said. "My child and I are among the people of x^0. You ought to get to know us better before you sign on with the one who wants to destroy us."

With that she put her arm around the boy and the two of them walked back toward the warmth of a nearby exhibit.

******

Vanida, the seventeen year old girl from Thailand, had traveled outside of her body for as long as she could remember. Now that she was more informed, she understood how the traumas of her youth had pushed her into developing her traveling skills. She supposed that was one good thing about being raised to shoot ping pong balls out of your vagina.

There were few people Vanida counted as friends, and the Yankee girl Michelle was one of them. Michelle offered her a lifeline to a world no one else bothered to tell her existed. Vanida knew Michelle had been damaged, but she also understood how those cracks could be mended. Vanida wanted to help.

The other American, Teda with the black curly hair, had formed a bond with Vanida too, in the Abode of Light and in their shared concern for Michelle. Teda was a traveler, innately kind, but what impressed Vanida was her willingness to fight for her friends' safety. Teda didn't seem to know a lot about fighting, at first, but in Vanida's opinion she was a quick learner.

Now, Teda and her family were in trouble of their own. Teda could be called upon to travel, possibly to dangerous places, even though she was still hesitant about it. Vanida was sure she could help if she were close by.

So far, her boss at c^3 had given her a lot of freedom. Could she convince her employer to send her to Texas, where she could help Teda and check in on Michelle? She'd get to see the U.S. Maybe visit NASA or ride on a bucking bronco or do whatever else people in Texas did. Eat bar-b-que. It sounded so exotic.

Vanida noticed verbal requests were often met with a "no", but a well-crafted written request gave the reader time to consider saying yes. Vanida picked up her laptop and began to type. Everyone always told her she had a way with words.

******

Saturday morning, Alex and Teddie left to run errands. Xuha and Lola sat at the kitchen counter, sharing coffee and getting caught up. Lola told him of x^0 and c^3 and then threw in the facts about Zane's ability to morph his appearance and Ariel's precognitive skills. Xuha took it all in stride.

"Five such amazing skills. Incredible, but it makes sense to me. I think as a family you've encouraged each other to develop your own strengths."

"That's a new theory." Lola was talking softly, hoping Maurice would sleep in, while she and Xuhu finished the conversation. "Others have asked me if we were all exposed to any unusual radiation. I don't think any of us has the personality to be, well, you know, a superhero. We want to be normal, so we denied what we could do, until each of us got forced into action."

"You're normal enough, Mrs. Z. I can understand how all five of you would want to keep it that way."

The second time he said it, Lola heard it.

"What do you mean 'all five of us?'"

Xuha was puzzled.

"What exactly does my husband Alex do?"

"Uh. Ah."

"Xuha?"

"If he hasn't told you, perhaps he doesn't want you to know."

Her eyes widened, and Xuha saw the storm clouds gathering.

"Or more likely he refuses to accept it himself."

She waited.

"Aren't you a telepath? Why don't you know this already?"

"I only know what someone thinks about at that moment. And, I give my family members as much privacy as I can."

"Wait, are you going to read my mind now to find out?" Xuha looked alarmed.

"I consider you family, and give you the same courtesy. But you are practically screaming the answer, so I'm afraid the cat is out of the bag." She paused, considering. "Time slows down for you? That's how you fight so well. You and Alex don't think of it as a power, but as doing what you need to do. It's how he got to be such a basketball star. How he rescued me on the river and stopped that teacher with a gun at that horrible school play.

Xuha gave a helpless grin.

"You pretty much got it. Please don't be mad at Mr. Z."

Lola's consciousness jumped to Alex. He was talking to Teddie. Lola had told him she was going to have this conversation with Xuha, so he was trying to tell his daughter in his own words exactly what it was he could do. Lola picked up on his emotions.

"He's embarrassed because we all do these cool things and he thinks of his as nothing?" Lola was incredulous. "Besides, he'd prefer to be considered a good athlete. Jeez, is that Alex or what?"

"Please don't tell Mr. Z I gave up his secret."

"Sorry, Xuha, but he has to hear about this conversation. Don't worry, he won't be upset with you. He'll know you couldn't have helped it."

"Okay," he said. "No secrets."

"I think we need to do better than 'no secrets,'" Maurice said, making his way into the kitchen. "We should consider training, or at least strategizing."

"Good morning, Maurice. Did you wake up on the paranoid side of the bed?"

"Not without good reason. I just got asked to weigh in on whether x^0 should implement a plan to neutralize the threat of the Entelechy or not. It looks like a consensus is being reached, and more members prefer to do *nothing*. Can you believe it?"

Lola didn't like this news. "So x^0 will ignore this threat? That makes no sense. I don't think Warren and his Reel News empire are going to go away and let us be."

"I know." Maurice went over to the sink to fill the tea pot. "But x^0 has a centuries long history of staying out of conflicts. I imagine Warren will try to get x^0 to engage by going after its members. Probably the members here in the U.S. that he knows about."

Lola stared into her coffee. "I can't believe I brought this down on everybody. On my own family."

Both men shook their heads.

"You did us a favor by finding this idiot," Maurice said.

"There isn't a family in the world better equipped for this," Xuha added. He looked a little embarrassed. "I've started consulting this Chinese fortune telling thing. Just for fun. There's a lot of wisdom embedded in it and helps me sort things out when I'm confused."

"You mean the I-Ching?" Lola asked. "I used to do that when I was in college."

"Yeah? Well, I did one before I came here and I got number forty six. It's called Sheng and it's a symbol of slow, organic growth. Rising and Advancing. Ascending. Sprouting from the Earth. That kind of shit. It didn't make any sense to me, but now it seems like it was exactly about all of us. We're people growing into our potential. Not powerful like we've been zapped by radiation but more like we're each improving naturally, in our own way."

"I like it," Lola said. "We're ascending the mountain. We just don't know it."

"So can I call us the 46. Ascending fighting force?" Xuha sounded eager.

"I think having a name is good. That's a fine one."

"Awesome. When does the rest of the team get here?"

"Well, Zane has finals next week and flies in Saturday. Ariel's on vacation with a guy who makes her eyes light up."

"Sounds serious," Maurice said.

"Could be. Her company is closing their office in Dublin, so she has to go back to pack up her stuff. She won't be here for another two weeks."

"How long will she stay?" Xuha asked.

Lola looked uncomfortable. "She can be a strange one. She told me she'd stay in Houston as long as we needed her. Actually, she said she'd be staying until 'it is over.'"

"Until what is over?"

"She didn't answer when I asked. I'm guessing until 46. Ascending finishes their fight."

<u>December 2012</u>

14. Breaking Even

"What the hell is going on?"

It was only ten in the morning, and already Warren had heard from six of his monads, each of whom was contacted by x^0 over the weekend. Reports were mixed as to whether the enemy was trying to recruit his men or gather intel, but either way, Warren considered this a direct attack.

"Like hell these people are peaceful. They're are coming after me and only an idiot wouldn't see it."

He paced around his office, impervious to the beautiful dark wood and the expensive Persian carpet. Part of him wanted to talk this through with Gabriel, but all the monads had returned home last week. December was a pivotal month, with end-of-the-year programs setting the tone for the public's memories of how the year had gone. Reel News had a moral obligation to shape those memories well.

So how did a leader deal with poachers? With pests? With competition to be beaten and eliminated?

******

The elderly woman in Bhutan who headed c^3 squinted at the request from Thailand. Vanida, an out-of-body traveler from Bangkok, wanted to go to Texas on her organization's behalf.

Yuden knew she would be passing the leadership of c^3 on to her grandson soon, as custom dictated. The grandson was a good man, kind and gentle, but he was so cautious.

This former sex worker, Vanida, had been unorthodox since c^3 discovered her almost a year ago. In her request to be sent to the United States, of all places, the girl was once again shaking up the ancient organization. Yuden, as the head of c^3, was pleased Vanida was fulfilling her destiny.

Yuden remembered her own recent journey on c^3's behalf. Six months ago she'd stayed at a home in India, working with the Texan girl Teddie and members of x^0 to thwart a sex trafficking ring. Yuden was happy she and her out-of-body travelers played a key role in the outcome.

A faint smile crossed the old woman's face. A little romance, or at least a little good sex, made the memory of any adventure all the sweeter. Her thoughts wandered back to Maurice, the family friend of Teddie's who'd stayed in the house as well. Sex for the elderly might be a gentler, slower affair, but it was as much fun as the passionate kind she remembered.

She and Maurice had stayed in contact. Would she get the chance to see Maurice again if she went to Texas with Vanida? Of course she would. Was that possibility in any way clouding her judgement? Maybe a little.

✱✱✱✱✱✱

The Ushuaia chief of police was a pragmatic man. When one of his officers was killed in the line of duty a dozen years ago, he'd made a show of offering the man's widow a job in the administrative section. He'd expected her to turn it down, understanding it was a political gesture, but she'd not only taken the job, she'd turned out to be competent at it. Now she was a fixture in the department, handling filing and dispatch duties and often filling in as surrogate mom and informal counselor as well.

The chief of police had no problem with that, except the woman was unusually inquisitive. No, that was too kind. The woman was nosy. Worse yet, she was talking to his officers and amassing stories from the locals about the questionable building practices of a certain worldwide media mogul who had paid heavily to build offices in Ushuaia, and then paid even more to make sure there was "no trouble" as he built the facility. The chief of police was all for no trouble. He needed a way to get Mrs. Delgado on board.

He thought he found the piece of leverage he was looking for. The woman had been nice enough to provide it to him.

"You know, my daughter in New York works for the same man who is building that place," he overheard her tell his men. "She's important, too. She sees Warren Moore all the time. I've asked her to find out what he's up to, and she's going to try."

Interesting. There had to be some to way to use this to convince Mrs. Delgado to show more discretion.

******

Monday night, Lola and Alex sat on the front porch, huddled together against the chilly December evening. Lola's twinkly Christmas lights made a festive backdrop to a serious conversation.

"I'm scared, Alex. We've got something dangerous coming at us. We've got to trust each other and tell each other everything."

Alex began his litany of reasons for why he'd never talked to Lola about his ability to slow down time, and Lola was wise enough to let him finish. She knew most of the facts already. She even understood them, and that made it hard to stay angry.

"No more," was all she said when he was done. "Everyone under this roof has to understand. No more secrets."

"You sound like you're getting ready to lead an army."

"I think I am. Xuha's already come up with a name for us." She laughed. "I'm afraid he's going to make us t-shirts next."

He wrapped both of his arms around her in the way she'd always loved, the way that made her feel so safe.

"Reporting for duty, commander." He whispered it in her ear.

They walked into the house a few minutes later and found Teddie, Xuha, and Maurice in the living room. All three faces looked up, relieved to see neither Lola nor Alex was upset.

"We have new house rules," Alex said.

"Figured as much," Teddie replied. "We've already been talking."

******

Maurice accepted that he and Lola were going to lead a breakaway faction of x^0. Luckily, the organization was flexible and members were free to act on their own conscience as long as they separated their actions from those of the group. Olumiji had a tougher balancing act, but even he made it clear he'd provide personal assistance in case of emergency.

Several hundred x^0 members had already announced they'd help Lola and Maurice any way they could. More than a thousand others wanted no part in this. The remainder were mostly were low ability psychics who hadn't yet learned of the conflict. There were a few higher-skilled members taking a wait-and-see approach.

"Are you up for commanding a team of superheroes?" Maurice asked Lola half-jokingly the next morning as she filled her travel mug with coffee before heading out the door for work.

"I'm warming to the idea." Maurice noticed she seemed less defeated than she had in a while.

"Do you think we can win this one, commander?" He winked.

She hesitated. "That could be my biggest shortcoming. I don't need to win; I'm okay with breaking even."

"Brushing up on your laws of thermodynamics?" Maurice laughed. "Don't sell yourself short. There could be wisdom in your approach. Tonight when you get home, let's talk about strategies to come out of this no worse off than when we went in. I'd be happy with that, too."

******

The x^0 member in Brazil who'd been asked to contact a monad realized she'd gone too far. The monad was attractive and more interesting than so many of the men she knew, and, well, talk had led to drinks, and drinks had led to sex, and sex had led to more sex. Three days later they were still at it, and it was pretty clear sex was leading to affection. Upon reflection, she should have backed off a lot sooner.

The monad, Fernando, had other feelings on the matter. For years now Reel News had been pushing his little broadcasting company in ways he didn't like. He'd gone along for the money, there was no denying that. More importantly, he'd gone along for the camaraderie. After a lifetime of thinking he was secretly a freak, it had been exhilarating to find more than thirty others like him from all over the world. Fernando assumed the cost of this support system was doing the bidding of Warren Moore. So he'd done it. Now this beautiful woman, who was his equal in psychic ability and more than his equal in other ways, was offering him an alternative allegiance.

She was an accountant; she claimed to be an excellent one. She insisted there was always a way to walk away. She was ready to help him sell the company back to Warren and, better yet, her group was ready to welcome him with open arms. The organization was larger, considerably more diverse, and had almost no rules. Fernando liked them better already.

He was on board with defecting, so to speak, when she got word from her organization to stand down.

"Too late," she told the leadership of x^0. "This one's ours and he can't wait to join us."

Tuesday morning, Fernando notified Gabriel he would be resigning from the Entelechy, while his lone attorney contacted Warren's office full of lawyers to begin the business negotiations. Warren heard about it from both Gabriel and his chief counsel.

As far as he was concerned, the seduction and removal of his Brazilian monad was a shot across the bow. The information obtained from Maurice's place indicated x^0 was an old and secretive organization with far more members than the Entelechy. Although their records made it clear they had low admission standards and most of their members weren't that powerful, in aggregate they appeared to be the stronger group. The Entelechy had reason to be afraid.

When Warren called Gabriel back, he confirmed a member of x^0 had reached out to him, too. Several other monads had similar encounters. Warren wanted a report immediately on each monad's experience and his response. He needed to know ASAP if any other monads were at risk. By his count, he couldn't afford to lose a single additional man.

Warren poured himself a scotch as he fumed and waited. Gabriel was no slouch; Warren had his report in twenty minutes. He read it over and shook his head.

Here he was, outnumbered at least ten to one, but x^0 was comprised basically of cowards. They used old people, young girls and pregnant women to hide behind. They appeared to have tried to pick off every one of his men individually. Then, for reasons that made no sense, they'd backed off from that with only the Brazilian lost.

Very well. He needed to send a message that further encroachment wouldn't be tolerated. He wanted to go after the head of the organization, like a man, but the information showed the group was really headed by a disconcertingly amoeboid blob.

Common sense dictated he go after those nearest and easiest to find. That was the lady from the interview and her family, and the old man he'd already kidnapped once. Hardly worthy targets, but what choice did he have? If the rest of x^0 was going to hide under a rock, he'd have to draw them out however he could.

"Get me everything you can on these people right now," he ordered his head of security. Then he called Gabriel back.

"Talk to Jerry in Dallas again. He's the physically closest. I know he's swamped with work, but he's got to get me some intel on what these dipshits are thinking. Tell him to drive to Houston and park outside the lady's damn house. They've taken away one of us, and I won't tolerate another loss."

Gabriel seemed amused. "They're probably as scared of you as you are of them. Why not leave them alone for a while? Let's finish our end-of-year business. Then we'll tend to this nuisance."

"What? And give them time to formulate another spineless plan to take away more of my men? I don't think so. If they won't come out and fight, I'll force them to."

Gabriel's sigh was audible.

******

Teddie's eyes grew wider as she read the message. It was true Vanida wrote her saying she hoped to come to Texas, but it had never occurred to Teddie she would actually do it, much less bring the formidable head of c^3 with her. Best find her mom and tell her about the visitors. Teddie had no idea if the arrival of these reinforcements would be welcome news or not.

She made her way out to the living room where the rest of the family was watching television. It looked like some sort of news program, and everyone was focused on it.

"Mom?"

"Just a second, Teddie. We're trying to listen to this. North Korea launched its first rocket today."

"Yeah?" Teddie squinted at the screen trying to figure out what could be so important about that.

Xuha turned to her and whispered. "They are trying to develop the technology to fire nuclear weapons at us."

"What? North Korea wants to bomb us and no one told me?"

Alex picked up the remote and hit the pause button. "I think they're more interested in being *able* to bomb us than in doing it. Relax, nothing's going to happen for years. Probably decades. What's on your mind?"

"Oh. I wondered how you'd feel about a couple more people getting involved with us here? I mean, people who want to help."

"That depends on who," her mom said. Teddie explained. As soon as she said Yuden's name, she saw the hopeful light in Uncle Maurice's eyes. Was Yuden coming to be with Maurice? That was weird.

"I was contemplating a trip to Bhutan in the spring," Maurice confessed. "I can't say this is bad news from where I sit."

"We can use allies. Especially such talented ones," Alex said.

"And my first thought was *oh no, not company now*. I may be too much of an introvert to lead anything." Lola laughed at herself. "You're right. We need help. Teddie, please tell them we say thanks."

She smiled at Xuha. "Zane will be here by then, too, so your 46. Ascending fighters will become a force of eight. But hold off on ordering t-shirts until after Ariel arrives."

December 2012

15. Too Many Telepaths

Gabriel didn't lie to Warren. The memory of a lie could waft through the brain unguarded when another monad was near. However, omissions were different. They could be swaddled in so many rationalizations no one could find them.

After all thirty-five monads were approached by members of x^0 seeking sympathy, Gabriel made his own tally of the results. One monad, Fernando, had left. Seventeen members of the Entelechy were offended by contact with this inferior group. Eleven, including Gabriel, found the encounter interesting and wondered why Warren was so opposed to learning more. The remaining six, including Gabriel's Filipino friend Rafael, were sympathetic to this accumulation of misfit psychics who lacked strong leadership or common direction.

"I can't imagine a less dangerous group," Rafael said when the two men spoke by phone. "This is like a small group of highly trained police dogs getting upset when they discover a dog pound full of mutts."

"Maybe some think the mutts' existence makes it less impressive to be a dog," Gabriel suggested. Rafael understood the analogy, even if he didn't admit it.

When Gabriel briefed Warren, he left out this conversation and many others. His report merely said about half of the Entelechy found the contact to be offensive, while the other half did not. The report reaffirmed no one except for the ill-fated Fernando was considering defecting.

Gabriel thought that was all Warren needed to know.

******

"So what are you are expecting to happen?"

It was Saturday morning, and Alex and Xuha were hitting tennis balls, the way they had two years ago when Alex was Xuha's physics teacher and tennis instructor. Back then they talked about the nature of time. Today, Xuha felt they were preparing for a battle, but he was having trouble figuring out what shape this fight would take.

"I mean, are people with mind powers going to invade your house?" Xuha punctuated his question with one of his signature exaggerated faces, this one of an imagined psychic psychopath. "I'm not sure I can do much about that, Mr. Z. Don't get me wrong, I'll try, but this reading minds stuff kind of creeps me out."

Alex had to laugh. "Me too. It's why I refuse to think of what we do as anything but a mind trick to play tennis better."

"But we both know it's more than that."

"Yeah, we do. We're one of the advantages Lola and Maurice have. No one knows about us. We're like secret weapons."

"Okay. But what is it we're fighting?"

"Near as I can tell, this guy Warren Moore really dislikes anyone who's not a hawk. He wants everyone to be armed and ready to fight. I understand conflict brings in viewers, but I think it's his philosophy of life as well."

"Your wife thinks most of his company's stock is held by people who sell arms, and provide mercenaries."

"That's probably part of it, too. Warren is entitled to his worldview; I don't have to agree. It's just unfortunate his media empire allows him to shapes the news as much as he reports it."

Alex hit the last ball into the net, gave his racquet an annoyed look, and began picking up the balls scattered around the court. Xuha started picking them up on his side. They met at the net.

"So how did the mind-reading Mrs. Z become part of this?"

Something in Xuha's tone caught Alex's attention.

"Does knowing what she can do bother you, Xuha?"

Xuha made another face, this time of exaggerated surprise. It hadn't occurred to Alex this could be an issue, but it made sense. Alex supposed he deserved the implied sarcasm.

"Yes, sharing a house with two telepaths is kind of creepy," Not to mention a girl who goes flitting about at night without her body. I'm glad these are people I already care about." Xuha paused. "Do you think if they saw me in action, they'd think I was creepy too?"

Alex smiled.

"Yeah, okay. Maybe they would. So, how did Mrs. Z end up on Warren Moore's shit list?"

"Kind of randomly. They were doing a fluff piece making fun of an article she wrote, and noticed her telepathic skills. Word is Reel News owes much of its success to the few dozen telepaths in charge of its satellite companies. They thought they were the only psychics. Lola and her friends were an unpleasant surprise."

"The surprise went both ways, didn't it? How did they not find each other for so long?"

Alex shrugged. "They were both so sure they knew how the world worked that they weren't looking for each other. Lola's group is into empathy, to the point where they find other telepaths by seeking out empaths. Warren's group is all about being superior. His guys are like these demigods. Smart, good-looking, athletic. They never expected a clairvoyant to be anything less."

"So why can't they just say hi and go their separate ways?"

"You'd think they could," Alex said. "But Warren seems to think there's only room in this world for one group. Lola and Maurice think he will try to draw x^0 into a fight."

"By doing what? Trying to kill them? Messing up their lives? Annoying them into surrender? What are you expecting?"

The balls were all in the basket now, and the two men were standing at the net.

"I have no idea."

In the bright sun Xuha noticed the age lines on his former teacher's face and saw the frustration in his watery-blue eyes.

"I know how to prepare," Alex said. "I'd do anything to protect Lola and all of you, but I don't know if I'm looking for a broken water pipe or a home invasion. I don't know where to start."

Xuha wished he had a way to comfort this kind man who'd done so much for him, but every response he thought of sounded dumb. He settled for the least stupid thing that came to mind.

"Let's find ways to prepare for anything, then."

Alex gave him a weak smile. "The best way I know to do that is to hit another basket of balls."

******

Warren knew he could have used a telepath at his side in New York. His skills at reading the market couldn't match those of his monads; he just didn't have the tools. Not to mention members of the Entelechy proved useful in difficult business negotiations and in providing leverage over reluctant sources. It would have made sense to put the New York office under a monad as well.

Yet the right man had not appeared. Of the two American telepaths who had emerged, Brett did an excellent job of running the LA office and overseeing West Coast operations while Jerry managed Dallas and kept watch on Houston and Atlanta, too.

Warren had pushed the envelope with Charlie in Chicago. According to Gabriel, Charlie had the necessary psychic skills and charisma, but in Warren's estimation he was as dumb as a rock. He kept Charlie on a short leash, giving him the most capable underlings he could find.

He didn't want to turn the reins of his New York company over to anyone like that, so he borrowed the talents of his monads as they passed through the main office. It wasn't a bad arrangement, really. He liked having some distance from these guys.

His strategy for dealing with the Entelechy was simple. Don't think much. It was lucky he already knew what he wanted in life. He wanted to be richer. He wanted respect. He wanted to make the world better. If some of his methods for attaining the last goal were questionable; they were justified.

To be honest, he was a little afraid of what he'd created with the monads, but he had a plan for that, and he shouldn't think about it now. Otherwise, his world was in order and there wasn't much to consider.

Which was why x^0 scared him. Good Lord, those people thought he would be willing be make *more* telepathic friends? Possibly hundreds more of them? He needed less people in this world to hide his thoughts from, not more.

Was he contemplating killing hundreds, maybe thousands of people to stay safe? No. Even he didn't have the power or money to get away with such a feat. He'd have to be satisfied with disbanding the group, forcing them to hide in fear and cease their contact with each other.

He thought he could live with a secret pact in which the Entelechy became the only psychic organization allowed, and all others had to hide what they could do. It would take some sort of scare campaign in the everyday sphere. Tricky business, but fortunately, scare campaigns were what Reel News did best.

Warren's hope was that behind the scenes, x^0 members would have to either swear loyalty to his monads or live in fear of being outed to a paranoid world. His men, and some of the lesser telepaths from x^0 who would undoubtedly defect, could police this new order, keeping it predictable.

Now that was a world in which Warren could relax.

As always, the devil was in the details. How was he going to start a worldwide fear of psychic abilities strong enough to scare all those telepaths into agreeing to his edict? That was a problem for another day. He'd already spent too much time thinking.

He picked up one of his word search puzzles and concentrated hard on the random jumbles of letters and words having to do with the Christmas holiday.

******

Violeta tiptoed back out of Warren's mind, as soon as she realized his thinking for the day was over. Tomorrow, she'd find a way to call Lola and explain the frightening details of what she learned.

******

"You know I'm in a difficult position," Olumiji said to Lola. The two of them were video chatting; Lola, from the late night privacy of the den after everyone else was asleep, and Olumiji from the dawn of a new day in Lagos.

"Many in x^0 think if we fail to engage with Warren, he'll go find something else to do."

"Doesn't it bother you almost anything else he does will add more strife to this world?"

Olumiji sighed. "Lots of things bother me, Lola, and yes, Reel News is one of them. But you know we've all sworn not to use our telepathy to try to shape the world to fit our own political or religious agendas. Hell, we don't even all agree on those things. So while I'm happy to provide advice to you as a friend, I'm obligated to honor the group's consensus to keep x^0 out of this fight."

She understood, but that didn't mean she liked it. She decided to try another approach.

"Maurice and I don't have the options you do. He's living with us now, for his own safety, until we get some idea of where this is going. Common sense would say they're going to come after Maurice and me, but we can't imagine in what way."

"That's why I called you. I can't involve x^0, but if I learn anything helpful on my own, I'm free to share the information with you. Many members of x^0 want to share what they learn, too. They're the ones who wanted to fight Warren head on. I'll be their messenger, passing along useful chatter. Do you understand?"

She did. Olumiji was trying to find a way to help, and she appreciated it.

"Stay safe, friend," he said. "You'll hear from me. Often."

At the time he said it, he really meant it.

December 2012

16. No Time for Comedy

The lawyer invited Violeta to have a seat in the grey leather guest chair in his top-floor office. He still had his suit coat on, and he checked his phone for messages as his admin left to get Violeta a cup of espresso. The combination of courtesy and rudeness was intimidating in a way Violeta couldn't explain, but she felt it was intended to be so.

"I see Warren often as I handle my responsibilities. I talked to him earlier this morning. If he wanted to tell me something, why didn't he say so?"

The lawyer smiled. "He felt this message was better conveyed in, um, a more formal setting."

There was something cold behind the smile and Violeta felt a flush of fear. This morning was not starting off well. The tiny cup of espresso was placed in front of her, then the admin closed the door as she left the office.

"Am I being fired?"

The man looked up from the device in his palm. "No, not today."

There was the smile again. He waited. She waited. He waited some more.

He doesn't know how well I can play this game. Violeta began to peek into his thoughts, when he chose to speak.

"It's important to Mr. Moore that he be able to trust all of his employees, particularly those, like you, with whom he has personal contact."

Violeta felt her insides turn squishy. Had they discovered her contact with Lola? How?

"Mr. Moore recently received a disturbing report about you, and has asked me to clarify the situation."

It took every bit of training Violeta had to keep the panic off her face and the fear out of her eyes.

"It regards your mother."

"My mother?"

"Yes. We understand she works for the police department in your hometown in Argentina. Is that correct?"

Violeta allowed herself to exhale slowly.

"It is. She's worked there since my father was killed in 2000. She does clerical work. Why would Warren care?"

The lawyer pursed his lips.

"Mr. Moore is building a rather extensive office complex in Ushuaia. He's chosen to keep this development quiet for now, as I'm sure you know."

"Of course. I heard about it from my family. To the best of my knowledge it's no secret there. Was I not supposed to talk to my mother about it?"

"Talking to one's mother is fine. Suggesting to one's mother that one will spy on their employer is not."

"I did no such thing!"

As soon as Violeta said it, she realized she kind of, sort of, had.

"I mean I was just, you know, humoring her. She gets a little, I don't know, excited about things sometimes."

The lawyer nodded, and Violeta felt the emotional temperature in the room go from freezing to merely chilly.

"That's what Mr. Moore hoped was the case. Nonetheless, it presents him with a problem. The Ushuaia chief of police understands Reel News wants no publicity regarding the construction of this facility. A formal announcement about it will be made when Mr. Moore feels the time is right. He needs to be sure you are on board with this."

"Of course I am. I've said nothing to anyone in New York. It was obvious Warren preferred discretion on this."

"Excellent. I'm happy to hear that. Unfortunately, there are those in Ushuaia who feel your mother is not showing the same good sense."

Violeta fought the urge to squirm.

"She's become a focal point for unfounded local suspicions. People in small towns do tend to amuse themselves with gossip, don't they? Mr. Moore has decided he has no choice but to ask the chief of police to fire your mother and any other locals showing a lack of discretion. He wants me to ensure you understand why."

"I see."

Violeta knew getting fired would devastate her mom, who relied on her job for far more than money.

"Is there anything I can do stop her from being let go?"

"Not really, no. The remaining question is whether two members of your family need to lose their jobs over this. Does Reel News have your absolute loyalty?"

"Of course they do." She said it without thinking.

"Good."

He stood as he answered, pushing a small button on his desk, as he gestured to the door. It opened on cue, and Violeta understood she was being dismissed.

She also understood her every move would be watched for some time to come. Thanks to the innocent reassurances she'd given her mother, there was no way she could call Lola today, or anytime soon. If she reached out to the woman with her mind, Lola could misunderstand and call her, which would be even worse. There had to be no contact. She'd wait for a better time to share the news of Warren's plans with Lola.

******

Ariel had known for a while the next several weeks would be difficult for her family. This was the problem with having precognitive abilities; it was hard to stay dumb and happy. Usually, as an event got closer, the probabilities began to collapse into a narrower range of outcomes. However, these possibilities just kept growing. That didn't strike Ariel as a good thing.

She did know the odds of a good outcome increased if she was with them. Her knowledge of the future was often set off by touch, so she supposed if she was there she could guide others.

She said a long, reluctant goodbye to her boyfriend and packed up or gave away everything in her little apartment in

103

Dublin. She'd do what she could to help her family survive the coming storm, then worry about a new job. Would she find one she liked?

Another problem with being precognitive was you didn't always get to know what you wanted. All the prescient people Ariel knew saw a certain distance ahead. Some could look seconds to minutes into the future, but no further. She'd also met those who only saw centuries ahead. At the extreme end was Cillian, an Irish prophet who was certain humans would face a near-extinction event in a few hundred years. Unfortunately, the man was also certain that the choices Ariel made with her life would weigh into the equation of whether humans survived. This knowledge was a burden Ariel could have done without.

Ariel's own knowledge of the future centered around a few weeks from now. So far, no information about a job had been forthcoming.

She sat down as new visions began to wash through her mind. She saw variations of her and her family under siege in Texas. Wait. What was Cillian doing showing up in some of the visions? The man had been blinded in an accident a few weeks ago. He shouldn't be traveling now. What's more, this fight had nothing to do with him. Yet his presence persisted, and in more versions than not. Often his friend Nell was there now, too. It made no sense.

Then she understood. Cillian wasn't there to help her family. He was there to protect humanity. It was his obsession, after all.

He'd made a science out of checking his visions, gauging whether the odds of species survival nudged up or down with this decision or that event. He was going to come to Texas and attach himself to her like a freaking heart monitor, making sure she did nothing to threaten humanity.

Shit. As if the next couple of months weren't going to be difficult enough.

Nell, of course, was coming to be Cillian's eyes. The good news was Nell was helpful, and useful in a fight. Actually, she was better than that. She was an accomplished actress who'd learned to alter her face, size, skin color, and body shape well enough to impersonate anyone. Much like Zane did. Zane's talents were useful. Two people with Zane's talents? More than twice as useful.

Ariel's phone rang. She was pretty sure she knew who it was.

"Have you had your visions yet today? You'd be knowing my plans if you had." The rich Irish brogue always made her think of the best whiskey.

"Yes, Cillian. I've seen you at my home in Texas."

"Don't blame me, lass. I've important work of my own to do, and I could be of some use to you while I'm doing it, you know."

"Cillian, don't make this trip. Please. I promise I'll stay out of trouble and live to fulfill my damn destiny, whatever it is. Okay?"

"That may not be a promise you can keep. I see a better chance if I'm there to guide you and yours. So call your mum and tell her to set the dinner table for two more. I promise we'll behave ourselves."

Ariel didn't believe that for a second.

******

By Saturday afternoon, even picking up Zane at the airport had become a discussion item. Was he safer in a cab? Teddie thought they all should go. Lola wanted to hire a private limo. Alex wanted to send Xuha and Maurice.

In the end, Xuha, Teddie, and Lola went. Maurice promised to monitor their journey from the house. Alex just wanted to open a beer and check out a few college games.

"It's hard to be keen without being paranoid, isn't it?" Maurice said as he opened himself a beer and joined Alex on the couch. "May I?"

"Sure, as long as you don't talk about anything except football. Unless, of course, you get vibes the family is in danger."

"Are they actually televising a UTEP game today?"

"Yep," Alex said. "And it's on now."

The two men smiled at each other. Neither said a word for the next half hour.

******

As soon as Ariel heard her mother's voice, she knew it was a bad time for a phone call.

"Honey, I'm in the cell lot at the airport, waiting to pick up Zane. Is everything okay?"

"It's fine mom."

"Good. It's chaos here at the airport. Talk later?"

"This is quick. I'm bringing two people with me to Houston for Christmas."

"You're what??" Then, with less irritation. "Wait, is one of them this young man?"

"I wish. These are friends of mine from Ireland, and it's kind of a long story."

Lola took a breath and reached out to her daughter. She got that Ariel wasn't happy about this and felt bad about springing it on her parents. She got that these two wouldn't be dissuaded from coming. They, too, had abilities that could be useful in the days ahead.

"Right."

"Did you just read my mind, mom?"

"An emergency decision, dear. This is not good timing for guests, but we'll make the best of the situation. When do you get here?"

"Friday."

"You know Teddie has people coming too, right? c^3 people. They get here Tuesday."

"It's all going to be okay. mom."

"Are you telling me that as a psychic, or as my daughter?"

Lola heard Ariel laugh.

"As your daughter. Our futures over the next few months couldn't be more confusing. I hope there will be more clarity once I get there."

The phone bleeped with a text message. Lola said goodbye as she made her way into the mass of cars picking up holiday travelers. She avoided those pulling out of parking and the others grabbing overstuffed luggage out of their car trunks, then sucked in her breath and hit her brakes as a small child darted out in front of her.

A traffic cop whistled and motioned at her to keep moving. Where the hell was Zane? He'd texted her, but now he was nowhere to be seen.

"Do you see Zane?"

"No," Teddie said. "But I see Xuha."

"That's not helpful. Look outside the car, please."

"I am, mom. I see Xuha standing over there on the curb."

Lola squinted where Teddie was pointing. A young man wearing Zane's jacket but looking remarkably like a taller Xuha was waving at them with a pleased grin.

"Oh for God's sake. This is no time for comedy."

Xuha stared at his double for a second, a strange look on his face. Then he broke into a laugh as he jumped out of the car to help Zane with his bag. The two of them climbed into the back seat still laughing as Zane's features dissolved into his own.

"Thought I'd start my visit off with some of that absolute honesty you've been insisting on, mom," he said.

"Can you do me?" Teddie asked.

"Of course, but it'd be better with a wig. You'd be surprised how much difference hair makes."

Lola glanced in the rear view mirror as Zane began to resemble Teddie.

"Would you like to be bright pink?"

"Oh please! No wait, lime green."

"Sorry, I can't do colors I don't have pigments for. You'll like the pink, trust me."

Lola heard Teddie squeal with delight. She shook her head as she merged onto the highway that led home.

This could be the longest holiday ever.

The Second Law of Thermodynamics

You Can Only Break Even
On a Very Cold Day

17. As Good as True

Lola sat alone on the porch watching the sun set. The day was nearly as short as it would get, and winter twilight held a mystical quality for her, with its soft purples and deep blues tinged with a touch of melancholy. Lola took a sip of the red wine she'd brought out and enjoyed the silence.

People she was close to in x^0 had been contacting her all evening offering aid, and dozens more she'd never met wanted to help too. Lola felt a soft touch of support from her Nigerian friend Somadina, and let her in as they shared a memory of how Lola had flown around the world with Somadina's sister in 2009, finally collapsing in Houston Christmas Day, barely awake enough to enjoy the feast.

"This year will be better," she heard Somadina promise as she exited, leaving behind the sensation of a gentle hug.

Lola was about to head back inside, when Xuha came out with the wine bottle. "Mr. Z thought maybe you could use a second glass."

She shook her head. "I think not. I'll be inside in a minute."

As the door closed, she remembered how Christmas of 2010 had been as difficult as the year before. Xuha had moved into their house, and a riled-up group of people held a protest on the lawn after a hateful teacher at Alex's school decided Xuha's abnormal speed was the work of the devil. Some of them returned on New Year's Eve and tried to burn the house down.

Stop focusing on the past. You have work to do now.

She took a minute to let the sky's deepening indigo engulf her with its peace. That's when she felt the man's presence.

Damn. She'd been so lost in reminiscing she'd let her guard down. Who was he? He must be close. Probably in that car parked over there. Was he sent to learn about her. Of course he was.

Get the fuck out of my neighborhood and my head, she spat at him silently, using a word she'd have hesitated to say aloud. She heard him laugh.

Happily. Leaving now. Then he was gone, his own wall up to keep her from learning more.

Lola walked back inside, angry at herself, but more angry with them. No member of x^0 would ever spy on her private thoughts like that. She was lucky she was thinking about Christmases past and not something important. She couldn't allow this to ever happen again.

So, they'd taken away her front porch, her wine and her alone time. Lola didn't know which one pissed her off most, but she was ready to fight these people now.

******

For once, Warren couldn't have been happier with Jerry, the large, happy-go-lucky monad from Dallas who never seemed to take things seriously enough. Jerry had driven to the Zeitman home and spent two days doing old fashioned surveillance in three rental cars. Warren got the impression the man enjoyed it.

"I even got to piss into a bottle. Just like in the movies." Warren supposed everyone was entitled to their own idea of fun.

Of course, Jerry's investigation wasn't standard. Once he made visual contact, he could tap into the person's thoughts. Wary of Lola or Maurice's detection, he'd sought out the others, looking for anything of use.

Warren read through the notes of mostly useless trivia. Daughter Teddie didn't like Brussels sprouts. Husband Alex thought there was a good chance this whole mess would blow over soon. Guest Xuha was secretly practicing his skills because he wanted to repay the Zeitmans for all they'd done. Warren circled that sentence. He needed to find out more about those skills.

The real goldmine turned out to be Lola. Jerry had dozed off and woken to her thoughts. His half-awake entry into her mind escaped detection as she reminisced. Two years ago, some neighbors thought the family was in league with the devil. Really? Never mind it was absurd. What better lead-in could he have?

Reel News could rediscover the story as a follow-up to their interview with Lola. Then, they'd pursue the facts. Did this family have some connection with evil? Did it give them powers even rational people should consider? Warren knew how to raise suspicion. If he kept at it, fear would follow. Even the skeptics would wonder, deep inside, the way they always did.

"Look what I've done," he'd say. "My reporters will never stop seeking out those in league with this woman."

Then, he'd find a way to communicate his ultimatum.

"I can expose everyone in x^0, in your own towns, at your jobs, and in your churches. Once the world knows who you are, I'll unleash the power of my broadcasting conglomerate, and before I'm done, even your friends will be scared of you. You may end up dead at the hands of an angry mob. Or imprisoned on bogus charges by fearful law enforcement. If you're lucky, you'll end up alone, looking over your shoulder for the rest of your life."

Warren liked the last bit. It was best when even the good news was awful.

Then, the choice would come. "There's an alternative. Demonstrate you harbor no evil by pledging loyalty to my Entelechy and you need never worry again."

That would work. Those who made trouble would be persecuted by others while the rest accepted Warren's patronage. Over time, the more trusted of them could be used by the monads in subordinate capacities. Eventually, a few would ferret out their former comrades. It always happened.

For the first time since he'd become aware of x^0, Warren felt at peace. There *was* a way to control this group, and he was in the perfect position to make it happen.

******

Tuesday evening, somebody had to go to the airport. Yuden and Vanida were arriving and the elderly woman from Bhutan and teen-ager from Thailand couldn't be expected get their own ride.

Lola felt Maurice become increasingly nervous. His brief affair with Yuden last spring had been a diversion for two people in difficult circumstances. Now, she suspected Maurice had more serious feelings, and wondered if Yuden shared them.

Teddie was nervous too. She and Vanida had never met in person, and their backgrounds couldn't have been more different. Once they stood face-to-face, Teddie wondered if they'd find anything to say to each other.

Zane suggested he and Xuha take the van to the airport, and Teddie and Maurice ride along. After they left, Alex began massaging Lola's shoulders and kissing the back of her neck. "You know, before things become chaos around here?"

"I have presents I need to wrap."

"Of course you do." Alex began kissing her with more intention. "They'll be gone over two hours. Plenty of time for gift wrapping." Hmm. He was right. How much time did she need to wrap gifts?

When the van hadn't returned three hours later, Lola contacted Maurice. The flight was late and the luggage was slow, but there were no other problems. Teddie and Vanida hadn't stopped talking since they met. Maurice gave no details about Yuden, but he didn't have to. His glow of happiness said it all.

******

What Warren's staff discovered couldn't have been better. Three years ago an orphaned Mexican with dubious citizenship transferred into Alex Zeitman's high school where he became the boy's teacher and tennis coach. The boy had a cocky attitude, and attracted the attention of a student watch group headed by a history teacher interested in promoting white pride. Some would call it a hate group, but Warren was more sympathetic to those trying to hold on to the cultural values that built this nation.

The boy went by Xuha, which he pronounced "schwa." When the illegals he lived with were deported, the Zeitmans took him in. He was a troublemaker, getting into fights at school and displaying uncanny speed in fending off his attackers.

A local church heard about the boy's Mayan roots and decided he was using some indigenous voodoo to fight so well. Warren assumed that was nonsense, but useful nonsense. A local group ended up on the Zeitman lawn a few days after Christmas, protesting that the family was harboring a devil-worshipper.

When someone emerged out of the bushes to confront them, the group gave conflicting reports. Some insisted it *was* the devil, with bright red skin and golden irises and heat radiating from his body. Others felt it was a young man dressed in a costume. Either way, the group became frightened and ran.

No news outlet would touch the story. Then, on New Year's Eve, a rowdy inebriated crowd showed up in response to the original incident. This second group wore white hoods and set a cross on fire on the lawn. Rumor was the participants were drunk and trying to be funny. Police tied the incidents together, concluded there was a lot of harmless bad judgment involved, made one arrest and closed the case.

The Houston paper carried a short article describing the arrested man. He'd hoped to make fireworks by igniting a sheet inserted into the propane tank. He claimed Alex came flying out of nowhere, throwing him to the ground, spraining his wrist and cracking two of his ribs. He sued Alex Zeitman for damages.

You have to love life in America.

But what about Alex flying out of nowhere? Had this kid taught his black magic to his coach? It looked like he had.

So, what if more than telepathy was going on? What if some illegals had brought in techniques of the damned and passed the practices along to Lola and Alex? The well meaning Lola could have innocently passed these practices onto her group. Hell, x^0 may have been no more than second rate all-American psychics until this diabolic infection spread through her organization.

Warren was liking this story. It would deflect fear away from the likeable Zeitman family and toward the shadowy others of different cultures. Did more powers lurk among those who were dabbling in these ancient rituals? No one knew better than Warren how well the unknown made people afraid.

He planned to go after Lola and Maurice once the holidays ended, but the timing of the original incident offered a special opportunity. People loved stories about what happened two years ago today. That gave Warren's staff a week to have this piece ready.

Would it all be true? Of course not. Various sources would speculate. Such sources could always be found. If the speculation was repeated enough, it became as good as true.

******

Late the next afternoon, Vanida sat cross-legged in the middle of the living room, leading an animated discussion about out-of-body travel. The petite young woman's English was excellent, so the older Yuden let her young protégé speak for them both.

Vanida wore her thick, straight black hair short with bangs, in a bowl shape around her young face. Her features spoke of the intersection of China, Burma, and India, where she was born, while her thick black glasses gave her an intellectual appearance.

Zane, Xuha, and Alex were listening, and Teddie and Maurice were nodding in agreement.

"I'm not getting how this is possible," Alex said. "I believe you and my daughter, of course, but it doesn't make sense to me."

Teddie responded. "Everyone's consciousness exists in their physical body and in a lighter body in a reality matching the heavy one. These two realities are linked. When my consciousness streams are split apart, they take in different input, because my lighter body is separated from my heavier body."

Yuden spoke up, leaning forward so she could be heard. The woman had chosen a beautiful purple brocade blouse for the day and had braided her long grey hair into several lovely, intricate strands. She spoke in a heavy accent.

"It is dangerous when the mind breaks into two."

"So both bodies have their own eyes and brain?" Zane asked.

"Yes, each in their own realm. But there is a physical entanglement between them. When you travel, they still touch, like two entangled electrons in particle physics."

Alex threw his long arms outward in delight. "Entanglement, yes! Einstein called it 'spooky action at a distance.' It is a real phenomenon."

The rest of the room seemed less delighted to find themselves discussing physics.

"The important point," Vanida said, "is the two brains must be reunited. Travelers learn how to separate our bodies at will and exert control over where we go. We've also learned how to remember what we see. Does that make sense?"

"It was a wonderful explanation," Maurice said.

"Uncle Maurice rode along in my mind when I was looking for Vanida and Michelle," Teddie added. "I think it's the only time that x^0 and c^3 have joined forces like that."

Maurice and Yuden exchanged a smile.

"After the girls were home safe, Yuden and I became intrigued with combining telepathy and out-of-body experiences. Both require a personal connection and we have one. So I've been riding along with Yuden while she travels. She can't tell I'm there, but afterward we talk. We've learned a lot."

"It's why I came here," Yuden said. "We've done much new. If bad trouble comes, we have a special way to help and it will work better with me here."

Lola had gotten home from work near the end of the conversation and stood in the entryway listening. So the two elderly lovers had found a way to push the boundaries of their skills. Lola felt a flash of pride in her friend, and a new gratitude for Yuden, who'd traveled halfway around the world for this.

******

Violeta knew she had to keep Lola from contacting her. If only they could communicate with their minds like the more adept members of x^0 did. Violeta wished she had more practice in sending messages and less in hiding them.

But she didn't. So how did one communicate in a world where everyone was always watching? Maybe it was time to leave telepathy and technology alone. She'd write Lola a letter by hand.

Should she tell Lola what Warren was planning? No, better not. Letters could be found; she didn't need Warren in a frenzy seeking the source of the leak.

She wrote it in a purple felt pen, with no signature or back address. Her name was Violeta. Lola would get it.

Then she called her mother. She expected her mom to be angry about being fired, which she was, but Violeta wasn't prepared for her mother's fear.

"I know these men. They don't fire me because someone asks them to or because someone pays them money, either."

"Okay, so maybe Warren threatened them. He's not above using intimidation."

"I don't get fired for an idle threat," her mother insisted. "It takes something awful to make them do this to me."

"I'm sure Warren saw it as just business. You were poking your nose into his affairs. He wanted you to stop."

"Somebody needs to stop him. But not you. As long as you work for these people, I fear for you."

"Don't be so dramatic."

She said it in the most soothing way she could. Her mother was being overemotional. Mothers got that way. The complex in Ushuaia was a private matter, not her concern. She was going to move her thoughts on to other issues, like what to wear to work tomorrow. Yes, she was focusing on her shoes now.

She said goodbye to her mom without changing the mood in her head. Then she let the thoughts of clothes swirl round until she felt Gabriel leave her mind as quietly as he had come.

Damn. That was the fourth time in three days he'd entered her head, wondering if she could be trusted. It was something he'd done little of over the years, and Violeta wasn't sure how much longer she could stay so vigilant. She *would* have to quit her job, and soon, before he learned too much. A letter of resignation timed to arrive after she was far away would be unprofessional, but best.

Going back to Argentina made the most sense, even though she'd just been there. It was a normal thing to do over the holidays. She could enjoy the comfort of her mother's house while she looked for another job. Best of all, she could snoop around Warren's complex in Ushuaia while she was unemployed.

Violeta looked at airfare. A last-minute holiday trip would clean out her savings, but rates dropped on Christmas Day. She could handle Gabriel's intrusions for another week. She made her reservation.

December 2012

18. Purple Angel

It was her last day before taking off for the holidays and Lola couldn't concentrate on work. Word of her predicament permeated through x^0, as dozens more members sent news or passed along their personal good wishes. Olumiji contacted Lola to let her know they expected Warren to use his media empire to launch a fear campaign against her and telepaths in general. No one doubted Reel News could make the world afraid of anything it pleased.

When Lola got home from work, she gathered everyone in the living room to tell them what she'd learned. They were all as concerned as she was.

"The worst part," Teddie said, "is if they put us in any kind of danger and we do anything unusual, we give them ammunition."

"If we all go home instead," Maurice said, "they can change tactics and find a way for each of us to have an accident."

"We've got three more people arriving tomorrow, and one of them can tell us when things will happen," Alex said. "That will help."

Lola noticed Maurice giving Yuden a concerned look. Yuden shook her head.

"I take care of myself for eight decades, buddy," she said, giving him a playful punch in the arm, enjoying her own joke.

Lola glanced at Alex, and he signaled his agreement.

"Yuden, if you'd like to stay here, in the guest room with Maurice, that's fine with us. I mean, you'd be welcome at our house. Assuming Vanida doesn't mind going to the hotel alone."

Vanida didn't get the chance to answer.

"Mom. There's plenty of space in my room. I bet Vanida doesn't mind an air mattress. That way, just in case, we're all here."

Vanida seemed pleased at the offer.

"Good." Lola agreed, getting up to pull the casserole Zane had made out of the oven. "So tonight, it's a slumber party. Tomorrow, we'll get a sense from Ariel of how this will unfold and we'll make a better plan."

"Why are two people coming with Ariel?" Xuha asked.

"One is a traveling companion, but from what I understand, she has something important in common with Zane."

"*That*'s who's coming?" Zane took more of an interest.

"Yes, and Ariel says she shifts her looks as well as you do. As to the other person, I'm not so sure. He was blinded in an accident a few weeks ago, but Ariel says he sees into the far future and insisted on coming as her clairvoyant body guard. Would not be dissuaded." Lola shrugged. "I don't see how having him here is going to matter one way or the other."

Later she'd wonder how she could have been so wrong.

******

Warren knew it was unreasonable to expect Jerry, the monad from Dallas, to remain in Houston for Christmas. He tried to listen patiently while a telepath explained to him, once again, the ways mind-reading worked.

"Now that I've made contact, I can find them. What I get may not be useful, but I'll keep trying through Christmas."

"Thanks. I won't expect much,"

But that evening Jerry called back. "You're not going to believe this!"

"Try me," Warren said.

"I found her daughter. Sitting bored at a school assembly. I'm thinking about their family, and she's thinking about the creep in the car who was spying on her mother. That's how this stuff works; it's not random you know. The daughter moves on to thinking about two house guests, and I find out one of them is a girl who can do what this daughter does."

"That's great. What does this daughter do?"

"I've no idea. She didn't give it any thought. Not only does the other girl do it too, but the woman who heads up the whole organization of people who do this thing is the other house guest! Then the kid got spooked because her mom told her not to think about this and she started concentrating on her schoolwork."

"Are we talking about something like telepathy?"

"I've no idea. All I know is the lady in charge of this thing is visiting from Asia. She's a Buddhist, for God's sake. I think she lives in a temple."

Warren hadn't known it was possible for a single fact to make him scared and delighted at the same time. He focused on the delight.

"Jerry, that's terrific. I've got a Mayan *and* a Buddhist doing secret rituals to harm the honest people of Texas. This just keeps getting better."

"I knew you'd love it."

After Warren hung up the phone, he faced the fear he'd put aside. Sure, the story against the Zeitman family was practically building itself. On the other hand, he *was* taking on hundreds of telepaths, two men who used some ancient Mayan magic to move at the speed of light, and a couple of teenaged girls who could do something unusual enough that there was an entire Buddhist organization devoted to it.

This was no time to get squeamish. He could be in so far over his head, in danger in ways he didn't realize. He had to hit this family, this story, with all the force he could, with no sympathy for anyone. Hell, his own survival could depend on it.

******

Saturday morning Teddie and Vanida were video-chatting with their friend Michelle, who wouldn't be back from California until after the holidays.

"I can't believe you came all the way from Thailand and I'm not there."

"I promise I'll be here when you get home. We'll get to—"

She was interrupted by the doorbell's chime.

"Teddie, get the door!" Zane yelled.

"I'm on the phone!"

The doorbell clanged again.

"So am I and it's for school. Mom and Dad are at the store. Get the door!"

Teddie gave Vanida and Michelle an exasperated shrug. She ran into Uncle Maurice in the front hall.

"I've got it."

It was two delivery men with a large Christmas plant, decorated with festive bows and lots of ornaments.

"Want us to set it inside?" They were struggling to hold it up.

"Uh, sure, I suppose. It's probably from Aunt Summer." Teddie let the men put the thing against the living room wall. "I like it better when she sends cookies."

One of the men had gotten mud on his hands and went to wash them while the first made small talk about all the last-minute deliveries they had to make. After they left, Teddie looked for the card. When she found none, she figured it had fallen off.

****

The monad Rafael was home in the Philippines. He called his friend Gabriel to wish him Merry Christmas and share concerns.

"If what I pick up is true, Warren has lost his mind."

"Maybe he has," Gabriel agreed. "He plans to introduce stories about these x^0 people over the holidays. His plan for containing their group centers around creating a fear of them. I advised him to wait, to meet with us first, but he wouldn't listen. I don't think he understands how personal this is to us."

"He can't understand. He runs the circus, while we're the freak show. You don't ask sensible men to add kindling to a fire capable of burning them as well. Do you think Warren has chosen this approach so he can control us better, too?"

"Maybe. If any of us gave him problems, a threat to throw us into the fire does work to his advantage."

"We can't let him go down this path."

"I don't know if we have a choice. Warren owns our companies. If he wants to air these stories, we do it."

"Why? He needs us as much as we need him."

Gabriel shook his head. "I'm not sure he does. His empire has its own momentum now, and he's a shrewd businessman. The way things are structured, he could fire any of us. We'd get generous severance packages, but he'd be left with the means to speak to the world."

"I hadn't looked at it that way. Can we change it so he can't take our companies from us?"

"We could pressure him to renegotiate our contracts, but he'd only consider it if he thinks he has our complete loyalty."

"Then we need to play along."

"We do. I also need to get a lawyer involved; we need to know our options. Before we go too far, we also need to figure out what we want. In the best of worlds, what happens to Warren? To x^0? To Reel News? To us?"

Neither man had an answer. Not yet at least.

******

A winter storm hit the Midwest and by Saturday morning flight were delayed across the country. When the exhausted threesome from Ireland finally arrived that night at eleven they were greeted by eight hungry people who'd waited for dinner.

Xuha started it.

"The way your mom describes how you see the future is so cool. Touch me first. I want to know what will happen to me." Xuha made one of his exaggerated comic faces, this time a look of amplified eagerness.

Ariel directed a fierce look of annoyance at her mother.

"We're in the middle of a crisis here," Lola said. "We've got a no secrets policy now. We tell everyone everything because we have to work together."

"That won't be possible," the blind Irishman said from the place where he'd settled in on the couch.

Lola looked at Cillian more closely. He was a tall, unusually attractive man in his mid-forties, with a rich brogue and the demeanor of someone of wealth and importance. He spoke like he was accustomed to being listened to.

"I beg your pardon?"

"Ariel will need to be selective about what she tells you. It's a pity you chose to share her feyness with the group, but she and I will find ways to manage that. She needs to check with me before she says anything more."

Lola knew she was tired. Hungry. Not used to strangers in her own house telling her what to do. She tried to soften her voice before she spoke, but didn't do a very good job of it.

"Ariel is my daughter and she will do no such thing. Her family is in danger and needs her help. What she does or doesn't do is not your concern. I'm not even sure why you're here, but you may stay if and only if you don't think it is your prerogative to tell us what to do."

The rest of the room went silent.

"That was an ignorant remark," Cillian said. The fatigue and stress were as clear in his voice. "You've no idea what you're talking about, woman. Unfortunately, I make things worse by enlightening you."

Lola turned to her oldest daughter in exasperation.

"Cillian sees the far future," Ariel reminded her. "He thinks I have an important role to play, years from now."

Cillian started to object, but Ariel kept talking.

"How doesn't matter, and he's right—the less you know, the better. The point is he came along to make sure I come out of this alive and this incident doesn't somehow, um, impact humanity unfavorably. I know that sounds farfetched," she said, looking at each member of the group for understanding. "He's got excellent reasons for what he believes. He's not here to help us, mom. He's here to guide me, regarding a greater good I know you would support if you knew more about it."

Lola was unconvinced, but Alex intervened.

"We'll find a balance between long-term and short-term survival. Right now, how about we eat?"

Zane and Teddie had already put the food on the counter, and Yuden and Maurice started to fill their plates. Vanida described the overcooked feast to Cillian, offering to bring him food and drink. He softened at her consideration, and a relieved Nell left his side to find the bathroom.

She was walking back into the living room as Zane got up. The two of them looked at each other as a slow smile spread across each of their faces. Zane set down his beer and his body began to shrink, until he was close to Nell's size. She rose a little taller in response, her breasts receding and her jaw widening. Zane responded by making his skin paler until freckles emerged on his face. The light blue irises of Nell's eyes became Zane's murky hazel. Zane's hips broadened as his waist thinned. Nell's nose lengthened and her eyes narrowed. Each kept improving in response to the other, and while neither was a perfect likeness, by the time they stopped, both imitations were remarkable The rest of the room watched in amazement.

"We'd be more convincing if we each had wigs," Nell said.

"Yeah. Clothes help too," Zane said. "Hey…"

He gave Nell a nod towards the bathroom. She smiled her agreement and the two of them ducked into the small room. A few minutes later two bodies came out, both with towels wrapped around their heads. One looked like Zane in Zane's clothes, the other like Nell in hers.

"Are you going to keep doing this?" Teddie asked. "If so, I'm going to give up and call you both Zell and be done with it."

"We'll get tired of it," the woman who looked like Nell said. She pulled the towel off her head to show off her shoulder length light brown hair. Zane removed his towel, revealing his short dark hair.

"Admit it. We had you guessing." They said it together.

The rest of the room laughed, and when Xuha started the applause much of the tension dissipated, at least for the night.

******

As Lola headed for bed, she saw the unopened mail next to her purse. The pile seldom contained anything but ads and bills, but today there was a hand-addressed envelope promising to be more interesting. She studied the thick, firm strokes from a purple pen and felt a familiar tingle.

By the time she had the one-page note in her hand, she knew. Violeta had turned to this to keep her message under the radar of psychics and technology experts alike. As Lola read, she understood her guardian angel was on the run. Warren and his staff had become suspicious and were watching Violeta, leaving her unable to aid Lola or even contact her.

Lola picked up the little lavender figurine on her dresser and studied it for a minute. It was hollow, with a small hole in the base.

"Stay safe, angel," she whispered as she folded the note into a tiny blob and tucked it inside the porcelain angel.

For a second she could have sworn she felt Violeta's presence and her smile at the idea of being considered a purple angel. There was a quick acknowledgement the note had been received and hidden in a worthy place. It was so quick Lola wondered if the exchange was no more than her own wishful thinking.

December 2012

19. Visions of Sugarplums

Lola got up early to put on coffee and throw together breakfast. Cillian and Nell had gone to their hotel late last night, but that left nine people to feed. She was emptying the dishwasher when Ariel came into the kitchen.

"Mom, we should talk."

Lola agreed. "Cillian had no idea what he was walking into, did he? He doesn't know about me or x^0 or Teddie or Zane or our troubles with Reel News, does he?"

"Mom, these aren't things I discuss. I came here to help you. Cillian guilted me into bringing him along."

"I understand that now."

Ariel gave her a sharp look. "You didn't look into Cillian's mind, did you?"

"Yes, I did." She tried not to sound as defensive as she felt. "Privacy be damned when I'm protecting my family. I will not do that from a place of ignorance."

Her voice had started to rise and she made a conscious effort to lower it back to a whisper.

"No, I didn't find out what calamity this man thinks befalls the human race, or why he's so hell-bent on protecting you. What I got is he's fanatic about his role, and will sacrifice anyone to protect this path he thinks we need to be on."

"He is a good man, mom."

"Maybe."

Lola was beating eggs into a scramble with an unnecessary amount of vigor.

"He's a scared man, I'll give you that," she said. "He's also frightened by his new blindness. I can't fault him for that. I'm willing to bet he behaved more civilly before his accident."

"He did. He's been through a horrible experience, so cut him some slack. I'm not going to run everything I do by him, but I will include him somehow."

"That's exactly what I want you to do. Fill him in completely, please, and Nell too. I want them to know everything this family has been involved in for the past four years. He can keep his secrets, but we'll have none, so if he can possibly be of help to us, maybe he will."

"Okay." Ariel stopped and stared at her mother. "We need to stop talking about Cillian and look at *your* future. I'm picking up things touching your utensils."

"Oh thank heavens. Tell me what Reel News is going to do."

"I can't. It doesn't work that way."

Ariel explained she saw future events the way others saw memories. Pictures, sounds, smells, and background knowledge combined to give a flash of information. Like a memory, the information was never complete.

"I call them premories," she said, a little embarrassed. "Had to call them something."

Ariel told her mom how the future always had multiple options, with likely events stronger and brighter. "I started assigning rough probabilities. There's never one premory, and sometimes there are so many I can't process what's going on."

"So how is tomorrow looking?" her mother asked.

"It isn't." She watched her mother's eyes widen in fear. "Wait. I don't mean it like that. I mean I can't see the next minute or tomorrow."

Alex had come in from the garage and was listening.

"I have a sort of window I see through. It starts several days out, nothing closer. It would be nice to know if it will rain tomorrow, but I can't do that. I can tell you there's a fifty-percent chance of rain on Saturday."

"I can tell you that," Zane said as he came into the kitchen headed for the coffee pot.

"Okay," Alex said. "How about you tell us about next Christmas. How likely is it we're are all here and happy?"

"I can't do that either. The furthest I see is around six months, and I don't do that far well. I can tell you next June is all over the place, with lots of wildly different scenarios."

Teddie joined the family. "What you do isn't as useful as I thought."

"I know. But touch makes everything more clear. Come here." Ariel opened her arms and Teddie smiled as she walked into the hug. Ariel held her sister tight for a full minute, while Maurice and Yuden came into the kitchen.

Ariel nodded as she let go. "I think I can make sense out of this, if I can get more." She turned to the elderly Yuden. It was surprising how imposing a woman less than five-feet tall and over eighty-years old could be, particularly in her pajamas. But Yuden oozed a silent dignity.

"I see you in so many of Teddie's possible futures. May I hug you, ma'am?"

A giant grin broke through the wrinkles.

"To tell my future? As they say here, hell yes." She threw her arms around Ariel.

The rest of the family got in line, followed by Maurice, and then Xuha and Vanida, who had joined the group.

Ariel grabbed a paper and pen, and began writing.

"Your futures all intertwine so much that what I can't make sense of in one place I can get in another."

"Are we going to be okay?" Lola asked.

"Probably." Ariel flashed her mother a grin.

"You guys go ahead and have breakfast. I'm going to try to figure this out. When I'm done, I'll tell you everything I know.

Ariel spent the morning diagramming what she saw, stopping only to call Nell at the hotel to ask her to keep Cillian away for the day. The two women held a hushed conversation, after which Ariel went back to work with renewed effort.

As her pages of diagrams grew, she took over the dining room table. At six that evening she told everyone it was more complicated than she thought and she'd need more time. Then, before they could argue with her, she went to bed.

She was back up a few hours later, making more notes. She moved on to larger and more elaborate diagrams in multiple colors on a large notepad her mother found for her. Occasionally, she'd walk around the house, touching things and sometimes hugging people. Late that night, she stopped, ate three bowls of cereal, and went to bed.

******

Ariel slept in the next morning, then came into the living room to face the wary crowd. Everyone looked at her, but no one asked.

"Merry Christmas, almost," she said. "My shopping was meager, but the good news is each of you gets your fortune told, as my gift to you. Cool, right?"

Smiles began to spread around the room. Ariel looked so much better than she had for the past day. How bad could it be if she was handing out fortunes as gifts?

"Me first?" Teddie said.

"Nell and Cillian are on their way over. I'd like to wait for them." She turned to her mother. "Nell gave Cillian a lot of information yesterday, and promises he'll play nice. He monitors his visions daily, checking for minute variations in far-off probabilities. He won't stop doing that, but will only speak up if we are significantly altering things for the worse. As of this morning, no change. "

"Then why does he have to come over?"

"Well, it's Christmas Eve, and he and Nell are thousands of miles from home. It seemed like the nice thing to do."

"Of course. I didn't mean to be thoughtless."

"Besides, he now believes any actions of ours affecting his visions for the worse are also likely to result in my or your untimely death."

Lola's eyes widened.

"Yup. He's decided if either me or you die young, things get worse. Interesting, huh? Given we'd like that *not* to happen also, I thought we'd listen if he advises against something."

"I see." Lola didn't look happy about this second piece of news, but she said no more.

✳✳✳✳✳✳

It's good to be me.

Warren was pleased as person after person took his call on Christmas Eve and each one found time to do is bidding. Some worked for him and had no choice, while others owed him favors. The remainder relished the idea of Warren owing them, or astutely surmised a man controlling a lot of the media made a poor enemy.

Whether it was a carrot or a stick, it worked. The tasks would be completed in spite of the holiday, mostly by relief staff filling in while the primary decision makers were out of the office.

✳✳✳✳✳✳

When Nell and Cillian arrived, everyone took a seat. All eyes were on Ariel.

"Okay," she began, sitting cross-legged in the middle of the living room rug. "Some of this is for everyone, and I'll start with that. Mom, your friends have told you Reel News will begin a fear campaign against us. That's true. They must be working on it now, because my closest in premories are all about that. While I don't know what they will do, I do know they try to get us to respond with something they can present as proof of evil powers."

"That's ridiculous," Maurice said. "They don't succeed, do they?"

"They do. I mean, there's over a ninety-percent chance they get something they can use. I don't think we need to worry about who gives them the material or how. I spent too much time trying to figure that out, but there are so many ways for them to accomplish it and there's almost no way to prevent every one of us from doing something unusual in a crisis. By the time my premories kick in, it's a done deal. I think we accept it happens, and plan from there."

"Do your premonitions tell us anything useful?" Lola said.

"They do. Your group x^0 is going into deep hiding. By next week they've vanished and you can't believe how completely they are gone. Telepaths do not exist."

"That's too bad."

Ariel paused when she saw the looks on everyone's faces. "Hey, a lot of this isn't going to be good news. You do get that, right?"

Everyone nodded.

"Okay, so, c^3 does the same. Poof. Gone."

Yuden and Vanida looked at each other.

"What about my job back in Bangkok?" Vanida asked.

"It's likely neither of you goes home for a while. It's hard for me to get details, because I know so little about what you do."

Ariel paused to take a bite of food and to look through the notes she had brought with her.

"Okay. Mom and dad. Let's start with you two. Have you made any travel plans?"

They both shook their heads, then Lola remembered. "When this started, we talked about going to Argentina, maybe over spring break."

"That must be it. I get a good probability you go to South America. At least fifty-fifty. Although I don't think it's spring break, and you don't seem happy to be there. Were you planning to go anywhere else?"

Lola and Alex looked at each other, perplexed.

"Not really."

"Well, I also see you guys on a cruise ship. Maybe cruising to Argentina?" She considered the possibility. "Do cruise ships go there? Anyway, it's a bad idea. A really bad idea. Don't go. If you do, I'm pretty sure you guys end up getting kidnapped because of Warren Moore, although obviously, he doesn't do it personally. And being kidnapped is not good. If it happens, you try to get away, and there's at least a one-out-of-four chance you both end up dead."

Her mom and dad exchanged a glance. "Cancel all travel plans through June," Alex said. He reached out his arm to Ariel.

"Can you do that touchy thing and see if, you know, the one-out-of-four chance of being dead has gone down?"

"I'd be surprised," Ariel said. She took her father's arm around the wrist, like she was taking his pulse.

"That's strange. The odds of your taking this trip have gone up now that I've told you not to go. Maybe I should stop talking."

"That would be my advice," Cillian said from his corner of the couch. "This visions of sugarplums nonsense you're doing inevitably makes things worse. I say shut up and let it happen."

Ariel gave Nell a meaningful look, and Nell bent down and whispered something in Cillian's ear.

"But don't listen to me. I'm just the resident prophet of doom."

Nell whispered again, and Cillian motioned a zipper across his lips. Lola had to smile.

"Thanks Nell."

"Okay. Zane." Ariel went on. "I'm pretty sure you'll miss the start of the semester. A couple of professors will work with you, but two won't, so you'll graduate a semester later than you planned."

"Shit."

"Yes, I saw you really pissed about it. Oh, and you may go to Argentina with Mom and Dad."

"Why would I do that?"

"We're not going now, remember?" Lola said. Ariel ignored them both.

"Don't you have any good things to tell me?" Zane asked.

"Lots of them, but they don't matter," Ariel explained. "I see you marveling at a sunset. Happy to be video-chatting with, ooh, some cute guy you met on a boat. He seems happy to be talking to you too."

Zane worked to cover up the blush appearing on his cheeks. "Okay, I get the idea. It's the bad stuff that's useful."

Ariel told Zane and Nell of the many premories she'd had of them impersonating multiple characters, including each other.

"Those were some of the hardest to sort out. I couldn't always tell where you guys were or even who you were. But I'd bet on you both doing more shifting over the next few months than you've ever done before."

Nell asked the question.

"Are we both alive in six months?"

"Probably. There's fringe stuff out there, of course, but if one follows the path of most likely, you both make it through. Not necessarily with ease, though."

Ariel went on to tell Teddie, Vanida, and Yuden that she'd also seen many visions of them having out-of-body experiences.

"One problem was my mind didn't know how to process it. I kept thinking you'd all gone to Argentina with mom and dad, which made no sense. Then I figured out I was seeing your, whatever you call them, your spirit bodies, not you. Maybe. Between that and seeing Zane and Nell morph their appearance, it was hard to make sense of it."

"So, how do things go in the end?" Teddie asked.

"You and Vanida do a *lot* of traveling. Like Zane and Nell, odds are you end up safe, but I see at least once when you fail to do one thing you think is necessary. It turns out it isn't. So if not everything goes right, keep on going."

Cillian snorted out a laugh.

"What about me?" Xuha asked.

"Wow, what you do is so cool," Ariel said. "I got to see you in action. You're amazing."

"So everything is good for me?"

Ariel shook her head. "These idiots at Reel News go after you, claiming you are some sort of Mayan cult leader. Were you involved recently in something involving an ancient artifact?"

"Yes, but so was your dad and lot of other people."

"I'm really sorry, Xuha, but it probably gets ugly regarding your heritage. Same for Yuden, and Vanida too. You ladies get painted as evil sorceresses playing Buddhist Jedi mind games."

"I like that idea." Vanida added a nervous giggle.

"Not the way they do it," Ariel said. "I don't think you die, Xuha, but there are some scenarios in which they mess up your life. Like, life-in-prison bad. Many where they don't, though."

Xuha exhaled slowly but said nothing.

Maurice reached out and touched Ariel on the arm.

"You can tell me," he said.

"How'd you know?"

"Even doing my best to stay out of your mind, I can't avoid the reticence you feel about talking to me. It's okay. You can say it."

"Oh, Uncle Maurice. I'm so sorry. There is at least a one-out-of-three chance that, come June, you're gone. There are so many ways it could happen, I can't get a handle on it."

Tears started to come into Ariel's eyes. Maurice laughed and gave her a hug, as she started to cry.

"My dear, I'm eighty-eighty. Even if I wasn't in the middle of this mess, I may not have a better chance of living till next June. Think about it."

"Oh." This hadn't occurred to Ariel. "That explains why I see the same for you, Yuden." She turned her gaze to the older woman. "I didn't want to tell you."

This time Yuden reached out to touch her.

"Thanks for the good news. I'm happy with two-out-of-three odds."

"Anything else of immediate help?" Alex asked his daughter.

"Not really. We know something unusual happens over the next few days that sets this in motion. The less we react the better. Oh, wait a minute, dad. Your school will be looking for ways to fire you."

"Forgot to mention that one, huh?"

"Sorry. And finally, nobody goes on a cruise. Nobody goes on vacation. Nobody goes anywhere near South America."

"Check in on how that's working out for you," Cillian said.

"Ignore him," Lola said.

"No, he is right," Alex said. "We should monitor this. We're learning about working with Ariel's visions." He reached out his arm to his daughter. "Are we at least below fifty-fifty for not ending up in Argentina?"

Ariel held on to her father's wrist for several long seconds before she answered.

"No, you're closer to sixty-percent now."

Cillian broke into a loud coughing spasm.

"Get him some water," Lola told Teddie in a stage whisper.

"I'd stop coughing *and* behave better if you made it a little Christmas brandy instead," he whispered back.

Lola rolled her eyes, marched into the kitchen, and came back with a bottle and a glass. She poured three shots into it and placed it in his hands.

"How's that?"

Cillian swirled the liquor around, feeling its weight. Then he took a sip and smacked his lips.

"Plenty of it, and not the cheap stuff, either. Thank you, lass. You've bought at least three hours of my best behavior."

"Great. Let me know when the meter runs out."

But the meter never did. Soon the rest of the family began preparing and consuming food and drinks as the spirit moved them. A round or two of presents were opened. Music played in one room and a card game got started in another as everyone did their best to put the future in the past.

When it got late, Nell turned to Cillian. "Okay, great prophet. Time for us to call for a ride to our hotel."

"I'm not going anywhere," Cillian said.

Lola started to respond with "Of course you are" but stopped.

"Analysis of Ariel and Lola's safety suggests I should stay here and not go anywhere for several days," Cillian said. "So I stay."

Is he working this prophet thing just so I'll keep him in whiskey?

I think it's possible. Maurice answered in her head.

"Well then, of course you stay," Ariel said. "Nell, I'll find you a place in my room. Cillian, I'm sure mom can get you things to make you comfortable on the couch." She hesitated. "Right, mom?"

"Of course." Lola was glad most of the people there couldn't read her mind.

20. Surely You Don't Believe

When the whimpering woke Lola a few hours later, she assumed someone was hurt. She scanned the household for anyone in trouble. Family and guests were all in deep sleep, but Lola could feel sorrow, fear, and rage, roiling around in an unintelligible mélange of agony. She sat up with a start.

"We have an intruder." She shook Alex to wake him.

"It's probably the cat."

"The cat died a year ago. It better not be the cat!" She paused. "It's coming from the front lawn, and it's several people."

She got out of bed, tiptoed into the hallway, and peaked around the dining room curtains. The first thing she saw was smoke. She rubbed her eyes awake and looked again. Either there had a been a freakish hail storm or there was dry ice laying on the front lawn. So it was mist she was seeing. Mist someone was creating. Why?

She squinted into it. A dozen people were on the lawn, dressed in grey cloaks, swaying and crouching in fear. Some were moaning in pain while others were grunting in anger. There was no obvious source of their troubles. Rather, it looked like an amateur acting workshop devoted to expressing negative emotions. Had this been staged to wake her and Maurice and make them afraid?

Alex came up behind her. As he looked out, a tall hooded man raised a dagger high above his own head and started to wail at the top of his lungs.

"What is this shit?"

"Maybe we should call 911," Teddie's voice was behind them.

"I wouldn't, unless you think they're going to hurt us," Zane said. "This has got to be what Ariel saw. Something to make our family look eccentric."

"Make *us* look eccentric? We're not the ones dancing around on the lawn making strange noises."

"How much do you want to bet that isn't the way the story gets covered?"

"Maybe if we all go back to sleep they'll get tired of this and go away,"

"The last thing we want is call more attention to them."

They were all speaking at once. Lola looked through the window. "If they get loud enough, a neighbor will call the police. Then what?"

Zane nudged in beside his mother and studied the scene. The man with the dagger was waving it in the air, and his sounds were becoming shrieks. Several of the others began to screech too.

"I could go out and spray them with the garden hose," Zane offered.

A lone, grey hooded figure emerged from the bushes carrying a tray holding a small, lifeless orange animal. The tray was laid in front of the dagger-holding shrieker as the four family members tried to get a good look at it through the mist.

"Please tell me that's a dead chicken."

"I wish. It looks more like the Nelson's cat." Lola said. "Hopefully only drugged."

The groans and screeches began to coalesce into chanting. It was a little free form, but the gist seemed to involve begging the Zeitmans to come outside and accept their sacrifice.

"They want us to stop the murder of this pet, by appearing with them," Zane said. "They're trying to force us to engage in this nonsense."

"I'll go out and do it," Maurice offered. He and Yuden had come into the front hall and were standing behind the others. "I'm not a family member, and we can't just stand here and let somebody's pet die."

"But you're a family friend," Yuden said. "Let me go."

"How about I go out there looking like someone else entirely?" Nell suggested as she came into the hallway. "Nelson Mandela? Nelson Spruce? Nelson Cruz?" She grinned apologetically. "I did hear you say it was the Nelson's cat, right?"

"Actually, you in disguise isn't a bad idea," Alex said. "Unless," he turned to Yuden, "you can go out there invisible and grab the damn cat?"

"She can't grab anything solid, dad. I thought you understood how this worked."

They all turned as a motion caught their eyes. A blur of something human-sized popped out of the bushes, exploded over to the tray, paused and almost became visible in the mist, and then burst back into the shrubs. All eyes turned to the tray, where the furry orange body of the cat was gone.

The hooded figures began jumping around in jubilation, chanting words of thanks to the Zeitmans for accepting their offering. The entire performance seemed scripted. Lola was certain of it once she saw the reporter and cameraman behind the fog.

"I think we played right into their hands." Maurice echoed her thoughts.

"Ariel told us we would" Nell said. "She was sound asleep when I left the room."

"She can sleep through anything. Who grabbed the cat?"

"I did," Xuha called to them from the kitchen. They moved towards his voice and they found him sitting in a kitchen chair petting the neighbor's groggy pet. "I was watching from upstairs and thought, *I can't let this little guy die*. I figured I could move so fast that no one would see me."

"You did, but it doesn't matter," Lola said. "Xuha, they got footage of a cat disappearing into thin air at our house. That's plenty."

"Even I couldn't sleep through this racket," Ariel said, coming into the kitchen. "Don't worry about it, Xuha. If you hadn't saved the cat somebody else here would have, and it all pretty much ends the same way."

Xuha gave Ariel a wary look. "Did I make things worse?"

She shook her head. "I've got a personal aversion to middle-of-the-night fortune-telling. Let's get some sleep. Please."

Lola poured a bit of milk out for the cat, while Alex opened the front door. The costumed crew had vanished, as had anyone else. The last bits of dry ice were disappearing, giving off tiny puffs of mist as they did. The cul-de-sac was silent, and the stars sparkled in the night sky.

Alex shrugged. "Some years you get Santa. Other years you get 'what the hell was that?'"

He held the door open as the fluffy orange cat licked up the last bit of milk then puffed his tail up straight and walked out into the night.

******

Violeta's mom Alma was up before dawn on Christmas day, humming in the kitchen as she finished last minute baking before she headed over to her son's house. She hadn't expected to enjoy the holidays much, what with losing her job and worrying for the town, but the news of her daughter's arrival brought more cheer.

Alma loved how the celebration coincided with the start of summer in her homeland and how the slow Christmas twilight extended almost to midnight. It was okay Violeta wouldn't arrive until after nine at night. There would be some of the day left to celebrate with her.

More important, Violeta would be far from that evil company in New York and the frightening people who ran it. She'd told her mother she planned to send her letter of resignation before she boarded the plane, and then stay in Argentina for a while.

Alma didn't care how or why Violeta quit. She was glad her daughter would no longer be working for the glib Gabriel, who acted so nice but had the heart of a snake. She was overjoyed her daughter's future would have nothing to do with Reel News.

******

Before dawn on Christmas Day, Olumiji got a call he hoped to never get.

The information came to him because another of the one-on-one contacts with the monads had paid off. He'd have been happier if this one hadn't been born of a sad loss.

Cenk, the owner of the Reel News media outlet in Istanbul, lost his son to a long battle with leukemia. In his grief, and in his son's memory, he wished to do something to yield less conflict in this world. He called the accountant, the member of x^0 who approached him earlier, and told him the specifics of Warren's plans regarding x^0. Then he instructed the man to leave and never speak to him again. The accountant gave Olumiji the details of the storm Warren was about to unleash.

Facing a credible threat of worldwide persecution, Olumiji contacted the other leaders. x^0 didn't have many rules, but they made an exception for such a dire case. Every member knew it. Many thought these extreme contingencies were born of unnecessary paranoia, but on this subject there was no room for dissent.

The leaders executed the ancient plan to move the shadowy organization further beyond the edges of society. Until the danger passed, every telepath was sworn to honor his or her pledge to the others, a promise to force their own memories deep into the haze of their unconscious minds.

Day-to-day contact between members ceased. All modern methods of communication were halted, written records were destroyed, and electronic records were erased. Doors were closed, windows were shuttered.

An organization of telepaths? How absurd. Surely you don't believe in that nonsense?

******

Yuden's grandson ran the day-to-day operations of c^3. He considered his grandmother's trip to the U.S to be more about late-life romance than c^3 business, but the communication he'd just received from x^0 leader Olumiji was of grave concern.

The code word, a rarely-used old Chinese hieroglyph, appeared three times in the text. Although the two organizations had grown apart, Lhatu knew what the code meant. It was taught to everyone who led c^3.

When it appeared three times, it meant disappear, deeper than you think you must. It meant do it now, even if it means leaving behind those you love. And it meant stay hidden, well hidden, until you hear otherwise.

Lhatu's heart sank. He wanted to contact his grandmother and others who might be left exposed, but he understood his responsibility. c^3, an organization with barely a footprint, suddenly had none. The blades of grass it had bent in its passing were made straight again, and the bits of dirt it had disturbed were dispersed into the wind.

An organization of mind travelers? How absurd. Surely you don't believe in that nonsense?

21. The Troubles that Passed

Everyone made their way into the kitchen Christmas morning, seeking coffee, juice or cereal. Each one wanted to talk about details from the night before with anyone who would listen. By noon, no one had anything more to add.

As the meal was almost ready, Lola noticed Cillian was quiet, and sent a worried probe his direction. He was sad, of course. Lola remembered he was recovering from trauma, far from home, excluded from the cooking, and surrounded by darkness in a strange place. She turned to Ariel.

"Is there a way to involve him in the festivities?"

Ariel raised an eyebrow. "He knows a lot of toasts. Could he lead off dinner with one?"

"Perfect. Ask him to do that."

The crowd grew quiet when Cillian stood up after everyone was seated. "I heard our hostess Lola traveled home from Nigeria three years ago today and her worried family met her at the airport."

"Yup," Teddie said. "We spent the day scared she'd been killed. It was the worst Christmas ever."

"Two years ago, I understand Alex rushed out the door for Belize and missed celebrating with you," Cillian said.

"Dad was chasing down an artifact and all hell broke loose around here," Zane said. "*That* was the worst holiday ever."

Cillian turned to Lola. "I heard last year you were huddled together in India, frightened by the kidnapping of one of Teddie's schoolmates and faced with leaving your teenaged daughter to fight for her friends' life in a way only she could do. True?"

"Yes," Lola said. "I've never been more scared by anything. That was the worst Christmas."

Cillian smiled. "Then this toast is for all of you." He raised his glass. "Always remember to forget the troubles that passed." He paused for effect. "But never forget to remember the blessings that last."

"That was beautiful," Lola said, and she meant it.

"Uh, mom."

Lola noticed her daughter was punching the buttons on her phone. "Can't that wait?"

"No, you need to see this now. Wait, let me get it up on my computer."

"I got four copies of it sent to me," Zane said. "Make that six. No seven."

Ariel opened her laptop to show a short news feature on Reel News, reporting on the strange events of last night. One hooded participant was speaking to a reporter, praising the Zeitmans for having developed supernatural powers and adding he was willing to do anything to convince the family he was worthy of being trained to wield the same forces.

The footage cut to a segment apparently filmed by of one of the women protesting on the Zeitman lawn in 2010. A creature resembling Zane was waving something and threatening people.

"Watch while we zoom in and enhance," a voice-over said.

There was no disputing Zane's sunburnt red skin had dark veins pulsing into thorn-like hooks raised off his skin. Two small horns sprouted from his head, and when he opened his mouth, smoke came out of it.

"I'm impressed," Nell said.

"How did one of those old ladies have the presence of mind to record you?" Ariel asked.

"What were you doing with my potato masher?" Alex wanted to know

Zane raised his palm to stop the questions. "Ariel decided I needed something to wave at them. It was the first thing she found."

"So you two put together this act to scare those women?"

"We wanted to make them go away before the rest of you got home," Ariel said. "We didn't want Xuha to see the horrible messages on the signs they were holding."

"I never thought it would cause this kind of trouble," Zane added as he started in on the mashed potatoes on his plate.

"It's okay. We all get to ruin Christmas dinner once," Teddie told him. After that, they all began to eat and no replays of the news were allowed until the last person finished their food.

******

The long twilight of a summer night was turning the pretty city of Ushuaia into soft purples when Violeta's plane landed. Twice while she traveled she felt Gabriel's touch; both times she filled her mind with thoughts of wanting to return home. She felt his growing conclusion. His assistant was a lonely woman, worn down by a stressful job and made anxious by the more powerful forces around her. She felt fondness on his part, perhaps the way one felt when deciding to let a cherished pet go live with a relative where it would be better off.

He was letting go of her. He was deciding his trust hadn't been misplaced. He was planning to find and train another assistant, this time one with no telepathic abilities.

Violeta smiled, working to keep the joy deep inside. She would remain vigilant, but it looked like the immediate danger was past. It was time to embrace being home and to enjoy the rest of the holiday.

******

Alex stopped counting how many times he saw a replay of the short news blurb. Everyone else seemed to own a device on which it could be analyzed, and by the next morning everyone had developed their own theory. Except for Cillian, who'd developed a liking for Lola's brandy, and was spending most of his time on the couch dripping the liqueur into a never-ending cup of hot tea refilled by Nell and Ariel. Now that it was noon, Alex was considering opening a beer and joining him.

"I'm positive this footage of me was edited," Zane insisted.

"Why didn't the reporter even consider this was staged?" Maurice asked.

"It's their snide remarks that annoy me," Nell said.

Meanwhile, Ariel tried to update her visions by walking around the house touching people and Lola went and sat on the front porch alone. She huddled into a hooded sweatshirt while she drank coffee and reached out for contact from her old friends. Ariel was right. The entire organization of x^0 had vanished off the Earth.

We can't sit here and let this nonsense go on. We could get hurt.

That's when the large black SUV drove up the driveway and five men in masks stepped out holding guns.

******

Violeta knew she'd made the right decision after she arrived. She felt safer than she had in a while. With her own well-being improved, she could better protect Lola in spite of the distance.

It was the beginning of summer. The usual wind from the west had been pushed aside by a cool breeze from Antarctica.

As Violeta sat on her mother's porch huddled into a hooded sweatshirt drinking coffee, she grew bolder and reached out to Lola. As she did, a flash of panic intervened. An image accompanied the spike of fear, and it showed men dressed in black, wearing masks, and holding guns.

For a second Violeta felt what Lola felt, then she felt nothing.

******

Lola went down when the drug-tipped dart pierced her sweatshirt. Before she dropped, she managed to send Maurice a warning. He used it, shouting, "Men with guns!" as he pushed

Cillian and Yuden toward the front hall closet. "You're both too important to lose," he said over their protests.

In the living room, Nell was morphing into something bigger and more intimidating, and looking for a weapon. In the hallway leading to the garage, Teddie caught Ariel as she fell, made dizzy by a low-level possibility turning into a full-fledged certainty. The intruders found the sisters first, and the darts found their marks.

In the kitchen, Zane, Xuha, and Vanida heard Maurice's yell and in the ensuing commotion. Xuha took off in a blur. The man leading the group hit the ground with thud.

The second-in-line put a dart into Xuha before he could charge the rest. When the remaining four men entered the kitchen, the only person in the room was Warren Moore, dressed in casual jeans, a t-shirt, and baseball cap.

"Mr. Moore?" The second man was confused.

"Go home, Bill. I've changed my mind. I came here to see this for myself. It's the wrong approach. Let these people alone."

Bill hesitated.

"Go on. Go," Warren repeated.

"That's not Warren Moore," the third man said. "See his brown hair under the cap? Besides, it's not possible. We just talked to him in New York. It's sorcery, like he warned us about."

Man number three shot a dart into Warren, and the falling body became younger and thinner as it hit the floor.

"See, I told you it was sorcery."

The fourth man found Vanida lying on the pantry floor, already unconscious. It seemed unnecessary to drug her, so he pulled her into the kitchen and left her next to the young man who had looked like Warren.

The fifth man headed to the bedrooms. They seemed to be vacant, but when he stepped into the largest one there was a rush of air and a blur of light. He had duct tape over his mouth, around his wrists, and around his legs, with no sense of how it got there. A shove landed him on the ground, and the bedroom door slammed shut.

The third man was alone in the kitchen and made his way into the living room, where he paused in confusion. A creature who looked a good bit like a monster from his worst childhood nightmare was sitting there waiting for him.

"Every time you're scared, you think of me, don't you?" It spoke with menace in its voice. "Big tough guy, but you're scared a lot and you've never lost your fear of me."

Man three stood with his mouth open. The next thing he knew, it was covered in duct tape and his hands were stuck together. A blur of motion later and his legs were wrapped in it and the floor was approaching his face.

Man four came into the living room to check on the noise and found his friend on the floor and a half-dressed woman who looked a little like a well known supermodel sitting on the couch making eyes at him. He blinked, which was all the time it took for his hands and feet to be covered in tape as well.

Bill, the second-in-command, came into the living room to check on his two partners, only to find Alex standing in the middle of the room with an empty roll of duct tape in his hand and a sad look on his face.

"I ran out of tape."

Bill laughed until the bottle of brandy hit him over the head hard. He joined his co-workers on the living room floor.

"I was hoping you'd put that brandy to good use." Alex thanked a pleased Cillian, as his diminutive guide Yuden led him back to the couch. Nell began to look less like a supermodel and more like Nell, as she worked on securing the last man down. Maurice stood up from behind the couch, where he had been busy reading minds and passing the information on to Nell. He headed off to find the man Xuha had tackled first, hoping to secure him.

He was a few seconds too late. The groggy man was getting to his feet and when he saw Maurice he ran to the front door. As he sprinted toward the SUV, Vanida yelled from the kitchen.

"Don't let them get away. They wore body cams. They transmitted this to equipment in their car. I saw it all."

But there was no way to stop the vehicle from leaving the premises.

"Damn," Maurice said. "He's delighted. That stuff they recorded was the whole point of this."

"I wouldn't be too worried," Alex said. "We've got four guys tied up here who broke into my house. I'd say we're on the right side of the law. I'm calling the police."

The only intruder without duct tape over his mouth was the man Cillian had knocked out with the brandy bottle, and he was starting to regain consciousness. Nell had tied his hands behind his back, but he laughed as he struggled to sit up.

"Please call the police. I'd feel a lot safer."

"Yeah, well, I don't treat home invaders so well," Alex snapped.

"What home invasion? We're a group of reporters who came to your door to ask some questions. You invited us in, then look what you did to us." He pointed to his friends on the floor.

"No one invited you in," Maurice said.

"Don't be so sure. We've got video to prove you did. If you liked last night's news, you'll love tonight's story. Please call the police and let's add 'claims of a home invasion' to make you sound even crazier."

"He speaks the truth," Maurice told Alex in a soft voice. "The less fuel we give this, the better."

Alex turned to Vanida, Nell, and Yuden. "Other ideas?"

Nell and Yuden shook their heads, but Vanida spoke up.

"I saw the equipment in their car, and recognized much of it. I work with photography, and I can promise you somebody somewhere is editing a video of this right now."

That was all Alex needed to know. "Vanida and Nell. There's another guy on the bedroom floor. Get all four of these men out of here, okay? Yuden, would you help me revive everyone that got shot with these damn darts?"

Yuden headed out of the room, glad to help.

Vanida turned to Nell. "We need to make sure we take their cell phones, body cams, and other recording devices away from them before they leave. In case it didn't all get sent already."

The intruder spoke up. "Wait. You can't take our phones. You guys live in the middle of suburbia nowhere. How will we get a ride?"

"Walk." Alex said it over his shoulder as he left the room.

✻✻✻✻✻✻

Two hours later, Lola's head still hurt from the drug, and she couldn't believe she'd lain unconscious while her loved ones were attacked. True, the many clever ways everyone responded brought her comfort.

Maurice's quick warning to all, Xuha's early ambush of the leader, and Vanida's finding a way to enter a trance in the middle of it and scope out the intruders' vehicle were wonderful, even though they paled in comparison to Zane's creative impersonation of Warren Moore, based on photos and video clips of the famous man. But the most impressive performance had to be the duet by Maurice and Nell, with Maurice reading an intruders mind well enough to coach Nell with whisper instructions into an impersonation as scary as it was personal. Of course, Alex's speed with duct tape and Cillian's well-timed aim with the bottle of brandy, guided by Yuden, deserved honorable mentions too.

Teddie seemed fine with not playing the hero, but Lola noticed Ariel was also irritated at having been downed by drug darts. Her daughter was treating her headache with some drink made from whiskey and bitters. It was working; Ariel's mood improved as she sipped.

Ariel turned to the group and tapped her glass with a spoon. The other ten people became silent.

"I can't see anything closer in than a week, but sometimes I see things that give me information about what's happened sooner. Does that make sense?"

Most of the group nodded.

"Good. There's going to be a feature at the end of the local news this evening. We need to watch it together. Be back in here a little before seven, and honestly, grab a drink. You'll want one."

"I do like you, lass," Cillian spoke up from the couch. "Seeing as how I'm a man who sacrificed the last of his liquid comfort to render an intruder unconscious."

"Of course you did, and you don't need to wait for the evening news, Cillian. I'll find you something to drink now."

22. Far Fringes

"Finally, tonight, we have a short but fascinating follow-up to last night's broadcast about the odd events at a Houston home," a newscaster named Julie said with perky cheerfulness.

Alex turned up the volume while the room grew quieter.

"That's right, Julie," her partner said. "If you remember, we came across disturbing video from two years ago in which someone dressed up as a devil tried to frighten off a group of women staging a small, peaceful protest."

The video of Zane's performance ran while the announcers talked.

"I remember it, Jim. It caught our eye when police reports came in early Christmas morning showing a far less friendly group assembled on this *very same* lawn.

The video switched to the grey-hooded group writhing and grunting in the Zeitman's front yard early Christmas morning.

"This creepy crowd claimed to be providing the hate and fear this family feeds off of. Watch what happens next."

The scene showed the unconscious neighbor's cat.

"They offer up this poor cat as a sacrifice to these people. I'd have thought it was all a bad joke, but look."

A fuzzy image of Xuha's body became visible as he swooped in and grabbed the cat.

"Our experts have been looking at this *all* day and calculated the boy was moving at least two-hundred miles an hour."

"That's not possible," Julie said.

"It isn't, so we sent a crew over to ask questions. You won't believe what happened. I must warn our viewers, it's disturbing."

The scene switched to Teddie answering the door. "Uh, sure, you can come in, I suppose." Maurice was standing in the hallway behind her.

"Now. Look what they do to our reporters."

The next scene showed Xuha plowing into the leader of the group. The man held a camera instead of a gun. The man behind him was holding a microphone and recording equipment.

"What happened to their guns?" Yuden asked.

"It's called Photoshop.

"After this wild boy attacks our cameraman, the crew heads into the house, looking for help. Each one of them is picked off and tied up by someone else exhibiting this same speed."

The film, run in slow motion, showed a crew member standing with his mouth open in disbelief, while a blurry Alex applied his duct tape.

"Our facial recognition experts are positive this is Mr. Zeitman, a local high school teacher. The boy is a former student of his who once was thought to be involved with a Mayan voodoo cult. We're trying to get more on that story."

"Why in the world would these people treat our news crew like this?"

"The crew wasn't sure. They said the house was full of people acting odd."

The video switched to a scene of Zane and Vanida lying unconscious on the kitchen floor

"Drugs? Trances? We don't know what's happening there."

The footage showed the news crew walking out of the house.

"So they got out safely?"

"They did. A couple of the women untied our reporters and let them go on the condition they not press charges," Jim said. "Our network says it will honor the promise, but I have to tell you these people scare me."

"You bet. They scare me, too. What if some poor child came to their door, I don't know, selling cookies or something?"

"Exactly, Julie."

"I know you'll think I'm silly, but I'm worried there's more to it. The unnatural speed, the connection with ancient rituals."

"It does seem like something not quite *right* is going on there," Jim agreed. "Of course, that's only speculation."

"Of course. Well, thanks for joining us. Remember, Houston, we're Channel 23 and we *don't* have a problem."

******

Violeta kept checking in on Lola. Once she knew Lola was conscious and out of danger, she sought out Warren and felt his sense of satisfaction. His plan had gone well. So, no harm was intended? What was the man trying to do?

Violeta searched for a way to comfort Lola. The smell of own her mother's Christmas pastries filled the house. Baking did have a way of providing cheer. Violeta concentrated on the smell.

******

Alex shut off the television. The eleven people in front of it were silent.

"Can they keep making up shit about us until they get us arrested or shot or something?" Zane asked.

"I don't see why not," Maurice said. "They're a reputable Houston station, and we're a bunch of kooks. I bet Reel News picks up the story, and this goes nationwide."

Lola rubbed her temples. The dull ache from the sedative was still there. She was considering pain killers, or whatever Ariel was drinking, or maybe both, when the soft scent of vanilla caught her attention. What was that smell? Sugar cookies? She shook her head to clear it, but the smell got stronger.

"Who's baking sugar cookies at a time like this?"

"No one, but it's not a bad idea," Teddie said, her mood lifting. "Would you like some?"

"Cookies fix everything," Nell agreed.

"Want some help making?" Ariel offered.

"Fine, go make cookies," Lola said. "I'll sit here and worry for all of us."

But the anxiety level began to drop as soon as the scent of vanilla made its way into the living room, and it didn't take long for the sisters to return with plates of warm cookies. As Lola reached for hers, Ariel touched her mother's hand and grimaced.

"Mom. I'm getting a two-out-of-three chance you and dad go to Argentina. What's with you taking this trip?"

"Stop worrying. I have no reason to go to Argentina." her mother said, her mood improving the second the soft cookie touched her lips. Lola noticed the cookie was lodged in her brain as well as her mouth.

Could the scent have come from someone she wasn't supposed to communicate with? Someone in Argentina, at the one place on Earth Lola wasn't supposed to go?

******

Now that the evil group x^0 was being forced into hiding, where it would be no threat, Warren knew he needed to reassure the Entelechy. They had to understand this fear of psychic powers he was fanning would pass and they would be safe in the end. No, better than safe. They would be in charge, and that was always better.

Having another in-person meeting soon wasn't realistic and he had to act fast. Yet recorded communication was dangerous. Warren Moore knew better than most how easy it was for words to be retold in the worst of ways.

He settled on using his highly encrypted company email server to send a message that couldn't be forwarded or copied, and would vanish in hours. A recipient could take a screen shot of it, but he hoped none of his men were *that* eager to have leverage over him.

Was it a safe assumption? He wasn't sure. All he knew was this was the topic he couldn't allow himself to think about for long. He had plans in place to detect disloyalty amongst his men, but he couldn't think about them either.

Warren picked up a nearby word search puzzle and sought out words having to do with household pets. Leash. Bowl. Collar.

He worked until his mind achieved stillness, then put the puzzle aside.

******

Construction in Ushuaia had paused for Christmas, but by December 27th the workers were back at the job, working to get as much done as possible during the long balmy days of summer. A generous year-end bonus was paid to all.

At the same time, several of the most inquisitive and least discreet of the workers were let go the day after Christmas. The rest of the staff got the message. People worked in silence after that and had little to say at the end of the day when they came home.

******

"Are we going to have to change our names and go live in a foreign country?" Teddie asked the next morning as everyone wandered into the kitchen to find something for a late breakfast. "You do know this is my last semester in high school, right?"

"We're not going anywhere," Alex assured her, as he put a plate of leftovers in the microwave.

"They wanted to drive my group x^0 into hiding," Lola said. "And they have. I've no reason to go anywhere."

"How about if they get angry people with pitchforks to come after you?" Zane asked.

"They'll never be able to prove Lola and I are telepaths," Maurice replied. "Hell, we can hardly prove it to ourselves."

"That doesn't matter," Nell argued. "You can't stay out of the news. They control it."

"True," Arial said. "Except of course on the far fringes."

"When you say far fringes, what *are* you talking about?"

"Oh, you know. Like, there's a tiny tiny chance North Korea drops a nuclear weapon on South Korea before New Year's Day. Then nobody on Earth gives a rat's ass about our family."

No one said anything for a minute. Lola reached for a second cookie.

******

The Filipino monad Rafael watched the newscast about the Zeitmans. It was sent to all Reel News outlets for possible use. Most outside the U.S. passed because people in Houston, no matter how weird, weren't as interesting as someone local. So stations under Warren's control found similar stories about a nearby person who aroused superstitious fears. Every place had such a character, and most could find several.

Rafael ran his story as instructed, but it left him wondering what constituted victory for the monads? How did this end well? Rafael only saw two possibilities. The first was things went back to the way they'd been, but that seldom happened.

The other good outcome was more unsettling. Warren's obsessive leadership had to come to an end. Probably x^0 had to be moved to the sidelines too, but that concerned Rafael less. They held their members to lofty ideals, so Rafael doubted x^0 would cause much harm. Warren, on the other hand, had money and influence and he knew how to use them. He was inclined to fight. He wouldn't give up being in charge without exacting a toll.

Common sense said if you couldn't go back to the way things were, you should move things forward all the way to where they needed to be. That was a world in which the monads ran Warren, not the other way around.

******

It was Teddie who asked the question. Her mother was booking Vanida a flight to Bangkok, and was irritated Vanida didn't want to leave until her friend Michelle got back next week.

"Mom? How does this end well? For us, I mean?"

Lola sighed. She really needed some time alone.

"Well, first we get Vanida home as soon as she has a chance to visit with Michelle. Yuden will stay in the U.S. longer, but she and Maurice will go back to his house right after New Year's."

"I don't mean when do people leave. Vanida has nothing to go back to. What will happen to Maurice in that narrow-minded town he lives in? No offense to where you grew up, but you know what I mean."

Lola did.

"Maurice is used to dealing with the challenges of a small town, dear. Vanida has her college classes to get back to. Now, I just need to persuade a certain Irishman that it's time for him to go and to take his nice friend Nell with him. We'll get Xuha back to school and everything will be fine."

"You're not listening to me. Nothing is going to be fine. I've had contacts over the past few days I haven't shared with you, but I can promise you my life will not be normal. Neither will dad's, not at school at least. Wait till you go back to work. Zane, Xuha and Ariel know what I mean; they just haven't talked to you yet. How does this possibly end well for us?"

"It blows over, dear. The TV stuff was nonsense. Any sane person will realize that. Tell people it was some awful prank, and they'll move on to the latest piece of gibberish about what some celebrity is wearing."

Teddie's expression was becoming more pained. "Ariel says Reel News is just getting started. She thinks the next piece will air tonight. What do we do when this keeps getting worse?"

Lola stopped to listen to the anguish in Teddie's voice. She felt the pain in her daughter's words and knew her daughter had a point. It wasn't likely things would return to how they were, but surely there was a way for this to end well. Preferably one that didn't involve a nuclear explosion in Korea or anywhere else.

******

"Remember that crazy story we ran two nights ago, Jim, about the Houston family sacrificing a cat on their front lawn?"

"I sure do, Julie. Even Houston has its oddballs, doesn't it?"

"Well, tonight, we have a follow-up. Our research department looked into who else lives at that house, and what they found will *really* surprise you. Stay tuned. We'll give you the whole story after this break."

******

The family gathered around the television. Ariel knew the broadcast would be bad; she just didn't know how. She knew its ramifications would reverberate into the weeks ahead but, as usual, her visions didn't supply the sorts of details she wanted.

******

"Okay, Julie, what is going on in this quiet Houston suburb?"

Julie smiled a flirty smile. "Did you watch Kung Fu movies as a kid?"

"Sure,"

"Well." She leaned forward, eager to share her news. "There is an old woman at this house who runs a secret Kung Fu group in Tibet. I'm serious. Our researchers say her organization is throughout Asia and strange feats are attributed to them."

"There's nothing strange about martial arts, Julie."

"There is in the way *these* people practice them. Supposedly they walk through walls, but that's not the bad part. Rumor is they have some sort of ties to human trafficking and child prostitution."

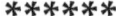

"What?!" Alex and Maurice barked it out at the same time. Yuden looked down in sorrow. Her organization's sole tie to human trafficking was to help rescue teenaged girls, but of course that meant ties could be found and misinformation spread.

******

"That's right. When our reporters were at the house, they photographed a young woman lying on the floor. She's been identified as a Thai citizen here on a travel visa. She was rescued from a prostitution ring in Bangkok. Here's the thing. She entered the country *with* the elderly woman. Authorities speculate she's being groomed for a management role in this group."

"That's so sad. We hear about how these girls often return to that way of life, because they have nowhere else to go. Is that what happened here?"

"I hope not. Whatever this old Chinese madam is doing, I can tell you the decent people of Houston have no tolerance for this."

******

Maurice wrapped an arm around Yuden and whispered something to her. Yuden stared straight ahead. Vanida went into the kitchen, and everyone heard pots and pans banging around. Lola thought maybe the young woman was emptying the drying rack while blowing off steam. Who could blame her?

******

"So do you think this family is involved in prostitution, too? I mean, I hope not. They have two daughters and a son of their own," Jim said.

Pictures of all five Zeitmans appeared on the screen along with their ages and full names.

******

"They can't do that!" Teddie yelled.

"Can we sue?" Ariel asked Zane.

"So far they've only speculated. I'm going to record the rest," Zane said, reaching for his phone.

"I'm already taping it," Alex said.

"I need a copy I can access back at school. Shh."

******

"We don't have enough facts to be sure," Julie said. "Given all the hocus-pocus this family is involved in, it could be less about crime and more about actual superpowers."

"That's silly, Julie. There's no such thing."

Julie giggled.

"However, I do agree they're a group prone to violence with all kinds of nefarious ties. Has an investigation been launched into this cult?"

"Not yet, but a source told me a prominent local authority will call for a full investigation after the holidays."

Jim smiled into the camera. "Stick with us for all the latest as this unfolds. Thanks for joining us. Remember, Houston, we're Channel 23 and we *don't* have a problem."

December 2012

23. A Walk in the Park

On the last weekend of the year, the monads Gabriel and Rafael talked on the phone in hushed whispers. Rafael had already sent information to Gabriel using his mind, amazed at how much better telepathy worked between the two friends as they became less suspicious of each other. Yet, some things were better said.

Gabriel listened to Raphael's concerns and agreed. A victory for Warren in this conflict with x^0 was not necessarily one for the Entelechy. Warren appeared to hold the best cards. He controlled the massive enterprise of Reel News, and could fire the monads one by one. However, he wasn't entirely the master of his own mind, and he knew it. Thirty-five other men had made a vital connection with him. They could invade his thoughts, learn his secrets, even feel his dreams. The Entelechy had to make it clear to Warren how unpleasant his life would be if he defied them.

"He has to agree to become a figure head," Gabriel said.

"What will we tell the rest of his management? We can't present this as a takeover by the company telepaths." Rafael laughed.

"Of course not. But we can be independent businessmen fighting for a bigger piece of what we've helped create. Many would sympathize. Others could be persuaded Warren has become unstable. We're stepping up to do what's best for Reel News."

"You and I don't have the business skills to pull off a corporate takeover," Rafael said. "But there are monads who do. The Saudi, Khalid, has excellent business experience. Juan, our Venezuelan, was once a lawyer in the world of banking. And

Johann, the Swiss? He has quite a bit of expertise in, uh, using personal information to persuade others to assist him."

"Really. I didn't know about Johann. All helpful, but the essential first step is demonstrating to Warren how we can make his life unlivable any time we want."

"You have a plan for making this clear?" Rafael asked.

"I think I know him well enough to produce an effective demonstration. The good news is it won't take much, because we scare him already."

"After we have Warren in our pocket, we'll be challenged by other executives. They aren't going to just let us have the world's largest news conglomerate."

Gabriel was thinking about that as well. "We'll insist Warren brush aside other usurpers as a requirement for his important title, high salary and peace of mind. Then, if we have to, we'll demonstrate our skill set on a case-by-case basis to anyone who insists on causing us problems."

"We'll need those monads I mentioned and more. Would you like me to begin rolling others in?"

Gabriel thought for a few seconds. Could he trust Rafael? It looked like he already had.

"Yes, do. Know there are some with no stomach for this, and others who will remain loyal to Warren. Recruit with care."

******

It made Warren sad. He always knew the balance between him and his monads wasn't stable. It couldn't last a lifetime, but he'd hoped it would for a few more years. By then, he'd have solidified Reel News as the dominant source of truth the world over. He'd have an ironclad corporate succession plan in place. He'd have completed that contingency work in Tierra del Fuego. He'd have sorted the few who could be trusted a while longer from the many who would get greedy first. He'd have been ready for this.

Then this other group had appeared, disrupting his delicate balance. Now the least trustworthy of his monads were forcing him into behavior he'd hoped to avoid for years. Very well, he'd do what needed to be done.

He saw one advantage to discovering x^0. He still needed the help of people with a skill he didn't have. This new organization did provide him with many more telepaths to choose from. If he couldn't count on his own men, he could find a way to use these others.

✶✶✶✶✶✶

Ariel avoided everyone all week-end, not wanting to share the many ways her cacophony of visions was growing darker by the hour. On her way to the kitchen, she noticed Cillian's head turn toward her as she passed.

"I'm learning the sound of your footsteps," he said, pleased.

Ariel thought it was the first time she'd seen him smile since the accident. She sat down next to him. He was the only person in the house who could understand the weight she carried.

"What I am seeing isn't good," she said. "In fact, it's getting so bad I don't know how to advise them."

"I understand. What I am seeing isn't good either. It's getting so bad I have no idea how to advise you."

"We make the nightly news again soon. Probably this evening," she said. "Should we even bother to watch?"

"You know my visions don't help with questions like that. Knowledge is generally an advantage, though, so I'd turn on the news."

A few hours later the wary eleven gathered around the big screen in the den. The crowd groaned when the Zeitmans were mentioned, and when the commentator said tonight's focus would be on the older daughter and an Irishman she'd befriended, Cillian yelled obscenities at the TV. Ariel sucked in her breath.

Cillian's father's financial advisor, a dour man named Doyle, was being interviewed at a Reel News outlet in Dublin. Cillian and Doyle had parted months ago, each accusing the other of various crimes. Ariel knew Cillian was innocent, and was pretty sure Doyle wasn't, but either way the hatred the two men had for each other ran deep.

Cillian rose to his feet as soon as Doyle's voice became audible. Lola jumped up, put her hands on his shoulders, and pushed him back into his seat as she said "hush" in the tone a mother would use with a small child. He hushed.

The group listened as Doyle spoke of how Cillian had been a disappointment to his father. The interviewer was barely interested and kept pushing for some other nugget. Finally, it came.

"Well, there was talk about how the boy was fey, you know. Some said he had visions; later in life I heard his friends called him a prophet. A prophet. Can you believe that?"

The announcer chose her words with care. "Do you think there may have been anything to those stories?"

"There's no such thing. Daft superstitions. God knows Ireland is full of them. But I think it made people a little afraid of him, so maybe he got away with things another boy wouldn't have."

"I see." The interviewer wasn't as interested in misbehavior as she was in the allegations of being fey. "Do you know how these rumors got started?"

Doyle shrugged. "I wouldn't have put it past the boy to start them himself. So he could get away with things, you know?"

The interviewer concluded with a tantalizing "You never know what the truth is," before they went to a commercial break.

"We're lucky Doyle was too dense to give her what she was after," Lola said. "They've gone after everyone except for you, Nell. Do you warrant your own program?"

Nell gave a shrug. "I'm an actress who's played many roles. A few of them could be trouble. Tomorrow is New Year's Eve, though, so no regular programming. Maybe we get a break."

"Never been one of my favorite nights," Zane said. "But I think we should figure out a way to celebrate."

"We could dance around drunk and naked on your front lawn," Cillian said. Everyone turned to stare at him.

"See." He turned in Lola's direction and winked. "Bet you thought I didn't know how to do that."

"Wink?" she said.

"No." He laughed. "Make a joke."

******

On the last day of the year, Violeta woke to the bright, cloudless blue of a cool day calling her to come out for a walk. Her days of hiking through the woods were over, but there was a park nearby with paths. Her mother helped her prepare for the outing, happy to see her daughter get out.

Tourists were everywhere this time of year and they filled the park. She didn't used to mind them; their money helped feed her and kept her dressed in judo gis throughout her growing years. But walking in crowds was more stressful now.

She strolled along for about fifteen minutes when her body let her know a rest would be good. She looked for a bench, but the few she saw were occupied. Some may have made room for her if she asked, but it still hurt to see the pity common on the faces of those who accommodated her. No, she could sit on the ground.

Unfortunately, getting up and down wouldn't be graceful, so she hunted for a place out of view. Fifty yards away was a small hill. Stepping through the grass, she set out for her private spot.

She hadn't quite cleared the hill when it became obvious what was on the other side. A small fence marked the edge of the park. Behind it, a six-foot-wide trench discouraged leaving the grounds, as did the numerous *No Trespassing* signs in many languages. The real showstopper, however, was the ten-foot-tall cinder block wall beyond, with its two feet of barbed wire on top.

Nobody in town had ever been this concerned about intruders. Violeta was willing to bet she'd found Warren Moore's new business complex. No wonder all of Ushuaia was talking about it.

******

Ken called Alex the morning of New Year's Eve because he needed to borrow a tool. Alex was pretty sure it was a pretext. Ken was the shop teacher at Alex's high school and he already owned every tool ever invented.

Ken and his wife Sara were friends of the Zeitmans. Alex was pretty sure they watched Reel News, yet Ken and Sara had more open hearts and minds than many, at least in Alex's opinion. He suspected the phone call was to offer support,

"Guess you've seen us on the news lately?" Alex decided to broach the topic.

"Ha. You guys have a way of igniting things, don't you?"

The affection in Ken's voice was clear. Alex breathed a sigh of relief.

"Is this still fallout from that peacenik article Lola wrote?"

"It is. Ken, this has gotten way out of hand. We have no idea how to stop this nonsense now."

Ken didn't say anything for a few seconds, and Alex wondered if he'd pushed the friendship too far.

"Is there something they want from you?" Ken asked, and Alex realized he'd been trying to think of a solution. "I say 'never give in to a bully,' but you could be fighting someone about three weight classes above you."

"I wish they did want something. It's more like someone at Reel News wants to ruin our lives. I'm starting to think they can do it, too."

"Have you heard anything from the school?"

"Not yet. I expect them to look for an excuse to cut me loose, though. If this keeps up, they won't have a choice."

"It's just wrong. I'll pick up that oil filter wrench tomorrow, okay? Can't believe those damn mechanics tightened it like that."

As Alex hung up, he wondered if Ken really needed the wrench. Nah. Ken hadn't changed his own oil in years.

******

Ariel was the last one out of bed on the morning of New Year's Eve. She kept one hand on her aching temple as she poured a bowl of cereal and took it into the dining room. When her mother followed her, Ariel wouldn't even look at her.

"Did I do something wrong?"

"Not yet, but you will," Ariel said. "The odds are huge you and dad screw things up over the next few days. No, I don't know how. Then, things are all over the place."

"Wait a minute," Alex complained as he joined his wife and daughter. "Your mother and I will not screw up anything. We're going to keep our heads down and stay out of trouble. Will you please stop saying otherwise?"

"What is it you think we do?"

Ariel's face had exasperation all over it. "I'm trying to tell you. It's three-out-of-four now that you're in Argentina next week. Tierra del Fuego, to be specific. What is it about that place?"

"She had a dream about going there. We talked about a vacation. Are you picking up on her dream instead of reality?"

Ariel shook her head.

"Okay, let's look at this another way," Lola said. "I've found out that is where Violeta, my contact from Reel News, is from."

"That is interesting," Ariel agreed. "Are you two in contact?"

"No. She's down there now, trying to get away from her former boss. He's been mentally spying on her, so she's avoiding direct exchanges with me."

"Could that change soon?"

"I suppose. Do I go to see her? No, of course I don't. Maybe you're picking up on our future mental contact?"

"I'm not."

Alex was about to argue when Teddie came into the room.

"Guess what? Michelle's back. They came home from California early. Okay if we head over there now?"

Alex, Lola, and Ariel all looked at each other and tried to think of a reason to object. None of them could.

"I'd avoid contact with neighbors on the way out," Alex said.

"You ought to warn Michelle's mom about the crazy news stories," Lola added. "I'm pretty sure she'll be sympathetic, but I don't want her blind-sided."

Teddie nodded, her thick black curls bouncing up and down. "Yes, yes. We'll be careful. We'll be honest. Come on, Vanida, let's get out of here before they change their minds."

No one could blame the girls for their enthusiasm.

"Well, if outings have been approved, how about I take my girlfriend out for lunch," Maurice said. "I'd like to show her something besides your lovely home while she's here. Maybe head into Montrose for a nice meal. We can find a place there where no one recognizes us and won't care if they do."

"It sounds like fun," Lola said. "Of course you should go."

"I could use a trip back to the hotel to get the rest of my clothes," Nell said.

"I'll drive you," Ariel offered. "Come on Cillian, you ride along and we'll get lunch at an American pub. You'll be surprised. We've got good ones here, too, even if most are chain restaurants."

"You haven't finished breakfast yet," her father said. Ariel smiled and picked up her mom's car keys.

Xuha turned to Zane. "Since they're handing out hall passes, want to go grab a beer somewhere? You know, celebrate the New Year before we go back to hiding under a rock?"

Zane reached for his coat in agreement. As car keys, hats, and purses were gathered, Ariel sat down and put her head in her hands.

"Now what's the matter?" her mother asked. "Maybe you should get a little food in your stomach before you go."

Ariel shook her head. "Vertigo. Things changing fast. It happens sometimes." She hesitated, as ten disappointed faces turned toward her, each expecting her to nix the bit of freedom every one of them craved. She couldn't do it.

"Okay, we should go out and enjoy ourselves, but we probably should be back here in a couple of hours. By then, I'll have a better handle on what made me so dizzy."

Teddie and Vanida were out the door before the sentence was finished. Ariel helped Cillian to her car while Nell tried to clear away the remains of their breakfast.

"Go," Lola waved Nell out the door. "Don't worry about this. Get out of here before she gets a new vision."

Maurice and Yuden weren't far behind, heading to Maurice's car when he erupted in an exasperated, "Not now!"

"What's wrong," Xuha asked, but then he saw. The back left tire held only a little air, the obvious result of a slow leak.

"We've got an air compressor. I'll have it filled in no time," Zane said. "No big deal."

It wouldn't have been, under almost any other circumstances.

******

Warren's construction manager called him back on the morning of New Year's Eve. Yes, a small wing could be cordoned off and finished over the next week if overtime was no issue. Yes, it could be secured so workers wouldn't need to set it foot in it again. Yes, the construction manager understood that Mr. Moore's special guests were not to be disturbed under any circumstances.

Once that was handled, Warren checked back in with the remarkably flexible security service he'd found. They'd turned out to be entirely professional about the whole unpleasantness resulting from the botched kidnapping of Maurice. They said they considered the handling of occasional glitches to fall with the spectrum of services they provided. Quite handy. Now this capable company was about to begin his newest undertaking.

"Just to confirm. You must have the lady of the house and the elderly man as, uh, guests in your new resort?"

"Yes. And her husband too. Make sure your men bring whomever else is there. I don't want witnesses or casualties. Having at least one of her children would be useful."

"Should we maximize the number of people we bring?"

"Hell no! I don't need eleven, uh, guests to get the job done. Just a few of them. Whoever is home. Keep it simple."

"Very well. We're watching them now. We'll wait until some leave, but the three you must have are there." There was a pause. "Are you sure you've told us everything? *Absolutely* everything?"

"Pretty much. I mean, the woman is kind of, I don't know, intuitive. She manipulates people. Her husband, he has some martial arts training, I think. No big deal, I'm sure."

The representative of Executive Security Associates cleared his throat. "We do watch the news, Mr. Moore. We'd appreciate knowing the source of the rumors concerning this family and their alleged superpowers."

"I'm the source of those rumors," Warren said. "Putting that nonsense out there was my Plan A. It's run into a few obstacles, necessitating Plan B. Do you have a problem with my Plan B?"

"No, sir. The superpowers we believe in here at Executive Security Associates are those of raw muscle and the occasional AK-47. We'll see to it your guests arrive safely in Tierra del Fuego by the end of the week. It should be a walk in the park."

December 2012 and January 2013

24. On a Very Cold Day

Rafael found out first, and called Gabriel.

"He knows what we're planning. He's thinking about how to deal with our coup. He tapped our phones."

"That's impossible. We watch him too closely. We'd have known."

"Not if he didn't let himself think about it, we wouldn't."

"Nobody can control their thoughts that well," Gabriel said. "People can't help what they think."

"Meet Warren Moore," Rafael replied. "I heard him. He listened when we explained we couldn't go mining for information, and he was sure he could develop the self-control to not think of this subject for more than a few seconds at a time. Odds would be miniscule we'd discover his suspicions. He *has* been monitoring us electronically because he was sure we'd try to oust him eventually."

Gabriel shook his head in disbelief while Rafael described how he'd touched Warren's mind while the man was speaking with a private security firm.

"You and I know quick surveillance is something I do well," Rafael said. "To be honest, I do it often with Warren, but I've never gotten a glimpse of this before. It was only dumb luck I hit him during the minute it took to make this phone call."

"So what's he going to do about this? About us?"

"I don't know. He wouldn't think about it. I'm telling you, this guy is a paranoid piece of work. All I could get was he doesn't trust us and is planning to get this Lola woman to help him. He hung up and started in on one of those word search things.

"We've got a bigger problem than we realized, don't we?"
It was a rhetorical question.

******

Violeta was insulted by how easily Reel News let her go. Gabriel had always been quick to dismiss her skills; now he attributed her resignation to a lack of emotional toughness. Ironic, given her martial arts background. He assumed she'd run home to her mother for comfort, jettisoning her career in the process. Violeta felt the derision inside the assumption, and it stung.

Warren accepted Gabriel's explanation for her resignation, and as far as Violeta could tell he hadn't given her another thought. She'd hoped Warren saw her value, even if Gabriel didn't, but no, apparently not. Lately he was more preoccupied than usual with his inane word search games.

Lola and her friends were respecting Violeta's request for seclusion. Their disappearance from her consciousness had been faster and more thorough than Violeta thought possible. The entire x^0 organization was as if it never existed. Except for the brief panic during the staged home invasion at the Zeitmans a few days ago, the minds of Lola and her teacher Maurice were hard to find also.

The more isolated Violeta felt, the more difficult it was not to peek into the heads of those she'd left behind. By New Year's Eve she was back to taking several quick scans a day, even though she realized she tempted fate each time she did so. The good news was the more she practiced, the more skillful she got at grabbing a glimmer of information without ever touching down. It was like a judo move, really. Her speed and dexterity grew until she could execute a barely detectable flit before she was gone.

Most such swoops made her feel connected but provided little new information. Then, on the afternoon of New Year's Eve, a skim through Gabriel's mind showed him deep in conversation with Rafael. No question, the two were afraid of Warren. They were no longer on his side. He wasn't on theirs. Something fundamental had shifted between the Entelechy and Reel News.

Violeta stifled her first reaction of sadness at being left on the sidelines. *Be glad you're gone. Whose side would you have taken?*

She thought about the arrogant monads, so certain of their superiority. She thought of Warren's need for power and control. She had her answer. *Neither. I hope they wipe out each other.* The thought came from deep within, from the place where people don't lie, even to themselves.

She turned to Lola, her newfound kindred spirit. Would this storm leave Lola and x^0 safe? She felt Lola look out of her living room window, watching while her son fixed a tire for her elderly friend. Such a good kid. Such a love-filled holiday in spite of the nonsense going on.

Then she felt the icy spear of panic that followed.

******

Lola often thought she didn't spend enough time being thankful. The warm cup of coffee in her hand was a sun roasted miracle, wrought by mysterious beans from the other side of the world. She savored the rich aroma as she watched her son repair a tire. He was kind as he listened to Maurice tell stories of flat tires from long ago. Lola was feeling grateful for them both and for the blue sky above when she saw the large black SUV.

Oh for God's sake, not you people again.

Maurice heard her thoughts and looked up, but there wasn't much he or Zane could do as the vehicle turned into the driveway and five men in masks carrying guns stepped out. Again.

Lola turned to yell to Alex, Xuha, and Yuden as she felt the familiar sting in her neck. *Not that again, too.*

It was the last coherent thought she'd have for a while.

******

Teddie and Vanida, came back to the house a few hours later and tried to figure out where the others had gone. By the time Ariel, Nell, and Cillian arrived at the house, they were becoming concerned. There was no note and no signs of a struggle.

Maurice's car sat in the driveway with a half-filled tire attached to a compressor hose. The compressor kept going off, causing everyone to jump, until Ariel marched into the garage and unplugged it.

Xuha's car was still parked on the street, and their dad's car remained. No one answered their cell phones. Messages sent via every possible app were ignored. After several hours they had to conclude the missing six people weren't coming back.

Ariel began to struggle with an onslaught of disturbing premories relating to the police. Soon after, Cillian became nearly hysterical, insisting the police could jeopardize the future of the human race. After listening to both psychics, Teddie, Nell, and Vanida agreed to not involve any authorities until morning.

By the time everyone was awake the next day, both Ariel and Cillian were more adamant about not calling the police. All five of them stayed home for the day, doing little more than worrying and waiting for some kind of ransom message. Nothing came.

******

Lola thought she'd woken up several times in the last few days. She had fuzzy memories of being led to a restroom and of having some fruit drink poured down her throat until she gagged.

She tried to move. A few blinks made it clear she was blindfolded. Her hands were loosely fastened in front to a belt, but otherwise she wasn't bound. She tried moving her shoulders, shaking her arms and legs. Her muscles ached, but not as bad as if she'd been more heavily restrained. So, her captors had some concern for her well-being. That was good news.

Her mouth wasn't taped shut. Had it been? She tried to remember, but couldn't. In fact, she couldn't remember much.

Scopolamine. The word popped into her head. She tried to clear out the fuzziness to find out why her subconscious had unearthed the chemical name for a common seasickness medicine. Was she on a boat? Yes. She could feel a slight rocking motion.

Wait. Hadn't stronger doses once been mixed with morphine to ease the pain of childbirth? Yes, and the scopolamine made the woman forget the birth, leaving her to wake with a brain full of cobwebs and a surprise infant. Scopolamine. Lola felt sure someone had been giving it to her, because that someone was thinking about the drug now.

Damn. Lola heard footsteps and felt the intention before she felt the sting in her arm. Scopolamine. She repeated the name as the cobwebs returned. Would she remember it the next time she woke? If so, she'd have the good sense to be still till she could learn more.

******

Rafael had done well. Twenty-one of the monads were vetted and briefed, and each was willing to do his part in the upcoming redistribution of authority. Many joined in on the ongoing effort to monitor Warren, but all anyone got was Warren's growing frustration with his inability to keep his mind off the kidnapping.

"He doesn't know what happened," Charlie, the monad from Chicago complained once the conspiring monads were all on a conference call. Gabriel had gone out of his way to ensure this one was secure. Charlie was the only member of the Entelechy who hadn't been made CEO of his subsidiary, and Warren's continued insistence he "wasn't quite ready" had provided the impetus for Charlie to jump ship.

"The man is keeping himself in the dark just to keep *us* in the dark. How stupid is that?" Charlie complained.

It wasn't stupid, it was frighteningly cunning, Gabriel thought, taking care to keep his observation under wraps. Warren was a more serious adversary than expected, and Charlie was going to be less useful than one would hope.

"If he didn't take all the family, then the others know who's missing," Khalid, the monad from Saudi Arabia spoke with impatience. "No one can locate the mind of the woman, her husband or her teacher, so why aren't we locating the others?"

"Jerry in Dallas is the only one who's made a connection with them, and we think he's loyal to Warren," Rafael said. "Besides, we don't care who Warren kidnapped or how they're doing. What we need to know is why Warren did such an outrageous thing in the first place."

******

Warren had a headache from trying to keep his thoughts off of the people being routed to Ushuaia, Argentina, at his request. It had seemed brilliant to ask Executive Security Associates to not contact him for three days after the kidnapping, but his abilities to stay distracted weren't as solid as he hoped.

His plan was to risk a quick phone call to get the facts, then space out his actions. He'd leave on a multi-leg business trip and only tell his closest assistants the journey would end in Argentina, to tend to business matters there. Once he was in Ushuaia, and made the new rules clear to his guests, he'd be able to think this thing through at his leisure.

It was a fine plan. He just hadn't counted on his own curiosity. Who'd have thought he'd be interested in discovering which members of the Zeitman menagerie would be his new pieces of equipment? Apparently, he was not immune to the lure of superpowers, at least when they were soon to be in his captivity.

The phone in his study rang, and he jumped.

"What did I get?"

"The three you asked for. Plus, the Mayan boy who fights, the son who did the devil imitation, and that Buddhist lady who does something no one has figured out."

"That works. Although it could have been useful to have one of the daughters."

"You didn't tell us that."

"No, I didn't. Hadn't really thought about it 'til now."

The lack of thought given this operation could turn out to be a liability. Well, no point in dwelling on it.

"Don't worry about it," he added. "You guys did great."

He hung up the phone and reached for his nearest word search book, opening it to a random page. *Words having to do with superpowers.* He threw it down and looked around the room for another distraction.

******

Those who remained at the Zeitman house were on edge. Teddie hadn't left her room in a day. She knew six of the people she cared about most were in serious danger. She didn't want to talk to anyone about it and she was too scared to sleep. She was mostly watching reruns of sitcoms on her computer.

By the third day, she tried to control her sense of helplessness She took a shower and put on fresh clothes. It was always possible to make a situation better. Always. She'd learned that.

Teddie could see how the timing sucked for Ariel. Her older sister was pushing her skills after barely escaping a situation a few months ago with her own life. Even though Teddie wanted her sister to go back to being the way she used to be, she knew Ariel couldn't do that anymore than she could. Ariel had to be more scared than she was letting anyone know. For the first time, Teddie felt protective for her older sister.

Teddie had been grateful when Vanida moved over to the empty guest room to give them both more privacy, but to be honest she hadn't given Vanida much thought after that. Teddie knew if she was in a strange country and couldn't go home, she'd be in a panic. How was Vanida staying so calm. Maybe she wasn't. What would help Vanida? The answer popped into her head.

Something useful to do.

Teddie found her sister in the kitchen.

"I was thinking maybe Vanida and I could do a little out-of-body reconnaissance. Maybe learn where mom and dad went."

To Teddie's surprise, Ariel liked the idea. Even Cillian raised no objection from his perch on the couch.

"Why haven't you tried this sooner?" he asked.

Teddie swallowed her irritation at the question.

"I don't like to travel. I have a problem with long distances and they could be far away. I haven't been able to sleep since they disappeared, and I can't do this when I'm exhausted. I've felt no pull from Yuden, which is disturbing, so, I'm also a little scared about what I may find."

"And you told us to not do anything and got agitated when anyone suggested any course of action," Vanida added as she walked in the room. Teddie was pleased to hear the sharpness in her fellow-traveler's voice.

"They make good points," Nell said, following Vanida in. "We've listened patiently to you, Cillian, while you lectured us on what we can't do. I want to talk about what we can."

Cillian raised both palms in an expression of surrender.

"Sorry, ladies. There are a lot of adjustments here I'm not handling well." He chuckled. "That could be an understatement. I'm sorry I'm screwing things up, but it's because I want so *badly* not to screw things up. Okay?"

"That sounds like another Irish toast," Teddie said, as heads of deep black, brown, and red hair bobbed in understanding.

"Then let's see if you girls can find our people," Nell said.

Ariel insisted Teddie and Vanida eat something first and rest so the travel could be as safe for them as possible. It was dark by the time they woke from naps, and the wind had picked up as a rare cold front blew into the Gulf Coast region. Ariel closed the windows and kicked on the heater.

"It's a cold day!" Teddie said as she stretched herself awake.

"Well, a cold night, actually, but I think that's as good."

"Is what you do easier in the cold?" Nell asked.

"Oh no. There is no temperature or wind on the energy plane. I don't know why Teddie cares."

"Thermodynamics," Teddie said. "Remember? The second law? You can only break even on a very cold day."

Ariel actually put her arm around her sister. "I think you're taking your physics class a little too literally, but hey, whatever brings you comfort."

The two travelers settled into a pair of chairs and moved into their trances. They went in holding hands, and their bodies of light started out their journey the same way. Traveling is hard to do with another, though, so they split up soon after, each seeking the ones they knew best.

Vanida's emotional connection with the elderly Yuden was strong enough to propel her forward as she sought the woman out. Teddie was emotionally close to the other five, and once she gave her body of energy permission to go, she sped off to the south, leaving Vanida behind. Teddie didn't worry. She knew Vanida would catch up.

While the girls were gone, Ariel, Nell, and Cillian were too restless to do anything. Ariel had moved into her parents' room, letting Nell have some space of her own. They tried to get Cillian to sleep in Zane's room, but he said he preferred the familiarity of the couch. As minutes turned into more than an hour, all three ended up at the kitchen table. They were discussing plans when they were startled by Vanida walking into the kitchen.

"Well?" Cillian demanded. "I mean," and he forced a friendly smile onto his face, "How did it go?"

"Teddie's behind me. She did the hard work. I'll let her tell you."

Vanida pulled up a chair. All three noticed she was shaking. Nell got up and grabbed a blanket off the couch and wrapped it around the girl. Ariel headed over to the microwave and popped in a mug of milk for hot chocolate.

"You okay?"

"A little shook."

"A little seasick," Teddie added, coming into the room. "How'd you get back so fast? Never mind. They're on a boat."

"A cruise ship?" Ariel groaned.

"No. Smaller, uglier, dirtier. A fishing boat, I think. They're down below, all six of them. First time I've been glad that travelers can't smell."

"They're all alive?"

"Oh yeah, very good news. Unconscious. Maybe sleeping, but I think drugged too, because we both called to Yuden to join us but she was deep under. They were tied up, kind of, but with no obvious cuts or bruises. It was like these people were just moving them. Like they were fish."

"And," Cillian tried for the smile again, "would you have any thoughts on where our fish are being moved to?"

Vanida did. "Teddie spent most of her time inside with them, so I snooped around. I know the stars because I use them when I travel. The boat is in the northern hemisphere, though not by much, and it's moving south along the western side of, uh, whatever continent it is along side of."

"That's impressive," Ariel said. "How'd you get that?"

"The North Star was low in the sky behind me and the land was to my left," Vanida said. "They were definitely on the ocean, though close to shore."

"Headed to Argentina," Ariel said. "Damn."

"Aren't they on the wrong side to go there?" Teddie asked.

"Not if they left from the West Coast, with plans to go around the tip to Tierra del Fuego," Nell said. "Ariel's right. This is what she's seen and is worried about." Her face softened. "Can you keep doing this? Follow their progress?"

"Yeah. It's pretty tiring but we can probably do this once a day." Vanida said. "But what good will it do?"

"We're working on that part now."

******

Violeta was at the sink, scrubbing the bigger pots and pans for her mom, when the word scopolamine popped into her head as clear as could be. What the hell was scopolamine? Sounded like a chemical.

Violeta let the biggest pot slide back into the soapy water and walked over to her computer to run the word through a search engine. Truth serum? Scopolamine was once used as truth serum. That was odd.

Violeta looked for the source of the input into her mind. Nothing. Try hard as she could, all she could find was a deep silence in the place the word had come from.

25. Talking with One's Hands

Ariel did her best to fight the vertigo engulfing her after her parents and brother disappeared. She drank club soda with a twist and left out the gin. She did every yoga balancing pose she knew until her ankles hurt. The dizziness would subside and her stomach would settle down, then she'd brush against Teddie or Nell and a new wave of possibilities would hit her. It was like trying to live in heavy surf.

The problem was the absurd fringes she avoided were converging with the highly probable into the oddest of stews. People in her visions appeared in unlikely places, and they morphed into each other in the way of dreams, not real life. At first only the travelers Teddie, Vanida, and the kidnapped Yuden did this, but now she was seeing Cillian, blind Cillian, running around Tierra del Fuego. It was preposterous. Or was it?

She stopped and listened to Cillian's voice in the next room. He'd been talking too soft for her to understand, but now he was agitated and easier to hear.

"No Nell, *you* are not listening to *me*. It's a brilliant plan. I know I'll be a burden and feel damn bad about it, but there is no, repeat no, other way. You go, I go."

Ariel took a deep breath and exhaled loudly through her mouth. She knew where they were considering going. It was a bad idea and she had to stop them. Cillian was a man of probabilities; surely she could use her visions to talk him out of this.

Ariel walked into the next room and put her finger to her lips. Without saying a word, she put the soft, sensitive skin on the inside of her wrist against Nell's arm and waited. Her friends understood, and let her be until she was ready to speak.

"Well, I didn't see what I expected," she said. "I saw a decent probability this time next week the two of you are at the tip of South America, weird as that sounds. Both of you. There is a much smaller chance you're there alone, Nell."

"I told you so," Cillian said.

"Just because you probably do go doesn't mean you should," Nell replied.

"It's okay. In spite of what I'd have guessed, I mostly I see you finding a safe place for Cillian to wait. I see a pretty decent chance of this idea of yours working, too. Jeez, that's one long shot of a rescue plan, but you may be able to do it."

The admiration in Ariel's voice was clear.

"What if she fails?"

"Then the probabilities explode, but not every shard is bad. You're likely safe no matter what, so there's no real reason for you not to go. No reason for you to go, either."

"Not that you'd see. I have my own reasons."

"Can you see anything that would help me?" Nell asked.

"Lots of little things. I'll write down what I can. One big thing, though. The odds of this working go way up if our people know you're coming and know what you're trying to do."

"That would obviously help a great deal," Cillian said. "But how? Your mother's telepath friends have disappeared, and your sister and her people can't deliver messages. You're not a telepath, unless you've been hiding something."

Ariel laughed. "No, my other useful skills here consists of being my mother's daughter. She told me she can't help checking in on her children. Teddie says mom is drugged now, but when they revive her, she'll look in on us. Once Teddie verifies mom is awake, I'll think about your plan every hour. Maybe every fifteen minutes. Actually, we should all think about it as often as we can."

"Sounds like great fun," Cillian said. "Won't that get damn tiring? It'd be nice to know when we can stop."

"We'll know. Teddie and Vanida can keep checking in on the captives. Mom will find a way to tell us she's gotten the message. It's cumbersome, but vastly better than nothing."

"I'll arrange our travel," Nell said.

"Great. I'll get you some of their clothes and stuff to take along. You and Zane will need all the help you can get to pass yourselves off as mom and Uncle Maurice."

Teddie joined them. She listened but said nothing.

"I'll also get you a bag of different looking clothes and some wigs so they can disguise themselves after they escape. Let's give them every chance we can," Ariel added.

Teddie looked at her sister in disbelief.

"Ariel, what about Dad? Zane? Xuha and Yuden?" She turned to Nell and Cillian. "What's wrong with you guys? How come you're only going to rescue Mom and Uncle Maurice?"

Cillian spoke. "We only have two shapeshifters to do the rescuing, lass. And at that, this Warren will lose your mom and Maurice, but gain Nell, which I'm not happy about. The plan will be to get everyone out, eventually, but first we have to make the other hostages useless, for their own sakes."

Teddie thought. "So only the telepaths are useful to Warren?"

"That's what we think," Nell said. "Here he is, a non-telepath dealing with mind readers. He doesn't know what our others can do or how he can use them. We think they're leverage, people who can be hurt to make our telepaths cooperate. Remove the telepaths; stop any need for hurting."

"But what if he gets angry when mom and Uncle Maurice escape? What if he kills dad? Or any of them?"

"That's a tiny probability," Ariel said. "Warren is far more likely to try to get his two useful captives back. While he's preoccupied with that, we'll get everyone else out."

Teddie looked somewhat convinced. "I came in here to tell you Vanida and I figured we can each travel to mom and dad every eighteen hours. We're going to start staggering our trips."

"That works," Ariel said. "We'll know within nine hours once mom is conscious and doing her mom thing."

Teddie had to smile. A year ago it had been disconcerting to find out her mom used telepathy to check on her every so often, but right now it felt comforting. She was going to joke with her sister about it, but something in Ariel's face stopped her.

"You look really tired, Ariel."

"This is wearing me out. I'll go lay down. Call me if anything happens. Or maybe don't."

******

Violeta couldn't imagine Warren had killed Lola, but that didn't mean Lola wasn't dead. Accidents happened, things got out of hand, drugs got administered in error.

She was most worried about the drugs. The more she thought about it, the surer she was Lola had been the source of the word "scopolamine." Had they given it to her to interrogate her? To make her forget? To keep her from getting seasick? Maybe it was merely an easy way to keep Lola sedated.

Violeta decided to risk checking on the woman often until she learned more. After a day of finding nothing but silence, Violeta expanded her search, seeking others in the woman's vicinity. Lola's teacher was nowhere near, unless he was unconscious or dead as well. She felt no telepathic energy near Lola, which meant her friend wasn't held by the Entelechy. Lola was either surrounded by strangers with whom Violeta could make no connection, or she was all alone.

That wasn't good. Violeta knew she had to be bolder. She considered seeking out Warren or Gabriel, but listening to either carried too high a risk of being detected. Who else could be helpful?

Violeta let her mind wander to Lola's family. She tried to remember the woman's husband, her house, her habits. The memory of the night Lola read her note surfaced, along with the little porcelain angel in the sparkling purple dress, and her own realization that Lola thought of Violeta as a purple angel.

Violeta saw the angel in her mind, then she saw it in the hand of a young woman. Her hand connected to a freckled arm with a bit of light red hair. Violeta was looking through the eyes of this young woman who was tired and overwhelmed, but trying to stay strong. She was worried about her family and friends. She was worried about Lola, because she was Lola's daughter. This daughter had picked up the little angel on her mother's dresser, and through the angel, Violeta had found her.

Violeta moved to shield herself from the girl's thoughts, then realized it was unnecessary. This one had no telepathic abilities, no sense Violeta was there.

Did she know where her mother was? Sort of. She wasn't thinking about her mother though. She was thinking about two family friends heading out to rescue Lola and her teacher. Well, that was great news. One friend had special skills for the job and the daughter was certain her friend would succeed. Even better news. The companion was special too, but for some reason he needed to be kept safe. Why?

The daughter studied the little angel, wishing she could send it along with her friends to protect them. They were going so far away, somewhere she knew nothing about. They were going to...

Violeta's heart began to pound. No.

They were coming to Ushuaia.

They were coming *here* because Lola was would be here. How did the girl know? She was sure of it. The friends would come to Ushuaia too and would need help from someone local, and this daughter was wishing she could find a way to provide it.

Violeta felt the girl put the angel on the shelf, and then lie down on the bed, discouraged.

You have helped them. You have. I can't imagine why Warren would move these people thousands of miles, but the idiot is sending them right to me. I live here. Now that I know your friends are coming, I'll be here for them. You don't know it yet, but I will be a large part of why your friends' plan succeeds.

******

Most of the monads were happy to join Gabriel and Rafael, but there were three exceptions. The Israeli monad, Ezra, baulked in spite of his irritation with Warren about the botched kidnapping of Maurice. He had no affection for Warren's politics, but was equally wary of Gabriel. The best they got from him was a promise of silence; he wanted no trouble with either side.

Hank, the Australian monad, gave a similar response, but in a more irritating fashion. He thought the group should have stopped deferring to Warren long ago and wondered what took Gabriel so long to reach this obvious conclusion. That said, he added he thought he'd do better on his own.

Cenk, the monad from Turkey who lost his son, was the third man to decline. Gabriel sensed his sorrow left him no room for involvement with any cause.

They'd already written off the Brazilian, Fernando, who'd picked this inopportune time to fall in love with a member of x^0. Gabriel was glad to not have the love-struck Brazilian or the grieving Turk on this team. In fact, they were better off without the aloof Israeli or the annoying Aussie.

Although they'd recruited Charlie out of Chicago early on, Rafael decided not to approach the other two U.S.-based monads; Jerry in Dallas and Brett in LA. Warren was closest with these two Americans, and both showed loyalty to him as well.

"We should stop," Rafael said. "There are only six others I haven't talked to, and my instincts tell me to wait."

"Who haven't you approached?"

"Nigeria. Italy. Canada. South Korea. Germany and Sweden."

"I like your instincts," Gabriel said. "We have enough; we can roll in more later if we want. Let's get this show started."

******

Lola faded in and out of consciousness. When she woke, it was to stomach pain and muscle cramps. Whatever they were doing to her, her body was starting to object. She forced her breath to remain slow and shallow, and her body to stay limp and still. She wanted time to think.

Her blindfold had slipped down, allowing a sliver of sight in one direction. She saw Alex, and beyond him, the crumpled body of Maurice. The lack of mental energy coming from them scared her until she saw the subtle rise and fall of their chests. They were breathing. Beyond them lay a tiny bundle that was Yuden. The woman couldn't have been more than a hundred pounds to begin with and didn't have the reserves to withstand this ordeal. What was wrong with these people?

She took a full minute to turn her head the other direction, not knowing if she was being observed. There was no sound in the room, and she could feel no other consciousness. She finally saw the leg of a fifth person on her left and recognized Zane's shoe.

She tried to keep her face expressionless as she felt relief. There were no others beyond Zane. Hadn't Xuha been at the house when this happened? Was he left behind or being kept elsewhere?

She fought to clear her brain, then heard footsteps. Xuha walked in. He went to Yuden and poured water into her mouth. Was Xuha working for their captors?

Lola felt his concern for Yuden and his worry she wouldn't survive the voyage. As he tried to get her to swallow the water, he thought about how he would be punished if she died.

So, Xuha had been coerced into caring for them. Threatened, Lola wasn't sure how. Used, because he spoke Spanish well. Scared, because he knew where they were being taken. More scared, because he knew his chief function once they arrived would be to serve as the most expendable person, the one to be harmed or killed first if Lola and Maurice wouldn't cooperate.

Every muscle in Lola's body stiffened. Someone, probably Warren, wanted Lola and Maurice to cooperate? Of course they wouldn't, unless he forced them to. Warren had four people to use. Lola's husband and son. Maurice's girlfriend. And Xuha. Lola felt a deep empathy for Xuha intertwine with her own fear and anger. What a horrible position for him to be in.

She felt Xuha turn in her direction, making sure she and Maurice were unconscious. She knew he was the one drugging her. He was doing it to keep her safe, having been told she'd be hurt if she achieved enough awareness to use her skills. She forced limpness into her body. There had to be a way out.

Then she felt it. Her. Teddie. Her daughter was here? Yes, the girl had been making trips to the boat as often as she could, for as long as she could, hoping each time to find her mother or Maurice conscious. Vanida had been doing the same.

They needed Lola awake so they could tell her something. Tell her what? Lola felt harder for her daughter's presence and waited for her daughter to think about the important message, but Teddie was busy being sad her mother was still unconscious.

Damn. She had to get Teddie's attention. Yet she couldn't move or Xuha would see. This was an impossible situation.

No. Teddie wasn't an ethereal entity when she traveled. Her body of energy had a position in the room. If Teddie was somewhere away from Xuha, Lola could motion to her without him seeing it. Where was Teddie's invisible body?

Lola looked through her daughter's eyes. Teddie was looking at Xuha's left side, baffled by his health and freedom. She could see Maurice's left side, too, and Alex's. She didn't see Zane.

Where am I in your point of view? Why don't you see me?

Teddie looked straight down and Lola had the disorienting experience of seeing the back of her own head. Teddie was floating right above her.

That means she can see my left hand and Xuha can't.

Lola began to make wild motions with all of her left fingers, adding wrist circles to accentuate the motion. The movement caught Teddie's eye. Lola felt her daughter's concern her mother was having muscle spasms. She tried to make the movements more regular and felt her daughter's worry dissolve into the realization her mother was conscious and trying to communicate.

Mom, hear me.

Teddie thought it and Lola waved her hand up and down in her best imitation of a hand nodding yes.

Got it.

Her daughter outlined a plan, a wild plan, for rescue. Lola was puzzled as the words and images tumbled through Teddie's mind until it began to make sense.

Nell was coming. She and Zane would replace mom and Uncle Maurice, shifting into their shapes and tricking their captors, so the two true telepaths could escape and run like the wind. Once Warren had no telepaths to coerce, options would improve.

Zane had to be told. Uncle Maurice had to be prepared. The others had to be brought in, so they'd cooperate with the deception. Mom was to check in often for updates.

She nodded her hand yes again, then added a thumbs up for good measure.

"I love you mom." The problem with being a telepath is you hear the emotions, all the emotions. Lola heard the affection, and the fear, worry and tears.

She crossed her fingers, trying to convey love and hope. She felt Teddie smile at the gesture, and then her daughter was gone.

26. Meet the Mapmakers

The first thing Lola noticed was stillness. The lack of a rocking motion was disorienting. She reached out a hand for balance and noticed the restraints were gone.

She felt stronger. Perhaps she'd been fed, even exercised. She tried to recall, but only found a thick, sticky syrup where her memories of the last few days should have been.

Scopolamine. Keeping five scared captives in a fog for a week had been no challenge for this drug. She started to laugh at the absurdity of it and a hand squeezed her forearm hard.

"Shh." It sounded like Xuha's voice. Wait, hadn't he been her captor? No, that couldn't be. Why would Xuha kidnap her?

She realized she was walking, blindfolded. Xuha's hand was on her left arm, guiding her with a firmness to keep her safe. She took a breath. She no longer smelled fish or the other unpleasant odors surrounding her for days. She heard a voice she was thought belonged to Warren Moore.

"That's good. Walk her in front of the chair and have her sit there. Remove her blindfold. You sit over there."

She felt Xuha's hands pull the covering off her eyes, and she blinked hard at the bright summer sun streaming through a window. She closed her eyes again.

"The light can be a little intense at first," Warren said. She felt his pride at having engineered this exact way to begin the discussion. "Truth can be like that. Hard to take in all at once, particularly when one has been in the dark for a while."

Lola felt Xuha's shame at having helped this man, and his helplessness at being forced to choose between cooperation or mistreatment of his friends. Later, she'd let him know she knew he'd done his best. Now, she had to pay attention to the asshole who wanted to give her a speech on the harsh truths of life.

She opened her eyes and looked at the floor while they adjusted. She didn't like how the maneuver forced her head into a subservient position, but it bought her a few seconds to look into Warren's mind. He understood human nature. He wanted to win her cooperation. He knew it was better to begin with an alliance because coercion brought out the fighter in most people but once someone had chosen to cooperate, they could be nudged along.

Lola raised her gaze, knowing the longer she kept him talking, the more she'd learn. She said nothing while he droned on about how a man like him was all that stood between civilized society and chaos. When the question came, she had her answer.

"A simple wall around my mind for half an hour is all I ask. I know you can do it, and I need time to sort through issues and make wiser decisions. Everyone benefits from that. Surely you'd contribute to the greater good by obliging such a minor request?"

She really wanted to answer "eat shit," but it wasn't her style. She settled for staring ahead and responding in a monotone. "I'm unwilling to do anything, no matter how small, to oblige you."

"We both know that won't last. If you insist, though, we'll do it the hard way." He turned to Xuha. "Take her to her guest room."

Alex looked awful, and Lola suspected he'd been given less care during the week-long voyage. He was more expendable. Her heart squeezed at the thought. He was pale, and his hefty body looked thinner as he snored on one of the two twin beds in the room they'd been given.

It was sparse, but more in the way of a hospital room than a jail cell. The floors were tiled and a row of glass blocks up near the ceiling let in a wedge of sunlight. A wooden table with a lamp sat between the beds holding a pitcher of water with two cups, and a bowl of fruit.

She was grateful they were in a room together, but considered how this arrangement served Warren. Was he hoping she and Alex would converse? Of course. She could sense him eavesdropping now, so the room had listening devices. But not cameras. He wasn't seeing pictures.

Warren would assume she'd seek out his thoughts; but it looked like he hoped she wouldn't do it often enough to become aware of his snooping. That seemed naïve to Lola, but perhaps such techniques worked better with his own telepaths. She could play his assumptions to her advantage.

She looked at Alex, remembering how firm she'd been in her refusal to help Warren. Maybe she should have been less stubborn. What if he harmed Alex and left her to sleep next to him and see his pain?

Surely not that. The response in her head came from someone else. Who?

She felt a small porcelain angel in her hand and saw the sparkly purple dress on the figurine through fresh eyes. Through her daughter Ariel's eyes. That made no sense. Ariel was no telepath. This felt like Violeta, who couldn't possibly be in Lola's bedroom.

Then she got it. Violeta had found Ariel, who was holding the angel. Then she'd found Lola.

Lola let her questions flow to Violeta and let the answers flood back over her own mind.

I quit my job with Reel News. I'm safe. Where? In the same city you are!

Lola saw the mighty Pacific Ocean pushing its waves against the Southern Atlantic, and she knew she was inside an office complex built by Reel News for reasons no one understood.

Lola answered by concentrating on Nell's rescue plan. She focused on her need to get word to the others about Nell's plan.

Yes. Violeta already knew of the plan. Ariel had been thinking of it. Lola should think about it more, with details.

Lola concentrated on what she knew, imagining Nell and Zane shifting to appear as much like her and Maurice as they could. Along with her images, she sent gratitude to this stranger who'd chosen to aid her.

No 'thanks' yet. There's more. Lola felt Violeta's impatience. *Listen.*

Violeta wanted to intercept Nell, and the blind man traveling with her, when they arrived. She could keep the man safe while Nell did her magic thing. Lola was amused at how Violeta considered her own telepathic abilities to be natural, but had classed Nell's skill set as magic.

Whatever. Magic or real, it doesn't matter. I'll give her information she needs about here, and will help her work to free you and the teacher.

Now do I get to thank you?

No. Thank me when I succeed.

******

When Nell led Cillian off of the small passenger plane in Ushuaia, she didn't have much of a plan. She'd booked a little rent by the week efficiency suite, thinking she'd get Cillian settled in and then find an English speaking local who could tell her more about the office complex of Reel News. Also, she hoped Lola and Maurice would find her, mentally, and somehow help.

As they made their way into the terminal, Nell knew she'd spent a lifetime relying on her strong self-confidence and her ability to improvise. It was entirely possible she'd ended up in a mess she couldn't push her way out of with sheer bravado.

Then as the Irish visitors cleared security, Nell saw a tall woman with long dark hair holding up a sign saying "Nell" in large purple letters. She looked at the woman with a question mark in her eyes, and the woman nodded. Perhaps daring had combined with dumb luck to work once again.

By the time the luggage was on the carousel, Nell had learned she and Cillian were in the care of Lola's mysterious Argentinian telepath, and they couldn't have found a better ally. The woman, Violeta, was familiar with most of Lola's situation, knew a lot about Warren and Reel News, and had grown up in Ushuaia. This had to be why Ariel thought this incompletely conceived rescue attempt had such a high probability of succeeding.

As the trio moved away from baggage claim, Cillian pushed impatiently against Nell's back. She turned to glare at him, then remembered her old friend could no longer see her expressions.

"You don't need to slow down for me. I can keep up."

Right. She'd noticed Violeta's limp and cane, but Cillian didn't know their host had mobility issues. *I'm so bad at helping him.*

"No you're not," Violeta said. "I think you're doing quite well." Violeta turned to Cillian and took him by the wrist. "Here. Feel. You can go fast, but I can't." She moved his hand onto her cane. He felt the handle, then nodded as he understood.

"So that's what the noise was."

******

When Yuden regained consciousness, her first thought was she would pass out. She turned to decades of training to slow her breath and her heart, and to bring strength into her body. When she felt steadier, she opened her eyes.

Well, this is a nice surprise. The horrible little room on the boat was gone. She was lying on a small bed, and a pile of clean clothes lay by her feet. Next to the bed was a wooden table with a lamp, and on the table were two glasses, a pitcher of water, and a basket of fruit. On the far side of the table was another small bed, and on it was Maurice.

He was alive but not moving, possibly sleeping, possibly drugged. Yuden turned her gaze back to the fruit and water, realizing how hungry and thirsty she was. The pears looked ripe. She munched on one as she considered her next move.

Maurice and his telepathic abilities would be helpful, but she thought it best to let him wake naturally, as she had. This would be a good time to go exploring. She lay her head back on the pillow and let her body of energy rise above her solid body with an effortlessness gained from years of practice.

Were the other captives nearby? She guessed they were. Every time she'd regained consciousness on the boat, the others were drugged. Even though she'd explored the small vessel, she'd learned little about her captors or their destination.

She moved out of the room into a sterile hallway, with doors on either side. This looked like a simple hotel. Time to find the other guests. The first three rooms she tried were like the one she'd left, but vacant. In the fourth one she saw Alex sleeping and a closed bathroom door. Lola?

Yuden dipped her head through the bathroom wall, and saw steam coming from the shower. Good news. If Lola was cleaning up, she was alert and well. Yuden moved on.

Three rooms down she found Zane sitting on a small bed rubbing his wrists and ankles. His restraints had been harsher than hers. Xuha was seated on the other bed talking to him. It looked like the two shared this room. Both young men were upset, judging by their animated discussion. Had they been speaking Bhutanese, Yuden would have read their lips, but she struggled with English even when she could hear it plainly. Again, she moved on.

She covered the building, first finding their guards, then finding Warren, his assistants and his bodyguards. She took a close look at all of the entrances and exits, committing them to memory. Later, Maurice could go over those memories with her until they became his own. Then Maurice would find a way to share her images with others and they'd be at step one of a plan to escape.

******

"What do you know about this business complex Warren is building in Argentina?" Khalid asked.

Gabriel felt absurd talking to the Saudi monad on the cheap device he'd been told was called a burner phone, but given the way the situation had gone, they needed to be careful.

It was the first Monday after New Year's Day. Gabriel was back at work on the top floor of his Buenos Aires office, and Khalid was in Riyadh.

"He's been pretty closed-mouthed about it," Gabriel said. "He had to confide in me, given it's in my country. I told him it seemed like a colossal waste of money. It costs a fortune to transport materials down there and if he had to have another office in Argentina he ought to consider Cordova. Even Mendoza would have been cheaper, and it has good wine.

"But he reminded me he had the money to spend. I decided it was a pet project, a cross between an exotic training center and a place to do business in case he has to exit the U.S. I think it's like one of those paranoid fantasies, where people build bunkers to hide in, in case of Armageddon."

Gabriel considered who was asking the questions. "Why your sudden interest?"

"Because it's where he is now."

Gabriel wanted to curse, but kept quiet. Warren was supposed to be in New York. How had he gotten away like this?

"His staff is keeping his whereabouts quiet, but I picked up he headed down there a few days ago, and didn't tell anyone when he was coming back. I think it's where he's stashing those people he kidnapped. He left his best New York flunkies in charge, ensuring nothing will happen while he's gone. Do you think he figured out what we're about to do?"

Gabriel ignored the question. He was in many ways the second-in-command of Warren's empire and it bothered him he didn't have any idea of what Warren knew. How had this other monad gotten so far ahead of him?

"We should consider beginning our processes without him," Khalid said.

"Not easily done. We don't have a single ally on his board of directors, or in the corporation. The only people on our side are us. We need Warren to be our mouthpiece and he knows it."

"Brilliant on his part. We can't threaten him if we can't talk to him. We need to consider persuading one or two of his board members. We could uncover information to buy us an ally."

Gabriel was sure this coup would require that sort of coercion before they were done, but he thought it unwise to use it as an opening move. "I want to hold off doing that and check in with others. Rafael has been talking with Juan, our Venezuelan. He's got a legal background in banking. Right now, you need to work with him to make sure we've got the money angles covered."

Khalid couldn't hide his frustration. Gabriel tried to reassure him. "I don't think Warren will hide in Ushuaia for long. It's not his way to stay away from the action. This will be so much easier once he returns."

Gabriel could feel Khalid's sigh.

"Suit yourself. Either way, our element of surprise is gone."

******

Alex regained consciousness after Lola got out of the shower. He looked dazed but sat up and tried to eat an apple and drink water while Lola told him of her conversation with Warren. She spoke like she didn't know the room was bugged, but saved the important news of Nell's rescue plan for later, when it could be whispered under the covers. Alex had little to say, and he dozed off again soon after. Lola let him rest.

She was starting to feel confined in the locked room when she felt Maurice's presence. He was conscious now, weak, but alive. She reached back to let him know she was, too. The information exchange that followed was filled with surprises for both of them. Lola was delighted to learn Yuden was with Maurice and had already explored the surroundings. It was a relief to hear Xuha and Zane were safe and housed together. Had they all been paired off in hopes conversations could be overheard? Probably. Lola and Maurice shared their frustration at having no easy way to communicate with Zane or Xuha.

Do we have to guard our thoughts? Does he have his telepaths here monitoring us?

No! Lola understood Maurice's worry and struggled to convey the complex situation. *He is fighting with his telepaths. He brought us here to help him. He feels vulnerable because he doesn't know what we're communicating with each other. It is why our rooms are bugged. Hopefully you and Yuden's conversations have only confused Warren, but be careful what you say aloud going forward. It's best if she explores and you observe in silence.*

She felt Maurice's agreement, then realized she had yet to share the biggest news of all. She concentrated on images of Zane and Nell morphing into her and Maurice. Then she concentrated on her and Maurice running. He was puzzled, but after a few moments he got it. She felt his amazement that a rescue mission was being mounted all the way from the U.S.

The things Yuden saw. It would help Nell so much if she knew them before she comes here, but I don't see a way.

Lola felt the soft tug of Violeta's mind, checking in to let her know Cillian and Nell were safe in Ushuaia with her.

Wait. There is a way.

Maurice, meet Violeta. Violeta, meet Maurice and Yuden. You'll want pen and paper so you can draw maps for Nell of everything Maurice and Yuden have to show you.

27. Give Me a Break

Gabriel took one problem and turned it into two.

The monads Khalid and Juan had explained to him the exact steps Warren would need to be coerced into so the Entelechy would control Reel News. Some actions needed Warren's signature, others merely the weight of his influence. The most important ones required the approval of the board of directors.

Gabriel put Rafael in charge of anything involving the board. Rafael had a deceivingly gentle manner about him that would be an asset with these powerful men, and he was the best at mining mental information. Gabriel paired him with Johann, the Swiss monad with experience using telepathy for blackmail. Together, they'd get board member support.

That left Gabriel with the Warren half of the problem. It appeared Warren planned to outwait him at the end of the Earth, so he'd go there. He considered bringing protection, but that seemed overly dramatic, given their lengthy partnership.

Gabriel planned to convince Warren he couldn't withstand a prolonged assault from his own Entelechy. They knew too much, and no distractions would protect him from a twenty-four-hour-a-day onslaught using every scrap they knew to make his life miserable. He'd show Warren what it was like when angry telepaths mocked his every thought and badgered him with unending insults and personal observations designed to reduce him to a sniveling wreck.

He might be resentful, at first, but he was practical. The position of reduced power they offered him was his best option. When he'd enlisted the power of a tiger, he knew the tiger would turn on him someday. Gabriel was counting on Warren's relief the tiger didn't want everything he had.

******

Xuha knocked on Lola and Alex's door. Lola smelled the hot meal as she opened it, but the pleasant odors were overshadowed by the fear she felt from Xuha. Then she saw the collar fastened around his neck, and she knew the apparatus was the source of his anxiety.

"Is he hurting you with that?"

Xuha jumped, as if he'd received an electric shock. Lola guessed he had, and it was meant as an answer to her question.

"He did that on purpose, didn't he?" Her temper begin to rise. "My God, he's got you in a dog fence collar!"

Xuha jerked again.

"Please stop asking about it, Ms. Z. Please."

She took a breath and stopped talking.

"It has a microphone on it. I'm being forced to wear it so I don't have conversations with you I shouldn't have. I'm only to tell you and Mr. Z to enjoy your dinner. You'll meet with him after you eat. He intends to, uh, let you know how he'll need assistance from you and Maurice."

Alex turned over in his bed, and his eyes widened at the sight of the food.

"Is that real cooking I smell? Xuha, did you bring us that?"

"Glad to help, Mr. Z. You enjoy your meal now."

Xuha put a finger to his lips and gave Lola a pleading look.

She nodded, but motioned for him to keep talking to Alex as she ducked into the bathroom. Xuha hid his look of bewilderment and tried to make harmless conversation with the groggy man.

When Lola came out a minute later, she gave Xuha a quick hug, and he thought she slipped something small under the collar. He'd have to find a way to check later.

"You hang in there." She made deep eye contact.

"I'll be back for you in a while," he replied in a monotone and closed the door behind him.

Lola let Alex dig into his bowl of stew served over noodles. He'd scarfed down half of it before he put down his fork.

"I think I'm going to throw up. You don't look so good either. You okay? We probably shouldn't have eaten so fast." Then he noticed her plate was untouched.

"Did you already eat something while I was asleep?"

"No, Alex. You were drugged more than I was; I've been clearheaded for twelve hours. I met with Warren last night and did *not* impress him with my desire to be helpful. Today, he put one of those collars on Xuha they use to keep dogs in the yard."

"Yeah, I've seen those. Gives the dog a mild shock." He noticed the way Lola was staring at him. "Of course it's a sick thing to do, but they're not strong enough to harm a human."

"Warren had the collar altered. He's been thinking about it for the past few minutes. He knows how fast Xuha can move, and it's his way of controlling him. He's proud of it. Oh, good lord."

Lola doubled over in pain.

"He put one on Zane, too. Alex, every time Xuha gets shocked, Zane gets one twice as strong. They both know it; Warren's been demonstrating. He figured Xuha might tolerate pain to help us, but wouldn't take chances with Zane's life."

Tears were starting to flow down Lola's checks.

"What have I done? The damn man has been thinking about this because he knew after I saw the collar on Xuha I'd come looking for information. He's running through his memories of giving the shocks, over and over and he thinks it's funny." Lola put her hands up over her ears in a gesture Alex hadn't seen from her since her early days of telepathy.

"Stop it!" she screamed.

Alex walked over and started massaging his wife's shoulders.

"Don't let him manipulate you," he said in the calmest tone he could. "Remember this guy knows how to deal with telepaths. Ignore him. Now. Go. Find. Zane."

Lola knew it was good advice. She sought out her son, felt his anger overriding his fear. Then, she heard his voice.

"Mom. If you can hear me, I'm okay. Xuha will keep me safe, and we'll manage this. Don't you dare let this asshole win."

Zane kept repeating those words in his mind, hoping she'd get the message. He understood Warren's plan; he knew Xuha was being sent to fetch her.

"Pretend anything you need to, mom, but in the end, don't give him an inch more power over anything."

For the thousandth time she wished Zane could hear her answer, could hear her say she'd do anything to keep him safe, and yet she knew he'd never be safe as long as Warren controlled her. She'd find a way to buy time, and to keep both boys' pain to a minimum. However fast Nell was coming, it wasn't soon enough.

When the knock came, she followed Xuha down the hall in silence, then sat in the chair Warren pointed to.

"I'd be disappointed if you didn't already understand most of your situation," he said.

"You've kidnapped six people. Moved us thousands of miles. You harmed a close family friend and threatened the life of my son." She tried to fill her voice with deprecation. "What does a rich and powerful media mogul like your need from the likes of me?"

He gave her a look of surprised appreciation.

"To the point. I like that. In spite of your childish pacifism, you have more stamina than I expected. I think you'll do nicely."

He waited. She waited. Then she realized he was expecting her to read his mind. She needed to adapt to dealing with a man so used to telepathy.

She felt... fear. Yes, he was trying to gain her empathy by showing her the exhaustion he felt at never being able to think about matters of importance. He was hounded by what he'd created. All he wanted was a little gauze around his brain while he tended to his business.

"You want me to hide your thoughts from your own telepaths?"

"You have no idea how tiring it is to never be able to concentrate. The fuzzy wall I asked you for last night is something you can do so easily. Why can't you and Maurice do the same for me? Take turns with twelve-hour shifts and give me a break."

Lola though about it. "That's really all you want from us?"

Warren nodded. "It's why I brought you here. I don't want you to engage with my telepaths. They'd best you if you did, leaving me in worse shape than I am. Once I get a few matters straightened out, you and those you care about will be free to go.

Lola searched deeper for any hint she was being lied to, and found none.

"I'm good at mental walls. If this is all you're after, why didn't you say so sooner?"

"You were so hostile last night. It seemed wise to put you in a more cooperative frame of mind. Will I have your assistance?"

"Mine, yes. I can't speak for Maurice."

"He's already said he'll abide by your decision."

"Fine. When do you want me to start?"

"Now. And Lola, I understand you know I have no immediate way of telling whether you are doing as promised or not. I can't feel your wall. Make no mistake, however. If you lie to me, or even merely fail at your task, events will make it obvious to me what has happened. I promise you such a lapse will cost you dearly, and I can and will be more specific if you need me to be. Do we have an understanding?"

"We do. I don't need to hear your threats. In fact, I don't want to hear them. Rather, I'll offer you a sign of good faith. Not only can I surround you with gauze, as you put it, but I'll know if any of your telepaths try to seek you out. I won't engage, but I'll give you that information if it would be useful."

"Of course it would. Why are you being helpful?"

She answered honestly. "Because while I don't like you, I also don't like them, and at least you and I have an understanding."

"Well said." He seemed pleased. "I do like a logical woman. I understand proximity is useful, so you will join me in my quarters for the night."

He waited. She said nothing.

"Good. You understand you needn't be concerned about any physical expectations on my part. I want your full concentration on your work. You have the," he looked at his elaborate gold watch "it looks like you have the 7 p.m. to 7 a.m. shift."

He turned to Xuha.

"Go tell the old man he's on duty at 7 a.m. sharp." His look softened. "Oh, and stop by and tell her husband she's safe for the night." He gave Lola a creaky smile. "A gesture of goodwill back."

"Your family is obsessed with math, aren't they?" Xuha said to Zane the next day as he dropped off a plate of fish and rice for his roommate.

Zane shrugged, wary of the penalties for prohibited conversation. "My family is weird. Why?"

"I was with your mom and dad a while ago. They seem fixated by equations. Here, you dropped your napkin." Zane looked down. How had a napkin gotten on the floor? The next thing he knew, the napkin was in his hand, much too fast for him to follow.

Zane wadded the cloth together, determined to examine it later. Based on what Xuha said, he was pretty sure whatever was pushed into his palm came from his parents. He doubted it had anything to do with math.

******

Violeta gave her guests the evening to settle in and the next morning she drove them around town. She felt the man's respect for the way she handled her physical challenges and realized he was new to his limitations. He didn't know it, but he needed examples of how to be stronger, not more helpless. Violeta liked being a role model. It sure beat being that poor woman with a cane.

As she drove, she told the visitors everything useful she could remember about Reel News. "It came together for me during that first interview with Lola," she said. "I watched this woman and thought *I'm not on the side of good here. How did that happen?*"

"So you became a random woman's guardian angel?"

"Well, she wasn't random. She was a telepath like me, and the first female one I'd encountered. I could tell her skills were strong, but her fighting edge was weak. I was afraid she'd get eaten alive. I thought I could keep that from happening."

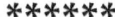

Ariel insisted Teddie go back to school after the holidays and that she also make excuses for her dad's absence. Teddie didn't want to jeopardize her own graduation, so she went to classes with her head down and avoided contact with all but close friends.

The woman who handled attendance told her after three days missed due to a health issue, the school required a doctor's note for teachers as well as students. Teddie was in the parking lot, thinking of forging a note for her dad, when she saw Ken, the shop teacher who was her dad's close friend.

"I've missed seeing your dad," he said. "He never called me back about picking up that wrench. Is your family okay?"

"Not really. But I've been told to be quiet and carry on. So I'm trying."

He didn't say anything for a few seconds. "Look, if you guys need anything at all, you can call me. Understand?"

Teddie did, but of all the things she needed, she didn't think her dad's friend could help with a single one. Wait, maybe.

"You don't know any doctors, do you? Dad, uh, dad is having trouble getting a note for the school about his health problems."

"My wife Sara works for an orthopedic surgeon. How about I take charge of updating the school on your dad's condition?"

"That would be great."

"Good. Tell him I hope his knee gets better soon. He's always had trouble with it. It's a shame it acted up at a time like this."

✶✶✶✶✶✶

Over the next couple of days, Nell learned more about Reel News and the role Warren's Entelechy played in its success. Warren had defied odds in broadcasting by defying odds in a far more fundamental way. He'd accepted the existence of an ability he didn't have and couldn't use, and he possessed the confidence to direct a group having this gift he didn't share.

Nell was intrigued by the differences in how Violeta viewed telepathy and the way she'd heard Lola and Maurice talk about it. Until recently, the monads were Violeta's only experience with other telepaths, and she'd adopted their secretive and even competitive views. The ongoing game of spying on Warren and

202

each other while feigning innocence contrasted sharply with the x^0 model of a cooperative conversation. Nell thought the different paradigms explained the issues Lola and Violeta had in communicating with each other. Yet, while Violeta was fiercely competitive, her behavior was guided by a strong moral code.

Nell noticed Violeta's pride in her decision to protect Lola. She noticed the trust growing among the three of them in a short time. And she noticed Cillian had asked for only two drinks since he arrived, and he hadn't finished either one. Also, he'd paid attention to every word Violeta said since they left the airport.

******

Zane was disappointed. It *was* an equation. The scrap of paper Xuha passed to him was toilet paper, and the math on it was done in tiny drops of blood.

Zane considered. The day after their arrival, Xuha was told to distribute DVD players to each room, along with a selection of old movies. He supposed their captor wished to keep them occupied. In spite of that, he'd not seen paper or a pen anywhere since he'd shaken off the drugs and regained consciousness. There was no reason to think his parents had access to a way to write.

One of them risked sending him a message written in their own blood. Why?

He looked at it again. Yep, it said "N.11 = L." Then it said "Z = M." What the hell had his parents meant by this nonsense?

******

Nell studied every scrap of information Violeta provided, going over the maps drawn from what Yuden saw and devising alternate routes into the heart of the complex. When Violeta visited Lola's and Maurice's minds, Nell incorporated the additional intelligence. She learned of the strange task the two telepaths were sharing, and she learned of the other hostages' situations. She memorized anything in their schedules that could be helpful.

Most of all, she was relieved to find out the rescue didn't have to be rushed because of danger to the hostages. It gave her time to prepare escape materials and devise hiding plans for Lola and Maurice. It gave her time to practice being Lola. Only one nagging issue remained. Lola had done her best to pass an idea of what would happen along to Zane and Xuha, but she had limited resources. Every time Violeta checked, both young men were still clueless. No one could think of a safe way to reach them.

The three of them were discussing options on Saturday morning over a late breakfast when Violeta slammed her fists down on the table. Nell and Cillian both jumped.

"He's coming here. He dares come to my town."

"Who? Why?"

"Gabriel." She was silent for a few seconds, and then she laughed. "But no, he's not coming for me. He only checked in to see if I knew anything; he doubted I did. He still thinks I'm mending from the ordeal of my high-stress job." She shook her head. "How little he understands me. But he has figured out Warren is here in Ushuaia. He's baffled he can't get any info from Warren, and he suspects Warren is using Lola and her teacher for that purpose."

"Well, he got that part right," Nell said.

Violeta cocked her head, as if she was trying to detect a faint sound. It took a moment but she understood.

"He's ready to take over Reel News. I think he's coming here to force Warren to comply."

"When?"

"He's preparing to leave now. He travels Monday? Yes, and hopes to confront Warren Tuesday."

"Looks like your rescue mission just got scheduled for Monday, lass." Cillian touched Nell on the wrist. "Just so you know, from where I sit, there's every reason for you to proceed."

28. Vanishing

Zane had of those annoying recurring dreams. This one was rooted in being the oldest child, often asked to do tasks his parents thought he understood, but he didn't. Someone had given him a tube of decorating gel and insisted he write "Teddie" on a cake while they did more important things. He tried, but the lowercase e's fused together and looked like big dots, while the d's looked like musical notes. He was pretty sure some variation of this had really happened.

Then he got it. No one sent him a note in blood saying N.11. The note said Noll. Or Nell. Obviously, Nell. It said Nell = L.

What the hell could Nell equal? Length? Longitude? A person could equal another person, he supposed. Whoever was writing didn't have the time or blood to keep giving whole names. So who was L? Not Dad or Mom or Xuha.

Zane laughed. His mom had a name. If L was Lola, then Z was Zane. M wasn't mom, so M was Maurice. This worked because Nell and Zane really could equal anyone. Nell could be Lola, except Nell was back in Texas. Zane could definitely be Maurice.

What the hell did they expect him to do with this information? Nothing. They wanted him to know it. They wanted him to cooperate with whatever happened. They wanted him to go back to bed, bury his face in a pillow, and practice being Maurice. Because somebody, somewhere, had a plan, and his part involved Z = M.

He could do that. With a little practice, he could do it well.

******

After Nell and Cillian left, the three young woman at the Zeitman house stayed home, except for errands and Teddie's time at school. Teddie's best friend Michelle came to over visit often. She was a contact point with reality and a reminder of how strange their circumstances were.

Teddie and Vanida kept making the long journey to check on the six captives in Ushuaia, and every day they reported back on the condition of Warren's prisoners. For safety reasons, Nell had decided to keep contact between her and the Texas household limited, but she sent a couple of oblique, reassuring messages from internet cafés.

The girls knew information was circulating between the elderly traveler Yuden, her boyfriend Maurice, and Violeta, a telepathic friend of their mother's who was hosting Nell and Cillian. The improbable coalition appeared to be putting together a viable escape plan, and the closer it came to occurring, the better they all felt.

******

Nell and Cillian met Alma, Violeta's mother, the day after they arrived, when she brought over a platter of homemade cookies. She spoke little English, and they spoke no Spanish, so the conversation mostly involved smiling and thanking her. When Alma called and insisted on seeing them again on Sunday evening, the night before Nell's rescue mission, Nell tried to get out of it.

"Please make up an excuse; I don't have time. I'm going to do this tomorrow when Maurice and Lola change places at the end of their 7 p.m. shift."

"You want to see her," Violeta said. "Mom has asked a lot questions about your visit and I know she's figured out more than I expected. Give her a few minutes of your time."

When Alma arrived, she brought along three former members of the construction crew who'd been let go after Christmas. They looked over the sketches Violeta drew from Yuden's memory and they made a few corrections. They gave Nell hats and ID badges, a worn tool box, and lunch pails and thermoses that looked like they belonged in Ushuaia. What a difference local details made.

"Please tell I thank her," Nell said.

"She knows. This brings her more joy than you know."

Monday afternoon, Nell began to morph her body plumper, and more male. She donned non-descript blue jeans and layered herself in four t-shirts of various colors.

Once she was near the compound, she hid in a clump of bushes close to the most-used exit and waited until 6 p.m. when the skilled laborers began to leave for the day. Her tool box was stuffed with colored hats. She'd long ago learned that shirt color and head gear defined appearance to a casual observer.

When an electrician in a bright blue baseball cap, jeans, and a black T-shirt came through the gate, she knew he would do. She let out a long breath, and closed her eyes to remember his face. Squarer jaw, higher cheekbones, narrower eyes. More arm muscles. This electrician worked out. But he was it; because she had a hat in the same distinctive blue. With any luck, the guard would wave her back in after she claimed she forgot something.

She expected her biggest issue to be explaining her return in passable Spanish. She and Violeta had decided on a few simple words combined with a cough, trusting on Nell's years in the theater to produce the accent and male voice.

She never got the chance. In the commotion of other workers leaving, the guard motioned her back in without asking for an explanation.

******

On the way to Ushuaia, Gabriel realized Violeta would have been helpful. He missed her prickly competence. Damn that woman could get things done.

Yet, she'd changed. It hadn't taken telepathic skills to know she'd fallen hard for him years ago. Obviously, he had no interest, but he'd been flattered. He'd watched her infatuation wane over the years, but a little of that initial crush always remained.

Until a few months ago. Her cooling loyalty was obvious and Gabriel had chalked it up to stress. Warren had become agitated when the liberal U.S. president he despised was re-elected and his frustration with events made him pull the reins tighter on the Entelechy. Then, this nonsense about another organization of telepaths had entered the mix and all hell had broken loose.

Gabriel assumed the proverbial kitchen had become too hot for Violeta. He'd checked in on her to see if she knew more about Warren and found her having breakfast with a couple of friends, making plans for the day. It looked like she'd slid back into the community from which she'd come. Well, maybe she'd give him a hand once he was in town. She owed him that much.

The late afternoon sun was bright as Gabriel walked down the steps of the small passenger plane. Once both feet were on the ground, he reached out to Violeta and was surprised to find her thinking of a construction worker at Warren's complex. Was she dating him? Maybe she was. He got a clear image of an electrician in a black T-shirt, with a bright blue hat and well muscled arms. Violeta was thinking of this electrician with affection.

Then Violeta's attention turned to another man, one who was sitting at her kitchen table talking with her. This one wasn't local; his fair, freckled skin spoke of the north. Gabriel could feel how his brogue enchanted Violeta. She laughed flirtatiously.

"I was caught up in beauty at one time," the man was saying. "My own good looks. Gorgeous women. Appearances mattered to me, you know, but now that's all changed."

What a bunch of drivel. Men will say anything.

"I think you're one of the most amazing men I've ever met," Violeta replied, and Gabriel could tell the woman meant it.

Good God. Enough of this bullshit.

He exited Violeta's mind as he made his way to the baggage claim area. His former assistant had plenty going on. Fine. He didn't need her help. He never really had.

Lola had been making mental gauze for a week and she was worn out. Yet she feared for Zane and Xuha if her protection failed. She knew her patience was fraying. As she checked in on the others, she saw they faced the same problem.

Yuden was exhausted from her mind-travel trips. Every day she found out more, and shared it silently with Maurice, who conveyed it to Violeta, who used it to help perfect Nell's plans for escaping a fortress.

Maurice was doing double duty, working with Yuden and guarding Warren's mind. Xuha did his best to endure the collar as he suffered through chores, cooking and caring for Warren, Warren's staff, and the other captives. Zane had been enlisted as Xuha's assistant as he lived in continual fear of Warren's demonstrations of the collar's power.

Only Alex was bored, left to amuse himself with an endless parade of old movies. Lola was having trouble feeling quite as sorry for him, especially when he tweaked up the volume on Ghostbusters as Lola was falling asleep. Yet she knew he, too, was anxious for this to end.

What kept them all going, was knowing everything would change soon. Today, soon had arrived.

Lola knew Nell planned to act when Maurice handed off his responsibilities to her. Thanks to whispered conversations under the covers and in the shower, Alex knew it, too. Maurice knew anything Lola knew. Yuden knew what Maurice knew, as whispered conversations were held in their room as well.

Zane, bless his smart brain, had finally deciphered her cryptic note, and been preparing to impersonate Maurice, although he wasn't sure when or why. Lola knew no one dared to talk to Xuha, but he was observant. Lola could tell how the odd gestures and facial expressions he saw had alerted him something was up. He was paying attention, ready to help in any way.

The impossible turned out to be remarkably easy, at least for Lola. When Xuha came for her that evening, a maintenance worker was with him. The worker pushed her gently toward the bathroom where they silently exchanged clothes, and a dark wig and bright blue baseball cap were pressed into her hands. By the time the three of them left the room, the maintenance worker was such a convincing version of Lola that both Lola and Alex found it weird.

In the hallway, her look alike pointed to a long, thick drapery, halfway down the hall. Lola understood. She went and stood behind it, then waited while Xuha and the new Lola made their way to Warren's chambers.

******

Violeta was learning the x^0 idea of telepathy, wherein friends used a ritual of knocking on and opening of a door to allow each other access to their thoughts. Lola and Maurice had praised the technique for achieving both privacy and closeness.

Violeta spent years sneaking in and out of minds, developing stealth techniques to cover her traces. Old habits were hard to break. The night of the escape, she checked on Nell as the shape-shifter made her way to the Reel News complex and through the gate. The planning, advance knowledge of the grounds, and the right clothes and props all contributed. Violeta could tell Nell was nervous, but elated, as she hid supplies for Lola and Maurice in locations Yuden had found.

Then Violeta sought out Maurice, who was finishing his shift as Warren's daytime guard. She felt him jump.

Excuse me?

His irritation at finding her in his head was impossible to misunderstand.

I'm sorry. I was making sure you were ready for this. Uh... in case I could help somehow.

He felt her embarrassment, and she felt him soften.

It's okay. I forget you operate under your own rules.

She felt his embarrassment too.

Stop it both of you. Lola's presence was clear. *Focus Maurice. Go away Violeta. We'll call if we need you.*

Violeta turned her attention back to Cillian, who was sitting at the kitchen table. He seemed to enjoy her company; maybe visiting would keep them both from feeling so nervous.

"Can I make you some tea?" she asked.

"No thanks. I wish I knew what you looked like."

"Would it matter?" she said, sitting down across from him. "Do you think you'd like me better if I was pretty?"

He laughed. "I like to think not, but it's probably not true. I was caught up in beauty at one time. My own good looks. Gorgeous women. Appearances mattered to me, you know, but now that's all changed."

"I think you're one of the most amazing men I've ever met." It popped out of Violeta's mouth without any thought. "I mean, the way you've adjusted to having no sight and how you've carried on trying to help your friends, coming all this way."

Cillian could tell she meant it, and although he couldn't explain why, he knew being admired by this particular woman at this particular moment meant the world to him.

He reached out and put his hand over hers, the way she'd done at the airport a week ago when they first met. She put her other hand on top of his, and they both knew where this was going to lead. As he reached out to touch her face, to try to decipher her features by their feel, he said, "Is this a bad time for me to take up your attention? What if they need you?"

"It's okay. I'll know if they do."

He believed her, because he wanted to.

✳✳✳✳✳✳

Warren looked up from his work. "You look tired," he said to Maurice. "Remember, I need you at your best." Then Warren grinned as something occurred to him. "That old Chinese woman isn't keeping you up all night, is she?"

Maurice managed a weak smile back, and tried to think of something useful to say now that he had Warren's attention.

"I'd sleep better with a little exercise and fresh air." He thought maybe he could coax an outing for those being left behind.

"Hmm. That makes sense. Okay, I'll look into it."

Warren was still looking at Maurice, but his thoughts were already back on Reel News. The door opened and Xuha walked in with a woman who looked like Lola.

"He's hard at work, Lola," Maurice said in greeting as he walked to the door. "I wouldn't disturb him now."

The Lola lookalike gave him a meaningful look back. "Putting up my wall now." She said it the way Lola always did.

"Make it a strong one," he replied, just as he did each evening before he left.

******

Gabriel had placed Warren under intensive surveillance before he left for Ushuaia, assigning shifts to the other twenty-two monads. They were each to try to penetrate the psychic wall the two x^0 telepaths were holding around Warren. Gabriel couldn't imagine two people could possibly maintain the concentration needed to shield Warren for that many days. However, every time he checked in, he got the same report. Warren was still dark.

Then, late Monday evening, not long after Gabriel arrived in Ushuaia, he caught a break. The monad from Thailand reported a sense of Warren feeling safe and protected in the completed part of his business complex outside of Ushuaia.

I'll take it from here. He sent the thought to the other twenty-two, then went hunting for Warren.

It was true. Warren could be found, sitting at the desk of his makeshift office in the business complex, feeling safe because he believed the woman telepath was protecting him. Only she wasn't. Yet the feeling of safety allowed Warren to ponder his decisions in a way he hadn't been able to for years.

Gabriel spent the wee hours of Tuesday morning laying on his back, listening in amazement to Warren's uncensored, undistracted thoughts. He learned more about the man than he had in the ten years he'd known him.

From the beginning, Warren had believed this time would come. His take on human nature was that a power struggle was inevitable. His number one goal had been to grow his communications empire to the point where he didn't need the Entelechy.

Warren was proud of developing a way to best a foe who outnumbered him and possessed a powerful weapon he lacked. He'd questioned of each of them until he was certain he understood the rules of telepathy better than they did, and then he used their blind spot against them, making his lack of telepathy an advantage. He let the monads believe they knew his mind, while ensuring they didn't.

Warren had picked favorites. Teacher's pets. Over the years, he'd rewarded four of the monads, enticing them to greater loyalty while encouraging them to be more cautious with their fellows. They were meant to form Warren's inner circle of protection when the battle came. Gabriel was excluded from it deliberately.

Who qualified? Jerry from Dallas was one, and the movie-star handsome Brett from LA was another. No surprise. The third was Cenk from Turkey, a barely willing monad kept cooperative by an ill child's need for expensive medicine. Warren thought because he kept the son alive, Cenk's gratitude would translate into loyalty. He'd misjudged. Warren didn't know it yet, but after the boy died, Cenk had no use for Warren.

The biggest surprise was the fourth monad. Chidi from Nigeria was ambitious and one of the group's strongest telepaths. The main reason he wasn't already part of the take-over was that his oldest daughter's wedding took place yesterday and he'd been participating in the lengthy traditional festivities in his hometown. Of all the remaining monads, Chidi was the one Gabriel had the least doubts about bringing in later.

Warren was proud of the relationship he'd cultivated with Chidi. He'd played to the man's ambitions, promising him leadership roles in exchange for complete loyalty.

I seriously underestimated how well he thought out his end game.

Warren was most proud of a final part of his strategy but before he could think about it, the woman telepath interrupted him. Because she was there with Warren, talking to Warren, Gabriel was able to connect to her. He flicked into her mind, thinking he might learn the cause of her lapse in protection. He expected to find Lola, but received the final surprise of an already astonishing evening.

Lola wasn't Lola tonight. She was a fierce Irish woman who hadn't a bit of psychic power to her, but who was pulling off the acting performance of her career. Gabriel could only guess at how the Zeitman family had managed this one, but he was glad they had.

✻✻✻✻✻✻

Lola was tired of hiding behind the drape. She was about to come out and look around, when she felt Maurice's presence in her head. He was coming down the hall, and he wanted her to stay put.

When he joined her, she whispered, "What gives? We can't hide behind this curtain forever. How do we get out of here?"

"Relax. Yuden's with us, in her traveler's body and in my head. She'll guide us. I'll hear her when she sees it's safe and I'll hear where to go. Warren thinks Yuden is back in the room sleeping, so there's no need to take chances by rushing. Nell is ready to buy us twelve hours pretending to be you."

Lola wondered how well Nell could keep up such a sustained charade, and what Warren would do if he suspected. Good thing it was the night shift; Warren slept part of the time Lola protected him. Only he wouldn't really be protected now, would he?

"Nell saw Zane before she came to your room." Maurice confirmed what Lola had already guessed. "Zane figured things out. She's moved him to my room and he's wearing my clothes. He'll try to get us even more time tomorrow."

Maurice felt his friends fear at the idea of her son's subterfuge. "He can do this Lola. The best thing we can do for everybody is be long gone once this is discovered."

Lola knew he was right. She felt Yuden's presence nearby.

"She says it's safe to go down the hall now," Maurice said. "Take the small hall on the left, go into the kitchen, and hide behind the work tables."

They went the forty-or-so feet, and waited for more directions. After a while, they made it out of a side door to the trash bins, then, after that, about fifty more feet to some bushes, via a path that avoided the new security camera.

Thirty feet to another building. Twenty crawling on the ground to avoid another camera. So it went, under Yuden's watchful eyes, until Warren's prized telepaths had disappeared into the warm summer night without a trace.

29. Run

Warren noticed Lola was unusually quiet, but he didn't think much of it other than to wonder how long he'd need to stay here, protected by the unwilling while he dangling himself as bait to his untrustworthy monads. If anything, Gabriel tended toward the impulsive. Warren had expected the man to show up and demand answers days ago. He wished he knew what was making Gabriel so cautious. Perhaps he'd somehow discovered Warren's plans to use the facility as a prison. That would certainly make for an interesting stand-off.

******

Nell opted to leave Lola and Maurice many small caches of supplies instead of a few large ones. It made gathering the provisions feel like an Easter egg hunt, with Yuden providing the clues. There were boots and a canteen of water there, a tool box stuffed with wigs and hats here, and a stun gun for extreme emergencies in yet another place.

As Lola pulled her hair up into a band, yanked a man's short grey wig over it, and donned a worker's baseball cap large enough to fit over it all, she realized how much thought was given to the supplies.

Rather than sneak out, the plan was to hide through the late-night dusk and then exit with the second shift of laborers leaving around midnight. Yuden guided them to a building from which they could blend into the crowd. Lola separated from Maurice, hunching her way into a group of men joking with each other. She stared straight ahead as she walked though the gate, and exhaled with relief as she peeled away from them. Maurice joined her a few minutes later, and as he did, a small black car turned the corner and approached. Maurice stayed quiet. Lola felt his calm as the front and back doors on the passenger side opened.

"Get in."

It was Cillian's unmistakable brogue. Lola leapt into the back seat and gave the man a hug. She wasn't sure if she'd ever been so happy to see someone she wasn't particularly fond of.

"You must be Violeta," Maurice said to the driver next to him. Lola looked in front and saw the woman she'd met a long time ago in a New York studio. At least it seemed long ago.

"Looking out for you is a full-time job," she said, and her voice carried the same cadence of efficiency it had back in New York. "But no time to catch up now. This is your rental car. There is a wad of pesos for you in the glove box. I'm dropping Cillian and me off and you, Lola, are driving as far out of town as you can. I don't want to know where." She gave Maurice a gentler look. "Yuden's presence is back in the compound now. She's exhausted, recovering in her bed in Warren's little prison."

"I know."

"Then you know once she's rested, she'll find you again and guide you, to help you stay hidden." Violeta turned back to Lola. "Gabriel and his monads are fighting with Warren. I don't know who's winning, or if I care. I'm still guarding against their mental intrusion, but it's easier now that they're preoccupied. Still, don't seek me out. I'll contact you when it is safe to do so."

"What about the rest of my family?" Lola asked.

"Don't check on them either. You and Maurice need to stay dark. Everyone is fine for now, and Warren has no idea what's been done."

Lola supposed that much was good, but she hated to think what would happen once he made the discovery.

"Lola." Violeta called her attention back. "Getting them to safety is the next thing we do. Your job now is to hide well."

******

Gabriel spent a few more hours waiting for Warren to focus on something interesting, but after his initial revelations, he moved on to his finances, then showered and watched a movie. Gabriel picked up Warren was trying to relax, going through a routine he practiced often. He went to sleep around 3 a.m.

Meanwhile, the Irish woman focused on looking and acting like Lola. She had a role to play, and wanted to play it well. She knew every minute she bought her friend would help.

Can't you think about where Lola is escaping to? No, you're on stage now, and you won't break character.

Gabriel fell asleep soon after Warren did, and tossed and turned his way through increasingly bizarre dreams.

******

When Xuha brought Maurice in the next morning, Warren knew something was off. The old man looked the same, dressed the same, and even moved the same. But he was different. Was his hair longer? Where were his glasses? That was it. He'd never seen the old man without his glasses.

He looked more closely. He'd also never seen the man turn up his shirt collar like that. Warren remembered reports about the boy, Lola's son. Surely his captive couldn't pull off a charade like this. Even if he could, why would he?

"Take off your shirt," he ordered Maurice, or whoever it was in his study. "Take it off now or I start in with shocks."

The old man sighed, and, without looking up, unbuttoned the top of his shirt. Warren could see the collar. Then the man pulled the shirt over his head.

Once his face was visible again, Warren was staring into the eyes of the devil. Not any random demon, but the exact same devil Warren had made famous by showing news clips over and over of the terrified protesters on the Zeitmans' front lawn.

The reddish face covered in dark undulating worms stared at Warren with yellow irises that appeared to be on fire.

"Eat shit," the devil said. "You don't have any telepaths to protect you. Now your own people will do worse things to you than anything you feared from us."

Warren watched as the face paled and the eyes became a serene, non-descript hazel. The young man stood tall and removed the nearly accurate white wig from his head.

"We forgot about Maurice's glasses. And my collar. But otherwise it was pretty damn close, wasn't it?"

"Very close," Warren agreed. "And you did this because, what? You were bored in your room?"

Then Warren got it. The devil had told him he was without telepaths now.

"Where is Maurice?"

"I have no idea."

"Where's you mother?"

"Gone, I hope."

"That's impossible."

Warren couldn't begin to imagine how two people, a woman and an old man, could have escaped from such a secure facility. But looking into the young impersonator's eyes, he knew they had.

Well, they couldn't have gotten far. The woman was in his chambers less than an hour ago. It was unfortunate he'd need to hunt them down, but he'd get all the assistance money could buy.

"Don't move," he said to the boy, as he reached for his phone.

✳✳✳✳✳✳

Teddie was in the second week of the semester, trying to focus on honors physics, survive calculus, and stay awake in the world's most boring U.S. Government class. She had no idea how to process the information that Nell was now some crazy man's prisoner while Teddie's mother and Uncle Maurice were fleeing to the tip of South America in a rental car. *What do you even say to news like that?*

Ariel had finally received another email, this one sent from their mother's friend on behalf of Nell. Instead of being relieved, Ariel was more agitated than usual after it arrived.

"What is *wrong* with you?" Teddie snapped at her sister while they waited for Vanida's lunch to heat up in the microwave." "For days you kept saying it all would be okay if this rescue worked, and now that it has, you're more upset."

"I'm not upset."

"Tell us what's going on." Vanida said it in a commanding tone people seldom used with Ariel. Ariel looked at Vanida, surprised. "Silence is brutal," Vanida added.

"Right. Okay. I've had this happen before, where I get two concurrent timelines going. That's happened for mom and dad. Two equally probable. One not awful, maybe even okay. The other really bad. The bad one jumped into high probabilities out of nowhere."

"What do you know about the bad one?" Vanida asked.

"In it, dad doesn't go. He has a chance to escape, but he won't, so mom and Maurice probably die and it's awful."

"And in the other one?"

"Dad does something he thinks is horrible. He's sick with guilt. But he's with mom and Maurice and his being there makes all the difference in ways I don't know. But whatever shitty thing he does, he *really* needs to go ahead and do it."

"Do you think dad kills Warren?" Teddie asked.

Ariel's eyes widened at the thought, but she said nothing.

"It doesn't matter," Vanida said. "We have to get word to your dad. Who can reach him?"

"Well, mom can't. Or Maurice, or Cillian, or that strange lady Violeta. The only people who can talk to dad are the people with him. Zane, Xuha, and Yuden. Nell, now, too."

"Yuden is our only option," Vanida said. "She reads lips. She understands pantomime well."

"You want me to try to meet her in the abode of light and get this across to her?" Teddie asked.

Vanida laughed. "How's your Bhutanese? She only reads lips in her native tongue. I speak some, thanks to my brother, and I've got more experience at this than you do. I'll go."

Vanida turned to Ariel. "What exactly is it I'm trying to say?"

Ariel considered. "Let her know my dad will have a chance to escape soon. He'll think he shouldn't, but that is wrong. Repeat, wrong. He has to go, no matter what it takes."

Vanida didn't look happy. "A simpler message would be better. How about 'Go, Alex. Ariel says run.'"

"My dad does okay with cryptic. That could work."

******

Later that afternoon, when all searches had turned up nothing, Warren went to see Alex, and learned the rest. The doors to the rooms opened from the outside, so he walked in, intending to question the man about his wife's whereabouts. He found the Irish woman talking to Alex.

"You're one of the people who was at the house back in Texas, aren't you?" he asked.

Then it started to make sense. The woman had somehow gotten into his complex. The only way she could be locked in this room with Alex was if she'd impersonated Lola last night. So the telepaths had left hours ago, probably at the start of Lola's shift.

He asked the next question before she could answer the first. "You're not a telepath, are you?"

Of course she wasn't. So if Lola left early last night, he'd been without protection for hours now. God, what all had he thought about? This was a security breach beyond belief.

"Come on," he barked at the two of them, motioning them to follow. "I'm getting the rest of you, and want you people to write down everything about how you pulled this off, and your best guesses about where the other two went."

As he walked to Yuden's room, he tapped the code into his phone to summon two guards.

"Come," he said as he pushed open her door. She was lying on the bed, napping again. She stretched awake and stood, as two flustered security guards sprinted down the hall toward him.

"I'm fine. I've got urgent business and need your help," he told them. "Get the two boys out of the other room, get these people pens and paper. Take them somewhere and watch them while they write."

"Yes sir. Where, sir?"

"I don't care. Anywhere. The courtyard. It's secure and maybe the fresh air will help them think."

******

Most of the group hadn't seen each other, or daylight, since they'd arrived. Mindful of the microphone on Xuha's collar, Alex hugged his son and Xuha in silence. He turned to Yuden, who was already scribbling away. She grinned and handed him a note. Alex read, "Your girl Ariel sees. You must run. Do not stop. Run. "

Shit. That didn't sound good.

Xuha, sensing the need for a distraction, began loudly discussing the assignment with Zane. "There's no reason not to tell him everything we know and be done with it," he insisted.

Nell was busy writing a narrative about her journey south and how she'd snuck in, desperate to help her friends. It elaborated on the two shape-shifters' clever impersonations, and finished with Lola and Maurice's lucky escape. It left out any mention of the many ways Violeta helped, as well as any mention of Yuden's talents. It concluded with Lola and Maurice fleeing on foot with no plan other than to stay hidden.

"Perfect," Alex said as he read it over.

One the guards took a phone call. "Come on, recess is over," he said, motioning them inside.

As he walked into the building, Alex noticed the door at the end of the long hall. He knew he could make it out the door before anyone could stop him. With the telepaths gone, Warren would have no need to retaliate against the others after he fled.

Then what? Hell, he had two telepaths who could find his thoughts and three traveling spirits who could see him, so somebody would surely help him get to safety. Then, instead of being a problem, he could rescue the others. He was tired of doing nothing. Ariel said to run. She'd hadn't said when, but this seemed as good a time as any.

He looked at the door and saw Xuha doing the same. That was even better. They could both run. No time for discussion.

He nodded. Xuha nodded back. The steps of the two guards and three other prisoners began to slow as if the air were becoming a thick syrup, while Xuha and Alex sprinted down the hall toward the doors, with Alex in the lead.

Please be unlocked.

Alex slowed a little and raised his arm for the impact. The door swung open wide, and he passed through, just missing another barely moving shape outside the door. He turned to see Xuha clip the side of Warren's body as both Xuha and Warren sprawled to the pavement.

"Stop!" One guard yelled, picking up speed as he moved toward them. Alex heard Ariel's words in his head. *Do not stop. Run.* He couldn't leave Xuha like this. Surely they'd punish him somehow. It wasn't right. *Do not stop. Run.* He had to trust Ariel. The guard was almost up to half-speed. Alex knew his window was closing.

Damnit, Xuha, find a way out of this.

He willed his body back to movement and time back to a viscous liquid as he headed down the path, hoping to make it out of the compound before exhaustion overtook him.

******

Zane, Nell, and Yuden all understood what was happening when Alex and Xuha took off down the hall, but only Yuden understood why. Vanida had traveled from Texas in her spirit body to convey Ariel's premonition to Yuden, and Yuden had passed it along to Alex. Run and keep running. And he had.

The guard who ran after Alex and Xuha helped an injured Warren onto his feet. The other guard locked the remaining three prisoners in a nearby office and stood watch outside.

This gave Nell, Zane, and Yuden a chance to share ideas. Thinking Zane's collar could have a mic, too, they augmented carefully chosen words with gestures and writing. Most of it had to do with the obvious question. *What about the rest of us?*

This has turned into a rescue yourself operation, Nell wrote.

Zane answered aloud. "Warren is pretty well alerted to what you and I can do. I don't think we can trick him again."

"Maurice told me Warren thinks I'm an old woman who sleeps all the time," Yuden said. Then she wrote, *Maybe sleepy old lady can find escape route?*

"I hear it's important for older people to get plenty of rest," Nell said. "You should nap often."

30. Not Really a Cruise

Warren was livid. The husband, arguably his best leverage, had managed to outrun his guards and was gone. The man had been so complacent, held in check by threats against the others, that he spent his time napping and watching old movies. Warren forgot how dangerous he could be.

He rubbed his hip. Damn, it had been bruised when that Mexican kid knocked him to the ground. He hoped he didn't have a hairline fracture. It sure felt like it.

He missed the people who looked after him; he even missed his wife. He'd been here ten days now, and couldn't keep up the charade of a business trip much longer. When the hell was Gabriel going to show up?

Well, at least he'd done one smart thing today. Getting the Ushuaia police to arrest the kid for trespassing and assault had been brilliant. He'd almost forgotten to remove the kid's collar, but caught it at the last minute.

"I'm going to tell them everything you've done," the boy said as the police drove up, defiance blazing in his eyes.

"Not unless you prefer the loony bin to jail," Warren had retorted. "You think the local police will believe a respected investor in their community kidnapped people and has been holding them as prisoners? Take your chances if you like, son, but psychiatric care facilities in this part of the world aren't up to U.S. standards, if you know what I mean."

The boy had kept his head down and said little as they took him away, only saying something in Spanish to the police, probably about how it had been an accident.

"That's not what Mr. Moore told us," the policeman replied in clear English, loud enough for Warren to hear. Warren was pleased by the courtesy.

No matter how much his hip hurt and how impatient he was for Gabriel, he felt better knowing he didn't have to worry about this kid's escape. Better to think about what he had left.

The old woman was a mystery. Rumor was she walked through walls, which would have been something to see, but she hadn't left her room once. The son was useful leverage. Warren was sure neither parent would abandon him here, and that would matter eventually. Of course, the boy and the Irish woman had their own talents, but Warren wouldn't be duped by them again. Maybe there was some way the imposters could help him? Hmm. He'd have to think about that one.

Meanwhile, he had the police chasing after the husband, accused as an accessory in the attack. He was a lone man on foot, an outsider who spoke Spanish poorly and lacked money or resources. Warren expected to hear the man had been picked up any minute now. The security firm overseeing escape routes for the two telepaths ought to get back to him soon as well. There were, after all, not that many ways to get out of Tierra del Fuego.

He rubbed his hip again. The medicine must be kicking in. It was starting to feel better.

******

Alex had never had a reason to see how long he could alter time. His need for speed was always in short bursts. Get the basketball down the court. Pull Lola out of a raging river. Tackle a man trying to blow up a tank of propane. That kind of thing.

Now he was running as hard as he could, trying to sustain the sense of urgency on which his time-altering seemed to depend. As he approached the gate, he was winded. He was pretty sure if he passed out all bets were off.

Pace yourself. Slow down, get out to a road, get on a side street, then stop. As he jogged through the gate, he noticed heads turning his way with bewildered expressions. The entry road was longer than he expected, and the street it opened onto was more barren than he hoped.

Jog slower. Keep moving. Just a little further. He was gaining on the vehicle ahead of him, but not by much, and it didn't look like it was going fast. As he approached the car on the passenger side, the back door flung open, blocking his path. He bumped into it hard, but before he could fall, a pair of hands grabbed him and pulled him inside.

He looked up expecting to see one of Warren's minions, or, worse yet, Warren smirking down at him. Instead, he looked into Cillian's concerned expression.

"*You* just pulled me into a moving vehicle?"

"Good thing my hearing and my instincts are intact. You're welcome."

Alex looked to the front seat where a tall, dark-haired woman was driving. Was this the lady from Reel News?

"I'm confused."

"I know you are," she replied. "Your wife asked me to look after you, so I've been in and out of your head since it occurred to you to pull that little stunt. That has got to be the most exciting run I have ever taken in my life."

She turned to the back seat long enough for him to see her grin. "I'd love to do it again some time when I don't have to worry about intercepting you." Then she added, "You are so lucky Cillian and I were out running errands and could get to you. What *was* your plan?"

Alex didn't know how to answer that. All he knew was the physical effort was catching up with him and he needed to get his breathing back under control.

"I didn't have one. Get away. Find help."

"Well, you managed both." Cillian stuck out his hand to congratulate him.

"Do *you* have a plan for me?"

"I'm working on one," she said. "I asked your wife to sever contact, but two sets of fugitives are twice as bad as one. I need to get you three together and out of here. Then we worry about the others."

"But I'd like to help with the others."

"I figured you would," Cillian said. "Look, I don't know a better way to tell you this. Your wife needs to stay alive. If you're not with her, she probably dies. You have to go with her, Alex."

"Does Ariel agree with you?" It was the only meaningful question Alex could think of.

"She doesn't see the things I do, but yeah, she agrees."

Alex tried to let that soak in. "When do I leave?" he asked.

"We're taking you to Lola now."

******

Xuha had trouble remembering all the bizarre events since he arrived at the Zeitman home in mid-December. However, one thing stuck in his mind with clarity. It was Ariel sitting cross-legged on the floor of the living room, turning her attention to him as she made her predictions.

"I don't think you die, Xuha, but there are some scenarios in which they mess up your life. Like, life-in-prison bad," she'd said.

Xuha hadn't told her how he'd rather she predict death for him than that kind of fate. Rather, he resolved to make sure he stayed on the right side of the law, no matter what else happened.

Yet, here he was, in jail. He knew nothing about how to survive such an ordeal, even in the U.S., and he knew less about prisons and the law in Argentina. He tried think of his advantages.

He did speak Spanish, even if he had a hard time understanding the heavy accents here. Being a guy his size meant he wasn't threatening. He knew how to keep his head down, and use humor to avoid a fight. He also knew how to fight, probably better than those around him, but that might be the option getting him into trouble in Ariel's vision. He had to avoid fighting.

He had friends who would try to help him, once they were able, and they would be able eventually. He was realistic enough to understand Warren was right: claims about being a kidnapping victim would do him little good.

His best bet was to continue to claim to be a lost tourist who'd gone exploring where he shouldn't have, and who was sorry to have done so. The harm to Mr. Moore had been unintentional. Why in the world would he pick a fight with Warren Moore?

It was a good story and his best move. It would work as long as nobody involved with law enforcement saw him having to defend himself.

******

When Gabriel woke four hours later, he was cranky. He needed his eight hours of sleep. This was supposed to be his big day, the moment he marched in and confronted his boss in ways that would change their relationship forever. But now he had to rethink the plan. Had Warren discovered the subterfuge of his captives? If he had, what would Gabriel be walking into?

Gabriel showered, fighting to clear his mind. He found Warren's thoughts as the man was telling police he'd been attacked by a tourist as he walked into his own building. Warren was in pain, because the Latino in front of him had knocked him to the ground. However, Gabriel could tell most of Warren's story was being made up as he spoke, in hopes the police would remove the young man who was no longer useful to him. *No longer useful?* Yes, now that the telepaths were gone, the boy and his skills were only a liability.

As Warren settled into the couch in his office, he was quite peeved the lady telepath and her teacher had escaped. To make matters worse, the husband had outrun his guards and gotten away, too. As Gabriel listened, Warren concentrated on who he had left.

The old Chinese woman. The son, still useful leverage. The Irish woman. Warren heard a soft knock on his door.

"Sir? The police have sent over a detail. They'd like to leave two men here for the day to make sure this kid isn't part of some larger group. Should I tell them no?"

"Don't do that. We value our relationship with the city police and don't want them to think we're ungrateful. Invite them in, and make sure you keep our remaining three guests out of sight."

"Yes sir."

"Oh, and we've lost our cook. Scrounge up lunch for us. No wait. Order in something nice. Call it 'police appreciation day.' I want them to be glad they look out for us."

The guard nodded. He understood.

Back in his hotel room, Gabriel sighed. He understood too. This was not going to be the day to march into Warren's office and inform him his special employees were banding together to take over his company and he'd be well served to let them do it.

Maybe tomorrow.

******

Lola hadn't expected to see Alex for days. He had important work to do to get the others to safety, and she had important work to do to remain hidden.

She'd given her job a lot of thought and decided they should act like they weren't hiding. Maurice agreed. Using hats and wigs from Nell, they'd gone out to dinner at one of the busiest tourist places. Then she, a brunette with her dark-haired father, got a cash room at a popular budget hotel. She booked them on an all-day bus tour the next day, with every intention of spending the wad of pesos from Violeta while behaving like every other Anglo in town.

Eventually, either Yuden or Violeta would to see a way to get them into Chile or on a flight out of South America. Until then, she and her dad would stay concealed in plain sight.

She was on the tour bus, listening to the English-speaking guide describe how Ushuaia had become a center for electronics manufacturing in the 1990s, when Violeta made a clumsy attempt to knock on the door to her mind. Violeta's greeting startled Lola. *What do you want?*

Sorry to interrupt your sightseeing. I have someone in my car I thought you'd want to see. It wasn't as clear as the words Lola substituted, but she got the tone and message.

Sorry to be rude. Who is it?

Get off at the next stop and find out.

Lola wasn't pleased, but she did as she was asked, dragging a baffled Maurice with her. Once she found Violeta, she was more confused to see Alex with her.

"What are *you* doing here?"

"Wonderful to see you safe and sound, too," he replied.

"Alex, you're not supposed to be here. I'm dong a great job of hiding, You're supposed to be rescuing others."

"I got reassigned."

"By who?"

"Your daughter Ariel."

Lola replied in the sweetest tone she could manage. "Why is Ariel messing with our plan?"

"Because she believes if she doesn't, you will die, and in spite of your unfriendly greeting, everyone, even Cillian, agrees that would be a bad thing."

"I don't need the sarcasm. And I don't need you to protect me."

"I don't think you do either. But Ariel does."

Violeta interrupted. "Do this later, you two. Get in the car."

"We're going to your place? Isn't that a bad idea?" As Maurice climbed into the car, he started to engage as well. "I'm surprised Warren hasn't been watching where you live. Are you sure he hasn't been?"

"First, we're not going to my place. Second, Warren doesn't know I'm involved. Much as it annoys me, I apparently didn't make it onto his radar screen. Even Gabriel thinks I've checked out from this mess due to job stress. Now hurry. We have to go shop for clothes."

Violeta stopped at a discount place along the docks and bought them all cheap duffel bags. Then she had them pick out a variety of underwear, socks, clothes, and jackets to stuff into the luggage.

"It will look suspicious if your bags aren't full. Get warm stuff," she told them.

Lola sought more information and found Violeta was keeping her and Maurice at a mental distance.

"Don't you think you should tell us what's going on?" Lola asked as she picked several pairs of ladies' wool socks out of a bin.

"Not now. I've got less than an hour to get you to the pier, and you people have an incredible desire to discuss everything. You have no idea how hard it was to get these last-minute tickets without having your name show up on a roster. I will not have you miss the boat."

"We're going on a boat?" Alex asked, emerging from the men's shoe aisle with a pair of work boots.

"Yes. Those boots will do nicely for you."

"No. I don't like boats," Alex said.

Violeta turned to Lola. "See what I mean. Let's pay for this and get you packed."

She looked at her watch for the tenth time.

"Your cruise boards in forty-five minutes. We've got to go."

"Oh, it's okay, Alex. It will be a big boat. We're going on a cruise."

Lola brightened up, then she remembered. Ariel's visions.

"Wait. We can't. That's the one thing we absolutely are not supposed to do."

"Don't be unreasonable," Violeta said. "It cost a fortune and took every favor my family could pull to make this happen for you. And, it's not really a cruise, it's more of an expedition. It's the only way to get you out of Ushuaia under Warren's watch, so don't argue."

"Where do ships go from here?" Maurice asked, but he remembered the answer before he finished the question.

Violeta waited.

"I've always wanted to go there," he said.

"Most people have. I hear the penguins are amazing."

"Hold on," Alex said. "Doesn't this ship basically go in a circle and come back here? I don't see how this helps us."

"We don't intend for you to return with the ship. Don't worry, we don't intend for you to stay in Antarctica either. We're working on a third alternative. I'll send Lola and Maurice information once we have it. Meanwhile, you stay safe."

Lola and Maurice were fine with that plan, but Alex was not.

Ariel was positive danger awaited them aboard ship. Even if she hadn't thought so, he wasn't fond of boats, he disliked cruises, and he definitely had no desire to go on anything called an expedition.

The Third Law of Thermodynamics

It Doesn't Get That Cold,
Even in Antarctica

31. What Will You Be?

"Damn them. What is it about parents? They never listen."

Ariel was pacing around the kitchen when Teddie came into the room to see what was the matter.

"What's wrong now?"

Ariel responded by walking over to the refrigerator and kicking it has hard as she could. "Everything in this house gives me information about them. I can't get it to quit."

"Isn't that good?" her sister asked.

"Not when they do stupid things. Things they were specifically told not to do. Things they *promised* they wouldn't do."

She put her head in her hands, and the bright orange strands of hair fell over her fingers as she shook her head back and forth. Teddie didn't think she'd ever seen her sister so distraught.

"I thought everything was going to be okay once Vanida got Yuden to understand about how dad had to escape."

"She succeeded alright. Dad must have managed it and kept running just like I said."

"So why aren't things better?"

"Because of the reckless thing he and mom must have decided on once they were together. Over the last few hours I don't see a single future in which they are *not* on a cruise ship."

"Oh dear." Now Teddie understood. "Yes, you were fairly clear about that, weren't you? Do you know where they're going?"

"Antarctica."

"Oh, Mom's always wanted to go there. She loves penguins."

Ariel didn't even look up.

******

The ship was a small one, with less than a hundred passengers. It was originally built for research, so it was less luxurious and more affordable than many. Lola realized if she'd ever indulged in such an extravagant trip, this was the boat she'd have picked.

She would, however, have picked a different cabin. The three of them were in a closet of a room on the lowest deck, with one small porthole and bunk beds. Violeta said a boat left daily during the January high season. Today's ship had last-minute space and was staffed by Ushuaia residents, allowing Violeta's mother to make a booking for friends lacking the usual paperwork.

Lola understood she was fleeing for her safety, so she stayed in the cabin as the boat made its gala exit from the pier. However, as soon as the shore receded, she couldn't sit still any longer.

"Where do you think you're going?" Alex asked as she reached for her shoes.

"Up top for a few minutes. I need some air. And yes, I want to hear the introduction. Alex, look at the program. They've got experts to talk about wildlife, ice floes, even weather at the South Pole. There's no reason we can't enjoy this."

"Maybe somebody will try to push you overboard. Had you thought of that? Am I supposed to jump in the water to save you?"

Maurice intervened. "Knowing your future is a two-edged sword, you two. Maybe Lola's potential demise comes from our being too cautious?" Before either of his friends could interrupt, Maurice raised the palm of his hand to stop them both. "We'd do best to act like what we're supposed to be. Tourists. Not those weird people in cabin 602 who never talk to anyone."

"I'm not saying we have to be surly. Just sensible."

"And I'm saying we're not without resources," Maurice replied. "We've eighty-five other passengers and thirty crew members, and I intend to meet every one of them. Lola should too. If anyone on this boat besides a well-trained telepath is harboring ill-will toward us, she and I will know about it."

"All right." Alex conceded the point. "You two need to mingle. Wait while I get shoes on. I'll go with you."

He ignored Lola's look of gratitude.

"Can't be a bodyguard if I stay in the cabin. Maybe I can spot some whales while you two work."

******

Yuden was discouraged. She'd been over every tiny piece of Warren Moore's construction site and knew the routines better than the workers did. Yet, they were three people locked in a room. The cleverest change in appearance wouldn't gain them anything and all the traveling in the world couldn't open the door.

Zane and Nell napped and visited while Yuden explored. She found out Warren had assigned his guards to other duties. Of course. Keeping the three prisoners in one room was easiest, so he hadn't bothered to move one of them. They were of no use to him, other than as bait to call the others back.

A guard appeared at the door to give them empanadas at lunch and a second round of cold ones for dinner. At least Warren recognized the bait had to be kept alive.

******

As Lola and Alex sat on the deck enjoying their little plastic glasses of champagne, Maurice moved to the front of the ship. He watched the late afternoon sun follow its low-angle path to the southwest as the bow turned to navigate into the famous Beagle Channel, named for scientist Charles Darwin's ship of nearly two-hundred years ago.

Sometime tomorrow, they'd leave the safety of South America behind, and move into the open sea to make their way across the Drake Passage. Their first destination was a small collection of islands scattered along the coast of Antarctica.

******

The young people had insisted Yuden take one of the two beds for the night. They wanted her to rest, but she planned to use the comfort to make longer trips that could provide them with more information. It was easy to find someone you loved, so she sought Maurice.

She expected to find him in hiding, perhaps camping in some abandoned shack in the countryside. However, Maurice was further away than she thought, and harder to find. She was traveling over the sea, waves crashing below her as she moved. Such things no longer frightened her, but she was puzzled. Maurice would never abandon them. What was he doing on a ship, moving farther away with each passing minute?

******

Late that evening, Maurice was back out on deck, staring out to sea as he searched for the mind of the woman he loved. In the late-night twilight, he found her and smiled when he realized she was thinking of him. Better than thinking. She was seeking him, moving over the ocean and nearing the ship, using his familiar presence as a navigating beacon. She was now hovering off to his right, where the planet Venus sparkled in the dusky sky.

He did what anyone would have done. He waved. He felt her surprise, then her acknowledgment.

Hi Maurice. That wave means you can hear me.

Maurice gave the air an exaggerated pucker of a kiss. Yuden responded with a girl's giggle.

Lover boy. When you get tired of staring at the ocean, would you check in on my captors and see if you can come up with an idea for an escape? We're out of inspiration.

He nodded. He felt her curiosity about what he was doing on a cruise ship, and tried to think of a way to pantomime an explanation. If only she could read his mind too.

He settled for a shrug, a point toward the cabin in which Lola and Alex were sleeping, another shrug with a helpless expression on his face, and then a giant air hug. He hoped she could make some sense out of it.

******

Of all the possible rewards for helping the U.S. woman, the chance to fall in love never made Violeta's list. The unexpected object of her affections was the furthest thing possible from the man of her dreams. Yes, the good-looking Irishman was clever and well meaning, but his new blindness challenged him physically and emotionally. She wasn't equipped to deal with either, and couldn't imagine they had a future together.

Yet here they were, on one of the beds in Cillian and Nell's efficiency suite, enjoying the first few moments after sex. Once again, it had been so wonderful words weren't needed. Lying on their sides facing each other, he was stroking her shoulder and arm, feeling the strength of her triceps.

"I like your arms."

They'd been stronger once, but she'd kept them up pretty well. The first few years after her injury, it had taken a lot of effort to relearn her body and adjust her attitude. She'd also had a newly formed hole in her heart where her father's love had been, so it had been a difficult time. Violeta wondered what tipped the scales toward her healing.

She hated to admit it, but some of it was Gabriel. Early on, when there was hope of winning his affection, he gave her something to work toward. Then Violeta realized it. She was serving the same purpose for Cillian. He cared for her, he wanted to impress her. His infatuation with her was prodding him to find ways to handle his disability and improve his mindset.

Pay it forward. She'd always loved the concept.

"Describe your skin to me," he said.

"It's, I don't know, skin. Browner than yours, I guess."

He laughed. "The entire world has skin browner than mine." He moved his hands to her face. "You feel pretty."

She studied his face. It looked different when it was this relaxed. Worry lines were already etched deep into it, but they softened when he smiled. She touched his face, his lips, and he kissed her fingers. She caught the flash of emotion before he spoke.

"We both know this can't last," he whispered. "But for now, let's pretend like it can."

She turned away from him, and then pushed her backside up tight against his chest and abdomen, pulling his arms around her. Her answer was in the way she snuggled into the curve of his body, and then lay enjoying the closeness while he held her.

******

As far as Gabriel could tell, Warren was hiding in his private building complex, guarded by hired men while he played endless word games and kept three hostages locked in a room. Gabriel guessed Warren's underlings in the U.S. thought issues in Argentina were taking longer than expected. Warren had made no effort to communicate with anyone in the Entelechy.

The monads didn't ignore Warren back. Wednesday morning, Gabriel sent Warren an email saying he was in Ushuaia to discuss important matters with his boss. When could he come over to the complex to talk? Then Gabriel had his monads resume their surveillance, hoping one of the twenty-two would grab on to a useful bit as Warren read the email. By the next morning, no one had heard anything helpful, and Gabriel had received no response. He guessed Warren never read his note. Fine. The man had a cell phone. He'd call him and set up an appointment.

Gabriel's phone was in his hand when he felt the sharp yelp of success from none other than his friend Rafael. The Filipino strategist was present when Warren made a crucial phone call. Now he knew something vital. Gabriel got this much before the phone rang in his hand.

"He designed the damn thing as a prison," Rafael said without preamble. "For us. He never wanted a fortress he could hide in. That was the story he told himself, over and over, so we'd hear it and make sense out of him building something so strange."

"A fortress makes more sense," Gabriel said. "What kind of man seeks out and trains others, then plans to lock them up?"

"A really paranoid one. Warren thinks people are inherently untrustworthy. He was sure the time would come when he couldn't control us. He figured you'd be the one to lead the troublemakers."

"I don't know whether to be flattered or insulted."

"Be both. His plan was to separate out us renegades, once we showed our true colors, and lure us down there for a meeting. He'd promise things like safety for our families if we'd join a 'special think tank' that would require our ongoing presence for an indefinite amount of time."

"He has to have known that wouldn't have worked forever."

"He did. He was going to have succession plans in place for non-telepaths to run our companies. While he held us captive, he'd sow the seeds of a worldwide fear of psychic gifts. He's been planning to run that scare campaign all along. Just not so soon."

"He always meant to use our gifts against us? That shithead. What was his end game?"

"He'd let us back out into the world, one by one, once he had enough to hold over us," Rafael said. "Any former monad who caused no trouble would be left alone as long as he sought employment in another field."

Gabriel got the picture. "Leaving Warren with a global media empire well beyond anything he could have built without us."

"Exactly. He did hope to end up with a few loyal monads to protect him. Then, he looked forward to remaking the world in his own scared and angry image, without our interference."

Gabriel finished his friend's thought. "So his well-thought-out timeline assumed it would be years before we tried to oust him. It got accelerated when he found x^0."

"Looks like it. He could have succeeded, too, if this worldwide organization of love and peace hadn't come along."

Neither man said anything for a full minute. They didn't have to. Their emotions were loud and clear. *What the hell is wrong with this guy? We have got to stop this.*

"We do. This is important, Gabriel. The last thing I got is he still plans to go through with this. He saw your email. He knows you're in town and he's happy you want to see him. He's waiting on something before he invites you over for a chat with the intent of seeing you don't leave."

"He's probably trying to get those two telepaths back first," Gabriel said. "Does he know I'm coming with an ultimatum for him?"

"He suspects you intend to threaten him and to try to replace him. Why else would you come all the way down here?"

Gabriel had to laugh. "Isn't it kind of a waste, blowing the big surprise of a prison on just me?"

"He wishes you'd brought more monads along, but he thinks he can hide that he's holding you against your will and get more of us there, as long as he has people to shroud your mind and his."

Gabriel sat in the edge of his hotel bed. This certainly changed his strategy. "I guess I'm not going to be the lone monad who shows up at Warren's place to confront him."

"Agreed. We need to find another way."

"I could ask him to meet me at my hotel. But why would he?"

"Don't. That request tips your hand. So far he has no idea you know his plans. Why not stay quiet while we learn more?"

"Wise as always."

✳✳✳✳✳✳

It looked like Alex spent a lot of time napping while he was Warren's prisoner, but he hadn't. Much of that time he'd been learning a new skill. He thought if he could slow down his own experience of time, so he had ten seconds while those around him had only one, then he ought to be able to do it the other way. It could be helpful to experience one second while everyone else endured ten. He hadn't expected his efforts to pay off so soon.

Alex had read how various latitudes had different reputations in the South Pacific. The equator was known for its absolute calm, while the windy forty-degree south latitude was referred to as the roaring forties. The even stronger gales to the south were called the furious fifties and those who sailed through the Drake Passage went through them. In fact, they spent two long days making their way through them.

Well, Alex would not. Once the presentation at breakfast keyed him into what was about to happen, he pulled Lola aside.

"You've picked up no ill will toward you, so it looks like you and Maurice will be safe while we're at sea. I'm going to go lay down for a while. I'll be up sometime Saturday morning."

She gave Alex a baffled look but said nothing.

"When you see me over the next two days, I'll barely be breathing. I'll have almost no pulse, and I'll seldom move. Please don't wake me unless it is an emergency, and please don't call the ship's doctor because you think I'm dead."

"Okay? What *will* you be?"

"Napping. For three or four hours, I hope."

"Are you serious?"

"Look, I've got no choice about cruising through this Drake Passage, but I'm the one person aboard ship who doesn't have to spend forty hours doing it." He gave her a peck of a kiss, as though he were leaving to run an errand.

✳✳✳✳✳✳

The security firm assisting Warren contacted him with their conclusions. They were sure his two missing guests were in the area and must have convinced or paid someone local to hide them. Although the firm didn't know how, they believed the man who'd run off on Tuesday must have linked up with the first two.

Warren listened to their deductions. He knew Lola and Maurice had no money on them, but they were desperate, and surely mind-reading was an advantage in petty theft, or in finding a local chump to care for them. As to Lola linking up with her fleeing husband; one would think any telepathic wife could manage that.

The firm wanted to offer a reward for information. Warren knew he needed to move forward with Gabriel soon, but first he needed these two telepaths back to weave their magic protection around his brain.

"This town isn't that big. Someone out there knows something," the security professional insisted. "We just need to give them an incentive to come forward."

"Do it. Make it enough money to get it done fast."

32. Not Particularly Nice

Warren didn't find his missing telepaths until Friday morning. Funny, the security firm had been dead wrong, and yet completely right.

Wrong. The two telepaths had left Tierra del Fuego and done it without being detected. Right. It was a small town and people did know things. For enough money, someone would talk.

"They're really on one of those cruise ships?" Warren laughed when he heard it. "That's insane. The ship just comes back here. Don't these people know you can't hide in Antarctica, even in the summer? Hell, I'd be inclined to let them die there except I still need their assistance."

"Our sources think they plan to escape when they return to Ushuaia, and you're not expecting it. There's some small chance they try to break away during the cruise and await rescue, but we can't imagine who'd be reckless enough to go get them. But, you never know, so we have a cruise employee keeping an eye on them. He'll alert us immediately if they disappear from the ship. The rest of our information is in the email."

"Thanks," Warren said. "You people continue to impress."

He opened the email and gave a surprised whistled as he read.

Violeta? That damn woman who worked for Gabriel? She'd been helping these other telepaths? Well, she was from this area. But how did she get involved with x^0?

Wait, hadn't she resigned around the holidays? Job stress? Yes, Gabriel said she'd gone home to recuperate. He'd have paid more attention, but there had been so much else going on.

It started to make sense. He *had* insisted the local police chief fire her mother along with several other busybodies who were spreading rumors. So, pissed off mom, pissed off daughter. Now they were together looking for ways to harm Warren Moore.

Sheesh, a man could make enemies without trying. But how had the angry mother-daughter team become involved with his American captives? Had word gone out seeking people who disliked Warren Moore? For all he knew, there was an entire hate group out to get him.

Well, the important thing was Lola and Maurice had been located. Much as he could have used them now, it made sense to collect them on their return. He'd find another way to make things work with Gabriel.

This early in the game, he hadn't wanted to use the few monads whose loyalty he'd cultivated, but one had to be flexible. They could provide him with mental protection so he could get the treacherous Gabriel over here and get this shitshow started.

✶✶✶✶✶✶

It had been the hardest few weeks of Olumiji's life. As a telepath with a leadership role in x^0, he did what the rules required. He drew thousands of people away from the support they were used to receiving and giving each other. Asking them to forsake two of their own was the most difficult; it went against the sense of loyalty at Olumiji's core. The fact that both were his friends made matters worse.

Yet in the end, he failed. He thought he had the self-discipline to do what was required, but after the holidays his brain began checking on Lola and Maurice with a will of its own.

He realized x^0 had investigated the minutiae of how telepathy worked, but spent little time looking into how it didn't. How did a telepath cease an activity that was second nature? Perhaps it wasn't possible.

At least, he found it more impossible each day. After a week, he was flitting into the minds of all of Lola's family, and then he was checking in on the rest of the unfortunate group. After that, he looked in on others who were involved in all sides of this mess.

Stealth was another area x^0 had spent little time analyzing. They'd never cared about how well telepaths could hide from each other. Were traces left behind? Could those in Warren Moore's organization tell what he was doing? How about others in x^0?

The last question was answered, somewhat, when he found himself mind-to-mind with another x^0 telepath who was cheating on the edict, too. Lola's close friend Somadina was a fellow Nigerian who'd inadvertently intertwined her mind with Lola's years ago. The two women had forged a deep friendship.

Now, in spite of the rules, Somadina was making mental contact with an Argentinian woman named Violeta, who was heavily involved in Lola's situation. Olumiji had found Violeta, too, and was about to give her mind a brief touch when he encountered the exiting Somadina.

They began exchanging embarrassed explanations, then stopped. There was no need to explain. They both understood.

Let's talk to this Violeta together. It was Somadina's suggestion. *She's struggling to put together a plan to save Lola. Let's tell her we have access to resources she doesn't. Perhaps we can help, as it appears we've been unsuccessful at not helping.*

******

Even as she secured the cruise tickets, Violeta knew how absurd her plan would seem. She'd grown up in a town where much of the revenue came from tourists, and much of the tourism came from those taking a once-in-a-lifetime trip to the most remote spot on the planet. She'd never felt the need to plunk down the cash to go, but she'd heard enough stories to feel like she'd made the trip more than once.

She knew the voyages had the feel of a polar adventure with almost none of the risk. Passengers were kept together, because having tourists wander off and fall into an ice crevice was bad for business. The first step of separating her charges from their shipmates would not be easy.

Then, finding a place for them to hide and await rescue presented more problems. Camping was not a good option, hotels didn't exist, and the few permanent buildings were controlled research areas that didn't accept random guests. Worse, no cruise ship could predict ahead of time the weather and ice conditions, meaning every cruise's itinerary was determined on the fly.

It appeared there was no realistic option other than to return from whence they came. So, if Warren was able to find out where his three escapees were, he'd simply wait for them to come back. She knew it was likely he'd find a way to get that information.

Obviously, the escapees had to go somewhere else.

Violeta sat at the table in the small efficiency, working out the details of her rescue plan while Cillian gave her a neck massage. She knew cruising to Antarctica and back was more involved than the uninitiated realized. The Delgado family had friends and relatives who'd worked in the cruise industry. Some worked in it now. Some had settled to the south. Some could be trusted to help.

Better than that, two old friends of Lola's made themselves known this morning, just when she thought there were no solutions to a few remaining pieces of the problem. As they made her aware of their resources, the last of the irregular little jigsaw shapes clicked into place.

Today, she would let Lola, Alex, and Maurice be, as they finished crossing the Drake Passage. It was 600 miles of the roughest stretch of water in the world. Everyone struggled with this part. Tomorrow, they'd hit calmer seas as they sailed into the South Shetlands, a dozen mostly ice-covered islands about a hundred miles off the white continent where remarkably consistent summer temperatures hovered right around freezing. They'd spend the day cruising around the beautiful flooded caldera of Deception Island, gasping in wonder at penguin rookeries and beaches covered by seals. That was when Violeta would reach out to Lola with instructions for the ensuing deception.

I don't know if the Entelechy is looking for you or if Warren has other telepaths seeking you out. So, hear me quickly. Don't ask questions. Don't tell your Maurice and Alex until you have to.

Yes, that is how she would begin it. Then she would tell Lola this.

Sunday, tomorrow, your ship will stop at King George Island in a permanent town. It has a shop and a post office and it will be the last time you're allowed to explore on your own. A man will

approach you and offer proof of his trustworthiness. Accept his
hospitality without fear and await information.

Would Lola trust her? Would Lola's companions go along as they would need to?

Violeta felt Cillian's hands move from her neck down to her shoulder blades.

"You're tense," he said. He used knuckles to dig in deeper around the bones. "These are your wings. They're getting tired."

"I don't have wings."

"Of course you do. You're an angel."

"It's sweet you think so, but I don't believe in angels."

"Doesn't matter. This isn't religious or spiritual. An angel is a creature that helps others. They do it because it needs doing and they're available."

"I don't think I'm particularly nice."

"You're not. You're a fighter. Certainly not mean, but not particularly nice. However, from where I sit, you make a hell of a good angel."

She was a little embarrassed by his praise and said nothing. His hands stopped their gentle kneading.

"Thanks. That felt good."

"Glad you liked it."

Then it occurred to her Cillian might have another motivation for his massage. "Did *you* like it?"

"Of course," he said. "I like touching you. You know that."

"That's not what I meant. You touch me sometimes to get data to feed into that psychic prediction machine living inside your brain."

Cillian gave an embarrassed smile. "Maybe sometimes."

"Lying to your telepathic girlfriend is a waste of time,"

"Oh, so now you're my girlfriend?"

"Don't change the subject. You know what I'm asking. Is what I'm planning going to work?"

"You know there's no absolute answer. And the psychic prediction machine in my head only sees possible futures beyond your lifetime."

"Yes, and I also know Lola and Ariel living out their natural lives makes your future possibilities more positive. So, you do have a sense of whether either of them dies prematurely, and an interest in seeing they don't."

He took her hand and kissed the tips of each of her fingers.

"You know so much more about me than you should. And yet, that seems to cause no problems. You make me happy. Giving you a massage makes me happy. Everything you are planning today makes me happy. How's that for an answer?"

"It will do. Promise me you'll let me know if something I'm considering upsets you instead?"

"You'll be the first to know."

✳✳✳✳✳✳

Gabriel wasn't sure who'd win a staring contest between him and Warren, but there was a good chance it would be Warren. The man was tough.

It was Friday already. Gabriel had wasted five days in this godforsaken town and Warren had still made no effort to contact him, even with a business-related email. It was the longest the two men had gone without communicating since they'd first met.

What Gabriel originally wanted with Warren was one private conversation in which he could use his powers to be menacing enough to convince the man that cooperating with the Entelechy was his best move. Warren wasn't going to give him that opportunity anywhere except at his own compound. Gabriel had known for two days now that if he showed up at Warren's door and made his threats, he'd end up a prisoner used as bait to draw in others.

Warren could have invited him over already, or even abducted him by now, but Gabriel thought he knew why the man hadn't done so. He was stalling, hoping to have his two coerced telepaths back to provide mental protection before he and Gabriel met. Gabriel wasn't surprised when he felt a reaching-out from Johann, the Swiss monad keeping watch.

Gabriel's phone rang as Johann opted for the ease of speech.

"Jerry and Chidi are on their way to Ushuaia. Warren didn't want to spill the beans to them yet about our suspected revolt, but with you in Ushuaia and his captives missing, he's moved on. They've both chosen to stick with Warren and are coming to shelter his mind until he gets the lady and old man back in his clutches. He knows they'll be more effective if they're closer."

"Got it. He'll probably invite me over soon, then. If I decline, he'll send someone to collect me."

It looked like he needed to blink first. Gabriel booked a seat on the next flight out of town. There was no way he was going to play Warren's game.

✴✴✴✴✴✴

Maurice thought about Yuden a lot; he had for the past year. Some days he made fun of himself, asking what kind of foolish old man fell for a lady who lived on the other side of the world. Actually, what kind of foolish old man fell for a lady at all?

As he lay in his small bed Friday night, enduring the never-ending rise and plunge of the ship, he'd have been happy to enjoy the combination of memories and daydreams that served as a nepenthe for most of humanity. But he couldn't. Every time he thought of Yuden, he saw her imprisoned while he was free. Well, maybe free was too strong a word; he *was* trapped on a heaving boat.

Lola had cautioned him about using his psychic abilities. No one knew what Warren's former telepaths were up to, but they probably weren't filled with good intentions for members of x^0. Maurice sighed. Being a telepath had been so pleasant until these people came along. Now there was all this hiding and sneaking around. It gave him a headache.

It was time to ignore Lola's advice, and find a way to help his beloved escape. She'd made his own getaway so much easier, guiding him and Lola away from danger. Yet she couldn't guide herself the same way because her solid physical body was immobile while she traveled in the plane of light. How sad.

Then Maurice remembered. There *were* two more travelers back at the Zeitman house: Teddie and Vanida. It wasn't trivial for their energy bodies to go all the way to the tip of South America, but it was possible. Maybe Teddie or Vanida could guide Yuden in an escape. It wasn't a plan, but it was a glimmer of an idea.

He made the quickest of contacts with Teddie, and found her filled with worry and anxious to help. That was a good start.

What other resources were there? Xuha was sitting in jail in Ushuaia. Maurice checked in and saw Xuha in a retention facility used mostly for drunk tourists and petty crimes. Xuha was orphaned as a preschooler and had navigated his difficult childhood with humor and intelligence. Maurice guessed Xuha had been relying on those skills now, because he remained unharmed and in good spirits. He'd even made friends among the other inmates and the guards.

Maurice also knew Xuha could fight two people twice his size, and he'd seen the boy run like the wind. If there was anyone equipped to overcome Warren's guards to allow Yuden, Nell, and Zane to flee, it was Xuha. Did Maurice want to ask Xuha to add escape from prison and a second charge of assault to his rap sheet?

Communication with everyone was the biggest limiting factor. Who could help with that? There was Cillian, the blind prophet left behind with the Argentinian woman. Maurice checked in on him and was surprised to find him entirely sober and quite smitten with this Violeta lady. Well, he was in no position to throw rocks at anyone concerning amorous issues.

What about Violeta? She could be useful as a telepath, but Lola had been extremely clear that, of all people, Maurice was to keep his mind away from her. She was the one known link to the Entelechy and the evil telepaths behind it. Under no circumstances was he to establish contact with her. Yet there was no one else.

At least there hadn't been until now.

Maurice had been friends with Olumiji long enough to catch the faintest wisp of his presence. It only lasted for a second, but Maurice knew what it meant.

You've broken your isolation?

I can't seem to maintain it. But I can't stay with you.

I'm working on something that will need your help. Come back later. Tomorrow morning. I'll make it quick then.

I will.

******

Lola was pretty certain the three of them were not going to finish the cruise. She paid close attention to the lectures and took advantage of all the reading material about Antarctica. She couldn't imagine what sort of escape Violeta had in mind, but there would be one. If communication was via telepathy, the more she knew, the better her chance of understanding what was being conveyed to her.

The two days of sailing across the Drake Passage were as rough as she expected. Maurice ate little and said less. No psychic powers were needed to know he was worried about Yuden. Alex did what he said he would. He lay in his bunk, never making a noticeable movement, and yet changing position over time, while emitting quiet, slow snores. It looked like he was having a fine nap, which was good, because he would have hated the two days at sea.

Lola tossed in her narrow upper berth, enduring the incessant rise and plunge of the ship. Maurice was deep in thought, and his wish for privacy was clear. She left him alone.

Years ago, she'd craved solitude and feared her developing mental powers would prevent her from ever having it. Tonight, with Alex unconscious, Maurice unavailable, and everyone else she knew continents away and mentally absent, she experienced an unfamiliar sensation. It was a little like melancholy, but with a trace of instinctual fear, flavored with something she couldn't quite identify. She turned it over in her mind, the way she might taste a new dish.

What was it? Lemon? Cardamom? Shallots?

She found the word for it, and understood. It was loneliness.

33. Not That Cold

As the sun crept above the horizon just after 4 a.m. Saturday morning, the ship docked at Deception Island, the first stop on the cruise. Most boats stopped here because it was not only beautiful, but the safest harbor in Antarctica, too. It was also the caldera of an active volcano, creating pools of hot water in which the island's more daring visitors could bathe. Violeta had forced swimsuits on them for this, and Lola was up at dawn, looking forward to the experience.

Alex awoke from his two days of sleep as the crew secured the ship to the dock. He was groggy but cheerful so Lola invited him to join her. It wasn't the sort of thing he liked, but he agreed. Probably his way of apologizing for sleeping through the past couple of days.

Maurice woke an hour later, in a far less jovial mood. Sensing her friend's unease, Lola went to get him a cup of tea from the galley and give him privacy to dress. When she returned with drinks and pastries for all of them, Maurice and Alex were talking. Maurice took a long sip of his tea before he spoke.

"Do you already know I've had contact with Olumiji?"

"What?" It was more of a bark than Lola intended. "I thought we were still being shunned. And you and I agreed we shouldn't have telepathic contact with *any*body." Her look was disapproving, but Maurice could sense her curiosity.

"It was quick, but I found out he wants to help us. So, I checked in on Yuden. She's learned so much, Lola, but Warren's put security cameras all around the building and she can find no way out of their room. I checked in on Xuha. He's fine. Teddie's good, too, but worried, and they're both eager to help."

"That much I know," Lola said. "Yes, I've looked in on Zane, Xuha, and Teddie. And Ariel, who wants me to, so I can use her premories to keep us safe, although she hasn't gotten much lately, and she is really angry with us for being on a ship." She gave him a half-guilty look. "I can't help myself—it's a mom thing. You don't have that excuse."

Maurice winked back. "I have a different excuse. Look, whatever Violeta is working on, I don't think we'll be on board when this boat returns to Ushuaia. No matter what happens with Warren, it can't be good for us to have people stuck in his compound once we're safe. So, I have a plan, and I just went over it with Alex. I don't need your help, but I do want your support. At least your lack of objection."

Lola had been afraid this was going to happen.

"It's a good plan," Alex offered.

"Well, that's encouraging." Lola surprised them both when she added, "In that case, why don't you *not* tell me."

"Seriously?" Alex had never heard that from his always curious wife.

"Seriously. I mean, unless Maurice needs something specific from me, and it sounds like he doesn't, my knowing is one more point of discovery. It's better to leave me out of it."

Maurice looked at his friend with appreciation. "You're right. You concentrate on Violeta's plan to get us to safety and we'll handle this other matter."

Maurice passed on the hot springs, so Lola and Alex set off with the rest of the giggling crowd to marvel at the chinstrap penguins roaming around. After a short hike through the mist, bundled in coats over swimwear, they made the dash into the hot water, and found their own corner of the pool.

Alex squeezed her hand. "It's okay you're enjoying this. What an amazing place. It's a shame Teddie's not here."

"Teddie? Aren't you glad she's safe at home?"

"Of course. I was thinking of her in my class. We never got to the third law of thermodynamics. You can't get to absolute zero. I wanted to teach it as 'it doesn't get that cold, even in Antarctica.'"

"Cute."

"Yeah, and here I am in Antarctica. Funny, huh?"

"Alex, we'll make it back and you'll get to finish teaching that chapter to Teddie, and to all your students."

Alex didn't answer. She started to say more, but felt Violeta's clumsy touch. Alex saw her sudden preoccupation and knew what was happening. He helped her settle deeper into the steamy water.

Lola closed her eyes, finding her head filled with images of tomorrow's stop on the largest of the South Shetland Islands. She felt happy to be shopping for souvenirs in Antarctica's only store. She saw a man approach her to offer his hospitality. He could be trusted. They should go with him.

"Got what you needed?"

"Yeah. It's not much, but I believe I do."

******

Olumiji spent a few minutes with Maurice, and afterwards he felt better than he had in weeks. The Entelechy of combative telepaths being at odds with Warren and his media empire was the best news yet. Perhaps the two factions would bring each other down and leave a world in which x^0 could reemerge in safety.

Meanwhile, acting entirely on his own, Olumiji was going to do something to make life better for people he cared about, and it involved no telepathy. He picked up his cell phone and called Teddie Zeitman, still in his list of contacts from a year ago. The young woman, had shown more good judgment then than many adults exhibited ever. Olumiji was counting on her to rise to this occasion as well.

******

Ariel hoped her mother was taking advantage of the one-way communication her telepathy allowed. She would have loved some news back, but the only information came from changes in Ariel's premories and from Teddie and Vanida's jaunts in the realm of light. Though energy bodies could travel at incredibly high speeds, they still had to cover the distance. Both girls found the repeated six-thousand-mile round-trip to be exhausting, particularly because the navigation over oceans and mountains took added vigilance.

Energy travel appeared to have one unfortunate thing in common with telepathy. Both yielded information on whatever was happening when you looked, or listened. If everyone was sleeping, eating, or watching entertainment, it was a waste. People spent a lot of time sleeping, eating, and watching entertainment.

Vanida checked in on Yuden almost daily and knew Xuha had been separated from the group. Ariel was pretty sure he was in jail and felt certain he was safe there, for now. A disturbing possibility in which he was free and got in a fight was starting to gnaw at her awareness. The bad outcome involved someone identifying Xuha to the police. She had to learn more.

Vanida was worried about Yuden, locked in a room with Zane and Nell, exhausted from seeking a way to escape. Vanida and Yuden communicated with pantomime and sign language, but Yuden had conveyed little other than her frustration.

Twice Teddie traveled to Antarctica, even though the journey over the wild waves of the South Ocean terrified her. She verified her mom, dad, and Uncle Maurice were on a cruise ship, and safe so far. Teddie saw them sleeping in their small cabin and saw Uncle Maurice and her mother dining. She was worried her father didn't leave his bed, but Ariel knew the odds of the them surviving had risen after the first few days of the voyage, even though she couldn't tell why.

Ariel knew Cillian remained safe, for she touched his belongings often. She was bothered by the odd possibilities emerging involving an Argentinian woman who seemed to care for him deeply. How had this happened?

All three girls were relieved when Teddie's phone rang Saturday afternoon, even after they discovered the caller was their mother's telepathic friend Olumiji, who tended to appear at the height of a crisis.

"I won't waste time. Teddie, I need your help and I can't go to the travelers in c^3, because they're in hiding too. Like me. So tell me the best way for you and Vanida to do this."

"Okay. What?"

Teddie listened for a while, offering ideas and weighing options. She asked questions of the two young women with her.

"Vanida? If we reduce the distance to Ushuaia from three-thousand miles to under a thousand and can follow a clear coastline with no mountains, how much easier will the trip be?"

"Much easier."

"Ariel? Do you want to come with us to Brazil or stay here?"

"You have to ask?"

Vanida and Ariel were packing before Teddie ended her call.

"We're going to Rio. Olumiji is sending the tickets by email and he's handling our visas. You should know we're going to be staying with one of those creepy monad people, except this one is a defector named Fernando. He fell in love with a lady from x^0, and he wants to help us. You guys okay with that?

"Sure," Vanida said.

Ariel didn't respond, but sat on the floor and put her head against her ankles.

"You okay?"

"Yeah, dizzy again. It's alright."

"Does this mean Olumiji is sending us into horrible danger?"

"Probably." Ariel laughed. "But it's okay. I'm dizzy because the odds of good things shot way up when we decided to go."

******

Xuha fared better than he expected. Years of living with his foster parents, who were in the U.S. illegally, left him with a deep fear of the police. Yet here, he was just another tourist charged with a minor offense. The jail keepers weren't sadistic or even particularly grouchy. A few even joked around with him.

Most of the other prisoners were in for public intoxication or recreational drug use. There was another assault, an indecent exposure, and a hit and run. Xuha got along with all of them, although the hit and run guy was a little stand-offish.

The others had one thing in common, though. Sooner or later friends or family came for them. Sometimes a lawyer showed up. Then, bail was posted. Nobody else stayed for more than three days, and he'd been there for five. The worst part was he knew there was no one who cared about him who was in a position to get him out.

To his surprise, Saturday afternoon one of the guards told him his attorney had come from Río Gallegos to see him. His attorney?

Yes. They were allowed to talk. The man said he'd been hired by the friend of a friend. Would Xuha like to be released on bail?

Xuha considered. He knew nothing about this man. Jail wasn't as bad as expected, and he could be headed into something worse. The attorney seemed to sense his reticence.

"I've been asked to put you up at a hotel and provide you with the means to confer with our mutual contact. He wants you to assist three friends of yours looking to leave the area soon."

Oh.

The man gave him a little smile. "The judge set your bail unusually high. I'm sure no one expects you to post it. What in the world did you do?"

"Not much, but I did it to someone with friends in high places."

"That can cause problems," his lawyer agreed. "You're being sprung because someone I respect a great deal needs a favor from you. I've been told it's one you'll be glad to provide. Shall I start the paperwork? I can get you out of here on Monday."

Xuha thought he had a pretty good idea of who he was supposed to help, and he was all for it. "Please do," he said.

******

Now that Lola knew something would happen tomorrow, she tried to focus on the needs of her trio.

"Tomorrow, we'll stop on King George Island, in one of the two towns in Antarctica. We need to stay together, even though we'll be given the freedom to wander around." She talked as the three of them made their way to the galley for dinner.

"Don't you think a few minutes on our own would do us each some good?" Maurice asked. Lola knew he needed solitude to recharge. Most telepaths did.

"Yes, but tomorrow isn't the day for it. Also, uh, bring as many personal items with you as you reasonably can, especially anything that matters to you."

Alex had to laugh. "I didn't get the chance to gather up possessions before we left Houston, remember? I do have the wallet Violeta bought me, the cash from her, and the toothbrush I bought. Oh, what the hell, I'll bring my extra socks and underwear, too."

They started out the day full of energy, disembarking in the Chilean settlement of Villa Las Estrellas. The town had about a hundred residents in the summer, mostly scientists and researchers.

Lola, Alex, and Maurice went to the South Pole's only post office, buying postcards and mailing them out like everyone else. Two restaurants in town vied for the tourist lunch crowd. Shipmates who weren't eating took turns visiting the tiny souvenir shop and photographing themselves in front of the many bright red buildings, designed to be visible in a white out.

As the afternoon wore on, all three began to worry some vital link in their rescue plan had failed. They were walking around the pier, reluctant to give up hope, when Maurice grinned.

"Well, I'll be damned. Alex do you remember how we were first introduced to each other?"

Alex thought. "I do. You called my home in the middle of the night about three years ago when I thought Lola was in Nigeria. I didn't know it, but she was getting off a plane in London. You asked me to name one large, visible item that would instantly identify the man holding it as a friend."

"Good memory. You told me how you'd fished Lola out of a raging river with a canoe paddle and thought that would work."

"Yes," Lola said. "I get off this plane, don't know where to turn, and this Brit says 'grab the paddle.' Just what you said to me in the river." She stopped. "Why are we doing this?"

Alex was smiling too. "Because there is a man two-hundred feet behind you, holding a canoe paddle and looking at us."

"Olumiji knows this story. He could have arranged this."

"I'm sure he did. Let's go find out."

Maurice and Lola were focused on the man holding the canoe paddle, but Alex turned to the ship and squinted at what he saw.

Three people, a middle-aged Anglo man and woman, and an older man, were making their way up the gangway and onto the ship. Their clothes were similar to those of Alex, Lola, and Maurice. As Alex stared at them, the younger man raised his arm and gave Alex a jaunty salute before he turned and walked aboard.

******

Violeta was sure Warren would eventually discover she was involved with messing up his plans. He knew too many people and asked too many questions.

Sunday, the day Lola, Alex, and Maurice were supposed to switch places with the Aussies on King George Island, she made a quick check on Warren and learned he'd discovered the role she'd played. She held her breath. He was a powerful man, and she had family to hurt. Maybe she'd risked more than she realized.

She took a second pass and discovered something interesting. Warren was fearful, but not vengeful unless it served a purpose. He viewed her assistance to his enemies as a logical response to his firing her mother. He expected nothing different, and had no desire to waste resources getting even.

Violeta exhaled. Then she remembered Warren still thought he was going to collect Lola and Maurice as they got off the ship on Friday. Would he be angrier, and more inclined to even the score, once he discovered his prized captives were safe elsewhere? Probably.

34. Watch Over You

Warren sat in his makeshift study late Sunday night, sipping on a fine scotch while he sorted out his thoughts. Chidi and Jerry arrived yesterday, and, after a good night's sleep, they were happy to take over the duties Lola and Maurice had been forced into doing. Their willingness to help him made Warren wish he'd never bothered with the uncertainties of using the coerced x^0 duo instead.

Now that he'd risked activating his loyal men, their care was such a warm blanket of comfort that he asked his third loyal member, Brett, to fly down from Los Angeles, so Chidi and Jerry wouldn't become exhausted. The remaining loyal recruit, the Turk, was too busy grieving his son's death to be of any use.

The practice of not concentrating on any topic for long had become such an ingrained habit he had to try to think things through. Given all that transpired, what should he do now? *Don't try to answer in seconds. Consider it for as long as you want.*

His security consultants reported Gabriel left the city yesterday. Warren presumed the man had learned the full extent of Warren's distrust. He could even have discovered the complex's ability to be a prison. It was best to assume he had.

Warren understood such a discovery meant he needed to let go of the years he'd spent hatching his plans here in Ushuaia. Such a shame; so much time and money was spent on this place. Was there another way to control the Entelechy, now that imprisoning them was no longer an option?

What about the rest of Reel News? It was time to get back to New York and reassure his executives and directors all was well. Perhaps monads working under Gabriel had already begun to recruit or coerce some of them. Warren supposed that was their end game. He had to assume a group of telepaths could gain the knowledge to effectively blackmail, entice, or threaten anyone.

Of course, once he went to back to New York, Gabriel would find a way to have that special, private conversation with him. If Gabriel was smart—and he was—he'd try to scare Warren, then offer him a reduced role at Reel News in exchange for cooperation.

Warren felt like the owner of a small restaurant who knew he'd receive a visit soon from an unsavory man making remarks like *Nice place you have here. Sure be a shame if it burned down.* A demand for protection money always followed. Why didn't the owner leave town, or go into hiding? Surely they realized once the threats were heard, their world shrank to three alternatives: Acquiesce, pretend to do so, or refuse. The middle option was a waste of time and the other two both ended poorly.

Warren wished he could keep hiding, but he couldn't. His company needed him at the helm, even though once Warren was in the office, Gabriel would see to it his world shrank down to bad alternatives. What a shame he couldn't put his hands over his ears and sing *I can't hear you* at the top of his lungs.

People couldn't do that. Unless...

Warren remembered the exhilaration he'd felt when he made the unlikely leap of accepting telepathy and resolving to use it for his own ends. He felt the same tingle now.

Telepathy wasn't the only improbable skill, and he had the captives to prove it. Down the hall was a sleepy old woman and two young people he'd watched on video as they morphed their features into amazing replicas of others. Hadn't the boy supposedly done a bang-up job of impersonating Warren?

So what if Warren went to New York and did the things he needed to, but Gabriel still couldn't talk to him? Couldn't reach him to make his threats and propose his deal? Because the person meeting with everybody and reassuring everybody wasn't really Warren, even though he looked like him.

This Zane kid could wear Warren's clothes, his expensive shoes, and wristwatch, and dye his hair. People would see what they expected to see. Zane would handle all of Warren's schmoozing while one of the loyals kept tabs on him. Meanwhile, the real Warren could remain in a hidden location, where no threat could reach him.

Didn't kings of old do this kind of thing, using stand-ins? It wasn't completely crazy.

Could he coerce that kind of cooperation from the boy? He could threaten to harm the other two captives. Would that be enough? It wouldn't have to be. He was going to collect the boy's parents as they got off that inane cruise. If Warren played this right, the boy would be a wonderful stand-in for him.

Of course, it wasn't a permanent solution, but it didn't have to be. With Chidi, Jerry, and Brett close by, Warren could think things through and not come out of hiding until he found a better way to solve this mess.

First, he and his stand-in had to get to New York.

******

Gabriel felt like a sucker for having followed Warren to the end of the Earth and then almost walking into a trap the man had been planning for years. A part of him had to wonder what would have happened if he'd obliged. Would some of his loyal monads come for him and gotten caught too? Would some have switched their loyalty to Warren? How many would have carried on without him, regrouping with Rafael, Khalid, or Johann running the show?

Probably most would have done the latter. Loyalty had never been one of the defining characteristics of the group, but ambition had. Even Warren overestimated Gabriel's popularity as a leader. If he'd been able to bring the entire Entelechy down there together and hold them captive, now that could have worked.

But he hadn't, and now Warren was out of moves. The man needed to get back to his company, do damage control, and be seen in New York. Nothing pleased Gabriel more.

Gabriel took a layover in Buenos Aires and arrived in New York Monday morning. All he needed was one private conversation with Warren, with no distractions. Warren's best alternative by far would be to take the deal Gabriel offered. Warren would know it, and Gabriel would know he knew it.

******

Lola, Alex, and Maurice spent a cold night huddled in a shed with sleeping bags and blankets, after their mysterious host with the canoe paddle led them away from the dock and between the brightly painted buildings. As he put them in the shed, he whispered to them to remain hidden and silent until the cruise ship was well on its way. Not knowing what else to do, they obliged.

Early the next morning he came to fetch them, obviously relieved the night had passed without incident. He took them to his home, and as he made them breakfast, he was more forthcoming.

He'd grown up in Ushuaia and gone to school with Violeta's mother. He explained the connection in broken but understandable English as he mixed powdered eggs and water. He'd fallen in love with a Chilean girl while studying oceanography in Santiago, and he and his biologist wife went on to spend much of their lives on this barely inhabited edge of Antarctica.

"So you're doing a favor for Alma, Violeta's mother?"

"I am. It's a debt I've owed for decades, and am glad to repay. She told me little about you, only that you could be trusted, and the less I knew, the better."

"How long will we be staying with you?" Maurice asked.

The man looked surprised. "You know less than I do? We've been asked to house you until you fly out Wednesday."

"You have an airport?"

"We do," he answered with pride. "The best one in Antarctica, with a gravel runway and the continent's only commercial flights. You'll be on an intra-Antarctic flight transferring research products and personnel."

"Do you happen to know where we're going?"

Their host laughed. "This is some strange business Alma has gotten involved in. The plane only flies to the U.S. McMurdo Station. Someone will meet you there and, for your sake, I hope they know where you're supposed to go next."

******

Xuha was nervous when he left his cell Monday afternoon and followed the lawyer down the hallway of the Ushuaia jail. So he was surprised at the surge of joy once he finished signing documents and put his foot outside the door. It was like sun breaking through after days of clouds. He wanted to sing or shout. He did neither, of course, but got in the lawyer's car, hoping he wouldn't be as eager to leave whatever came next.

Once the man pulled into traffic, he was more talkative. He *was* a real lawyer, from the larger Argentinian town of Río Gallegos, a few hundred miles to the north. He was a friend of Mrs. Z, at least telepathically, because he was part of the organization of mind readers that had abandoned her, although the lawyer didn't see it that way. He thought the organization had been disbanded for safety reasons. His legal services were requested and paid for by Olumiji, the Nigerian telepath, with no telepathy involved.

The business arrangement included the lawyer caring for Xuha's needs for food and housing, and giving him a phone on which he could talk freely to Olumiji, who would fill him in on particulars his lawyer didn't need or want to know. The only other instructions were Xuha was to be careful not to violate the terms of his parole. The lawyer's job was to delay Xuha's trial for as long as possible, and then, of course, to get Xuha acquitted.

******

Early Tuesday morning, Ariel, Teddie, and Vanida arrived in Rio de Janeiro. The two flights were long and cramped, but after being confined in the Zeitman home for three weeks, no one complained. A gorgeous Brazilian man with golden skin, large expressive eyes, and long lashes waved at them as they exited customs, and an equally beautiful woman who could have passed for an international model waved with him.

"Those people are friends of mom's?" Teddie whispered to her sister.

Ariel looked closer but, before she could answer, both Brazilians were engulfing them in hugs as they moved them toward the parking garage.

"You are okay for a long drive, yes?" Fernando asked.

"How far are we going?"

"Almost to Uruguay." He laughed. "As close as we can get you to Argentina, so you can do this thing you must do. Camila has booked us a cabin on the beach. Very private, very secluded. We will be safe, and have a good time too."

Well, what was not to like about that?

"It's a two-day drive, on mountainous roads," Camila added.

******

Warren's security group contacted the cruise ship every day to confirm the three Americans were still aboard. On Monday, they were told the trio had come down with a virus after their day on shore. They took their meals in their cabin, but were definitely aboard ship. On Tuesday, each one emerged on deck at least once to enjoy the scenery, well bundled against the cold.

That was all Warren needed. Sources said there were even slimmer chances for escape once the ship was in Antarctica proper, so the task of gathering his hostages up at the end could be delegated to others.

He called his assistant in New York and told her he'd be flying back to New York the next day. He wanted to travel by private charter. If she found the request odd, she didn't say so.

As an afterthought, he called the Ushuaia police chief. He wanted a little added security around the complex in his absence and it never hurt to let law enforcement know Warren valued their relationship. Eventually, someone needed to buy this monstrosity, and the city of Ushuaia was his best candidate.

He was making idle conversation when he said, "I hope the boy you arrested for assaulting me hasn't caused more trouble."

"We thought you knew. He got out on bail yesterday."

"What?"

"That's right. Some fancy lawyer showed up, had everything in order, there was nothing we could do."

"Well, I guess it doesn't matter," Warren said. "As long as he doesn't hurt anyone else."

"Don't worry. We'll keep an eye on him for you. Have a safe trip home."

******

The two-day mountain drive was breathtakingly beautiful and queasiness-inducing at the same time. Teddie had trouble with vertigo and the steep drop offs, Ariel with her stomach and the never-ending hairpin curves. Only Vanida seemed unaffected, staring out the window with a pensive expression and saying little. Ariel knew Vanida hadn't traveled much and guessed she was transfixed by the mountainous beauty.

It was dark when they arrived Tuesday night and found their bungalows, equipped with kerosene lamps and an outhouse.

"Beach cabins tend to be primitive here," Fernando explained as he saw the looks on their faces. "In the morning, you'll see how beautiful it is. It will be okay tomorrow. I promise."

Teddie and Ariel were willing to take him at his word and get some rest, but Vanida was anxious to feign sleep while doing some travel reconnaissance.

"Don't you think you should wait 'til tomorrow?" Ariel asked, worried the fearless girl from Thailand was rushing things. "How can you be sure you can even find them from here?"

"I can find Yuden from anywhere. I want to see how they're being guarded, and check out a route Xuha can use. With any luck, we can do this tomorrow night."

Then Ariel got it. "You weren't watching the scenery because it impressed you. It made you homesick, didn't it?"

Vanida looked happy to have been understood.

"The mountains here and the mountains in Thailand, they're not so different. These made me realize how much I miss the life I have. I had. I don't accept that life is gone. I want to get this done, then fight to get my life back."

Ariel could identify. She had new premories to deal with tonight and a life of her own to rebuild when this was over.

"You're right. This nonsense needs to end. While you travel down there to find an escape route for everybody, I'll try to figure out why I keep seeing Xuha back in jail. Let's get this done."

******

Wednesday morning, Zane woke to a sharp knock on the door, then it opened. He was lying in front of it, trying to sleep on the linoleum floor, bundled in a wad of blankets and sheets. He scrambled to get out of the way.

He assumed breakfast was being delivered early. Food, usually take-out and often cold, had appeared twice a day since the others escaped. Other than that, the door never opened. Yuden kept busy with her daily journeys in the energy realm, but it was fair to say Zane and Nell were so bored a knock on the door at dawn was a welcome diversion.

Over the last few days the food was delivered by one of three men. This morning, it was the one who dressed and looked like a movie star.

"You," he said, pointing to Zane. "You need to come with me."

"Where are we going?"

Brett threw his palms up like he couldn't think of a reason not to answer.

"New York, I think."

Zane looked at his two companions.

"Go and be safe," Nell said.

"Don't forget, those who care *will* watch over you," Yuden added.

Zane smiled. Of course they would.

<u>**January 2013**</u>

35. Keep Going

Zane wasn't sure what he was expecting when he was led into Warren's makeshift office, but it wasn't this.

"You want me to imitate you?"

"I hear you already have, and did a fine job of it, with little preparation. I assure you, this time I'll make it worth your while. You'll be in a better situation, and you'll also buy improved treatment for the two ladies here. Quite possibly even their eventual release."

Warren waited.

"Even if I wanted to," Zane said, "I couldn't. You don't understand how this works. I can keep up someone else's appearance for a while, but not all day. It'd be like, I don't know, holding my arms up over my head. The muscles give out, no matter what I do."

"I see. So, you'll have frequent rest periods. I'll develop some minor health problem. Stomach issues work well. No one wants to hear the details. Oh, and you'll need a hand injury, maybe a dislocated right index finger, to explain your poor signature. Jerry can see to that."

Zane winced. He had to talk the man out of this.

"What about the things about you and your business I don't know? I'll give this whole charade away the first time I open my mouth."

"No you won't. Zane, we have three entire advantages you're not considering. The first is me. I'm going to brief you all the way to New York and tell you everything I think is essential. I know what you need to know."

Zane considered that but said nothing.

"The second asset is you. I've learned you're an uncommonly smart young man and can remember most of what I'm going to tell you. You're clever enough to fake what you can't. Trust me, I'm going to keep you highly motivated to do that."

Zane didn't like the sound of the threat, but he still said nothing.

"The third advantage is we have three capable telepaths on our side, and two of them will come to New York with us. Brett here has dabbled in acting, and he'll be with you every moment you're on stage. He'll even be in your mind. If he feels you go blank, or consider any ill-advised statement, he'll chime right in. See, that's the kind of advantage people don't usually have. So I think we can pull this off."

"But what about the other telepaths, the ones who are trying to take over your business? They're going to know I'm not you."

"Oh, they certainly are," Warren said. "That's exactly what I'm counting on."

✱✱✱✱✱✱

Wednesday morning Vanida was exhausted. She'd made three trips from Southern Brazil, traveling more miles in one night than any traveler had been known to do.

However, she now understood what was happening in Ushuaia. She knew Warren had reduced his nighttime security to a single guard who mostly watched the feed from new security cameras. She'd watched him make physical rounds around midnight and 2 a.m. It would be best to attack him when he was outside. Xuha could dash in, disable cameras, subdue the guard, and drag him inside into a closet. Then he could use the guard's access card to open the door to free the captives.

But part of Vanida's mission had failed. She couldn't roust the traveling body of a tired Yuden, who remained in a deep sleep. That meant she hadn't been able to warn the trio they would be escaping, or to confirm Yuden knew of good places for them to hide and at least one way for them to leave the grounds. Should

270

they wait and keep trying to communicate with Yuden? Every day they delayed they risked more variables coming into play.

What was it Ariel had said during her Christmas fortune-telling? "I see a time when you fail to do one thing you think is necessary. It isn't. So if not everything goes right, keep going."

That was it. Keep going. Yuden could handle it.

******

Late Wednesday morning, Lola, Alex, and Maurice were bundled in warm clothes, driven to the airport, and put on a plane for the ten-hour flight that would take them a third of the way around the giant continent of Antarctica. Their hosts had been kind, but both Lola and Maurice could sense their overwhelming relief at having the danger move elsewhere.

They were warned the flight would be long, cold, and uncomfortable, and were given ear plugs and medication to make them drowsy. Alex and Maurice took their pills without hesitation, but Lola held off. She hadn't had a minute alone in days, and she wanted to savor the solitude as she checked in on the rest of the family.

She squirmed in the thick parka and uncomfortable jump-seat buckle, but settled in well enough to relax. She found her two daughters and friend Vanida sipping rum drinks on a beach in Brazil. What? Where? And wasn't it kind of early in the day for rum drinks?

Well, at least they were safe. But what were they doing there?

They were part of a plan to rescue Zane, Nell and Yuden. Not a plan—*the* plan—the one Maurice and Alex weren't telling her about. It was going to happen tonight. Tonight?

She better leave this alone. She let her consciousness settle back into the rough vibrations of the ride.

What about Xuha? Was he okay?

Eggs. She smelled eggs. Xuha had ordered a late room-service breakfast and was dipping his toast into a sunny-side-up concoction. Okay. What about Zane? He was being served food, too, but by the co-pilot of the private plane Zane had boarded a few hours ago for New York. Why was he going to New York? On a private jet? He wasn't thinking about that. She felt her son recline into the plush seat and sip his hot coffee.

How had so much changed so fast without her knowing about it? She reached a gloved hand into the knapsack her hosts had given her and found an energy bar. As she chewed the sawdust-like contents, she wished she had eggs and hot coffee. Maybe even coffee and rum. She took one of the airsickness tablets, hoping she wouldn't wake up for another thousand miles.

As she started to doze, she had one last groggy thought. How could Zane be rescued in Ushuaia if he was in New York? Why was no one else worried about that?

******

Violeta and Cillian enjoyed their days together, days made sweeter by pretending this never had to end. As the plan to get the rest of the Zeitman clan to safety took shape, the end date became more apparent to Violeta.

Gabriel and his loyal monads were hell-bent on taking over Warren's business. They seemed to have dismissed Violeta from their minds. She was doing her best to keep it that way.

However, Warren was now well aware she was involved. As long as he was getting his way, he didn't much care, but he'd take a closer look at her when his three remaining captives disappeared tonight. Once the other three failed to disembarked from the ship on Friday, she expected to have his full attention.

That meant she and Cillian needed to flee with Nell, Zane, and Yuden. Her plan was to get them all into Chile and find a place where they could lay low. Once they were safe, Violeta would leave and try to draw Warren's attention elsewhere.

"It's the only way and you know it," she said to him. "Please don't try to talk me out of it."

Then she realized Cillian already agreed with her.

"Wait. You know it's the only way, don't you? Your prophet sense has decided we have to part soon. Hasn't it? I can tell from the way you're not arguing with me."

He didn't say anything for a minute, but he didn't have to. She felt his sadness, and his undercurrent of anger that this couldn't turn out differently.

"I considered not telling you," he said. "If you found a way for us to get out of here together, I thought about staying with you and never going home. Maybe we'd have many happy years and you'd never know the cost of it."

"What cost?"

"It's no sure thing, but what I do over the next decades ups the odds of keeping the human race alive through the dark times. Ups it a fair amount, really, because I alone can detect whether a path is productive or not, and change course if it isn't. That enables me to do a lot of positive things."

"Why can't you do positive things with me?"

He heard the trace of anger in her voice and he understood it.

"I'd think I could do more with you, but although my skill is far from detailed, I know I need to return to Ireland. I don't know why. Maybe I die young if I stay with you. Maybe you do, and I can't recover. Or maybe I'm so happy with you I stop worrying about the future. I can't tell. All I know is the life I need to have isn't one you'd be happy with, and I can't stay here and be part of yours."

"It doesn't mean we can't see each other again, though, after this whole thing with Reel News ends?"

"No, it doesn't. We're free to drag out our good-byes as long as we like. Years, I suppose, if we wish. That's up to us. Eventually, though, there are two paths. On one, I'm known to have lived in Ireland all my life and lived without a love by my side. Far down that road, I see the light of civilization. On the other path, no one remembers me or anyone else, because there is nothing left of humanity to see. I've tried to come up with other interpretations, but I can't."

She didn't ask any more questions after that.

✳✳✳✳✳✳

Ariel found what she was looking for, on a near fringe she hadn't paid attention to earlier. It was Xuha, free and safe after the daring role he played in the final escape from Warren's prison. What made this scenario different from the others?

She knew it as she watched the premory. No one had been able to identify him. He wore a ski mask, because he'd seen it in the lost and found and thought it was a good idea. Such a trivial thing. Such a vastly different future.

Ariel knew they weren't supposed to communicate by telepathy any more, but this was an emergency. Camila was part of x^0 and she knew Olumiji. Couldn't she reach out to Olumiji for a second and let him know Xuha had to look through the lost and found box in his hotel? Take the ski mask. Don't go without one.

******

Xuha played with his runny eggs the way a little kid would. It felt good to be eating food he liked. It felt good to be eating alone, not rushed, or watched, or nervous. Although the jail in Ushuaia had been the best of prisons, it was prison nonetheless.

The hotel room his lawyer got him was elegant. The food was marvelous and the bed superb. But Xuha understood all the finery came at a cost.

Tonight, he'd be required to do something well beyond anything he'd ever attempted. According to Mrs. Z's friend Olumiji, he'd get a call in the middle of the night. Once he was told the night watchman was headed outside, he'd have a few minutes to crawl out his window, run more than three miles to Warren's compound, find a gate somebody was going to leave open for him, and run through fast enough that he seemed like no more than wind. Through his phone and ear buds, he'd receive guidance from Olumiji, who'd be listening to Teddie. Teddie, in her traveler's body, would give directions on how to find and turn two cameras, where to physically subdue an armed guard and hide him, and how to open a locked door with a key he hoped worked, because there was no Plan B for that.

Then he'd have seconds to explain to three baffled people how they needed to get the hell out of there. He'd run the three miles back to his hotel, climb in his own window, and go back to sleep like nothing happened, because Ariel was positive he couldn't be associated with this escape in any way.

He was exhausted thinking about it. He dipped the last bit of toast into the last bit of egg, then savored it in his mouth, slowing down time as he did, to make the enjoyment last.

Once the eggs were finished, he headed into the lobby. He'd lost a pair of sunglasses the lawyer bought him, but it hadn't occurred to him to check the hotel's lost and found. Now, this Olumiji was insisting he do so, saying he would find a ski mask there and should take it.

His glasses weren't in the box. Well, he hadn't expected them to be. But mixed in with the socks and gloves, there was an old navy blue ski mask. It had to be the one everyone was insisting he should wear.

******

Teddie had a lot of reasons to be nervous. The fate of people she cared for rested on her young shoulders and she knew it. She'd sworn to stop this whole traveling thing when she returned from India, and as far as her own peace of mind went, that was a good idea, even though the decision had left her out of practice until recent weeks. Finding her parents and Uncle Maurice was easy because of the strong emotional ties, but now she had to find others. She had a small connection to Yuden, and none, really, to Nell. Zane was her best hope.

"Take me to Zane," she ordered, with all the confidence she could. Then she added, "Somadina, I hope you're listening to me and are ready to go."

That, of course, was the other reason to be nervous. She'd agreed to allow a telepath to enter her mind, and she was pretty sure there wasn't an eighteen-year-old in the world who wanted someone else hanging out in their head. At least not one who was best friends with their own mother.

"Don't think about anything you don't want mom to know," Ariel had advised. *Real helpful.* Now *all* she could think about were things she didn't want her mother to know.

At least Somadina was there for a good purpose. Seeing through Teddie's eyes, she'd know the exact moment the guard left the building, and that timing could be communicated to Olumiji and on to a waiting Xuha.

She relaxed the way she'd been trained. She rose out of her body, and stifled a giggle at the familiar tickle as she passed through the walls of the hut on the beach. She began to move along the Brazilian shore line, a comfortable fifteen or so feet in the air and picking up speed. It took a few minutes for her to notice the moonlight on the water off to her right.

Off to her right? Wasn't she supposed to be going the other way. You know, south? That was where the South Pole was, wasn't it?

Stop! This wasn't working. Her energy body thought Zane was north, and she didn't have time to argue. She thought of Yuden with all the fondness she could muster. Yuden had helped her last year in Bhutan. Yuden had made it possible for Teddie to save two of her friends from horrible situations.

"Take me to Yuden," she said. Her body of light shimmied for a few seconds, hovering in indecision. Then it turned and began to move, following the ocean waves breaking into foam as they rolled onto the sand. Sand that was to her right. A moonlit ocean that was to her left.

"I'm going south. South to Yuden." Her training took over as she put everything else out of her mind and held the thought of Yuden firm in her head and heart.

******

Somadina was in a village in Southeastern Nigeria, lying in her bed. It was morning and there were butterflies outside her window. She knew it would be hard to communicate telepathically with Olumiji while she held tight to this teenager's thoughts, so she had him on her cell phone, set on speaker as she talked.

"She's on her way now; I'm with her."

Olumiji listened as he drank his morning coffee in Lagos. He knew enough not to interrupt.

"Wait. She stopped. Something's wrong. She was going north. The problem is with Zane. She has no idea why, but now she's seeking Yuden."

"Stay with her and proceed as planned," he said. "I'll look into what's happening with Zane."

******

After multiple refueling stops and changes, Warren's charter jet finally approached the Teterboro Airport in New Jersey for a convenient, middle-of-the-night landing. Zane found it interesting Warren was able to handle his "lost" passport as he and Warren were waved back into the U.S. along with Jerry and Brett,

It was good the aircraft was well stocked with coffee. Warren had spent twelve of the eighteen hours on the plane educating Zane on every aspect of Reel News. Zane could retain a lot of information, and he wondered if he did know enough to run Warren's company. The time spent together had an added benefit; hours of observing Warren up close had equipped Zane to be more accurate in his impersonation. Surely this whole thing would be less awkward if he was believed.

After landing, Zane considered trying to run for it, but he couldn't imagine what he'd gain. His best bet seemed to be to go along with Warren's preposterous scheme while he looked for ways to make the situation better.

36. Not Really a Crime

Although it seemed like hours to Teddie, she knew from experience it hadn't taken her that long to get to the dark, sterile hallway and be ready to pass though the steel door. She didn't like the feel of metal, especially steel, and its presence was probably what brought her to a complete stop. She looked more closely. The walls were covered with painted drywall, but as she moved her hand she felt the concrete blocks reinforced with steel cables. Somebody had built a serious prison here.

Well, she could pass through it, and the cables were better than solid steel. She thought of Yuden again and moved through. Yuden appeared to be asleep, but her energy body was rising up to greet Teddie, a grin on her face.

Teddie looked around. Nell was asleep in the other bed, and Zane was nowhere. Yuden saw her searching the room and flapped her arms like wings. Zane had grown wings? Yuden kept flapping. However he had done it, Zane had flown away. Now, she had to explain what was about to happen to them.

She pointed to Nell. She pointed to Yuden. Then she started to flap her own arms. Yuden clapped her hands. *Either she likes the performance or she understands. Maybe both.*

Teddie nodded that Yuden had it right. She pointed to Nell's watch. She pinched her thumb and index finger close together, to mean a little. In a little time.

Yuden nodded and waved goodbye to the room to show she comprehended. Then she slid back into her solid body as Teddie watched.

Geez, I hope we understood each other. Teddie saw Yuden's physical body jolt awake and move to wake Nell. Both women were talking as they pulled on pants and socks and shoes.

Better go find the guard. Looks like I've set an escape in motion.

******

Somadina had been a telepath for as long as she could remember, and she found it painful to watch Yuden and Teddie struggle to communicate simple concepts. *Non-telepaths faced so many challenges.*

Somadina experienced Teddie's distaste as she went through the dreaded steel cables and she watched as the girl explored the rooms until she found the night watchman. She waited with Teddie for ten long minutes as the man kept one eye on the camera feed and the other on a rerun of an old comedy show. He kept looking at his pack of cigarettes. Somadina felt his yearning, and his determination to wait a full two hours in-between smokes. Eleven minutes after Teddie arrived, he decided it was close enough. He picked up the pack and headed out.

"Now, now!" Somadina yelled it into the phone to Olumiji. "Tell Xuha to start running."

"I just did."

******

Xuha didn't let the absurdity of what he was doing soak in until he approached the gate. It was supposed to be opened by friends of the mother of someone Lola knew, but what did he do if it was closed? No one had given him alternatives.

Yet, the gate set wide open. He rushed through and found the guard with no trouble. Xuha left him in a closet secured with duct tape. He'd be sore but there'd be no permanent damage. The key card worked, and the door opened to a waiting Yuden and Nell, dressed and ready to run. Their only question had been, "What do we do once we're out?"

Xuha was puzzled. "No one told me. I thought you guys knew that part. I'm sorry, I have to run because the gate I'm supposed to go through closes in two minutes."

"Go," Yuden said. "We'll figure it out."

He ran as fast as he ever had in his life, until he was back in the hotel bed ten minutes after he left. Had he just committed a crime? It didn't seem to him like he had.

Something else kept nagging at him. What was it?

Of course. He should have asked them where Zane was.

******

The worst seat on the most crowded airplane was going to seem like first class after this ride, Lola decided as she got off the plane and stepped into the blinding white of an Antarctic summer afternoon. After ten hours of sitting in what felt like an over-enthused massage chair, she was ready to hear silence and be still.

"Are we looking for more people with canoe paddles?" Maurice asked, as he pulled the ear plugs out of his ears.

"Probably looking for him." Alex pointed to a man in a thick black and orange parka holding up a sign saying "Zeitman." Later they'd learn the man was clad in the traditional colors of Scott Base, the nearby New Zealand research outpost that occasionally welcomed visitors.

He stepped forward when he noticed their attention, explaining he'd been charged with meeting them and seeing to their night's lodging before they boarded the cruise ship for the journey they were joining in progress. Apparently, they were off to visit Tasmania's Macquarie Island, halfway between Antarctica and New Zealand.

"Fascinating history there, the way they've eradicated all those outside pests, but I'm sure you know all about that if you came this far to visit the place."

"I'm a geologist," Lola said, trying to think of something that wouldn't show how ignorant her little group was of the locale.

"Oh, then you'd be here to see those rocks from down in the mantle that are exposed over there."

"I read about those," Maurice said. Lola sent him a quick mental thank you, and a request to sound more informed.

"Geologists come a long way to see those outcrops. I'm a meteorologist, so they just look like rocks to me, you know. Hey, you people must enjoy rough seas to fly over here from the peninsula to make *this* trip. You do know you spend eight days at sea getting to New Zealand, don't you?"

Lola watched Alex's eyes widen, but her husband said nothing as the threesome put on protective gear and got into the vehicle. They were safe, away from Warren, away from being used in any way that could bring harm to her family or friends.

Remote was good and there couldn't be a place on the planet more remote than this.

******

Neither Nell nor Yuden panicked easily, but each came close when Xuha said he had to be out of the compound in two minutes then vanished in a blur. Then they began to take stock.

"No one will know we're missing for a while," Nell said, closing the door to their prison room and pocketing the key card.

"I know the layout of this place as well as my own home," Yuden said. "We can avoid people and cameras."

"I hid lots of supplies for Lola and Maurice less than two weeks ago, and I can find those spots. I doubt they used everything."

"I know where we can find one of those golf carts the guards drive around in," Yuden said. "It might be unattended."

"If I have the element of surprise, I can kick the arse of anyone guarding that cart," Nell responded. "Then, I can look like the guard whose arse I just kicked while I drive you out of here."

"I can direct us somewhere safe once you drive us off of the grounds." For a second the old woman blushed like a young girl. "And then, I have a boyfriend who can find us."

"You do, don't you?" Nell laughed. "Okay, let's go. We're not in half as bad a situation as we thought."

******

Teddie stayed to watch Xuha arrive, put on the ski mask, and then subdue the guard. She tried to stay calm as he spent precious seconds giving the half-conscious man a gulp of water.

She was proud to see Nell and Yuden waiting at their door ready to run, like they'd understood her every gesture. She vacillated between following Xuha back to his hotel or sticking with Yuden and Nell to make sure they got off of the grounds, and decided on the latter.

The two women were funny together, so different in every possible demographic. Yet the tiny, ancient Asian woman who knew every inch of the compound and the feisty Irish actress who could fight as well as she could act formed an impressive duo. Teddie gave them a silent laugh from the abode of light as she watched them drive through the front gate in a golf cart, dressed as guards. As they abandoned the cart and took off on foot, Teddie sent them an invisible wave before heading north.

Shaken but elated, she made her way to the coast and began moving along the shoreline. She focused on her sister, speeding back to Ariel to get a full account of how successful the mission was. She was a ways from the beach huts when Vanida's traveling body flew out to meet her. Vanida turned several cartwheels in midair, did a few backflips and finished the greeting by giving Teddie an ethereal hug. Teddie was pretty confident that meant it had had gone well.

As her eyes fluttered open, she saw Fernando and Camila smiling at her.

"I'm guessing we did it."

"I've been in touch with Olumiji while you were gone. Xuha is safe," Camila answered. "Olumiji has heard from Maurice, who is monitoring Yuden. He reports she and Nell are hidden and awaiting pick-up."

Teddie turned to her sister, who was sitting cross-legged on the floor. "How are things looking now?" This was the question that really mattered.

"Not all bad," Ariel said looking up. "There's a lot going on. Good news. Xuha did it. I no longer get a future where he ends up in jail. Instead, I mostly see him back in El Paso at school, leading a boring life. A boring life is really great."

No one in the room argued with her."

"I see pretty good probabilities of Nell, Yuden and Cillian together next week and safe, although I'm getting a lot of funny stuff about the Argentinian woman who's with them. Nothing is sure for that group. Their exit from Argentina has iffy parts."

"Okay. That's the best we could hope for, right?"

"Probably."

Camila interrupted. "x^0 is still officially vanished, but more members have emerged, wanting to help your family. Thanks to them we've found your brother. He's in New York."

"That makes sense," Ariel said, "because all hell is going to break loose between Warren and his telepaths and no matter how it goes down, Zane will be in the middle of it."

"Unfortunately, Warren's telepaths are watching Zane's brain closely," Camila said, "so we have to keep our distance. We don't want them to find out we know where he is."

"Will Zane be okay?" Teddie had to ask the question.

"I'm not sure," her sister said.

Teddie let that sink in. "Mom? Dad? Maurice?"

Ariel shook her head. "I've never seen anything like this. They keep avoiding disaster, only to walk into potential for a new one. I told them to stay off of damn cruise ships and I was so happy when Olumiji told Camila they'd disembarked. But it looks like they're getting on another cruise ship, because I'm getting a fifty percent chance of something awful happening to mom and half a chance again of it killing dad as well."

She put her head back in her hands.

"But there is fifty-percent chance she is okay, right?" It was the best thing Teddie could think of to say.

✳✳✳✳✳✳

Violeta realized she'd never appreciated what a resourceful woman her mother was. True, she'd never seen her mom so motivated. The woman blamed Reel News for firing her, and apparently she'd despised Gabriel for years, being more aware of the dynamics between Violeta and her boss than Violeta would have guessed. Her mother had also become a proud citizen of Ushuaia protecting her home.

It seemed like the entire tip of South America knew Alma and owed her a favor or two. The woman had managed to get an old school chum to shelter Lola's traveling trio in the South Shetland Islands and another to open a gate for Xuha at a vital time. Now, she'd secured a vehicle for Violeta to use as a getaway car to take her friends out west of town in the middle of the night. There, they could board a fast, private boat that would maneuver through the fjords of southern Chile and deposit them safely in Punta Arenas, Chile's most southern city.

Okay, mom hadn't known anyone who could come up with such a boat, but Violeta's newfound contact—this man Olumiji from x^0—appeared to be as resourceful as her mother. As Violeta drove the old pick-up truck her mom had found down the deserted road in a light rain in the wee hours before dawn, she hoped this telepath was as reliable.

An old woman named Yuden sat next to her and seemed totally exhausted. She was sure Nell and Cillian, huddled together under a tarp in back, were as tired and even more miserable. She didn't want to show up in the middle of nowhere only to wait in the rain for hours and finally turn around.

The dark sky was starting to show a hint of violet to the east as she rounded the last curve leading to the small dock. She turned off the engine and bright lights came on. Her first thought was the police were waiting for her and this whole drizzly getaway had been for nothing. Then she realized the lights were on a boat.

A little cigarette boat sat waiting. It looked like the craft had led a hard life at sea, but it would hold up to six passengers. The captain was giving them a friendly wave.

Violeta wasn't used to checking in with other telepaths, but she took a second to send a thanks to Olumiji, her mysterious x^0 benefactor, and another pause to breathe a sigh of relief.

It was the middle of the night when Warren got into his hotel room, and it took him a while to fall asleep. It would have been so nice to have been in the comfort of his own bed after more than two weeks away, but given the subterfuge with Zane, he thought it was better to be difficult to locate from the start.

He woke to the sound of his phone ringing and answered it out of habit, forgetting his calls were being routed to Zane, and that only a small group had access to his new number.

"Yes?"

As soon as he heard the voice he remembered. The call was from one of the few who'd been authorized to reach him.

"We have a situation here in Ushuaia."

"You've got to be kidding. I haven't even been home for a day."

Warren was not happy to hear a janitor had found the night watchman tied up in the cleaning supply closet. The man said he'd been attacked by a boy in a ski mask who'd apologized and then taken the key card to the room holding the two remaining women. As suspected, the women were gone. A thorough search of the grounds was in progress.

"Jeez, what is it with these people?"

"There is simply no way they could have left the premises," the man reassured him.

"Why not? Everyone else seems to have had no problem doing so. Go check on that boy I had arrested. He's got to be involved with this somehow."

"We already did, because he was the only likely suspect. Front desk at his hotel says they saw him going into his room alone around ten. Never left after that. Meanwhile, the guard's key card was used to open the room at 2:14 a.m. The boy was still in his hotel room a bit ago when we knocked on his door."

"I don't believe it," Warren said, then he paused. "You know what? I don't believe it and I don't care. Unless you find an easy way to ID the kid, drop the charges and don't waste more manpower on him or the two ladies, either. They were bargaining chips, nothing more, and I'm not going to need them."

"Seriously?"

"Yup. I want you to focus on picking up the three that went to Antarctica. They are the only ones that matter now. Secure the woman and her husband and the old guy as soon as they get off of that cruise ship, okay? And keep me posted."

Warren hung up the phone and stared out the window. Damnit. He was way too agitated now to go back to sleep. He reached for a word puzzle book, then stopped. There was no need to do this; Jerry was in a room across the hall, keeping him safe. It was a habit he needed to break. Or did he?

He tried to imagine how two ill-equipped women had been able to flee into a foreign countryside. Maybe he was up against something stronger than he imagined. Maybe more people than he realized wanted to ruin him. Maybe, when it came down to it, he shouldn't be trusting anyone at all for anything.

He lay in his bed and shivered under the blankets until the first touch of light in the sky signaled a winter dawn.

37. Are You You?

Hank, the monad from Australia, worked for Warren for years, and he had a pretty good idea of how the man's mind worked. Like most important people, Warren expected things to go the way he expected them to go. He was not going to be pleased when he discovered Hank, who was one of his own, and Hank's missus and his old man, had been occupying the Zeitman cabin on the Antarctic cruise ship since it stopped in the South Shetland Islands six days earlier.

Hank laughed. He'd had enough of Warren's airs long ago and been looking for a right dramatic way to exit for a while. Casting his lot with the likes of Gabriel and his ilk looked to be nothing but more of the same, under new leadership. No, striking out on his own was the way.

When x^0 approached him last December about switching sides, he'd given it fair thought, and they knew it, too. So, last week, when a fellow Aussie from their organization rang him up and offered to send him and his own off on a cruise of a lifetime in order to pull one over on Warren, Hank had appreciated the humor of the situation. He'd scrambled to get out the door and to the remote Shetland Islands to make it happen.

There had been a bit of the odd about it, but the three of them managed to have some fun. They'd stay covered in hats and glasses, kept to themselves, and talked like Yanks when they had to talk. Only one person, a young girl maybe ten years old, had surprised him one morning at breakfast by asking him outright.

"Aren't you a different man than the one that used to be staying in your cabin?"

Her parents looked horrified, but before they could say a word, Hank answered.

"No. Are you a different girl than the one that was staying in yours?"

She giggled and said no more. After that, if any adult had been wondering, they were too polite to ask.

Now, Hank had to figure out the best way to exit the ship and get to the airport in Ushuaia, all while keeping himself and his rellies safe.

"I say we walk off looking unmistakably like us. No caps, no sunglasses," he told his family. "You show off your blonde hair, dear, and dad, you let that bald head of yours shine. And give everyone your real name. That's how we're registered."

The disembarking process was easy enough, but once they were outside and moving toward the cab stand, three large men stepped in front of them and spoke to his wife.

"You're to come with us, Mrs. Zeitman."

Hank could feel their hesitation, and he was never prouder of his missus than when she used her strongest Australian accent to indignantly reply, "You've got the wrong lady, Bub. I'm Mrs. Cook, I've got the ID to prove it, and if you lay a hand on me I'll scream bloody murder."

Two of the men peered into a photo on a cell phone.

"They are the only three it could possibly be," the third man said.

"I told you, she's not blonde and she's not an Aussie. And look, that guy's not bald. These are the wrong people."

"Let's go," Hank said to his wife, side-stepping the men and heading toward a taxi. One of the men reached out for Mrs. Cook's arm as she passed by and she shrieked. "Don't you dare touch me!" as she marched to the cab.

Hank couldn't resist enjoying the confusion filling the minds of Warren's goons. He hoped word of this got back to Gabriel, too. There may not have been a better way to have quit the lot of them.

Friday morning, Xuha's lawyer got word all charges against his client were dismissed. He phoned Olumiji, the man who'd hired him.

"I have no idea what this Warren man is thinking," Olumiji said. "If Xuha is truly free to leave the country, part of me says get him out of there on a plane today. But let me talk to Xuha, because if my friends in Argentina encounter more problems, he's a great asset to have nearby."

When asked, Xuha was not only willing to stay, he insisted on it.

"Just for a few days," Olumiji said, "until we get our arms around what's going on and make sure you're not needed."

"Uh," Xuha began, and Olumiji picked up on the young man's embarrassment and its cause.

"Of course, I'll have your lawyer prepay your room before he leaves town and have him leave you with some cash."

"I don't want that—I don't want any more charity from you."

Olumiji understand Xuha's discomfort.

"Trust me, it's not charity, but I have another idea. Maybe a better one. There is a lady in town who's been helping us. She's the one on the boat with Nell, Cillian and Yuden."

"Yes. Ms. Z's friend from Reel News. Her name is Violeta."

"That's right. Violeta's mom lives in Ushuaia. She could be in danger over the next several days. I bet she has a spare room and wouldn't mind having company while her daughter leads a group on a daring escape into Chile. What do you think?"

"I think that would be good for both of us."

Olumiji could feel Xuha's relief all the way across the Atlantic Ocean.

******

Zane woke up Friday morning after half a night's sleep, and as he reshaped his body to fit into Warren's best hand-tailored suit, he knew it was show time. The monad Brett would remain nearby, listening to Zane's every word and making sure he behaved. Meanwhile, the real Warren would be hidden at a location unknown to Zane or Brett.

Warren had made appointments for Zane, starting with ones likely to be easy. First up were the non-telepathic executives who oversaw Accounting, HR, and Legal. Each needed some of the big boss's time to approve things and be reassured Warren's unprecedented absence for the past two weeks had been necessary and the issues in Argentina were resolved. His executive assistant needed time with him, too, and Zane guessed she would be the toughest one to deceive.

But really, what was she going to say?

"Are you sure you're Warren?"

He already knew how he'd answer.

"Yes. Are you sure you're Denise?"

The conversation would probably never happen. People saw what they expected to see.

Zane studied the wristwatch that probably was worth more than his rent for a year and did his best to get in character.

"Hi Warren. Welcome back."

A bald, well-dressed man with thick glasses entered the office at exactly 9 a.m.

"Did you guys straighten out that mess yet with the 1099s from last year's consultants?" he snapped at his Senior Vice-President of Accounting.

"Yes sir. Handled last week. Should never have happened."

"No, it shouldn't have."

So the day went, as executive after executive left Warren's office without a trace of suspicion.

******

Nobody in Ushuaia wanted to make the call to Warren.

It was one of those things. Nobody's fault, really, and everybody's, sort of. They'd all had expected Lola, Alex, and Maurice to walk off of the ship. Sure, they might try to disembark before or after everyone else, or try to blur their identities with disguises, or get off individually to be less obvious. But when exactly eighty-five passengers disembarked at the same time, and none of them were the three in question, the guys who'd been sent did the best they could and followed the three most likely. It was a good choice. Only the three hadn't been the right people, and now no one had any idea where the trio was.

The head of security made the call early Friday afternoon. To his surprise, he had to be patched in to a special line with an unlisted number. He was curious about why, but this was no time to ask questions. Once he had Warren on the phone, he explained the situation. Warren's silence spoke volumes.

"What do you want me to do, sir?" he finally asked.

"Search the ship. Now. I don't care how you do it. Get the police involved if you have to."

"Yes sir."

"Get someone to search every damn port the ship stopped at."

"Yes sir."

Warren paused again, considering something.

"Where do *you* think they are?" he asked his head of security.

"Me, sir? What do I think?"

"You heard me. If you had to bet, where would you put your money?"

"I think they had local help, sir. It's the only way, really. Maybe they never were on the ship to begin with."

"That's an interesting theory. I want you to find out everything you can about an Ushuaia woman named Alma Delgado and her daughter Violeta. The daughter used to work for me. Get surveillance on them both. I want to know where they are now, who's with them, and everything they've done for the last week. I need that information by tomorrow morning. This must be resolved by Sunday. After that, I'll be even more difficult to reach. Do you understand?"

"Yes sir," he said, even though he didn't understand the last part at all.

******

The real Warren had scheduled the meeting with Gabriel late in the day, well after all the other major players were reassured. He knew Zane would be tired by then, possibly exhausted, and he was okay with that. If the young man was going to fail in his impersonation, this was the time to do it. But Warren didn't consider the other ways fatigue affects behavior.

"Thanks for making time to see me," Gabriel said as he walked in for his 5:30 appointment, his sarcasm obvious. Then he looked closely at the man behind the desk.

"It's been a busy few weeks," the man said.

"I don't think so. You've been avoiding me, and you went to end of the Earth to do it."

"Really? How far have you gotten with your plans to take over my company?" Zane asked. "That is what you've been doing in my absence, isn't it?"

Gabriel looked closely at the man again. "Who are you?" He said it in almost a whisper.

Another imposter would have answered differently, but Zane had some recent experience with telepaths. He couldn't resist toying with this man.

I'm your worst nightmare. He thought as hard as he could.

Gabriel's eyes widened, and then he laughed.

"Unbelievable. And well done," he added. "But where the hell is Warren?"

"I've no idea," Zane said. "I'm being forced to do this, he's holding my family, and he's got someone listening to every word I say."

******

"Zane didn't plan to say that. This has worn him out so badly that he's punchy," Brett said into the recording he was making for Warren. "I'm going to get him out of there."

******

"What does Warren want you to do?" Gabriel asked.

"Not much. Act like him to everyone else. That mostly involves bossing people around in rude ways. I think he really wants me to tell you to piss off, but he didn't tell me that, at least not explicitly."

Gabriel was grinning. "Well, this is a refreshing bit of honesty. How long do you think you'll be around?"

"Decades, I hope," Zane said, a worried look on his face.

Gabriel laughed again.

"You need some rest, kid. You're young, aren't you? I can feel it. And worn out to your core. What I meant was how long are you going be here as Warren?"

"Oh. I've no idea."

******

"Wait," Brett said aloud. "I'm going to hold off a minute. I'm not sure this conversation is going all that poorly."

******

"Tell the real Warren he can't hide from me forever," Gabriel said. "Tell him he needs to come over here and deal with me because two can play his stupid game. Tell him if he keeps this nonsense up, I'll find a way to hold more leverage over you than he does, so you will do exactly as *I* say, including signing away his company to me while you impersonate him. Make sure he understands the message."

Zane may have been weary, but he heard the last bit and was alert enough to not like where this pissing match was going.

"Small problem here. I've got no way to get any message to Warren."

"Oh, of course you don't. Warren's clever enough to have established a convoluted path to make it harder for me to threaten him. But I'll bet old Brett there in the next room can get him the message." Gabriel looked in the direction of the camera hidden in Warren's office. "Hi Brett, you pretty lapdog. You're getting this on film, too, aren't you? Excellent. Make sure you pass on what I said. Warren has got the week-end to sort it out. If I don't see the real Warren by Monday, I'll have an alternative plan that will work every bit as well for me. I promise Warren will like it even less."

******

Lola was fascinated by Scott Base. Under any other circumstances she'd have wanted many more days there. But, if she, Alex and Maurice had been able to fly in, then others could too. She felt vulnerable at the base in ways she hadn't while aboard ship.

Friday morning, when the three of them were taken over to join the New Zealand cruise in progress, she felt a giant sense of relief. One look at Alex showed he didn't share her perspective. His reluctance to leave solid ground was written all over his face.

It seemed so unnecessary for Alex to be here. Could Ariel's premories have been wrong? Or maybe he'd already averted some disaster indirectly, saving her life in a way she'd never know.

Maurice wasn't looking so good either, Lola noticed, and she considered how hard this must be for a man his age, even one in as good a shape as Maurice. Of course, his ongoing worry about Yuden didn't help. Lola was painfully aware Maurice's love was as old as he was, and at the moment she was charging through the ice-cold waters of Tierra del Fuego in a speedboat. Not exactly a calming situation.

It was helpful that their quarters on the ship were more spacious than their previous ones. The other passengers greeted them warmly, accepting the story about two geologists joining the group. Lola racked her brain for everything she could remember about the Earth's mantle, while hoping for unusually calm seas.

******

Gabriel could have found the Texan lady telepath any time he wanted; he had no reason to bother. She was irrelevant. At least she was until her son showed up doing a perfect impersonation of Warren. Warren was not irrelevant.

He would have gotten Rafael to probe her mind if discretion had been important, as his Filipino friend had the precision of a surgeon when it came to stealth telepathy. But he didn't care whether she sensed his contact or not. He had no reason to fear her. He entered her mind and simply asked the question.

Where are you?

The reply was instantaneous.

What the hell are you doing here? Get the fuck out.

He laughed. So she knew who he was, and even middle-aged women used foul language in their own brains.

I just want your location.

Instead of her answer he felt the power of her mind, a growing strength pushing at him, driving him out. The intensity of it shook with her effort, but she succeeded.

Damn. He wouldn't have thought she was capable of that. He went back in. Or at least he tried, but he found nothing but a grey fuzz. He tried her teacher and found the same.

Okay. There were plenty of others. Somebody somewhere knew where that woman was.

******

The Chilean city of Punta Arenas couldn't have been more than a hundred miles from Ushuaia, if one was a bird. Nell wished she was, because a fish, or a boat, had a several-hundred-mile journey twisting along the breathtaking fjords of southern Chile.

They traveled all day Thursday, bundled up and hunched together, stopping for bathroom breaks and to stretch, and to pour more petrol into the gas tanks. Their captain said little, talking occasionally to Violeta in Spanish. He obviously knew his route well. Anyone who didn't would have been hopelessly lost.

They anchored for the short night, and got a few hours of cold and miserable rest in their seats. Friday, they resumed their journey as dawn filled the northern sky. Nell, Cillian, and Violeta huddled together in the back, while Yuden sat in the co-pilot seat wrapped in blankets.

Nell was sleepy, stiff, and sore, but recognized she was seeing beauty few humans got to experience. As cliff after cliff made a stunning drop to the sea, she focused on appreciating the sight. It was all the more poignant because she was enjoying it next to her dear friend Cillian, who couldn't share in her awe. He was cold and tired, too, as his misery radiated from him.

Nell understood Cillian's melancholy went well beyond his inability to see the view. Cuddled against him on his other side was Violeta, and the affection that had sprung up between them was obvious. So was the fact that they were slowly saying goodbye to each other with every touch and every word.

Nell thought of her own love, a wonderful Icelandic woman waiting for her to return. Love was what kept her going. She couldn't imagine how Cillian was coping. She gave his hand a squeeze and he squeezed back. Sometimes, between old friends, no words were needed.

Friday afternoon, they began following an inhabited coastline. Violeta told them they were about fifty miles south of Punta Arenas, and would stop to eat at a small town aptly named Port del Hambre, or Port of the Hungry. Instead of more dried snacks, they'd have a hot meal before speeding on to their destination by nightfall.

38. Not How It Was

Friday evening, the five people camping on the beach in Southern Brazil were gathering up their things to make an early morning departure easier. Ariel knew it was time to go home. Teddie and Vanida had done what was needed to free Nell and Yuden, and Xuha had done his part without risking his future. Everyone was on the road to safety. Mom and her telepaths could regroup to fight Warren's people another day. There was no reason to stay.

At least, that was how it should have been. But it wasn't how it was.

Ariel had brought a bag full of stuff from everyone and she resorted to holding various combinations trying to coax out visions. There weren't a lot of scenarios that looked like they'd gone the way they should have. The danger to her parents was growing and a there was a second danger point caused by someone intending to hurt them. Uncle Maurice stood a good chance of being collateral damage.

Zane was absolutely not in South America next week. He was surrounded by wealth and intrigue at the core of these events, but she was having a hell of a time seeing him. Had he shifted to become someone else? Why?

The escape Teddie, Vanida, and Xuha worked so hard to set in motion seemed destined for trouble as well. In one horrible set of probabilities, Cillian had already drowned at sea along with Yuden and Nell.

"I can't leave here," she told the group as they got together for a last walk on the beach.

"Me neither," Teddie said. "This has got to be the most beautiful place I've ever been."

"Beaches in Brazil have a magic allure," Fernando agreed.

"I didn't mean that," Ariel said. She saw Fernando's face fall. "I mean, yes, it's beautiful here, but I can't leave because I can't be on the road, not until things settle down. Heavy shit is coming next week, and it affects us all. I can be of more help if I'm not bouncing around in a car. Can't we stay longer?"

Camila considered. "I'm supposed to be at work on Monday, and so is Fernando. But, people do get sick on vacation." She glanced at Fernando. "You look like you're feeling poorly."

"Thanks," Ariel said. "I promise I'll work hard at this tomorrow. Maybe we can leave Sunday morning."

She wandered into the hut she shared with Teddie and Vanida, and sat at the little wooden table. She was trying to save the last bit of battery on her phone, so she dealt out a solitaire hand from a deck of cards left behind. Maybe this would relax her.

She started the game by doing the obvious things. Put the red five on the black six. Wait, which red five? They were identical choices. She went down one path. Not so good. Try the other. Much better.

This game is like my life with premories. One choice doesn't matter and another makes all the difference and you can't tell the two apart. It's not always about good decision-making, either. Sometimes it really is random.

She kept dealing, thinking and replaying. Soon she wasn't paying attention to the cards but was in a sort of trance. Teddie was the Two of Clubs and her mom was the Queen of Hearts, and, for some reason, she was the Nine of Spades. The man who ran Reel News was the King of Diamonds, of course, but there were two of them. No, not really. The Jack of Diamonds was pretending to be the King. That had to be Zane.

The worst of it was the Ten of Clubs was trying to get the Jack to kill the Queen of Hearts, who could only be saved by the King, but he wouldn't know it, and the Jack of Clubs, who seemed to be mom's friend Violeta, could stop the King of Diamonds, but only if the Queen of Clubs, who was Yuden, did some random thing she probably wouldn't do. Then Nell, who was the Jack of Spades, had to pretend to be the Queen of Hearts again.

Ariel leaned forward, put her head between her knees, and took deep breaths until the dizziness passed. She could use this.

She dealt again. And again. A sense of how events tied together began to emerge as the cards unraveled a complex tapestry that would have confused her logical mind. It reminded her of Tarot cards, which she'd seen friends use over the years and found amusing. Now, the richness of that other deck inspired her. Multiple characters and meanings danced through her head. Why had the Kind of Diamonds disappeared? Here at the end, why was the Queen of Hearts always upside down?

Dark comes quickly near the equator. After a short while, Camila came in and lit the gas lamp, saying nothing. A little later Fernando brought her a sandwich. She mumbled thanks but never touched it. She just kept playing. Not long after, Teddie and Vanida tiptoed by her as they went to bed. Sleep comes early, too, in a world without electricity.

After another hour, every card had taken on an identity or location, and almost all of it made sense to something deep within her brain. She hoped the few remaining puzzles could be solved later. She took the lamp and went to wake Camila.

"You contacted Olumiji for me once. Can you do it again?"

"I shouldn't. x^0 is in hiding, but I did it because you said it was an emergency." Camila was groggy but trying to wake up. "Why?"

"Well, I have another emergency. We either need to drive to phone service or you have to get a message to someone, and I'm not sure we have the time to drive. Please."

Camila was reaching for more clothes while she listened.

"If it's that important, of course. Tell me what and who."

"I need to pass information on to this lady named Violeta, my mom's friend from Reel News. Can you do that?"

"I'll contact Olumiji. He'll find a way. What do you need her to know?"

Ariel sighed, trying to think of an easy way to say it. "The sun is still setting down where Violeta is, and she going to get off a boat. An elderly woman named Yuden is one of the passengers. Yuden's cold, and the captain of the boat will offer her a dry baseball hat from his pack. She probably won't take it, because she's proud, but she needs to. She needs to tuck her hair under it, and keep wearing the hat, and do anything else she or the others can think of to make people think she is an old man. Not a woman. But the baseball hat really is the key."

"Are there more messages?"

"Yes. Tell Violeta I'm sorry, but Cillian and Nell need to room together, at least as far as the hotel staff knows. They need to pretend to be married and conceal the fact that Cillian is blind. Hats and sunglasses for everyone. Anything Nell can do to look like my mom is helpful. Or Cillian to look like my dad. The rest can wait until morning."

"That's complicated and way too specific," Camila said. "I'll do my best."

✶✶✶✶✶✶

Early Saturday morning, Warren had his report from Ushuaia. There were holes in it, of course, but he could fill them in. Alma was still in Ushuaia. Last night she had a house guest, and it was none other than Xuha, Warren's assaulter and former captive.

I knew these people were involved with each other. Now he's her bodyguard. That complicates matters.

The report said Alma had recently purchased an old truck from an acquaintance and it had been found on Friday, abandoned at a dock twenty miles west of town.

That's how Violeta got them out of there. They left by boat! Lola, Alex, and Maurice never even boarded that damn cruise ship. They sent imposters as decoys. Clever.

So, Lola, Alex, and Maurice were almost certainly on the small speed boat that left the dock Thursday morning, along with the problem-causing Violeta. What about the other two women who escaped? Surely they were aboard too?

No, the report said the boat had docked late last night in the Chilean city of Punta Arenas. Lodging had been secured for the captain, a tall Argentinian woman with a limp, a foreign couple, and an elderly man. The report noted the boat could only hold six people.

"So, they had to leave one or both of the other women behind. They must have left them both."

Warren considered searching for Yuden and Nell, but why? He'd be better off securing Lola and Alex, making sure he, not Gabriel, held this ultimate leverage over Zane.

******

Saturday January 26, Lola turned fifty-three. Or at least she thought she did, because there was some chance it wasn't Saturday. The international date line ran all the way to the South Pole, and she thought they'd crossed it once, maybe more. Perhaps her birthday was tomorrow. Or maybe she'd missed it.

She didn't get seasick, but this rough ride was challenging. Waves were unusually high, so only a continental breakfast was being served. To mark the day, she picked the most decadent-looking pastry out of the basket in the ship's galley. She took a small bite and grimaced. It wasn't chocolate chips; she'd been deceived by raisins again.

Well, at least Gabriel hadn't been back to bother her. What had he wanted, anyway? She tried to reach out to her children for information, but the effort only added to the queasiness.

Alex had been lost in his own time-warping nap since yesterday, and it was unlikely he'd wake up before tomorrow. Last night, Maurice had taken all the motion sickness medicine the ship's doctor would give him, hoping to sleep through this storm.

Tomorrow, they'd be at sea all day, then Monday they'd go ashore at Macquarie Island. After that, it would be another five long days to Invercargill at the southern tip of New Zealand. The seas would be calmer by then, though, and once they were at Invercargill it would be easy get to the U.S.

She was ready to go home. This had gone on forever. She wanted her family safe, her life back, and for the ship to hold still.

Maybe she should lay down. Her body had no idea if it was morning, noon, or evening, not that there was much difference between the three, with the sun low in the northern sky no matter what time of day it was.

She curled up under the covers and considered her next move. She was pretty sure it was nine in the morning, on her birthday, and she was back in bed for the day.

Alex was snoring in the bunk next to her. So peaceful. She peeked into his mind and rode the wave of his deep slumber for a moment. When she blinked her eyes open, the little clock said ten-thirty. Whoa. That worked well. It hadn't occurred to her that when Alex's mind moved at a different speed, hers could too.

Would he care if she did more of that? Of course he wouldn't. She got out of her own bed, crawled into his narrow bunk, curled her body around his backside and held on while her mind melded into his. Then she rested while the miserable day flew by.

******

Warren spent more time sleeping on Saturday than he intended, but no where near as much as Zane did. Brett reported to Jerry that Zane slept almost the entire day. Jerry, of course, reported it on to Warren.

Warren assumed the young man was worn out from impersonating him for hours on end. That was fine. He didn't need Zane till Monday, and he had plenty of other matters to tend to.

He contacted Jerry to increase the level of his mental protection, and then he used his new secure line to make calls to board members and friends, soothing ruffled feathers and establishing he was still in charge. A few warned him something was afoot with the heads of his subsidiaries and he'd do well to watch his back. He thanked each, knowing it accomplished more to be grateful than to tell an ally he was sharing old news.

He made careful note of those who didn't warn him, or, worse yet, those who went out of their way to imply all was well. There were ways to find one's enemies without telepathy.

He realized with some embarrassment that he'd forgotten about his wife. She was likely to hear he was in town and wonder why he hadn't come home. At least he hoped she'd wonder why. Well, this was the sort of situation text messages were made for. He composed one filled with apologies about urgent business and a need to stay elsewhere, added a few expressions of his affection and gave it to Jerry to send on.

Then he turned his attention to the Entelechy.

Gabriel's threat had been passed from Brett to Jerry, as it should have been. However, Jerry had passed it on to Warren.

"That is *exactly* what is not supposed to happen. It is why I'm in hiding. Why Zane is here. You are not supposed to let Gabriel threaten me."

"But what if I didn't tell you and Gabriel did something awful to mess up your plans? You'd be livid."

Jerry had a point. His men wanted to look out for him, so they couldn't serve as a filter. The wall between him and Jerry had to be such that Jerry had no way of passing along a threat.

That meant Warren had to hide somewhere Jerry couldn't discover. That could only happen if Warren didn't know where he was himself, because Jerry could read his mind. So, he had to be taken somewhere he couldn't identify, by somebody Jerry didn't know. Under those circumstances, Jerry could keep up a wall around Warren's mind but have no way to relay threats on to him, no matter how much he wanted to.

Well, plenty of ready cash could buy such a crazy scenario.

Meanwhile, Jerry had to focus his full attention on keeping a shroud around Warren's brain, taking only short, cautious breaks when Warren slept. That was going to be tough duty, but Jerry was a tough guy.

This would all work better, of course, if Brett couldn't relay threats on to Jerry either. Warren was pleased with his own brilliance. He could do a double filter. He'd hide Jerry somewhere too, in a place Jerry didn't recognize and Brett couldn't find. Under the circumstances, this added layer seemed worth the effort.

Didn't anyone else notice how complicated telepathy made everything?

By Monday morning, he had to be able to trust, one-hundred percent, that Zane would do exactly what Brett instructed him to do. So it was imperative he get his hands on Zane's parents before he and Jerry disappeared.

His sources said their getaway boat remained docked in Punta Arenas and the captain of the vessel, the tall Argentinian woman, an Anglo man and woman, and an elderly man remained at the hotel. They spent most of the day resting after their ordeal of travel. A hotel employee confirmed the group had arranged to check out Monday morning.

Very well. He had until tomorrow night to get this whole situation under control again. He picked up the phone and called Chidi, who was in Ushuaia waiting for instructions.

******

Gabriel didn't want to spend all day Saturday trying to find Lola, but he did. He started with the obvious, making more attempts to connect with her, her teacher, or her husband. Either the woman had some powerful way to make all three people appear to be asleep, or all three of them had really slept for the past fifteen hours. Gabriel didn't think either was possible.

Zane was easy enough to find. Ongoing checks revealed he was wary of Gabriel and displeased with the ongoing charade he'd been forced into, but he had no idea where his parents or anyone else in his family was. In fact, he wished he knew. Gabriel wished he did, too.

Locating either of the two sisters could have been useful, but without some direct connection Gabriel couldn't find them. It was possible Warren knew something, but Warren's mind was now under the protection of the monad defector, Jerry.

Monad-defector. Gabriel ran the words together and fought an impulse to spit. Who'd have thought there'd ever be such a thing? Yet, there'd been more than one. Rafael, his Filipino friend, had taken on the job of tracking the loyalties of the others. It was time he checked in with Rafael to see how the unknowns were stacking up, and how efforts to influence the board of directors were going.

"I have information to help you," Rafael began. Gabriel marveled at how fast his friend discerned the purpose of the phone call. "First, the other twenty-one members of the Entelechy who swore allegiance to our takeover all remain loyal. Good news. The bad news is none of them have the information you want. Further bad news is Warren thinks he has gained the cooperation of four monads, which gives him far more power than he'd otherwise have. Jerry and Brett are with him, as you know. Jerry provides him with a shield around his mind. Brett is babysitting Warren's imposter. I think it would be dangerous to try to obtain information from either of them."

Gabriel agreed.

"He's bought the loyalty of two others," Rafael continued. "He's holding the Turk in reserve, thinking he may be useful once his grief subsides. We think not. Our best bet is Chidi, the Nigerian he left in Ushuaia to look after his interests. Warren has great trust in Chidi. We should look closer look at what he knows."

Gabriel sent his agreement and thanks. Rafael was impressive in his competence.

"There's more. To my surprise, five monads have left us and claim loyalties to no one, while another four have openly sided with x^0. Someone in that group may know something. I'll look and let you know what I learn."

After the phone call, Gabriel took a welcome break and headed to the hotel gym. As he stepped onto the treadmill, programming in his cardio, he had two tiny, nagging thoughts.

Was it possible Rafael was more capable than he was? And why hadn't his old friend asked him about how things in New York were going? Gabriel had to guess it was because Rafael already knew.

By the time he got back to his room he had three text messages from Rafael. They said: "Fernando w/ Zane sisters in Brazil," "Our Aussie Hank took the cruise," and "Chidi helping Warren find Lola."

That was encouraging. He hopped in the shower. By the time he got out there was another. "Lola on ship from South Pole to NZ. Ashore Macquarie Island Monday landfall NZ Friday."

Finally, he had something. He'd dry off, then find out where the hell Macquarie Island was, what ship was docking there, and how he or someone else trustworthy could get there by Monday morning. He was pulling on his pants when the final text came.

"Warren thinks Lola is in Chile! Let's keep it that way."

This just kept getting better.

39. No Such Thing as Cold

Warren was pleased with Chidi, his Nigerian monad. Early Sunday morning, the man booked a mid-day flight to Punta Arenas for himself and two of Warren's locals. Better yet, he made it clear to Warren he understood he'd be approaching three telepaths and a man capable of lightning speed. He was confident he could prevent the telepaths from sensing him and planned to drug the other man.

"Have no worries about what these people can do. It is handled."

After all the past bumbling, this was a refreshing start. It seemed to Warren his problems resulted from being too soft. He'd gone out of his way not to harm people, and they'd responded by finding ways to thwart him. It was time to face facts. He was at war, fighting for his way of life. He needed to think like a warrior.

"I only want the parents of the young man," Warren told Chidi. "I don't want the other two."

Chidi asked what he should do with his former coworker Violeta and the elderly teacher he'd already kidnapped once and rather enjoyed meeting. Warren said nothing.

"I will not kill them."

"I'd never ask such a thing of you. I'll arrange for one of the other men to handle it. You don't have to know anything about it."

"I don't see how that's substantially different."

"And I don't know of another way to make sure they can't *possibly* follow you, or *possibly* ever make trouble for me again." The irritation in Warren's voice was clear. "I'm sick and tired of having these people make a fool of me. Your job is to get them together and subdued, and bring me the two I need. Let me worry about the rest."

This time it was Chidi who said nothing.

******

Sunday morning, the captain of the small charter boat checked out of the hotel in Punta Arenas to return home. Violeta went to work. Her short to-do list included sending the first man she'd loved in a decade back to Ireland with his friend Nell. Yuden had to leave, too, but Violeta was delaying that problem because it wasn't clear where the woman should go. Yuden wanted to go to Texas, but the people she knew there were scattered around the Southern Hemisphere. Yet, returning to Bhutan meant possibly abandoning her love for Maurice forever. Violeta had no trouble understanding the woman's dilemma.

Another item on her to-do list was maintaining the illusion that Yuden was an elderly man. That, along with the illusion of Nell and Cillian being a married couple, was important. No one had bothered to explain the reason to her, but it wasn't hard to guess somebody somewhere thought she'd fled with Lola, Alex, and Maurice instead of Nell, Cillian, and Yuden. Someone on her side wanted to maintain the deception.

For the past couple of days, Violeta had been relying on information from the Nigerian telepath Olumiji. She still found his style awkward and his communication confusing, but Lola trusted him, so she did too. She would have preferred to deal directly with Lola, but she saw the wisdom in keeping Lola as mentally isolated as possible. Wherever Lola was, whatever she was doing, the less anyone knew about it the better.

******

Lola was napping. She never slept well when the sun was up; she tended to lay there and think of what she ought to be doing.

307

She was making an exception for this trip, however, often crawling into Alex's mind to make her nap last longer.

The storm had been relentless and by early Sunday morning the seas were dangerous. Passengers were asked over the ship's PA to remain in their cabins. Crew members would come by with food and supplies. Patience was appreciated. Waves were expected to diminish by nightfall.

Maurice and Alex both slept through the announcement.

Lola couldn't go back to sleep after the speaker crackled off. She tossed around as she thought about Teddie's reaction to the laws of thermodynamics. It reminded her of the hours she'd spent in high school agonizing over whether she existed or not. What happened to that first blush of angst? As people aged, did they decide big questions didn't matter? Who cares if you aren't real or if the universe is in a slow fizzle when you have bills to pay? She rolled over and stared at the water outside the gray porthole.

Maybe it *was* all becoming increasingly disorganized, destined for a long, sad end. Or maybe we didn't understand the universe. Maybe we only got a small fraction of it. Could Alex's many timelines produce a multiverse ending in something better than a whimper?

The ship took a particularly nauseating drop, and Lola grabbed onto the rails on the side of her bed. *Keep thinking about something besides this ship.*

How did one get multiverses? All that matter popping out of nowhere. It made no sense. Then again, matter popping out of nowhere one time made no sense either. Plus, matter might not even exist. Could be it was all energy. Nothing more than waves.

She felt the ship twist as it lifted high and she braced herself for the plunge she knew would follow.

Don't think about waves. No waves. Hell, there was no way *not* to think about waves right now. If the damn universe was going to descend into disorganized nothingness, why didn't it get it over with?

A series of sharp knocks on the cabin door woke her two companions. A pleasant young man, at ease on the heaving ship, brought in a tray of dry snacks, cartons of water, and more motion sickness treatments, as well as extra pillows, cushions, and more bungee cords.

"We're in a bit of a lull," he said. "The captain says if you want a quick spot of air on deck, now would be the time."

"I'll pass," Maurice said, "but I will take a look at your pill selection."

"I could really use the fresh air," Lola said. She looked at Alex. He knew how hard it was for her to stay in the enclosed cabin.

"Let's both go."

After that, their recollections would always be different.

She'd remember wanting to leave the cabin before he changed his mind.

He'd remember wondering why she didn't stop to put on something besides those stupid cheap slippers.

She'd remember hurrying down the hall, because she wanted to catch the heavy metal door before it latched behind a couple coming back inside.

He'd remember being annoyed at having to hurry to keep up with her, as he felt a gust of wind blow through the open door.

She'd remember bounding outside, then looking up and being overwhelmed at the sight of the huge wave on the other side of the ship. She'd recall its roar, its froth, and her own fear as she started to slide with the tilt of the deck.

He'd never see the wave. As he reached the door, he was looking down, watching her momentum carry her into a slide, as she slipped in those stupid shoes along an improbably tilted deck toward a rail that came only as high as her knees for Christ's sake but stuck out over the ocean. What kind of guard rail was that?

She wouldn't remember a guard rail, just a second of terror, a realization she was going overboard.

He'd see her slow down, way down, almost stopping as she hung there.

She'd remember Alex grabbing her arm so fast she thought he'd dislocated her shoulder, then both of them slamming onto the deck and sliding backwards toward the door, with Alex grabbing on to something as the boat made a high-angle lurch the other way and then a few more frightening tilts back and forth.

He'd remember time speeding back up as she cried and shivered with the cold and the shock. He'd remember thinking he'd almost lost her again.

She'd only remember telling him that she loved him.

He'd remember holding her to warm her and hoping she understood how much he loved her too.

******

"I've just lost a quarter of the probabilities I was seeing." Ariel announced it on Sunday afternoon.

"Oh my God. That sounds awful," Camila said.

"Sorry. I wasn't clear. I've lost the quadrant containing some of the worst outcomes possible. Based on something that happened, everything in it is no longer an option."

"That's good then?" Fernando said.

"Absolutely. Mom, dad, and Maurice still could die, but one whole group of dire scenarios just vanished."

"Does that mean we're leaving?" Teddie looked sad as she asked, but Camila and Fernando were less dismayed, so Ariel addressed her answer to them.

"Not quite. I've been following this well enough to be sure we're close to this all resolving. Can I have until tomorrow?"

"We can push it a little longer."

******

Back in the cabin, Lola was covered with all of the blankets they had, but she still couldn't get warm. Alex wanted to go get her some hot tea, but passengers had been asked to stay in their quarters given the "unpredictability of today's seas."

He tried to say something to help her feel better. "You do know technically there's no such thing as cold?"

Many people would have replied, "I'm shivering with cold, you idiot," but Lola understood.

"I know." She gave a weak laugh. "Only more heat and less heat. Or no heat at all, which is absolute zero, but you can't get there from here. Or anywhere." Her teeth were chattering as she said it.

"Knowing there is no such thing as cold is scant comfort to someone freezing to death," Maurice said, as he wrapped an extra jacket over Lola's legs.

"It's okay. Humans die from insufficient heat or too much heat. Cold is like dark, really," she babbled. "No such thing as dark either, just more or less light."

Maurice relented, thinking the discussion could help her. He tried to take it further. "No cold. No darkness. How about no hate?"

"Even better. No evil. Think about it. Lots of love, or too little love. People do awful things because they lack love in their hearts. There's no force called evil."

Alex saw how she was still shivering, and pulled out his extra pair of socks and gave them to her. "Put these on over yours. Most religious leaders of all faiths disagree with you about no evil."

"I know. I'm just saying it's a different perspective." She was shivering a little less now. "You can fight evil, but maybe you should be encouraging love. It's not the same thing, because there's no enemy to fight, just something lacking."

Both Alex and Maurice noticed color coming back into her cheeks. She shrugged off a blanket as she sat up straighter. "I was thinking about this while you guys slept. Maybe instead of dying I get to keep being me in all those multiverses you love, coming back over and over, trying to do it better. With more love."

Both men looked at her and, for an instant, between the heaving waves and the shivering cold, it clicked together for her.

"That's it."

"What's it?" Alex asked.

"You know, I wise up and do the best me possible, and after that I come back and get to start doing you. Or Maurice. Or whoever. Until I get that right. It all ends eventually, but it's a long, long path and my death here means little. Somewhere within in it all may be a place where all of creation comes together perfectly."

Alex reached out and took her hand in his.

"You're warming up," was all he said.

She gave him a pleading look. "It's more than that. When this is over, and life's normal, don't let me forget that for a few seconds the universe made perfect sense to me."

He gave her hand a squeeze. "I'll remember that, I promise. On every timeline I can."

******

Because Chidi was concerned about Lola, Maurice or Violeta sensing him, he didn't try to get information from them ahead of time. He only made a fast sweep to verify they'd be where he expected, and he made his plans.

He and the two Argentinian thugs would approach the foursome while they eating at the hotel. Chidi would drug Alex, then force the group upstairs where he'd be expected to drug Lola as well, so the two groggy captives would be docile enough to transport without incident. Lola and Alex would be flown out on a charter to Panama. Warren had made arrangements already.

Chidi knew one of the men with him had a second set of syringes to be used to kill Violeta and Maurice after Chidi left. He considered trying to dilute or replace the liquid but he had no idea where these syringes were kept and he knew he lacked any expertise to deal with them if he found them.

So his plan, such as it was, was to improvise and find a way to keep Maurice and Violeta alive. He wasn't happy about the many ways *that* could go wrong, but he didn't have a better idea.

******

By Sunday afternoon Zane felt rested. He put on a news program in his room and did some stretching exercises. A peek outside the door revealed the two guards were still there, so he ordered lavish room service on Warren's tab and considered his next move.

Warren was using him to buy time while he found a way to oust his two-dozen-or-so disloyal telepaths without letting them have the means to oust him. What exactly did Warren plan to do with these people if he succeeded? They didn't seem to be the sort to just go away.

Even if they did, what next? Would Warren pursue his agenda of stirring up paranoia about psychic phenomena as a way to control them? Would that carry over to persecuting his mother's x^0 group and the Zeitman family? Or would Warren return to stirring up fears and starting wars in order to keep the money flowing? The latter was the best scenario, and it wasn't that good.

What if Warren failed and Gabriel and his monads took control of Reel News? What was their agenda? They'd already used their telepathy to make the network wildly successful, but reading minds could yield a lot of information. Had they blackmailed reluctant sources into talking? How about coercing cooperation from those with facts that didn't fit their narrative? These men had not only covered the news for years, they'd shaped it. Until now, that shaping supported Warren's agenda. Without him, they'd advance their own desires. What were those?

Zane recalled his mother describing the monads as a group of self-centered men interested only in their own egos. Maybe that was being a bit hard on them. Such a group wouldn't have a philosophical agenda, so perhaps they wouldn't be as dangerous.

Or would they?

Would he rather give power to a zealot wanting to manipulate the news to support his own fear-based vision, or to a group of egotists with no belief system other than their own gratification?

Neither. Neither was an acceptable choice for wielding this much power. Somebody else had to run this network.

Then he realized it. Tomorrow morning, that person was going to be him. If he chose, he could go right ahead and run Reel News.

Granted, by tomorrow, Warren hoped to have the means to coerce Zane. Gabriel hoped to have a way to override Warren's threats. But what if Zane refused to be threatened by anyone or anything, no matter how horrible?

That could end very badly, of course, for him and those he loved, but a bad ending wasn't a given. He had a lot of capable people on his side. He could do what was right in the hope they'd find a way to protect themselves while he did. In fact, he could up the odds of them managing their own survival if he let them know what he was considering.

The most compelling argument to go this route was that giving in to threats often ended as poorly as resisting did. He and those he cared for may not be any better off if he complied. Zane was warming to the idea of being a man who couldn't be coerced.

Yet, if it all worked out, he couldn't keep impersonating Warren. Tomorrow's version of Warren needed someone else worthy of taking over the company. He needed to find this person fast, before either side put a stop to his short reign.

A couple years prior, Zane had watched the president of the company he worked for make a death-bed decision to pass the helm of his corporation over to someone unexpected. Zane still had contacts who were well versed in exactly how it had been done. No one would think the twenty-seven-year-old law student impersonating Warren would have the first inkling of how to accomplish a corporate takeover. Surprise would be one of his best weapons.

He could start with a couple of phone calls tonight to set matters in motion. He could call an old friend or two on the hotel phone and maybe even use it to call Nigeria. It would all be traceable, of course, but he couldn't see why it mattered. He was only passing the time, sneaking in a call to a friend of his mom's in hopes of getting word about how she was doing. Wouldn't it be more suspicious if he didn't do a few things like that?

40. Take the Helicopter

Violeta was getting ready for dinner when she felt Olumiji's presence.

I'm about to call you. I've much to tell and it's too important for misunderstandings.

I thought that phone calls weren't safe?

They weren't, but everything is about to change.

Her phone rang.

"Hello?"

******

Chidi was in the restaurant, standing behind the man who could move fast, about to inject the sedative into his neck, when he realized something was wrong. He felt the man's sense of panic and knew it involved being unable to see. The man was blind.

Chidi looked at Violeta, who was seated next to the blind man.

"You've been tricked," she said. "The people you want are nowhere near here. Tell your men to keep their weapons hidden and come upstairs. We need to talk."

Chidi agreed. Why not? It made no sense to drug this blind man, and going upstairs was what he'd planned on doing all along.

Once they were in Violeta's room, she demanded everyone's weapons before she would say a word. Chidi motioned to his companions to comply. One handed over a small hand gun with relief. The other laid down his gun, a knife, and the two fatal syringes while eying Violeta with anger and Chidi with contempt. Chidi added his own syringes filled with the sedatives to the pile.

Violeta was blunt.

"Before dinner, I was contacted by the man who runs x^0. He confirmed what I suspected. Zane's parents, Lola and Alex, are safe elsewhere, as is Lola's teacher. Warren was deliberately misled to think they were with me. Instead, I have three of the others Warren took from Texas, and they're of no use to you."

Chidi saw his hopes for making a safe exit from Warren's clutches withering. It was time to improvise. And bluff.

"We could overpower you," Chidi said. "Even kill all four of you. Give us the parents' exact location and we'll spare you."

She laughed.

"You don't have to threaten me to get it. Right now, the three you want are on a boat in a heavy storm somewhere five days south of New Zealand. Warren can't get to them in time. However, I'm willing to offer you a different deal. Probably a better one."

She picked up that Chidi was interested, and it didn't surprise her. He'd always looked out for his own self-interest, but tempered it with ethics. She repeated her offer in Spanish. The two Argentinian thugs with Chidi had less to gain, but one was curious about her proposal, while the other was looking for a way to get his gun back. She felt his hope of earning Warren's favor by taking down two disloyal employees and four hostages.

Yuden took off her sunglasses and removed her baseball hat, letting her long braids fall to her shoulders while she studied all three men. Nell had made an effort to look more like Lola at dinner, and now she relaxed back into her own features.

"Yes, I do see how we were misled," Chidi said. "What could you possibly have to offer us?"

"A better alternative than doing Warren's increasingly distasteful bidding, or even pretending to do so. Instead of running from him, a chance for a place in the reorganized Reel News."

"You do not have this to offer," Chidi said.

"But I do. Tomorrow, Warren will take steps to turn the company over to me. I'm far from a likely choice, but I was on a short list. Most of Warren's officers and board of directors don't trust Gabriel or his group, yet they sense Warren is losing his influence. The man who picked me doesn't care for the monads *or* for Warren. The board will be coaxed into welcoming me in an unexpected development."

It was Chidi's turn to laugh.

"Why in God's name would Warren do such a thing?"

"Because he won't really be Warren."

Then Chidi understood. The young man they were trying to control was, in fact, going to be able to single-handedly change the course of the company tomorrow. Warren wouldn't be able to stop him because no one could reach Warren to tell him what was going on. But surely it wasn't that simple.

"What's to keep me from telling Brett all this right now? I bet Brett could stop Zane."

"Your own common sense and self-interest should guide you. Gabriel *will* get to Lola and Alex because he's known their location since yesterday. If you contact Brett and gum up the works, Gabriel will assume control of Reel News with or without Zane's help. It's a takeover he's planned well. The first thing he'll do is deal with you monads who defected. He's disgusted with you, and his plans aren't pleasant. I know you don't like him and you've lost your regard for Warren, too."

Violeta gave one of her sweetest smiles.

"So why not join the winning team?" she said. "We actually value the loyalty you showed to Warren, and we don't... intend... to... treat... him..." Her words slowed down as she felt the angry thug begin to inch toward the weapons. Two guns, three syringes, and a knife all lay there. Where was the other syringe? Who had it? She felt Yuden's pride at having snuck it into her palm.

The man made a sudden lunge for his guns, then sprung up, and pointed it at Chidi's head.

"La gallina," he said. Chidi knew the Spanish word for chicken.

Violeta felt Nell's pulse rise. Yuden had passed the syringe to her, but she was too far from the man. She was considering passing it to Cillian, who was closer.

Violeta felt the man preparing to pull the trigger, steeling himself to do the most unthinkable thing humans do. He intended to shoot six times before he could think about it and then make a triumphant call to Warren.

His finger twitched, and Violeta flew at him, decades of judo training overcoming her own fears and pains. She landed on top of him, pushing the barrel of the gun to the floor.

Cillian landed next to her, the syringe in his hand. He couldn't see where the gun was pointed, so he just reached out for the man's neck and plowed the needle of into it. The man spasmed under Violeta's weight, then lay silent.

"That wasn't a sedative," Chidi said. "Those blue ones held lethal doses meant for Maurice and Violeta. I intended to prevent them from being administered."

No one said anything. Cillian put both of his hands on the body for a minute and bowed his head. Violeta thought he was saying a prayer. At the end of it, he seemed to have reached a conclusion.

"I will take responsibility for what I've done," he said. "No one else here needs to be involved with this death."

"What do you mean?"

"As far as most people know, I'm not here. I'm already leaving at dawn for Ireland." He held up his hand to keep anyone from objecting. "Leave the syringe next to the body so it's obvious what happened. Find it all tomorrow after Nell and I land in Panama and tell the police you think I got into an argument with him. Explain Yuden is your friend, but you didn't know us; you only brought us along because we were stranded in Ushuaia too. You had no idea I was capable of this."

"They'll figure out the flight you left on and come after you."

"Once we're in Panama, we'll disappear. I'll get a hold of my own people in Ireland. They'll get us home."

Violeta looked at Cillian. "You won't want to be making visits to this part of the world after this will you?"

"No, I doubt I'll even want to be seen in New York romancing Ushuaia's newly famous CEO. You have important things to do, Violeta. So do I."

He reached his hand toward her and pulled her face closer. "I didn't realize leaving you was going to be so hard to do."

"Yeah. If I'd known about this, I'd never have met your damn plane."

"Let's go to my room and give them a minute," Nell said.

Chidi turned to the other man who'd come with them, remembering he spoke only a little English.

"Are you okay with this? Listo? To switch sides?"

"I am okay," the man replied.

"We're sorry for your friend," Yuden said.

He pointed to the dead man on the floor. "Not a nice man. Not a friend."

Chidi understood.

Later, he'd ask Violeta to give the man more details. Right now, there were so many things he wanted to ask her. How was this transfer of power going to take place? What role would he play in the new structure? What would happen to Warren?

But it didn't take telepathy to recognize Violeta had no interest in answering questions at the moment. She'd wrapped her arms around Cillian and was clinging to him with all her strength, tears running down both cheeks. Chidi could only see the back of Cillian's head, but he was pretty sure the Irishman was crying at least as hard as his Argentinian lady.

✶✶✶✶✶✶

Gallows humor ruled the breakfast table aboard ship Monday morning, as passengers enjoyed their first hot meal in days and exchanged tales from the weekend. Dangerous falls, extreme sea-sickness, and bruises from unexpected encounters with flying objects were described with exaggeration and laughter. It was a hearty group, one that had expected a difficult voyage. With the hardship over, they reveled in sharing their stories.

They became more somber, however, when they heard of Lola's poorly timed entrance on the deck just as the largest wave yet had tilted the ship far enough to have frightened them all.

"How did you get all the way over there to grab her in time?" one passenger asked Alex. "That sounds impossible." Alex froze.

"I'll never know how he managed, but I'm sure glad he did," Lola said. More laughter followed. Of course she was glad, and if the couple had overstated the story, what was the harm?

After breakfast, Lola, Alex, and Maurice prepared for their first journey ashore. They joined the other passengers in wiping their gear and putting on sterilized boots to protect the isolated ecosystem they were about to enter.

Boarding a Zodiac in high seas was no trivial matter, but the experienced crew walked them through the maneuver without a hitch. It was a short ride to shore. Even Alex's face lit up when they stepped out on a beach covered with friendly king penguins who looked at them with curiosity and began to follow them around. Before long, they were talking to the penguins and posing for pictures with them. It was hard to say whether the penguins or the humans were more amused by the encounter.

Because geology was part of their cover, the trio made a point of examining one of the famed rock outcrops formed from oceanic crust squeezed all the way up to the Earth's surface. Maurice and Lola asked as many informed questions as they could. Lola was relieved to sense the geologist who spoke with them felt no reason to question their expertise.

They were enjoying a late lunch when a member of their ship's crew approached Alex.

"You folks are requesting a chopper ride on to Auckland Island?" He sounded bewildered.

Alex shook his head. "Not me. It's true I'd be happier than most to avoid the next stretch of sea, but that's out of my price range. Plus, my two geologist friends here are in no hurry to go."

"Cost shouldn't be a concern. We were told friends of yours wanted to do this for you. They're worried about your wife's close call at sea yesterday and are trying to get you home sooner."

"Oh heavens, we don't need a helicopter," Lola said, ignoring pointed glares from both of her companions. "We're fine."

"Well, the soonest one could make it would be early tomorrow morning, and we're not sure one is available. Plus, the ship leaves tonight, so we'd have to make arrangements for you to overnight here on the base." His tone made it clear this exception was not always granted. "I'll tell you what. You go enjoy your afternoon and I'll check in once we see if it's even an option. You can decide then."

Alex and Maurice said no more, as the three of them joined the other passengers in the Zodiac headed to the penguin rookery on the other side of the island. These penguins were even more inquisitive, coming up to the passengers' phones and cocking their heads to the side with puzzled expressions, making for countless hilarious photos.

"You know, this is just the kind of thing Olumiji would do," Maurice said. "I have no idea how that man finances his exploits but I would be so like him to decide to fly us off of here. I think we should consider taking him up on his offer."

"But we're not even sure it's him. Are you positive he knows we're here?" Lola asked.

"He's the *only* one who knows we're here. Well, he and Violeta. He worked with her and her mother to do this. Before Gabriel tried to get into your head a few days ago and you put a wall up around us, he and I checked in with each other. He knows how tired I must be. I suspect he's doing this for me."

Alex raised his hand. "He may not know it, but he's doing it for me, too. I'm worn out, dear. If someone wants to throw us a lifeline by sending a helicopter, I say take it."

She didn't reply. Everything Maurice and Alex said made sense, but it didn't feel right. Maybe it was her pride; she wanted to finish the journey.

When they got back to the Zodiac, one of the ship's crew was on the radio. She waved at Lola and Alex.

"You guys are in luck. They've found a long-range chopper, and the base has three beds they'll let you use. Are you a go?"

"Give us a minute," Lola said.

"Are you nuts?" Alex asked her.

"I just want to contact Olumiji and make sure this is his idea." She closed her eyes, holding on to Alex's arm to remain steady. "Damn. He's sound asleep."

"Try Violeta," Maurice suggested.

She nodded, then shook her head. "Is it the middle of the night all over the world?"

"I've got people waiting on the radio," the crew member shouted over. "Yes or no?"

Maurice and Alex both gave her their best puppy eyes.

"Yes. Of course. Thank everybody for their trouble."

"Oh, cheer up," Alex said. "You're getting to spend the night at yet another Antarctic research station. That's cool, isn't it?"

Lola tried to look happy, but Alex was the one whose spirits had risen considerably.

******

The next morning, Chidi wanted to make sure his Argentinian accomplice understood what he was getting into. To do that, he needed Violeta as a translator. He knew she'd just put Cillian and Nell on a plane, but he'd given her all the time to cry that he could.

When she answered her door, Chidi was relieved to see her eyes were dry and her voice was steady.

"Make sure he understands I called Jerry last night and lied," he said, pointing to his accomplice. "Jerry had no reason to suspect me, so Warren has now closeted himself away somewhere even Jerry can't reach him. No one can reach Jerry either. Brett has been assured I have the boy's parents with me. Tell him I told Jerry that you and Maurice were already dead and Lola, Alex and I are leaving this morning on a charter for Santiago. Tell him instead it needs to be me, him, and Yuden. The charter will only count passengers and note genders."

"So now you want him to help you with this deception?"

"I do, but not for long. He just has to ride on the plane. Tell him last Friday Warren arranged for Zane to meet with Gabriel at ten tomorrow morning New York time to discuss changes to the company's leadership. Once we land in Santiago, I'll be patched into that meeting. He can go find a place to lay low. All hell is going to break loose then, so tell him not to go home until things blow over."

Violeta understood. She started talking to the man in Spanish. He asked a few questions. She answered them. Chidi followed along telepathically.

"He wants to know where you and Yuden will go after he leaves you."

"Tell him I want to get this grandmother safely back to the U.S. where she knows people. Me, I'll make my way to New York, where I hope to play a key role in a new organization." He gave her a meaningful look. "I hear I'll be working for a talented lady who I've always admired. I was pretty sure you were telepathic, you know."

"Really?"

After Gabriel and Warren's brush off, it hadn't occurred to Violeta that others in the Entelechy had noticed her skills.

"Gabriel is a vain ignoramus, all the more so for not appreciating you. How soon will you be in New York?" he asked.

"I'll clear up matters with the police, and check in on my mom. Xuha is with her. Once I'm sure she's okay, I'll head out."

"Sounds good. I'll see you in New York, boss."

He grinned, and Violeta couldn't remember when she'd seen Chidi so happy.

After he and his helper left, she checked the clock. She dare not get the police involved for another hour. All morning Chidi had been holding up a wall around them to keep Gabriel and the other monads at bay, but now she was on her own.

She reached out. It was two hours earlier in New York and Gabriel was sleeping. Zane was awake, working through a complex plan to legally change the course of a company in ways that couldn't be easily undone. How had a twenty-something learned to do that?

Right now, he was worried she would be unable or unwilling to handle the burdens being foisted on her. She didn't blame him. He'd chosen her because he couldn't think of another option.

When Olumiji contacted her on Zane's behalf yesterday, she'd agreed to Zane's plan without much thought. Most of the intervening hours had been focused on her goodbyes with Cillian and, of course, on the three men who'd been sent to murder her.

Now that she had a moment, she realized her acceptance of this challenge ran deeper than feeding her own pride or winning out over those who'd wronged her. This was a job she could do and would enjoy doing. This was a job she could do well.

She reached out to Olumiji, still unsure of the etiquette for doing so.

Yes? She almost heard the word in her mind.

Please. I need Zane to know I have given this more thought and I am more certain. He need not worry. I can and will do this.

She felt reassurances he would pass along the message.

Violeta was about to move on to other tasks when she decided to give Yuden a quick check. Yuden been through a great deal, and Violeta needed to look out for her. She moved cautiously into the previously unexplored mind of the elderly Bhutanese woman and was staring at Cillian's face. Her heart stopped beating. What the hell?

Then she felt the unfamiliar feel of Yuden's thoughts, in a language far from her own but with emotions that made sense. Yuden, lying in her bed, was using her abilities to check in on Cillian and Nell. Yuden was concerned about their safe exit from Chile, and hoped to bring back news of well-being to Violeta. She was worried about Violeta, who'd been through so much lately.

What a lovely gift. Violeta lingered a few seconds longer, studying the familiar features of Cillian's face. Then she exited Yuden's mind. It was time to put together the details of the story she'd tell the police.

41. Do What You Will

It was Monday morning, and Ariel showed no signs of being ready to leave. Fernando got up early to drive till he found cell reception, so he could call both his and Camila's bosses. Camila stayed to help Olumiji handle telepathic communications.

Teddie and Vanida tried to relax on the beautiful beach, but felt like they needed to be helping somehow.

"I understand," Fernando told them once he returned. "I'm not close enough to the right people to be able to form links and help Camila. It's frustrating not to be able to do anything."

"I'm going to go find Yuden," Vanida decided. "I know she's supposed to be safe in Chile, but I want to see for myself. Maybe I'll learn something useful while I'm there. I'll be back in a while."

"That's what I was thinking." Teddie said. "I mean, I'm going to go look in on my mom and dad. I know they're on a boat and I hate going over oceans, but I need to see them."

"Can I help you somehow?" Fernando was so sincere.

"Keep bugs and animals away from my body while my mind travels," Teddie said.

"You've got my permission to check in on me, you know, mentally, while I travel," Vanida said. "If you see something that matters, or even hear me thinking something useful, get it to Camila to pass along."

Teddie gave a long sigh. "Okay, me too. I mean, watch for crawling insects first, and mind-read second. But you do have my permission to do both."

******

Lola tried to ignore the sinking feeling as she waved to the Zodiac pulling away from the beach and the other passengers waved back. These were people she would have liked to have known better. With five more days at sea, she could have made new friends. She certainly could use some, after all that had happened. But, she wasn't on vacation. She was an escaped kidnapping victim trying to get home. Anything making the journey faster was to be welcomed.

She followed her host inside to see the quarters. They'd go to bed early, as their chopper would arrive at 4 a.m. It would be a long ride to Auckland Island and another one on to Invercargill on the southern tip of New Zealand. After that, well, she didn't want to think that far ahead.

The guest quarters were in a cinder block room with no windows and poor ventilation. She fought her claustrophobia from the start. It resurfaced every half-hour, when she woke to look at the clock.

Alex and Maurice were on adjacent cots, and she could tell they weren't sleeping well either. But they passed the night in silence, each hoping the other two were getting more rest than it seemed. Three groggy people made their way to the heliport in the haze of a slow, lavender dawn.

The chopper had already refueled and engines were on as they approached. The door to the passenger's side opened, and the co-pilot waved them forward. Alex grabbed the man's hand and hopped on board. Maurice shouted into Lola's ear, trying to be heard over the sound of the chopper.

"No mind."

"Huh?"

"They… have… no… minds."

What was Maurice talking about?

Lola reached out to her friend mentally, but his focus had changed to watching his own footing as the co-pilot helped pull him aboard.

As the co-pilot grabbed her hand next and yanked her forward, she reached out to the mind of the pilot, and understood what Maurice meant. His brain was surrounded by soft grey fuzz. So was the mind of the co-pilot. She buckled into her harness and placed the headphones over her ears.

Why would Olumiji keep a protective wall around the people he sent to fetch us?

The helicopter lifted into the air.

He wouldn't.

She heard a thought from Maurice. *Oh shit.*

He'd obviously reached the same conclusion.

******

Zane kept dreaming about corporate training. He was at some wilderness course zip-lining and solving problems with blocks of wood. The team building exercises were exhausting and he woke up annoyed. It took a long, hot shower and two cups of hotel coffee before he saw the humor.

He was about to go into a meeting where two rivals were each going to threaten to kill his family if he didn't do what they wanted. He could not possibly please them both, so he intended to please neither.

His plan was simple. He would tell them both to go to hell, and then he would produce the affidavits from his board of directors supporting his decision to appoint Violeta Delgado as CEO of Reel News, assuming Olumiji had managed to get the affidavits prepared overnight. He was betting the Nigerian telepath had.

He thought back to Yuden's words as he was taken from the compound in Ushuaia. "We will watch over you."

He believed her, and he believed in her. As Olumiji had reassured him, these talented people whom Warren and Gabriel had taken on as adversaries were capable of saving themselves and more. He was betting their lives on it, and quite possibly his own.

In other words, he was about to take the greatest trust fall of his life. No wonder he'd dreamt about those damn team-building exercises all night.

******

Warren worried Gabriel would find a way to get to him before the meeting. The papers giving Warren absolute control of each subsidiary had been drawn up and he was trusting Brett and Chidi, two of his best, to see to it Zane signed those documents this morning, in front of Gabriel. But this worked only if his adversary had no way to contact him.

Chidi assured him last night he and Zane's parents would be ready for a video chat from Santiago at 10:00 EST. Chidi confirmed he was prepared to inject both father and mother with what he would claim was a lethal cocktail if Zane didn't do as Brett instructed. As extra insurance, an uncooperative Zane would get to watch his parents spasm and struggle for air while Chidi offered to inject an antidote in return for cooperation.

Warren couldn't imagine it would get that far, so he agreed to allow the dose to be less than fatal. Chidi had a point. In the worst of scenarios, having no dead bodies would keep things simpler.

Once Zane cooperated, which he would, then a majority of the board had already assured Warren they'd support him at an emergency meeting afterwards. HR was prepared to fire all the disloyal monads, effective immediately. Gabriel and his ungrateful telepaths could bloody well go find another company to run.

After the monads were escorted from the building, Brett would insert a specific television commercial into the show being broadcast. It would be Jerry and Warren's signal to emerge from their rooms, discover their locations, and get cabs back to the office. Neither would try to learn their whereabouts until then.

It was as ironclad as Warren could want, but it didn't mean Gabriel wouldn't be trying to break through Warren's defenses and get his icy claws into Warren's mind. Warren shuddered. He could almost feel the dark tendrils reaching out to capture his thoughts.

Thanks to technology, Gabriel had eyes in the helicopter as soon as the three were aboard and he was annoyed Maurice ended up in the middle. He couldn't imagine Zane was going to give him any trouble once he saw the live feed from the chopper, but on the outside chance Zane balked, he'd wanted to be able threaten Maurice with falling out of a malfunctioning door.

Gabriel couldn't imagine Zane would call his bluff, but in the worst of cases, he was willing to follow through on his threat. Maurice was old; he'd had a good run. After the horror of something so extreme, Zane's full cooperation would be a given.

But the pilots had been preoccupied with taking off in the high winds and had forgotten that part of his instructions. He supposed he should count his blessings. Finding two chopper pilots in that location on short notice who would do *anything* he asked had not been easy. Fortunately, money had been no object. Now he had to hope Zane was as reasonable a young man as he seemed.

Once the chopper was airborne, Gabriel eased up on the protective wall he'd been holding around the pilot's minds. It really didn't matter now what Lola or Maurice discovered.

Gabriel reached out to Warren, thinking it would be amusing to hear his old boss's smug belief he was about to best his own monads. Or would his self-satisfaction be engulfed in a fuzzy wall held up by the exhausted Jerry?

Neither. Warren was back at his word puzzles, circling letter combinations without a care in the world, happy to be giving Jerry a break. Unbelievable.

Where are you hiding, you old fart?

Gabriel didn't have to wonder for long. Warren was thinking about how Gabriel couldn't find him, because he had no idea where he was. None whatsoever. And he had no idea who had brought him there, either.

Clever trick. Good thing you don't matter anymore.

Gabriel turned his attention back to what did. He noted someone in the helicopter, probably Lola, was shielding the trio's thoughts from him. She needn't have bothered, but she didn't know about his video feed.

Once Zane understood his options, he'd sign the paperwork, leaving Gabriel CEO of Reel News. Warren would retire, effective immediately. Warren's man Brett would be left fumbling, until

Gabriel had the security guards remove him from the building. Gabriel figured it would all be over by noon.

******

Vanida had never used her energy body to travel to someone who was on an airplane, so she was alarmed when she ordered her body of light to seek out Yuden and she began rising thousands of feet into the air. It took effort not to panic and not to snap back to her physical body resting on the beach.

Once she saw the plane approaching, she realized why she was there. The skill with which her energy body matched the speed and direction of the craft amazed her. She was able to cross through the metal as if it had been sitting on the ground.

Inside, she found Yuden resting and an African man fretting and writing ideas down on a pad. Next to him was a Latino man who was sound asleep. Who were these people? Where was the rest of the group Yuden had traveled with? She tried calling out to Yuden, hoping the woman would respond.

After a few seconds, Yuden's energy body rose in the air, visible only to another traveler. Yuden gave Vanida a grin hello and a happy wave. The two of them had become proficient at communicating without words. A shrug from Vanida asked: *What's going on?* A point toward Chidi followed by a hug said: *He's on our side now.*

Vanida drifted over to see what he was scribbling on his pad. It took a few minutes to sort out. She wished she knew if Fernando was following along in her mind. He could be with Teddie, now. Best to head back with the news.

A point to her temple and a nod said: *I understand.* She waved goodbye, then sought out the golden cord connecting her entangled two bodies. She willed an emergency snap back to the physical plane.

"You okay?" Camila asked as Vanida came to with a spasm.

"Yeah, fine. That fast return is hard on everything. But I learned something. You've got to let Olumiji know there is a guy from Africa who works for Warren. Warren is counting on this guy to do something big this morning. He's not going to do it. He's already not done it. That part is confusing, but the point is Zane does not have to worry about him."

"That's interesting," Ariel said, getting up from the hammock where she was resting. "I kept getting this one set of timelines in which everyone says, 'If only Zane had known.' Maybe this is what he needed to know. Camila, can Olumiji contact Zane now?

"He can call him," Camila said.

"That's perfect. Make sure Zane knows Warren's man from Africa is on our side and—this part is important—no one else but Zane knows it."

******

It was an odd group in Warren's office at 10 a.m. Zane was there, looking like Warren and holding on to a folder full of papers like they were spun from gold. No one knew what he was holding.

Two newly hired security officers stood on either side of him, and each held a smart phone. They'd been hired by Brett to do the bidding of the real Warren. One guard was to give documents to Zane to sign, while displaying a video call with Chidi. Chidi's purpose, of course, was to persuade Zane, if necessary.

The other guard was to take a video of Zane signing Warren's documents while Zane explained to everyone what he was doing. He'd apologize for the shaky signature caused by his injured hand, and he'd express regret that his partnership with the monads no longer served the best interests of his shareholders. The video and documents would allow the board to support Warren's plan at the emergency meeting that would follow.

Once done, the guards had been instructed to escort Gabriel and his companions from the building and to ensure the paperwork made it to the board meeting. This, at least, was the plan from the Warren camp.

Gabriel had a different view. He'd been invited to bring two monads with him, and had chosen Khalid and Juan, the two with the most business expertise. Khalid held the documents giving Gabriel control of Reel News. Juan had been asked to tape the signing for much the same reason.

The phone Gabriel held would connect with the real location of Zane's parents and show the potential tragic accident awaiting them over icy seas. He figured the threats could be easily edited out of Juan's recording later, and if Brett's two guards caused the Entelechy trouble, they could be handled, too.

Gabriel knew the board would have to approve his changes, but he didn't consider it a problem. Johann had done an excellent job of gathering personal details about each board member and it would take an hour or two at most to persuade enough of them to lend their approval.

"Gentleman." Zane addressed them all. "We're here today to witness my instigating major leadership changes at Reel News. Warren," he cleared his throat, "uh, I, wish to restructure the organization to run without independent subsidiaries and without the Entelechy. The guards behind me have brought that paperwork, but I understand you have an alternative to present first."

If the young man who appeared to be Warren was frightened, he didn't show it.

Gabriel looked at him. "Someone is holding a wall around your mind."

"That's true. A few of my mother's old friends thought it was the least they could do for me today."

"I see," Gabriel said. "It doesn't matter. This won't go as planned, because you won't want to do as Warren wishes. Your parents are not where Warren thinks they are." He turned to the two guards. "Don't believe me? Make your phone call and find out."

The one to the left of Zane typed in numbers. Chidi answered.

"What's going on there?" the guard asked Chidi.

"We've run into some technical difficulties and I won't be able to provide the original programming as requested."

"What's that mean?"

"It means we're offering an alternative to our viewing audience. It's me sitting here telling you Warren was deceived. I believe the vernacular is 'he's screwed.'"

The two guards looked at each other. Gabriel burst into a laugh.

"Good show, Chidi. You had us conned into thinking you'd defected to that old fart. There you were, looking out for us all along. Well done."

"I couldn't risk telling you," Chidi answered. "Not with the other defectors being real and watching me."

"I'm impressed," Juan said. Khalid smiled his agreement.

"Now, you gentlemen do your part and get that company put into our hands," Chidi said.

Remember he's really on my side. Olumiji said he's playing them, too.

"As I'm sure you know," Gabriel turned to Zane, "I have an alternative set of papers for you to sign."

"What happens to me after I do that?"

"You walk out of here. I've no quarrel with you. Now take your pick. Sign. Or make me threaten your parents, then sign. Maybe you'll feel better doing it that way. Surely you're not going to actually make me kill one of them, then force you to sign documents you don't even care about in order to save the other?"

"What if you kill one of them and I still don't sign?"

Gabriel looked at Zane in disbelief. Was he trying to make a joke? There was no expression at all on the face that appeared to belong to Warren.

Zane reached under his desk and pushed a button. As the door began to open. Gabriel pounded his fist hard on Warren's desk.

"You bring anyone else in this room and I will kill your parents immediately."

"Relax. It's Denise, my personal assistant, and she knows what's going on. She's only here to assist me, not to cause you any trouble." He turned to Warren's two hired guards. "Or you guys either."

"Here's what's going to happen," he continued. "Denise is going to tape me signing the documents *I'm* holding. I'm going to tell you what they say as I sign them. You're all going to hold off doing anything until I'm done, because you may not mind what I'm doing and it's in your best interest to at least find out. Once I've done what I'm going to do, then you do what you will."

"I have to admit I didn't expect this. Do you hate your parents?"

Zane stared straight ahead and said, "Denise, please begin filming."

42. Upside Down

Teddie was in the helicopter, trying to maintain her energy body in the tight space between the two front seats. She really didn't like the sensation of having things or, worse yet, parts of people, going through her, but there was barely room for her, so the seats and pilots' elbows both kept intruding.

Was that a camera on the dash? Sure looked like one. The recording light was on, too. Hooked to a satellite feed? Why was this being transmitted?

She wanted to leave, but the fearful expressions on her mother and Maurice's faces made it clear the group was in danger. Was there any way she could help?

******

Gabriel was not impressed with Zane's solution. "Violeta Delgado? My old assistant who once had a crush on me? You've got to be kidding. She wouldn't know the first thing about how to run this corporation."

"I've done some checking," Zane said. "Others disagree."

"This is not an acceptable compromise. Tear those papers up and sign what I need you to sign or, seriously, your dad is about to have a most unfortunate accident." Gabriel's swallow after he said it gave away how agitated he'd become. "Don't make me do this."

"It's too bad. My dad's a very good guy. I'll miss him."

Zane said it and folded his hands in his lap. It took more courage than he thought he possessed to stare straight ahead and wait. And trust.

Warren's two men exchanged puzzled looks. Nothing in their instructions covered this scenario. The look that passed between Juan and Khalid was as perplexed, but it held a trace of panic as well. Neither had seriously considered a situation in which Gabriel had to make good on his threats, much less one in which he actually did so.

Yet, Gabriel's pride appeared to be mutating into anger at the possibility of Zane forcing his hand It seemed possible he'd do whatever it took not to lose this game of chicken.

******

Teddie watched the co-pilot turn to the back seat. He had a resigned look on his face and held a box cutter in his hand. In one expert move he cut her father's harness, ripping into his parka in the process. Why? She could see all three passengers yelling now, but couldn't hear a word. Then the back door on her father's side popped wide open and the helicopter began to make a turn. She watched her father grasp the torn harness for something to hold on to, and watched Maurice grab on to him.

The co-pilot said something into his mic then nodded as he listened. The angle of the craft steepened as the co-pilot turned and cut the strap again, this time where it met the seat. He batted Maurice away as he did it. Alex began sliding out the door.

She saw the look of horror on her mother's face and Maurice's anger and frustration. The co-pilot had one more quick exchange with whomever he was talking to. He didn't look pleased as he said something to the pilot. The pilot nodded and brought the chopper almost sideways with a look of grim determination on his face. As Alex's fingers vanished, he brought it back to level again.

Needing to know, Teddie passed to the outside, where she saw her father resting rather snuggly inside the landing skids, a satisfied grin on his face. How had he done that? It couldn't have been easy, but, to a man who could slow down time as much as he needed, it must have been possible.

She watched him try to pull his hood tighter around his face, and worried the wind chill might do what the icy waters had not. This nonsense had to end quickly.

******

"Your family friend could be next, but I don't have all day. I'm going to go straight to your mom."

Although Gabriel stated it matter-of-factly, Zane could hear the man's underlying fury. Well, halfway through a trust fall is no time to stop. He said nothing.

"Is this really necessary?" one of Warren's two men asked.

"Are you kidding me? Weren't you people planning on doing this exact same thing?"

Juan interrupted, speaking softly. "Your threats aren't working, Gabriel. Surely it's pointless to go on."

Gabriel studied Zane's face. There was no hint of expression. None at all.

"I'm not so sure. This next one may bring him to his senses. Damn that wall those x^0 people are keeping around him. The only way to know how he'll react is to continue."

******

Lola dropped her mental wall to get information. She felt both pilots' hesitation at killing her. So, she was next. She guessed she had cultural biases to thank for being the second parent to be dumped into the ocean. Not that it mattered.

She found Gabriel and felt his determination to punish Zane for his lack of cooperation. She sought out Olumiji, Violeta, Maurice—anyone who might have an idea.

Your husband is hanging on underneath. He's reconstructing a harness for himself, and doing it at lightning speed. If he ties himself on tight enough, he thinks he can reach out and grab you as you fall.

At the speed of thought, she knew the information had come to her from Olumiji. He'd gotten it through a telepathic link with Camila. Camila was standing on a beach in Brazil, and she knew what was happening because she was listening to the voice of Fernando, her boyfriend.

Fernando, meanwhile, was in the mind of Teddie, and he was describing everything he saw out loud. And as for Teddie? She was right here with them in the helicopter, watching it all.

******

Ariel followed along as Fernando communicated with Camila every way he could. He was standing on the beach shouting with his eyes closed and making huge wild gestures while using telepathy. Ariel got out of the hammock as soon as she realized he was witnessing her parents' probable death through Teddie's eyes.

She heard him yell about her father being under the chopper and shout Olumiji's advice to her mother. That was when the logic of the last card she'd played the other night made perfect sense.

It was one of the few things she hadn't been able to figure out. Why was the Queen of Hearts always upside down? In Tarot, upside down gave a less favorable interpretation, but she was sure this upside down was good. Necessary. Only it made no sense until now.

Fernando was hollering about her dad's crazy plan of grabbing onto her falling mother. But it wouldn't work if mom simply slid out of the chopper and reached out to her husband with her arms. She had to get him her legs, and she needed momentum when she did it.

If she went out the door head-first, against all logic, swinging her feet over her head to gain momentum, and then swung her heels back under the chopper it would work. It was like a trapeze trick. They grabbed each other like that all the time because it was easier. Her mother had to be a trapeze artist.

"Go out upside down! Do a trapeze show! Let Dad get the back of her feet—he can take it from there. It's the only way it can end well. Upside down!"

Now she was the one screaming to Camila, saying it over and over, trying to drown out Fernando.

"Stop it!" Camila yelled to them both. "I got it. She needs to go out head first, face down. Turn a summersault and use its momentum to swing her legs far under the chopper. Like a high wire act. Swing her feet to Alex."

"Oh thank you. Thank you." Ariel sat in the sand and put her head in her hands.

******

Lola. Go out head first, face down. Hold on to the door jam and do a somersault. Then swing your legs backwards as far as you can under the chopper. Let Alex grab your feet from the back.

Olumiji's voice was clear, just as the co-pilot reached back to cut her harness and the chopper began a steep turn in the other direction.

I haven't the vaguest idea what you're talking about.

But I do. It was Violeta. *You need to use momentum. Like in judo.*

I don't know anything about judo.

I do. Go limp. Let me control your body. I can do this.

Lola wasn't sure that was even possible, but as the harness fell away from her and the tilt of the chopper increased, she didn't see a better option. So she slid toward the door without fighting to hang on. When Maurice didn't try to grab her, she knew he was listening in.

Then, she did two of the most difficult things she'd ever done in her life. The first, and the easiest, was to slide out head-first toward the icy Southern Ocean. The second was to give up complete control of her body as she did so. It was a sensation that felt more like dying than anything she'd ever experienced.

As she let go of her physical self, her body executed a maneuver of incredible beauty and grace. Her awkward fall turned into a slow-motion dive followed by a flip that left Alex with two easy-to-grab ankles swinging towards him. Her body used its own momentum to swing on upward to the relative safety of the skids.

All she knew at the time was she was terrified, and more graceful than she'd ever been in her life. Then she was safe as Alex moved in a flurry to secure her under the chopper. His movements slowed to normal as he pulled her clothing tighter around her. She wondered why he was bothering with something so unnecessary, then she felt Violeta relinquish control, and the wind and freezing cold slapped against her hard.

"Out of ideas here," Alex shouted into her ears, bringing her back to reality.

"Me too," she shouted back. She did her best to calm her racing heart and to let her mind reach out.

"But not everyone else is," she yelled to him. "Maurice has got things now. He says hold on tight. Make time go fast for us, like you did with those naps. He'll handle the rest."

******

Teddie watched horrified as her mother slid out the door toward the sea and Maurice did nothing. What was going on here? Dismay turned into amazement as her not-particularly athletic mom executed an incredible gymnastic maneuver that landed her safely under the helicopter's landing skids, where she was secured by her father, who'd acted with all the skill of a trapeze artist. Where had her parents learned to do this?

She turned her attention back to Uncle Maurice. Was he going to be next? Would her dad be able to catch him, too?

Wait. Uncle Maurice had somehow ended up with a gun. It belonged to one of the pilots? Maybe he hadn't been doing nothing while her mother fell to her death.

Teddie watched him point the gun at the co-pilot and speak. Even with no sound, she had a pretty good idea of what sort of thing he was saying.

******

Now that the impact of what he'd been forced into doing was sinking in, Gabriel was livid. This cold-hearted young man had egged him on to committing murder, twice—a fact he'd now be covering up for the rest of his life.

"Both your parents are dead, son. I hope thwarting us was worth that price. Go ahead and take your plans to your board of directors today. I wouldn't be too happy about it if I was you. We *will* control every member of that board before long, and we *will* reverse everything you've done."

Gabriel stood up, motioning to his two companions. "Let's give this asshole some time to think about how his day went."

Juan looked dazed, and Khalid looked like he might be sick to his stomach, but they both followed Gabriel out the door.

After the three monads left, Warren's two hired guards gave each other a puzzled look. One turned to his phone where Chidi was still listening in. "I have no idea what we're supposed to do now," he said.

"Do whatever the man there tells you to," Chidi replied.

The second one turned to Zane. "You're not really the guy who hired us, are you? Do you know where we could find him?"

"Actually," Zane said, "he doesn't even know where to find himself right now. Look, I could use you guys for a couple more hours. After that, you take rest of the day off. I'll make sure Warren knows you two did your best under the circumstances."

"Works for me," one said.

The other nodded. "Were those really your parents?"

"Oh goodness, no. Hired actors from a stunt company. Don't worry about it. No one died."

Both men let out an exhale of relief. "We guessed as much."

Denise gave him an expectant look.

"You take the afternoon off too, of course, but first I do need you to go down to HR and make sure they fire all the monads exactly the way Warren requested. They're not to come within a thousand feet of the building or of any employee of Reel News. Then, go enjoy the rest of your day with my thanks."

"You sure?"

"Yeah. I've got some advisors who will walk me through the procedures with the board this afternoon, but I could use your help tomorrow while I finish things up. Violeta should be in New York by Wednesday. I know she hopes you'll get her oriented."

"I'll see to it she succeeds," Denise said. "I'll enjoy that."

"I believe you will."

******

"You're not going to shoot us," the co-pilot said. 'We die, you die."

"Yup. That's why I wouldn't have considered pointing this at you if the others were still aboard. They had a lot left to do. Me, it's been a great life, but after what I've seen today, I've got no problem shooting you both and facing the consequences here on Earth and anywhere else. In fact, shooting you sounds like the most satisfying thing I can think of doing right now."

"You're going to kill us for spite?" the pilot said.

"Possibly. It does bother me I never got to see that rock outcrop of oceanic crust back on Macca, though. It's supposed to be great, if you're a geologist. Something to see before you die. So, while shooting you would be satisfying, if you fly me back there nice and steady and let me hop off the chopper, I don't think I'll shoot you."

"You're hijacking us?" The pilot turned to his co-pilot. "Do we have enough fuel to do that?"

"With just the two of us aboard after that, we should," his co-pilot answered.

The pilot looked at Maurice and considered his response. Here's how this goes: We'll report turning around and letting you hop out because you feel ill. Not enough fuel for us to land proper. As far as anyone knows, your missing friends are still aboard. You claim anything else and we'll call you crazy. You understand?"

"It won't be a stretch for me to feel ill," Maurice answered. "And how you handle things won't matter to my friends now, so it doesn't matter to me either. I suspect you two will become difficult to find well before any investigation into their deaths happens."

He looked at the gun in his hands. "So then. The three of us live if you take me back to Macca now."

"We can do that."

S. R. Cronin

****

Zane called Olumiji as soon as Denise walked out the door. His hands were shaking.

"Well?" He let the panic he was feeling overtake him.

"They're fine. All fine. It got far more dicey at the end than anyone would have liked, but it worked out." Olumiji said.

Zane felt his knees turn to jelly. "Do I want to know how?"

"I'm sure you'll get a different version of the story from each member of your family. Suffice to say it was one of the most incredible scenarios I've ever watched."

"Where is everybody now?"

"Let's see. Your mom and dad just jumped off the undercarriage of a helicopter onto a sub-Antarctic research station. They're both suffering from hypothermia. Maurice hopped out of the same chopper, and the two pilots who are flying it just looked down and realized they were deceived. They aren't happy, but are heading away with all possible speed."

"Somebody is there to help my folks?"

"They are. A puzzled team of medics is on the runway already. They thought Maurice was having a medical emergency, but they'll tend to everybody."

"Teddie?"

"Her traveling body was on the helicopter when both your parents were pushed out. She's had a pretty traumatic day, but she was the only one who could see what was happening under the chopper. She let Fernando ride along in her mind, and he sent what she saw on to all of us. We couldn't have managed without her. She is safe now back on the beach in Brazil."

"What's she doing in Brazil?"

"She's with Ariel, who just added Tarot readings to her repertoire."

"My sister doesn't need Tarot cards."

"No, she doesn't, but she used them to figure out some amazing complexity in her visions. She saved your mom's life."

"Wow. Everyone else is okay?"

"They are. Xuha is safe in Ushuaia, and his charges were dropped. He's going to spend a couple more days at Alma's house, keeping an eye on her until everything settles down. Violeta will fly to New York tomorrow. I'm guessing the Brazil group will leave for Rio later today. Nell and Cillian have landed in Ireland. Yuden is in Santiago and heading back to Texas. You're the only one I'm still worried about."

That made two of them. Zane was worried about himself, too.

"I've got a couple of guards Warren hired who are willing to escort me to the board meeting. Can you guys keep this fuzzy wall thing around me through tomorrow? This is complicated enough without having to worry about warring telepaths in my head."

"You got it," his mother's friend said. "May I also continue to keep watch over you until you finish what you've started?

"You most certainly may. I've got dozens of heads of subsidiaries to issue restraining orders against. Then, I've got a gun-loving board of directors to soothe while I explain to them why it's a good idea to turn the company over to an Argentinian woman."

"Then you need to get the hell out of there, and turn back into you."

Zane didn't even mind it when Olumiji finished his thought.

✳✳✳✳✳✳

Ariel stood up and screamed at the top of her lungs. Fernando and Camila couldn't tell if it was pain, frustration or, maybe, joy. Vanida sat up and stared. It sounded to her like a shout of ecstasy.

The yell brought Teddie back to her physical body with a snap. She came to with a spasm and an irritated look on her face.

"What did you do that for? I wanted to make sure mom and dad got treated for hypothermia," she complained to her sister.

"They do," Ariel walked over, and, for once, she hugged Teddie hard. Tears were pouring down her face. "They do."

"You okay?"

"Never better. You did great. Zane and Uncle Maurice and Violeta and mom and dad all did great. I promise you, everybody is going to be fine. Wonderfully boringly fine."

43. One of Three

Back in her own kitchen, Lola sipped coffee while marveling at how her simple morning ritual was fantastic beyond belief.

Last night she'd spent the first night in her own bed in a month. This morning, she called her boss and discovered how well Ariel handled her mother's absence. Lola would be back at her desk Monday, with more explaining to do, but at least with a job.

Her daughters got back from Brazil yesterday. Teddie went to school this morning, hopeful she could stay on track to graduate in May.

Zane flew from New York back to law school, citing his classes as the reason, but Lola suspected it was more complicated in his case. His bluff had turned out to be brilliant, but it could have gotten them killed instead, and they all knew it. She thought he needed time to come to terms with the chance he'd taken.

Xuha had flown from Argentina straight to El Paso, where he hoped to salvage some of his semester, too. Each of them wanted their old life back. Nothing made one appreciate normal more than a close, hard look at the alternative.

Only two family members remained unsettled. Ariel's company had closed their Dublin office and she'd opted to take severance pay and find a new job. Obviously, she hadn't had much time for job-hunting, but this morning she was on her computer hard at work. Or at least Lola thought she was. She listened to her daughter's laugh as she video chatted. No, she probably wasn't talking to a prospective employer.

Lola went to her bedroom, where Alex was under the covers. He'd born most of the burden of holding the two of them under the helicopter in the freezing winds. It hadn't been a long trip, but it was terribly cold and dangerous, and Alex had struggled to warm back up ever since. Most of it was psychological, of course, but what did that matter? The man was still cold.

Lola suspected he dreaded making contact with Hope High after he'd been accused of so many things in the Reel News smear campaign. He was facing disciplinary action and possibly dismissal. She couldn't fault him for wanting to stay under the covers; she just hoped he'd eventually tire of it.

Her cell phone rang, and she smiled when she saw it was Maurice. She felt him notice her worry about Alex, and felt his hesitation to intrude. She answered the call.

"Just wanted to let everyone know Yuden and I are safely back in West Texas. She seems to like it here. Says she's never seen so much nothing in her life."

"There is a lot of that there," Lola agreed. "So, she's going to stay?"

"For a while at least. I'll do what I can to help her coax c^3 out of hiding. Those people take instructions to disappear pretty damn seriously. We'll probably end up going to Bhutan to work on that."

"Vanida ought to be home in Thailand by tomorrow," Lola said. "Teddie says she'll be doing the same thing there."

"I know. Yuden hopes to coordinate with her."

"If you go, how long will you be in Bhutan?" Lola had trouble imagining her friend feeling at home in a mountainous kingdom halfway around the world.

"Don't know. Guess one thing this little adventure did for us was make it clear we'd be smart to enjoy the time we have. So, wherever we are, we're going to both be there, if you follow."

As Lola ended the call, she wished events had brought her and Alex closer, too. Here she was, anxious to get back to her old life, and there he was, huddled under blankets, avoiding his.

She heard Maurice's words again. *So, wherever we are, we're going to both be there.* It was good advice, and it didn't have to mean traveling halfway around the world. She went back into the bedroom, and crawled under the covers. She snuggled in next to Alex.

"I thought you had a million things you couldn't wait to do today," he said.

"I do. But they can wait. Let's warm each other up."

******

A couple of hours later, Lola woke to a soft knock on her door. It was Ariel.

"Mom. Dad. I've got the noontime news on TV. I think you want to wake up and see this."

Lola grabbed her yoga pants and t-shirt and headed for the living room. Ariel had hit record, and backed the show up as her mother entered.

"Is everyone okay?"

"They are. It's about Warren."

A perky newscaster was telling her viewers about the unexpected discovery of the former head of Reel News. He'd been found in the middle of a paranoid breakdown while hiding in the honeymoon suite of a suburban discount hotel chain. This morning, he fired shots at police responding to another call. He injured one policeman while screaming at them to go away because telepaths were trying to find him.

Inquiries at Reel News revealed Warren had secretly and unexpectedly turned the reins of his entire conglomerate over to a former employee from Argentina on Monday and the Board of Directors had approved the action in an emergency meeting later that day. Warren had not been seen since.

Word was the company had been under pressure for weeks, as Warren and the various heads of his subsidiaries underwent an internal power struggle. Observers reported Warren appeared to have been slipping into an unstable condition during that time, making unusual and unfounded accusations about his employees and even about people in the news.

The reporter went on to add that much of Warren Moore's breakdown appeared to center around a growing irrational fear of paranormal activity. He'd urged his broadcast outlets to seek out locals accused of having ties to the occult and to present their stories in an unfavorable light. This request appeared to have exacerbated the problems with many of the network's subsidiaries.

Lola turned around and saw Alex had joined them.

"We just received a tip about one such family, living here in Houston, who disappeared for weeks after a particularly vicious set of reports about them surfaced around Christmas. Friends of the family have told us they left town for their own safety, taking an extended vacation with relatives in another state."

"I wonder who told them that?"

"I think Ken did," Alex answered. He had his phone in his hand. "He just texted me. It says, 'watch news ur good ur sub sucks come back.' Think I should check in at school?"

"Of course you should. But, if we go this route and agree we chose to leave town, we lose any chance to bring charges against Warren," Lola said.

"Why would we want to, now? We're safe. People think he's crazy. Thanks to him shooting at the police, he'll be locked away, even if it's in some nice facility."

Ariel jumped in. "Mom, if we go to the police, we're back in the limelight, going through this shit again. It's pointless."

"I know." Lola understood them both. "But I don't think somebody should get to do something so awful to people and not face consequences. Like those two helicopter pilots. Nobody has found out who they are and *they* tried to kill us. It's not right."

"It isn't," Alex agreed. "When I thought there was any chance of Warren doing something like this again, I felt differently. But now, he's lost his company, his dignity, some of his fortune, and all of his freedom. He *is* being punished."

Lola was going to answer when she saw the television screen flicker and a smiling Violeta looked right at her. Lola reached for the remote and turned up the volume.

"Thanks for taking a minute to speak with us, Ms. Delgado. How does it feel to find yourself at the helm of such a powerful company?"

"Honestly? It feels good."

It looked like she was standing in Times Square. The reporter giggled. "Are you planning a wholesale housecleaning?"

"Oh, heavens no. Reel News ran well because it was blessed with many capable, hardworking employees, perhaps more than Warren realized. I hope to give them more running room to let their skills shine."

"What about the heads of the affiliate companies? Word is a powerful internal struggle was what precipitated Mr. Moore's, uh, illness. He wanted more control of the smaller companies and their heads resisted. Will you be keeping the original structure or carrying out Warren Moore's wishes?"

"Some of both. I'll evaluate each subsidiary and its management and do what makes sense on a case-by-case basis."

"I see. One last question. Many would say that Reel News always had a particular slant on things. Do you expect that to continue?"

"No, I don't."

"Well, there you have it," the reporter told the audience.

Lola turned to say something to Alex and Ariel, but Alex was gone. She heard his voice coming from the kitchen.

"Sure. I can come in this afternoon and discuss the situation with you. Yes, it was traumatic, but I'm up to it. No, I don't think I need my rep there. We'll just talk. Sure."

Lola looked at Ariel with questions in her eyes.

"You still see nothing but blue skies ahead?"

"Mom, assume I do. You don't want me weighing in on every little decision; you really don't. If I need to speak up, I will."

✱✱✱✱✱✱

While Alex was meeting with the principal at Hope High, Lola decided to make a difficult phone call before it was bedtime in Nigeria.

"I was going to call you tomorrow," Olumiji greeted her. "Have you been following the developments in x^0?"

"No. I haven't been invited back, yet."

He laughed. "Forgot about that. First things first, then. Consider this your official invitation to rejoin."

"I'm thinking about starting my own organization." The words tumbled out, but as they did she realized they were true.

"So we're going to have the Entelechy, x^0, and a *third* group of telepaths? Why?"

"The Entelechy is going to be allowed to continue?" she countered. "Why?"

"That was what I wanted to discuss with you. But first, Lola, let me tell you I'm sorry x^0 made things so difficult when this all started. You've always acted in ways you believed were right, and I know that."

"Apology accepted. And I am sorry for the problems I caused. I appreciate all you did in the end to get us to safety. We probably owe you our lives."

She paused as she felt the healing of the rift between them.

"So, what is happening?" she asked.

"Well, we're officially out of hiding and all normal activity has resumed. What a relief. I don't know a single telepath who didn't hate the experience."

"I suppose you'll never hear from the few who found the peace and quiet more to their liking."

"Good point. We may have lost a few members, but we're going to gain a few, too."

"How so?"

"We're negotiating with Rafael, the monad who's become the new leader of the Entelechy. He's a saner, more analytical alternative. His group can't believe Gabriel allowed you and Alex to be killed. The fact that you survived doesn't exonerate him. Under Rafael's direction, they're discussing appropriate disciplinary action."

"That's refreshing. So what happens to these monads?"

"Well, eight of them have joined x^0 and more are considering it. Rafael is making no moves to stop them. We plan to welcome in those who are sincere. I believe Violeta intends to keep those eight on, if they want to stay with Reel News. She says x^0 imposes a value system that discourages poor behavior and she likes that. There are also a handful now who want no affiliation with anyone, and we've all agreed to respect their wishes and leave them be."

Lola did the arithmetic in her head. "Doesn't that leave at least twenty more of them?"

"It does. Jerry and Brett, the two that worked with Warren, are guilty of almost as much as Gabriel. The Entelechy is holding an internal trial. Rafael says he'll establish ethics guidelines for his remaining group and work toward realistic policing procedures. I think we need to give him a chance to make good on his word."

She was surprised. "So we really are attempting to co-exist with a competing group of telepaths?"

"That's the idea. Most of x^0 and the remaining monads think we can make this work, and at least stay out of each other's way. Unless, of course, your new group gums up the works."

Now Lola understood his frustration with her plans.

"I don't think I'll gum up anything. I guess I had an eye-opening experience bouncing around on the Southern Ocean. For a few minutes out there, I even thought the universe made perfect sense."

"Really? Can you explain it me?"

"I can't even explain it to myself. But I did come out of it sure of a few things. One of them is I want to use my telepathy for more. Not world domination more, but an end hunger and attain world peace kind of more. I don't agree with hiding when things get difficult. I don't want to be fearful about being *found out*. I need to discover my own way to do this, and it's going to be one that makes more of a difference."

"I see. It sounds like the rescue work I do," Olumiji said. "Walking through ruins after earthquakes, trying to sense life trapped under the rubble, that kind of thing."

"Yes. It is like that, but on a larger scale. Back before this nonsense with the Entelechy got started, Xuha told me about this I-Ching hexagram. It had to do with going towards the light and ascending mountains to become all the things you were meant to be. My idea is to provide resources and direction for telepaths who feel like I do, and maybe members of c^3 and people with talents like Zane and Alex and Ariel we don't even know about. I think a lot of folks have quirky skills they could contribute. I'd like to welcome all of them and find ways to make the world better."

She felt his amusement.

"You want to form a league of superheroes. Where have I heard that idea before?" He laughed. "You'll get no objection from me, just a warning to be careful. Take a cue from the comic books. It requires an exceptional moral compass to pull this off."

Then he considered who he was talking to.

"You know what, Lola? I think you're the perfect person to do this. I see no reason three groups of telepaths *can't* get along. Maybe it will be easier for x^0 to be one of three than it was for us to be one of two. Is membership exclusive or can I be part of both?"

"Definitely both. Like the Elks, Shriners and Knights of Columbus back in my home town. Maybe they didn't get along back when, but today they march together in local parades."

"Then we'll march together, too. Many paths to the top of the mountain, right?"

"Exactly.

He didn't have to say it. She heard.

I love it. Sign me up.

44. The Blessings That Last

Lola glanced at her phone. Alex had left for school two hours ago and there was still no word from him. She was happy to fuss around her kitchen while she waited, taking dishes from where the girls had stashed them and putting them back where they belonged. She felt good getting her life in order. She felt better after the conversation with Olumiji. There was one more difficult phone call left on the list.

Why was she so hesitant to thank the woman who'd saved her life?

Perhaps she didn't want to bother her. After all, the lady was in the process of becoming one of the most powerful women in the world. She was being tracked down by reporters for interviews as she walked through Times Square. She didn't have time to chat.

No, Lola thought, that was only part of the problem.

The mental exchanges the two shared were uncomfortable from the start. Their relationship was based on Violeta's gallant determination to protect Lola, even though Lola hadn't asked for help. Yet she'd needed it, desperately needed it in the end.

Her phone rang.

"There will always be a connection between us now," Violeta said.

"Were you just in my mind?"

"Barely. I wanted to know if it was a good time to call."

"You need to learn more about protocols."

"Exactly. I've been on the phone with Olumiji. I've decided I serve the telepathic community best by joining x^0. I need to learn your conventions. Olumiji tells me it's common for new members to have a mentor and I want mine to be you."

Lola felt her discomfort with Violeta soften.

"I'd be honored."

"I may not be the best student, though. Free time will be a little scarce for me."

Of course. She's got to learn to run a corporation.

"Besides that, I've got *three* other projects. One is to learn about x^0. Another is to locate some of those adept female telepaths we decided must exist. I think I've found one already, and I want to get you involved with her, too."

"That's great news, and something I'd love to do. And your third one?"

"I need to become a member of the Entelechy."

"What? And, they're going to let you in? I thought it was a boys' club."

"It was. The new leader, Rafael, will be turning the group to more of a business focus. Telepaths with influential roles in industry, that kind of thing. He's got a lot of ideas and thinks it's important I be part of it."

"You'll be a bridge between the groups then?"

"One of them, I hope. I think we've persuaded Olumiji to join the Entelechy, too. He'll fit in well, and probably be a better bridge than me."

"Olumiji? Part of the Entelechy? Amazing. But now that I think about it, he *will* be good at forging cooperation."

"I'm also going to be occupied with changing the direction of Reel News. With Warren gone, many of our big investors will go elsewhere. I've already sought counsel on how to better diversify our board of directors as well as our investment community. We'll get free of obligations to support any specific political philosophy."

"That would be impressive."

"Well, I have an idea to help make it happen. Rather than push out the old and leave a vacuum in its place, it's better to have a new sense of direction. I hear there's an up-and-coming *third* telepathic organization. Possibly called 46. Ascending?"

Lola had to laugh. "Word travels fast."

"Yes, at the speed of thought."

"My group isn't going to be only about telepathy, though. It's going to be about everyone using their talents to make positive things happen. No particular political or religious slant, just people who want a gentler, kinder world."

"That's what I was hoping. We'll have to work together on timing, but I'd like Reel News to champion your organization. Maybe undo a little of the harm it's done over the years."

"Wow. That would be great." Lola didn't know what else to say.

You don't have to say anything. Work with me. I'll work with you. We can be friends.

I'd like that. Oh, and thanks. For, you know, saving my life.

She heard the garage door open and knew it was Alex. "I better go."

"I understand. Tell your husband I say hello."

Alex walked in as she hung up. She looked at him but didn't say anything.

"Don't read my mind."

"I'm not. It's hard, but I'm not."

"Okay. They offered me my old job back"

She studied his face for a second, trying to figure out if this was good news. Damnit, it would be easier to read his mind.

"Are you going to take it?"

"I'm not sure. A lot has happened."

"It has."

"But I always thought I'd be there when Teddie graduated, sitting up there with her, you know, as one of the teachers. I guess it would make me sad if I wasn't."

Lola didn't say anything. He was still deciding.

"I think I'll go back for the rest of the year. After she graduates, we'll see."

Lola walked over, put both arms around him, and held him for a full minute. After all they'd been through, she figured it was going to take a lot of hugging before they both felt warm in the middle the day.

******

Ariel had been exchanging texts with Nell and knew her two Irish friends had arrived home safely a few days ago. The police in the small town in Southern Chile had either been disinclined or unable to track the unnamed Anglo responsible for the death of an Argentinian criminal. Nell thought as long as Cillian avoided the southern tip of South America, he'd be fine.

Ariel decided it was time to check in on him.

"You still have your own ringtone. You always will," he greeted her. "How did this all end for you?"

After a few minutes of exchanging stories, Ariel cut to the chase. "What's changed?"

"A lot actually. You may not think so, but once things get going on a different path, I do see the effects hundreds of years from now. Different scenarios become far more probable."

"Okay. Like what?"

"Well, there's c^3, this group of people who mind-travel. I get a whole swath where they never come back, and it's not good. The world needs them. So I've been in contact with Vanida and she's going to be working harder to get things going again."

"Well, that's good."

"There's more. Violeta." Cillian paused and Ariel thought he sounded a little choked up. "Violeta is likely going to do a hell of a job running her company, because I can see those effects down the road. Far better than if Warren or Gabriel had stayed at the helm."

"That's easy to believe."

"Me and you, we helped set her on that path, you know, along with the others. Big positive changes."

"That's great." Ariel recognized this was an emotional topic, and she didn't want to sound too enthused.

"Oh, there's one more thing. Your mum."

"My mother?"

"Yeah. I found her a little annoying, to be frank, but I have to give her credit. She can get things done. She's got some group she wants to start. 46 Ascending? Make sure she does it."

"Really?"

"More than really. Encourage her. It's likely to catch on well past anything she expects. If it takes off, it's as good as any idea I have. In some scenarios, it's the single biggest game-changer and it wasn't even a possibility before this nonsense with Reel News. How's that for irony?"

"Reel News helps save humanity by being a war-mongering firm specializing in frightening its viewers? Yeah, it's pretty rich. Okay, I'll encourage mom's idea anyway I can."

"Let your mum know I respect the way she wants to take this awful experience and turn it for the good."

Ariel had to smile. "You could tell her."

"Nah, that's okay. But let her know that if we ever meet again, I want to lift a glass together. We'll toast how a rocky start sometimes is the very thing that gets you to those blessings that last."

45. Okay in the End

The purple magnet had been on the refrigerator for years. Today it held the postcard she'd sent from Antarctica. On it she'd written "The laws of thermodynamics are wrong. It does get that cold in Antarctica."

The magnet itself held her interest today, though, as her family put their Christmas dinner on the table.

They were a family of cooks, and were showing off for new guests. Xuha had brought his girlfriend; she was as charming a young woman as Lola expected. Maurice and Yuden were there, back in the U.S. after a few months in Bhutan. Teddie, who'd managed to graduate on time and start classes at UT, was putting the finishing touches on her cupcakes while chatting with Yuden.

Xuha was setting the table. Maurice put out the glassware while he told Alex how glad he was everything had settled back down at Hope High.

"My company pretty much ignored the Reel News smear campaign," Lola said as she took dishes out of the oven and moved them to the serving table. "They put me back at my workstation like nothing happened. But that's the oil business."

Alex looked up as he put the finishing touches on the mashed potatoes. "Not a lot of conversations at school either. Got a few words of sympathy from teachers I know, but that was about it."

"I hear Warren was released from his psychiatric facility," Ariel said as she came into the room. She'd been video-chatting with her boyfriend Mikkel. Last April, she'd found a job in New York involving a lot of travel to Europe. Her long-distance relationship appeared to be going strong.

"You mean Warren is back home like nothing happened?" Maurice asked.

"Word is he's on probation. They say he wants to get back into broadcasting, but he'll never build a company like the one he had, particularly since mom's friend is running his old business better than he ever did."

As Ariel began pouring ice water into the glasses, Alex gave Lola a careful look.

"It's okay dear. I've made peace with our decision about Warren. I still struggle with how gently Rafael is handling the situation with Gabriel, but that one is out of our hands."

"Olumiji is pushing him to do more," Maurice said. He'd moved on to putting serving spoons in the food.

Lola pulled the gravy off of the stove. "Hey, we're all healthy and together for this celebration. I'm not complaining."

"Is 46. Ascending still growing by leaps and bounds?" Xuha asked. Lola noticed he was putting packages wrapped in tissue paper by everyone's plates. Something cloth, smaller than a towel.

"You did the t-shirts?!"

He laughed. "A year late, but they're still timely. I may have to start a cottage industry making these for your organization."

"She can hardly keep up with how fast it's growing," Alex said.

Zane, who'd been out on the porch talking on his phone, came inside.

"Say, young man, did you finally pass all the classes you fell behind on?" Maurice asked.

"Got one more to take this spring, then I'm good. Almost back to normal." He looked around for something remaining to be done, but dinner was ready.

"Normal." Teddie said the word out loud like she was hearing it for the first time. "Do we even know what normal is?"

"Let's find out."

Ariel laughed. "Right. We'll sit down to Christmas dinner and if no catastrophe happens, it will be our first normal holiday in five years.

Everyone took their seats. Lola had the magnet with her.

"I bought you that," Teddie said. "It says, 'Everything will be okay in the end. If it's not okay, it's not the end.'"

Lola held it up for all to read. "It does."

Xuha looked around, wiggling his eyebrows, faking suspicion. "Looks to me like everything is okay."

"I hate to jinx it, but I agree."

They waited.

Nothing happened.

At all.

"Everything is okay?"

"Yes."

"Sure."

"Looks like it."

"Completely."

"Unless we let the food get cold."

Lola ignored the last comment.

"So it *is* the end. Let's enjoy it."

Defying
Entropy

46. Three More Non-Mutually Exclusive Endings

March 2064, on this timeline

The Real Ending

In March of 2064, Lola Zeitman died.

Teddie delivered an unusual eulogy at the large gathering that was held afterwards. She began by holding up the little magnet she'd bought for her mom over fifty years ago.

"It says, 'Everything will be okay in the end. If it's not okay, it's not the end.'"

The crowd laughed a little.

"We all know it isn't true. One's story ends when everything is not okay. Light and life go, and in that instant the laws of thermodynamics appear to triumph over the beautiful complexity of biology. Physics wins.

"But let's not leave it there. I'd like to share something a teacher of mine told me long ago. Ask people if an apple will always fall to the earth once it breaks free from the tree and one-hundred normal adults will say it will. But a child will say maybe not, because it could float into the hand of a magic genie. A mystic will tell you she could levitate the apple if she wanted to. A physicist (like my mother) will instruct you on stronger and weaker gravitational fields and then move on to warped space.

These people are all scratching at the same truth, that the universe is more complicated than our day-to-day experiences lead us to believe.

"I once asked my parents if there was a way to defy the laws of thermodynamics, because I found them depressing. My mother told me our understanding of the universe is part of a larger story. It's brilliantly correct inside a limited range, but only a piece of the full picture.

"I liked her answer. So today, I celebrate my mom for many things, but none more than her understanding of how a larger truth lies somewhere beyond our answers."

Teddie pulled an apple from her bag and held it out.

"So. Will the apple always fall to the earth?" She smiled, then tossed it high into the air. "We don't know. Maybe ... someone will catch it as it falls."

She grabbed the apple as she said it, then studied it for a second in her hand. "Then, maybe they'll eat it." She took a bite out of it, gave the audience one more smile, and sat down.

She knew it was a little showy, but it was still a hell of a good ending.

The year 3346 on this timeline

Another Kind of Ending

Lola sat on her front porch, sipping a Sauvignon Blanc and thinking the geraniums could use a little water. She stood up to get the pitcher and was startled by someone standing behind her. The young woman wasn't familiar, and looked bothered by having scared Lola.

"I'm sorry. I didn't mean to startle you. I thought you'd know I was here."

Lola studied the woman. She was tall, a black-haired and tan-skinned mix of ethnicities. She was dressed in a sparkly gold evening gown. An evening gown?

"Can I help you with something?" Lola didn't know what else to say.

"Of course you can. I didn't realize I'd have to explain this. I thought you'd know." The woman seemed frustrated. She looked up into the air. "Can we start over or something?" Nothing happened. The young woman gave an audible sigh, turned, and handed a round metal plate to Lola. "You're supposed to give this to me. Nice and slow so we get good vid."

It was Lola's turn to be annoyed.

"What is this thing and why in the world would I give it to you? For that matter, what are you doing on my porch?"

The young woman looked ready to cry. "I'm graduating, dammit. I get one shot at this presentation and it's costing a fortune. I spent weeks learning your antiquated dialect so we could do this authentically. Everybody I know is wired in watching. You're supposed to hand me this, tell me I did wonderful and say congratulations. Is that so hard?"

"Doesn't your school give you your diploma?" Lola was baffled.

"Oh my God. We are really going to have to start over." The young woman looked around the porch. "Can I sit down? Better yet, can I have some of that wine?"

Lola saw she had a second glass, though she wasn't sure why. Was Alex home and planning on joining her? He usually had beer. Well, it was good the glass was there. She shrugged and poured the stranger some wine.

"What's your degree in?" she asked, trying to be polite.

"Obviously, it's on you and your family and the effect your 46. Ascending organization had throughout my timeline and …"

Lola started to feel dizzy as she lowered into her chair.

"You have no context at all, do you?" The girl looked almost apologetic. "You're not real, Lola. You're a computer simulation. A very good one. We had your DNA preserved and so much information about you because of your daughter on Mars, so they thought they could make an unusually high-quality simulation of you, especially for someone who lived before the troubles. I mean" the young woman looked embarrassed "almost everybody springs for a virtual presentation with some sort of context. My parents insisted." She hesitated. "None of us knew it would be this good."

"I'm not real?" Lola said it like it was the only thing she'd heard. "How can I not be real? I feel real."

"I don't think you are supposed to feel at all."

"Well, I do. Do you feel real?"

"I am real… oh, this is ridiculous." The woman looked up into the air again. "Seriously? You made some kind of mistake here. You're going to make me explain this whole thing to her?"

A few seconds of complete quiet passed.

"Fine." She turned back to Lola. "My name is Zho. And obviously if I want good vid I need to get you to understand. Somebody, somewhere, probably thinks this is funny. Well, it's not funny for you or for me. Let's make the best of this."

"Okay." Lola's irritation was giving way to curiosity. "Explain away."

Zho took a sip of wine and smiled as she swallowed.

"Whoa. This tastes like real old-fashioned wine. I've had it a few times. Whoever created this part knows their stuff."

Zho took a second, bigger sip and started to talk. Lola listened more or less calmly to the young woman's story of her years of efforts to get an advanced degree. Then Zho said it was the year 994.

"No. You're not making sense. I'm not born until 1960."

"Oh, wait. You actually think like Lola. I mean, you use her calendar. Of course you do. Then to you it's—let me think— 3346. You see, we didn't start to recover from the troubles in year zero for a few hundred years, and we didn't begin to understand timelines until the fifth or sixth century. Some places on Earth still use your calendar."

"But most of my world vanishes in these troubles?"

"No, some of your husband's work was well preserved. He was an amazing pioneer. His thinking was nearly a millennium ahead of his time.

"Alex? My husband, Alex?"

"Yes, but of course he's a bit overshadowed by the rest of you. Did you know that, on almost a quarter of the accessible timelines within one standard deviation, you and your family are considered to be no more than a myth?"

"I'm not real *and* I'm a myth?"

"On some lines. You make a big difference, Lola, on a lot of them. Some even consider you a goddess, usually of kindness or compassion."

"You've visited these other timelines and come back and written a dissertation on me?"

"Of course not. That's impossible. Rather, the coming back part is. Your husband postulated that. Wait, maybe he hasn't done it yet, but he's is going to."

Zho looked around the porch with growing understanding.

"Wait. I bet you think it's 2008, don't you? Before it all started. Damn. They gave me the early Lola. You were supposed to be ten years older and know more about what was going on, so when you gave me my diploma you could, you know, comment on my research."

Lola got a funny look of realization on her own face. "Wait. Aren't you telling me things about the future I shouldn't know? Like maybe this meeting here will mess everything up?"

Zho laughed. "That's the old way of looking at it. We know better now. First of all, if I'd done something as stupid as go back in time, I'd have launched a whole new timeline; one in which you maybe find out things you shouldn't and who knows how occurrences play out then. Nobody, including me, is ever dumb enough to jump backwards and get thrown off of their own line. No, Lola, we study other lines through observation portals. All look and listen. No touch."

She was going to add it wasn't really 2008 and this simulated Lola wouldn't exist long enough to mess up anyone's future, but given how real the woman felt, pointing this out seemed hurtful.

"So, you've seen variations of me and my family on all sorts of these line things?"

Zho was pleased Lola understood. "Exactly. I've spent years watching you." She stood a little taller. "I'm now this line's leading expert on you."

Lola was seldom speechless, but it took her a few seconds to think of an intelligent response. Finally, she asked, "Am I on *every* timeline?"

Zho laughed, and Lola thought it was to the young woman's credit that she worked to keep condescension out of her answer.

"Earth isn't even on most timelines. There are a bazillion of them out there where the Milky Way never forms. But who cares? The multiverse is huge, full of boring stuff. I'm a historian. We never go more than two standard deviations away from our own. It's just not relevant."

"I see," Lola said, though she didn't see at all.

"So now, do you think you could, you know..." Zho gestured toward the plate she'd laid down next to the wine bottle.

"Do they charge you by the minute for this? Because if they don't, I'd like to ask you another question."

"Go ahead. There will be a renegotiation of these charges anyway, given the irregularities."

"Thanks. You got, what, hundreds of me out there, right?"

"Trillions," Zho corrected. "A new one for every different decision made by you and others who affected you. We use neural nets of course, to select a few hundred to study. So many are almost identical, and so many more are irrelevant outliers."

"Okay. Whatever. So, of these hundreds of Lolas you studied, how do you know which one is the real me?"

Zho looked like the question made no sense to her. "They all are."

"They can't all be real.

"Of course they can."

Lola tried again. "Which one came first?"

"They all did. I mean, they come at the same time. Wait, that may not be true. You're talking philosophy here, and that's not my field, but I do know some philosophers think some lines are more evolved than others. They think everyone has some sort of, I don't know, essence or soul that learns and does the same person better in the next line. It's only a theory. Sort of like another theory you'll encounter soon that there is only one human soul and it reincarnates as every single human in this line, growing with each life."

"Is that true?"

"I've no idea. I'm a historian, remember? I only know about it because the theory usually has a large influence on you."

Lola reached for the wine and poured them both another glass. This time she made each glass a little fuller.

"Could they both be true? I mean, maybe I do me on all these timelines, then I come back and do somebody else on all of them and then another person? This could keep me busy for a while"

Zho nodded. "You do love philosophy. It's a part of you I really enjoyed, and they did it so well with this reconstruction."

Zho reached over and patted Lola's hand. "Hey, it wouldn't have to go in that order, you know. You could do everyone on this line and then do everyone on the next line and so on. Everyone improves a little when you go to the next line. That works too."

"Yeah, it does. Oh, I wish you could tell me how it really goes."

"I can't. We've no idea how people are interconnected and how the lines relate to each other. If at all. I mean, this isn't my field, but I'm pretty sure that for all our advances, we're not a whole lot closer to understanding the important things about the universe."

"No, I guess you wouldn't be."

Lola noticed the sun had set and the pinks and corals in the sky were turning darker.

"I guess we'd better get this thing done for you," she said, sadness creeping into her voice. "It's been fun to meet you and amazing to find out someone, someday is actually going to study me. It's wonderful to know I make a difference."

A thought occurred to Zho. "Was it cruel to do this to you?"

"Do what?" Lola didn't understand.

"Make you alive. Give you a few moments of sentience again. I never guessed they'd bring you back as fully as they did, but now, well, once you give me my diploma I think you go away. I don't want you to go, Lola. I've enjoyed talking to you. It was much more fun than watching you, and there's so much more I wish I could ask you."

Once again Zho looked like she might cry.

"Oh now, don't start." Lola laughed but tears were forming in her eyes too. "We all live knowing we're going to go away at some point. I mean, usually it's not in seconds, but then again, this is kind of like a bonus thing for me, right?"

"Yeah. I guess."

The tears started to run down Zho's face. Lola reached out to wipe them away, and then they started to run down Lola's checks as well. She tried to gain her composure and to hand Zho the plate, but then both women started to laugh. Lola gave up. The two women simply hugged each other as the tears flowed.

At that moment, there wasn't a soul in the universe who could say with certainty which set of tears, if either, were real.

<u>**February 1986, on another timeline**</u>

A Better Ending

In February of 1986, Lola Zeitman had her first telepathic experience. It lasted about three seconds and she ignored it.

The next morning, at nine months pregnant, she made a presentation to the president of her company. It involved everything she'd done so far as a newly hired geophysicist and it went well, if one ignored the smarmy jokes the executives made about her advanced state of pregnancy. It started when the head of her division introduced her.

"Our fourth prospect today will be presented by Lola Zeitman. Lola got her master's degree just eighteen months ago from UT, and she has done a great job here despite a little, uh, inconvenient medical situation which we hear can be remedied."

There was assorted laughter.

"Please gentlemen, do not say anything to upset her," the division head continued. "The last thing any of us wants to do is to deliver a baby here in this room today!"

Slightly louder and more boisterous laughter followed.

"No, no, no," the president surprised his entourage by throwing up his beautifully manicured hands in mock agitation. He was in a good mood today.

"Say anything you want, gentlemen. Talking is not the activity that sets off labor with a very pregnant woman," he chuckled knowingly. "Trust me, I know what really sets labor off."

The chuckle spread to others and took on an even more knowing tone, first from those who knew what he meant and somewhat more slowly, from those who didn't have a clue.

Lola, knowing damn well what activity he was referring to, became increasingly uncomfortable as the laughter and muttered comments continued. She knew no offense was meant, but it seemed smarmy, like she was the butt of a mildly dirty joke she'd been forced to listen to without being permitted to respond.

People were always telling her she had to learn to play along. Yet she felt like she'd tried that approach, and it didn't work. Not for her, and not for others, either.

"I know you don't mean to, but you're making me uncomfortable." She said in a gentle voice, but the room went silent. Lola could feel the tension. Before anyone could respond, she went on. "I'm here today to recommend we make a substantial bid on a block in southern West Cameron. The map behind me shows a faulted four-way structural trap with sizable potential."

Her delivery was professional and she kept to the facts. After a few minutes the tension eased. When Lola finished, she knew she'd done well enough that she'd receive no worse than a reprimand from her superiors. Let them lecture her, she thought. She felt better for having said something.

She started back to her office, but decided to grab a soda first. The geoscientists who'd finished were in the break room, kidding around, giddy with the relief of being done.

"Hi, Lola." A young geophysicist named Frank welcomed her into the circle of laughter. "Got a joke for you."

He looked at her, and told her a disgusting racist joke. Lola was so surprised she froze, with no idea of how to respond. Then she knew what had to be said.

"That is the stupidest, most hateful excuse for humor I've ever heard. How could you say something so awful?"

Everyone else in the break room looked at Lola. Unspoken office rules were if someone made a joke, even a bad one, you laughed. Frank stared back at her.

"I think you're better than that, Frank."

He gave a sheepish shrug. "It's my brother-in-law's joke. He can be kind of a jerk."

"Doesn't mean you have to be one."

No one looked her in the eye, but Lola saw satisfied expressions on many of her coworkers' faces. They'd hated the joke too. She felt better as she headed back to her desk.

Halfway there, she stopped as she saw none other than the president of the company walking into her office. How had he managed to lose his entourage? Was he so angry he wanted to fire her in person?

"Would you mind closing the door behind you?" he asked as she walked in. "I'd like this conversation to be private."

She went numb as she pulled the door shut. One of the secretaries walked by. Lola watched the woman's eyes widen as she figured out who Lola's visitor was.

"Please. Sit down." The man gestured Lola toward her own chair. "I hope you understand no offense was meant when you began your presentation."

Lola nodded. "I know. I just thought —"

The president held his hand up to silence her. He was a man used to silencing others with a gesture.

"Just because offense is not intended, doesn't mean it can't be felt. I realize that."

Lola kept nodding. Behind the man's head she saw the secretary and two of her coworkers peering in through her glass pane from a safe distance away, trying to figure out what was going on.

"When you said what you did, you made me think of my own daughter. She works in aeronautics, and puts up with crap you would not believe."

Lola was pretty sure she'd believe it, but she didn't say so.

"You got me thinking. I wonder how often the guys she works with don't realize it. They're talking to each other; they forget she's there. I'm going to tell her this story. Encourage her to speak up more."

Lola noticed the secretary and two coworkers had now been replaced by her boss, two other supervisors, and the chief drilling engineer. All of them were watching her.

"Speaking up is kind of a dangerous," Lola said.

"It is. It works better if you can manage not to be angry but that can be difficult. You did it well, by the way."

"Thanks."

Two vice-presidents and a general manager had now joined the group in the hall. The older man noticed Lola's gaze and laughed.

"Yes, I'm sure by now they've figured out I didn't go to the men's room." He stood up to leave. "I just wanted to thank you in person. For the gift of a better perspective."

Later, when Lola left for the afternoon, her spirits were buoyed by the odd sensation that she'd done this day well. Maybe better than she'd done it before. That was ridiculous, of course, because she'd never done this day before.

She ran into her friend Mary as she was leaving.

"Ready to stop playing the game for today?" Mary asked.

"I've got a doctor's excuse to do it." Lola patted her stomach. "But 'you have to play the game' *is* the zeroth law of thermodynamics, isn't it?"

"Yup. I just think playing it may be more complicated than we realize."

"Couldn't agree more."

"I have a question for you," Mary said. "This baby. You know your whole life changes after this. So how do you see this? Is it a beginning? Or is it an end?"

"Good question." Lola placed her hands on her belly and knew her answer. "It's both."

More Stories

One of Two is the last book in this collection. If you've missed any of the previous books, you may enjoy reading them now. Each one is a stand-alone story containing twists and turns not revealed in this novel.

Consider Layers of Light, Teddie's tale of how she uses her innate skills for out of body experiences to save her friends from a human trafficking ring. You may enjoy Shape of Secrets, Zane's story of how he uses his ability to alter his appearance to find a murderer in the South Pacific. Try Flickers of Fortune, Ariel's story of discovering other precognitives and the importance of her unique skills.

You may prefer Twists of Time, a novel about Alex learning to use his ability to warp time to protect the students at his high school. Or go to the first novel in this collection, One of One. It tells of Lola discovering her telepathic abilities as she becomes the unlikely hero in a rescue mission in Nigeria.

Why Call This 46 Ascending?

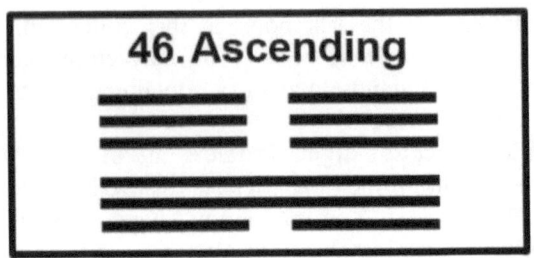

It started in 2010 when I decided my six proposed books could be made into an I Ching hexagram. I gave those with a female protagonist two lines, and began with book one at the bottom. I looked up the hexagram and it was called Sheng.

I suppose I was worried writing these books would change me in ways I wouldn't like, and there'd be no going back. Sheng answered the question bothering me most. It wasn't "Will I sell a lot of books?" or "Will these be good books?" or even "Will writing these books make me happy?" Those would have been fine questions, but *my* question was "Should I do this or not?"

Researching Sheng, I read it refers to a time of development and progress, when a steady progression occurs and the predicted outcome is positive. That sounded good to me.

I learned Sheng is also called the Symbol of Rising and Advancing, Ascension, Promotion, Sprouting from the Earth, and Organic Growth. Who can argue with those? In other words, everything I read about Sheng told me "Write the damn books." So I did.

If you asked me then what this collection of books was about, I would have told you it was about how we humans have so much more potential than we realize. We can improve. We can rise. We can ascend. Climb the mountain. Move toward the light. You know. Grow.

So, I'd not only found this I Ching hexagram that got me off my butt and writing, but happened to also describe what it was I was trying to say. Go figure.

It seemed reasonable to name the collection of books after it. When Lola wanted to copy my idea and use the name for her organization, I didn't argue.

Thanks

I'm blessed with five people who love me enough to take my early drafts and read them, helping me find errors in my reasoning, emotions that don't ring true, and proclamations they are sure I never intended. These alpha readers are also known as my husband, my sister and my three children. I thank each of them for hanging in there for six whole books.

I was lucky to find my editor Joel Handley while I was writing the original x^0. I thank him for the many ways he's made this collection better.

Beta readers let me see my story through the eyes of others, allowing me to tweak my book so it can put its best foot forward. Thanks for beta reading this novel go to John Ryan, Debby Gates, Fred Morgan, Jill Florio, Steve Wilcox, Vickie Caligure, Carol Meier, Kathy Byland, and Dhivya Balaji.

When I finally get to my *this is it* version, one last set of eyes always scans my books a final time. My greatest thanks go to this final reader, my husband. He is my alpha and my omega, and on the timelines where I'm not with him, these books probably don't happen.

About the Author

Sherrie Roth grew up in Western Kansas thinking there was no place in the universe more fascinating than outer space. After her mother vetoed astronaut as a career ambition, she went on to study journalism and physics in hopes of becoming a science writer.

She published her first science fiction short story long ago, and then waited a lot of tables while she looked for inspiration for the next story. When it finally came, it declared it had to be a whole book, nothing less. One night, while digesting this disturbing piece of news, she drank way too many shots of ouzo with her boyfriend. She woke up thirty-one years later demanding to know what was going on.

The boyfriend, who she'd apparently long since married, asked her to calm down. He explained she'd gone back to school and gotten a degree in geophysics in a fit of practicality. She'd spent the last 28 years interpreting seismic data in the oil industry. The good news, he said, was she found it mildly entertaining and ridiculously well-paying. The bad news was the two of them had still managed to spend almost all the money.

Apparently she was now Mrs. Cronin, and the further good news was they had produced three wonderful children whom they loved dearly, even though to be honest that is where a lot of the money had gone. Mr. Cronin turned out to be a warm-hearted, encouraging sort who was happy to see her awake and ready to write. "It's about time," were his exact words.

Sherrie Cronin discovered Sally Ride had already managed to become the first woman in space and done a fine job of it. No one, however, had written the book living in Sherrie's head for decades. The only problem was, the book informed her it had grown into a six book collection. Sherrie decided she better start writing before it got any longer. She's been wide awake since, and writing away.

The Telepaths of Reel News
(see next page for everyone else)

Monad: a single individual acting alone. In music, it is a single note, in biology, it is a one-celled organism, and in Pythagorean philosophy, it is the single entity from which all else grew. Yes, it rhymes with gonad.

Entelechy: describes realization as opposed to potential. It is pronounced en TELL eh key

Monads of the Entelechy mentioned by name:
Brett: *LA man with ambitions to be an actor*
Cenk: *Turkish father with a dying son*
Charlie: *Chicago newsman struggling to prove himself*
Chidi: *Nigerian man who prefers no trouble*
Dave: *Canadian who meets a child telepath at zoo*
Ezra: *Israeli former interrogation specialist*
Fernando: *Brazilian who falls in love with x^0 telepath*
Gabriel: *Argentinian journalist who heads the Entelechy*
Hank: *Australian who gets to take an unexpected cruise*
Jerry: *Dallas man who spies on the Zeitman family*
Johann: *Swiss expert in using telepathy for blackmail*
Juan: *Venezuelan former lawyer in the banking industry*
Khalid: *Saudi with a background in business*
Rafael: *Filipino expert at telepathic reconnaissance, Gabriel's one friend*

List of Main Characters
(see previous page for all monads)

Alex Zeitman: *a high school physics teacher in Houston who has an odd relationship with time and an even odder family*
Alma Delgado: *Violeta's mother*
Ariel Zeitman: *Lola and Alex's middle child, a technology expert who remembers the future*
Camila: *Brazilian x^0 telepath who seduces Fernando*
Cillian: *An Irishman with visions of the far future (pronounced Killian)*
Lola Zeitman: *A geophysicist from Houston who developed telepathic abilities a few years ago*
Maurice: *An friend of the Zeitman family and the telepath who helped Lola learn to control her skills*
Nell: *An Irish actress who can morph her appearance*
Olumiji: *A Nigerian telepath who serves as an informal head of the organization x^0 (pronounced oh loo ME gee)*
Teddie Zeitman: *Lola and Alex's youngest child, a high school student with a flair for out-of-body experiences*
Xuha Santos Rojas: *A college student who briefly lived at the Zeitman home and shares Alex's odd relationship with time (pronounced schwa, rhymes with spa)*
Vanida: *a young Thai who has had out-of-body experiences since early childhood. (pronounced vuh NEE duh)*
Violeta Delgado: *An Argentinian telepath who works for Reel News (pronounced vee oh LAY tuh)*
Warren Moore: *Creator of the Reel News media empire*
Yuden: *a Bhutanese out-of-body traveler, the head of c^3*
Zane Zeitman: *Lola and Alex's oldest child, a law student who can alter his appearance but would rather not*

Who has what superpower?
(see previous page for list of characters)